Red-hot ra
Lou

TOO HOT TO TOUCH

"*Too Hot to Touch* is a satisfying, emotional and touching read."
—*Read, React, Review*

"I can see that this series is going to be another keeper on my shelves. A great start to this new foodie series, it makes me want to learn to cook . . . almost."
—*Smitten with Reading*

"Edwards always amazes me with her descriptions in the kitchen and food. Be sure to read this book on a full stomach, or else the hunger pains might get ya!"
—*The Book Pushers*

"Jules and Max scorch the pages . . . very well-written characters with flaws, issues and depth."
—*Badass Book Reviews*

"I loved this book. It was funny, sexy, the love story was touching, and the characters were likeable. As a fan of contemporary romance, this is exactly what I'm looking for when I buy a book. I can't wait to read the next installment. This one is a keeper so don't waste more time and go get it!"
—*Romance Around the Corner*

"If you like food, televised food shows (especially the popular Bravo series *Top Chef*) and books with happy endings, you're in for a treat."
—*San Angelo Standard Times*

"Scorching romance and delicious passions ignite behind the scenes of a high-stakes culinary competition. Today's hottest chefs vie for fame, fortune . . . and each other's hearts."

—*Fresh Fiction*

"Yowza! There's nothing like romance in the kitchen to get juices pumping and hearts pounding, especially when the writing sizzles like it does in Edwards' latest."

—*All About Romance*

"Every woman who's made the painful discovery that great sex is not enough to make a man realize he's in love will sympathize. *Too Hot to Touch* flips the power balance."

—*BN.com Romance Reviews*

"I enjoyed the banter between all the characters. We get a little hint as to whom Danny's heroine will be as his book will pick up where this one leads off. It's overall an enjoyable read, and I'll be picking up Danny's book when it comes out."

—*Happily Ever After Reads*

JUST ONE TASTE

"The third addition to Edwards' contemporary, culinary-based love stories is a rare treat that is certain to satisfy readers with its delectable combination of lusciously sensuous romance and irresistibly clever writing." —*Booklist*

"Laugh-out-loud funny, *Just One Taste* [is] a surprisingly tasty story of two unlikely people meeting and falling in love . . . A fun, light read with plenty of humor and passion, *Just One Taste* makes it to my keeper shelf and has me searching for the book preceding [it]."

—*Affaire de Coeur*

St. Martin's Paperbacks Titles by

LOUISA EDWARDS

Can't Stand the Heat

On the Steamy Side

Just One Taste

Too Hot to Touch

Some Like It Hot

Some Like It Hot

LOUISA EDWARDS

St. Martin's Paperbacks

This is a work of fiction. All of the characters, organizations, and events portrayed in this novel are either products of the author's imagination or are used fictitiously.

SOME LIKE IT HOT

Copyright © 2011 by Louisa Edwards.

Excerpt from *Hot Under Pressure* copyright © 2011 by Louisa Edwards.

For information address St. Martin's Press, 175 Fifth Avenue, New York, NY 10010.

EAN: 978-0-312-53439-4

Printed in the United States of America

St. Martin's Paperbacks edition / December 2011

St. Martin's Paperbacks are published by St. Martin's Press, 175 Fifth Avenue, New York, NY 10010.

10 9 8 7 6 5 4 3 2 1

For Deidre Knight, the savviest agent, sweetest friend, and best honorary big sister a girl could wish for. I'd be lost without you!

Acknowledgments

First of all, thank you to Deidre and my editor, Rose, who love Eva Jansen as much as I do! Thanks, both of you, for allowing me to tell the stories that excite me and play with the characters who make every day of writing more like fun than work.

Also on the make-work-fun side of things, a zillion thanks to my besties Roxanne St. Claire and Kristen Painter! I honestly don't know how anyone makes it through a draft without you two.

The first draft of *SLiH* would've stayed a messy, ugly draft without the beta reading talents of Kate Pearce, Bria Quinlan, and especially Nic Montreuil. Kate, you never hold back, and I love you for it. Bria, your insights and speed-reading make you a treasure I totally cherish, and Nic. Honey. What can I say? Sometimes I feel like you know these characters better than I do. Thank you for helping me stay true to them! (Winslow thanks you, too . . .)

Thank you to the Peeners—you dirty girls know who you are—for invaluable advice, venting sessions, and dick jokes.

Thank you to all the readers and reviewers who read *Too Hot to Touch* and said, "We want more of Danny. And OMG BECK!" The rest of the Rising Star Chef trilogy is for you.

I can't let a book go by without thanking my parents for everything you've done (and continue to do) for me. You make us dinner, you bring us veggies from the farmer's market, you walk the dogs, you find the best Mexican restaurants, you entice me away from my desk to swim… how did I go so many years living so far away from you?

And last but never least, thank you to my handsome husband, Nick. Your support and encouragement mean everything to me. And the fact that after more than a decade together you can still make me pee my pants with laughter? That's what convinces me true, deep, everlasting love exists.

Chapter 1

So this is what it's like to leave home, Danny mused, narrowly avoiding a collision with a woman who seemed to have forgotten she was pulling a wheeled carry-on case behind her.

LaGuardia was packed. Every bank of waiting room benches sported at least a couple of people sleeping out the wait for their delayed planes, while the terminal seethed with chaos and confusion as flights were called, boarding was announced, and everyone rushed to find the right gate.

Danny Lunden, who'd never been out of New York, took it all in and tried to ignore the chills of excitement down his back.

They were on their way.

A panicking voice rose above the din of bustling passengers and PA announcements about not leaving bags unattended.

"Where's my ticket? Please tell me one of you—oh, there it is. Okay. Thanks, Danny."

Patting his jittering friend's shoulder was a little like grabbing hold of the business end of a hand mixer.

"Winslow, cool it. We're all good. We're at the gate in plenty of time."

Which had to be some sort of miracle after the adventure of wrestling luggage and carry-ons through the New York City public transit system and pushing through airport throngs walking slower than the tourists in Times Square. Danny did a quick head count to make sure he hadn't lost anyone in the subway tunnels or security lane.

Beck, their resident master of fish cookery, was always easy to spot in a crowd, since he topped the mere mortals around him by about four inches. The big guy caught Danny's eye and gave him a silent nod of acknowledgment. Beck was solid, as always, standing like an oak planted in the middle of a rushing river, carrying everything he'd packed for this adventure in a single duffel bag.

Next to him was Danny's oldest friend in the world, Jules Cavanaugh. Her dark blond hair was caught up in a messy ponytail, and her eyes glittered with the thrill of finally embarking on this trip they'd been anticipating ever since they won the chance to take on the Rising Star Chef competition.

She glowed with happiness, spilling her warm light all over the guy beside her, who was busily soaking it up like a sponge cake doused in amaretto.

Max Lunden, Danny's brother. His older brother, in fact—and Danny had teased Jules about him for years before her unrequited crush turned into completely requited forever-hearts-and-flowers love.

And wasn't that a rolling pin upside the head, because Danny never thought he'd see the day when his wandering prodigal brother would settle down and commit to anything—much less to winning the RSC, his family, and a woman all in one fell swoop.

But Max had.

Danny watched the way they leaned into each other, their wheeled bags bumping and threatening to trip them when they got too close, and tried to be glad the team had two such passionate, inventive chefs in charge, and ignore the unidentified tightness in his gut.

It wasn't jealousy—knowing about her long-standing crush on his clueless brother, Danny had never been able to see Jules as more than a friend. Hell, Jules had been the next best thing to a sister for years, long before Max swooped back into town. The fact that Max would eventually be the one to make it official didn't bug Danny.

He wasn't sure what was bugging him, really, so he shoved it aside and turned to the guy next to him: Winslow Jones, the fastest knife on the team—and the one who'd nearly been grounded by security for pleading to be allowed to carry his knife roll on the plane with him—was still vibrating under Danny's palm.

And Danny was the pastry chef. So that was everyone. He relaxed minutely, a fragment of tension going out of his shoulders.

The gang's all here.

A nasal voice over the loudspeaker broke into Danny's thoughts.

"We are now boarding flight number fourteen twenty-two to Chicago O'Hare International. First-class passengers only, please."

"Well, that ain't us," Beck said, settling onto his heels with the look of a man accustomed to waiting.

"Have you ever flown first-class?" Jules asked, staring up into Max's eyes.

He laughed. "Hell no. An airplane with toilets on it is a luxury to me. I did most of my traveling through Asia on crowded buses or in the back of a truck transporting live goats or something."

"Sounds smelly." Winslow wrinkled his nose, making the darker freckles stand out on his light brown skin.

"You have no idea," Max told him. "But this." He gazed around the busy airport. "It's something else."

Danny looked around, too, at the walls of glass and metal, at the reasonably clean floor and the people chatting as they rode the moving walkways, and figured he knew what Max meant.

This was something outside all their experiences. Because they weren't just embarking on some little pleasure jaunt to see the sights in the Windy City.

They were headed to meet the teams they'd be up against in the Rising Star Chef competition, the other chefs who'd be cooking their hearts out and giving it their all in the hopes of coming out on top.

The significant cash prize didn't hurt anything, either.

The newly minted East Coast Team stood in a loose huddle staring at one another nervously. Someone ought to say something, Danny realized, with a visceral pang of yearning for his dad's gift of effortless inspiration, or his mom's serene calm in the face of any crisis.

"Gus and Nina should be here," Jules said, in one of those weird moments of reading Danny's brain like an open cookbook. She'd been doing it since they were in elementary school together, and it still freaked him out.

Shaking off the emotion as if he were flicking whipped cream off the end of a whisk, Danny did what he did best.

"Mom and Dad wish they could be with us," he soothed. "But somebody's got to stay home and run Lunden's while we're off winning the Rising Star Chef and bringing glory to their restaurant. I know this is kind of a crazy situation, and we're all a little worked up, but we just have to stay focused on bringing home the prize. For Lunden's. For my parents. For all of us."

As Danny glanced around the team, making sure to lock eyes with each person in turn, he could see them shedding their nerves and standing up a little taller. And a bit more of the tension rolled off his back, because if he could keep everyone together and zeroed in on the goal, they were going to be okay.

Danny knew he'd have to work hard to take his own advice.

Stay focused. This is for the family, for the restaurant, for the future.

To Danny, they were interchangeable.

When it was their turn to board, he herded his group over to the flight attendant, produced all five tickets, and got the team and their assorted carry-ons down the jet bridge and onto the plane.

After some confusion over the seating arrangements—Max and Jules weren't technically seated together, but were still in that phase of the relationship when they couldn't bear to be parted for the hour and a half it would take them to fly from their home base of New York City to the unknown wilds of Chicago—Danny had everyone situated.

Max, Jules, and Winslow were clustered on one side of the plane while Beck and Danny were in the slightly more spacious pair of seats on the other side of the aisle.

Beck asked to sit by the window, and Danny readily agreed. He buckled himself in, stowed his satchel holding the precious tools of his trade under the seat in front of him, and was ready to go by the time the rest of the passengers finished boarding.

But they didn't go anywhere. The plane just sat there. And sat there. And sat there.

Danny craned his neck out into the aisle to get a better view of the front of the plane. What was the problem? Were there electrical issues?

Finally one of the flight attendants, a skinny young dude with unlikely yellow hair and an earring, grabbed the handheld microphone and stood in the aisle to make an announcement.

"Sorry for the delay, ladies and gentlemen," he said smoothly, "we're just waiting on one passenger, then we can get under way."

Blithely ignoring the ripple of exasperated sighs and groans, the flight attendant hung up the mike and went back to passing out blankets and pillows.

"Well, this sucks," Danny said, impatience simmering under his skin. "Let's get the hell off the ground, already."

"If they're lying about waiting for a passenger because there's actually some kind of systems failure, I'd personally rather they figure that shit out while we're still on the ground."

Blinking, Danny turned to study his seat partner, taking in Beck's rigid posture, the cold sweat dotting his hairline.

How did I miss this?

"You're afraid of flying," Danny said, disbelief sharpening his tone.

Beck stiffened even further. Danny worried for a second that the big guy might Hulk out and break the arm right off the seat between them.

"I'm not afraid of flying," Beck grated out. "I'm not even afraid of falling—that would at least be a quick and relatively painless way to go."

Danny went into caretaker mode. "Okay, you're a tough guy, everyone knows that. I didn't mean anything by saying you were afraid."

Beck shook his head, the loose waves of his longish dark hair hiding his face for a second. "It's not that I don't—look. Everyone's afraid, sometimes. I'm no exception. Fear is a survival response; it's healthy. It can keep you alive. I just meant, it's not the flying that wigs me out so much as it's . . ." He swallowed audibly, his Adam's apple moving in the thick column of his throat. "It's kind of cramped in here. Not a lot of air movement. I don't like that."

Danny processed that quickly. There was a lot they didn't know about Beck, the taciturn chef who'd joined the Lunden's kitchen crew only a few months before Max came home. There had been rumors—mostly started by Winslow and his overactive imagination—that ranged from *ex-con just out of prison* to *foreign prince in exile*. Danny had never paid much attention to them. So long as Beck did his job, banged out the straightforward, excellent fish dishes on the Lunden's menu, and got along with the rest of the crew, Danny didn't much care where he came from.

The claustrophobia, though, was a new piece of the Beck puzzle.

Setting that aside for the moment, Danny said, "Would it be better if you were on the aisle? Might give you a little more room to stretch out."

Gratitude flashed in Beck's hooded eyes, but it must've been for the lack of further interrogation on his issues, because he said, "Nah, that just puts me in the middle of the big metal tube with no escape hatch. At least here, I can look out and see the open air, even if I can't touch it. I'll be fine, man. As soon as we take off and get on our way, I can start counting down the minutes until we're in Chicago."

Danny returned the tense smile with the most reassuring expression he could manage—and when it came to reassurance, Danny was the ninja master. Usually he'd start with a pep talk, but from the way Beck was white-knuckling it, the guy needed action more than words.

Unbuckling his seat belt, Danny stood up, the familiar

comfort of a sense of purpose filling him with determination.

"Where are you going?" Beck asked.

Danny straightened and stepped into the aisle. "To get some answers."

The blond flight attendant with the earring was fooling around with the coffeemaker when Danny marched up the aisle to the front of the plane, but when he saw one of his passengers bearing down on him, his eyes widened.

"Sir, you need to sit down."

Danny had a couple of inches on the kid, but he did his best not to loom in the cramped confines of the airplane's prep area. "Listen. My friend's not a great flier and he's starting to get anxious. Is there anything I can tell him about when we might be taking off?"

"We're nearly finished with the boarding process, and we can't push back from the gate until all passengers are seated, with their seat belts securely fastened," the attendant parroted.

"Yeah, but see, we've all been doing exactly that for the last twenty minutes, and the plane's still parked at the gate. What, exactly, are we waiting for? I mean, you've already made, like, four pots of coffee. I bet you're getting sick of the smell of burnt coffee beans."

The flight attendant's gaze flickered, and Danny pressed his advantage with a smile.

"I don't really know," the kid finally said. "I got a call from ground control to hold the plane for a late passenger; she's supposed to be on her way."

Danny stared. "You're serious. You weren't lying, trying to keep us calm while we waited to find out there's a pigeon in the engine or something?"

"We're pigeon-free, as far as I know."

It obviously wasn't this kid's fault, but Danny was starting to get pissed. One of his guys was stuck feeling like shit for an extra half hour, and as far as Danny could tell there was no legitimate reason for it. "Is this standard practice, holding up a whole plane full of people for one passenger?"

Earring glinting as he shook his head, the kid shrugged helplessly.

"It is when the passenger is me," purred a low voice from behind them.

Danny whirled, nearly clocking himself on the jutting refrigerator cabinet, to see a svelte woman dressed in something complicated and elegant that wrapped around her slim body like some sort of chic lady mummy costume, only in dark blue.

The color set off her pearly smooth skin, making her a study in rich jewel tones, from the scarlet curve of her smirking mouth to the shiny brown hair angling bluntly down to her chin. She looked as if she were on her way to opening night at the Met or something, not a commuter flight to Chicago.

Recognition fired one instant after the instinctual spark of visceral desire, and Danny clamped down on the dizzying combination.

Clenching his teeth, he faced the woman whose millionaire restaurateur father had founded the Rising Star Chef competition twenty years ago.

"Thanks for waiting," she was saying to the flight attendant. "God, Daddy getting on the airline's board of directors is the best thing that ever happened to me. Unlike everything that happened this morning! I had to avert a professional disaster, then there was a mix-up with the car service and I had to take a taxi. My assistant is so fired. Well, not really, I'd be a mess without him, but I'm cutting his chocolate budget. No more candy on his desk until he figures out how to get me to the airport on time!"

She smiled, perfect white teeth flashing. Before the dazzled flight attendant could gather his wits off the floor, Danny had stepped between them.

At a deep gut level, all he could think was *mine*.

And, close on the heels of that thought, *Uh-oh*.

Chapter 2

"Nice of you to finally join us," said the hottest pastry chef Eva had ever seen—and she'd seen plenty.

This one, though? Was pretty memorable.

"Where's your seat?" His sensual upper lip curled in a slight sneer that sent a zing through her nervous system. "I'm assuming it's one of these empty ones in first-class."

She resisted the urge to tuck her hair behind her ear and struggled not to let on that she was out of breath from her mad dash through the airport.

Holding out a hand she desperately hoped wasn't sweaty, Eva gave him her most brilliant smile and said, "Daniel Lunden, right? I remember you from the East Coast finals. Is your whole team here? What a wacky co-incidence!"

Lunden narrowed his gorgeous blue-gray eyes at her, his firm, chiseled mouth flattening to a straight line.

Whoops, looks like someone's a little ticked.

"Um. Maybe we could save the joyous reunion for after we're in the air?" The young blond guy who'd held the plane for her suggested it with the air of someone used to being ignored.

Eva turned the brilliant smile on him, since it didn't seem to be working on Lunden. "You're absolutely right"—she peeked at his name badge—"Patrick. I apologize. I'd like to make it up to everyone. How about mimosas for the whole plane, on me?"

"But that's . . . five dollars per person for everyone in coach," Patrick stammered. "Even not counting the minors, it's going to be at least five hundred dollars!"

Cheap at twice the price, Eva thought, feeling her embarrassment at being late ease. "That's totally fine. Do you want my credit card now?"

Patrick beamed at her, apparently undaunted by the task of opening fifty half-split bottles of mediocre sparkling wine, but Eva could feel the stiff disapproval radiating off the man at her right shoulder.

Or maybe that was his body heat. The guy must have converted his body to some sort of furnace, with the amount of warmth he was putting out.

Eva wasn't short, especially in her favorite five-inch bronze patent-leather platform Louboutins, but Daniel Lunden was taller by at least three inches. Leaner and harder, too, she noted, casting a practiced eye over the way his black Henley shirt pulled across his broad shoulders and gaped at his sturdy collarbones, showing a tantalizing slice of smooth, tanned chest, and his faded blue jeans hung low on his narrow hips.

Nice.

"As far as I'm concerned, the apology alone would've done it," Lunden said. "That, and an acknowledgment that your time isn't more valuable than everyone else's."

Not so nice.

"Look," she said, spreading her hands. "I said I was sorry. And I'm happy to pay for my crimes! I'm a businesswoman—let's put a dollar amount on the time everyone's spent waiting here at the gate for me. Less than an hour, correct?"

"About thirty minutes," Patrick put in.

"Minimum wage would be seven twenty-five for the full hour." Eva furrowed her brow, pretending to count on her fingers. "So . . . how about five dollars per person, in the form of a nice glass of champagne and orange juice? I think that's reasonable for punitive damages."

"More than reasonable!" Patrick was starting to lose patience with the negotiation.

Lunden cocked his head. It was entirely unfair that even in the harsh, unforgiving fluorescence of the airplane lighting, he looked golden and perfect, from the tips of his spiky light brown hair to the hint of a cleft in his well-shaped chin.

He clearly wasn't buying it, but all he did was turn to Patrick and say, "My team and I are in row fourteen. You can skip the mimosas for us, thanks." Giving Eva one last stern glance and an ironic twist to that decadent mouth, he said, "Enjoy first-class," and stalked back up the aisle.

Lowering her lashes over what she knew was probably a smoldering look, Eva paused for a moment to enjoy the view.

It was distracting enough that she almost didn't notice her best friend, Claire, giving the group of them one of her patented wry looks from the window seat in the second row.

Not for the first time, Eva envied Claire Durand her smooth air of sophistication and maturity. Nobody did suave like a forty-something Frenchwoman.

Which Claire proved once again by responding to Eva's

bounce down the aisle with a mere arched eyebrow and a laconic "If you're quite finished ogling one of your contestants?"

"One of *your* contestants," Eva was quick to stress. "Unlike some people, I'm not a judge—merely the lowly panel moderator, there to set up a nice patter and keep the action moving. I'm the Vanna White of the Rising Star Chef competition! There are no rules about me keeping my hands off the chefs. And I should know. I was there when Dad wrote the rules."

Claire snorted. It was another one of those things she could only get away with by being French. "Yes, I'm certain of that. Your father would never make a rule that disallowed him from chasing after any segment of the female population." Skewering Eva with an ice-pick glare, Claire continued, "That doesn't signify that you are obliged to emulate him."

Eva pouted. She couldn't help it, even though it hadn't worked on Claire since Eva's nineteenth birthday. Despite the gap in their ages, it had been years since Claire had bothered to treat Eva like a child.

"Thank you, Patrick," Eva said while the flight attendant fell all over himself to help her stow her beloved Louis Vuitton tote bag in the overhead compartment.

She settled into the deep leather comfort of her first-class seat, head still full of the stern set of Daniel Lunden's indescribably luscious mouth, the firmness of his clenched jaw.

As Patrick stepped smartly into the aisle to do his safety dance, the plane pushed back from the jetway and the passengers in the back started a cheer that only got louder when he paused in his demonstration of the oxygen masks to tell them they were all being offered complimentary mimosas to make up for the delay.

Satisfied that she'd compensated for at least some of the annoyance she'd caused with her tardiness—and ooh, her assistant, Drew, was in big-time trouble—Eva picked up the conversation where she and Claire had left off.

"There's just something about a male pastry chef," she tried to explain.

"Pastry chefs are like any other man in the professional kitchen." As editor in chief of *Délicieux,* an internationally renowned food magazine, Claire knew from chefs. "The successful ones are arrogant, overbearing workaholics with egos large enough to crush innocent bystanders. If you're as smart as I've always thought, you will not allow yourself to be sucked into it."

Eva, who'd started learning the business of opening and running restaurants at her father's knee, knew a lot of chefs, too. "In my experience, people who deal with the delicate chemistry of desserts tend to be perfectionists. Regular chefs have their charms, of course—creativity, passion. But pastry chefs . . ." Eva smiled. "They take their time. They're meticulous. Thoughtful. Focused."

And those qualities sometimes spilled over into . . . other aspects of their lives.

Allowing herself a delicious little shiver as she recalled the electrifying moment when his body had brushed hers as they maneuvered in the cramped confines of the airplane, Eva tried to remember the last time she'd had a pastry chef in her bed, with all his delightful thoroughness aimed at her. It had been a while.

Maybe it was time to remedy that.

"I know that avaricious look in your eye." Claire clicked her buffed nails on the armrest, sounding resigned. "It's the same expression you get in the Bergdorf's shoe department. My little crazy person, don't you have enough stress and drama to suffice you already? Running the most prestigious national culinary competition on your own for the first time isn't enough?"

"Oh please." Eva waved a dismissive hand. "A little seduction is a stress reliever, Claire, everyone knows that. The thrill of the chase, the joy of the hunt—it's invigorating! And the fact that, at this moment, Daniel Lunden thinks he doesn't want to be caught? Well. That just adds an extra spice to the whole thing. And you know how much I love spice."

"I do. I also know how single-minded you are when in pursuit of what you want. Do you expect this particular pursuit to at least go quickly and smoothly?"

"Probably not." Eva sighed. "He doesn't like me one bit. He thinks I'm a spoiled brat who kept a whole plane full of people waiting, just for funsies."

"Why were you late, incidentally?"

Slumping back, Eva experienced again the sickening vertigo that had dizzied her the moment she took that panicked phone call from one of her RSC judges.

"Devon Sparks's new wife is pregnant. They just found out, and now he's freaking about leaving town. Even though she's not due for months! Men. He actually tried to back out of being a judge. Can you believe it?"

Claire blanched, satisfyingly horrified. "You managed to talk him out of it, surely! It would be a nightmare to replace our celebrity chef judge at this late date."

"Yes, thank goodness, I did, although it took some fancy footwork and a lot of soothing—Devon's kind of drama-rama, isn't he?—but finally I convinced him that, you know, women have babies all the time and everything would be fine for the next couple of months. It helped that I could hear Lilah laughing at him in the background."

She'd also had to promise that Devon would have several long weekends off to fly home to New York for visits, which would take some intensive schedule juggling and might cost some money in terms of production time with the television crew, but that was okay.

She'd make it work. She had no other choice. She couldn't risk losing her biggest Cooking Channel draw, especially if that might mean the television producers deciding not to film or broadcast the RSC.

Her father had been very clear when he handed over the reins of the competition this year. It was her job to increase the RSC's visibility, and getting on TV was a big part of that.

Eva tightened her fingers on the stem of her champagne flute. She refused to let him down. Whatever it took to convince the Cooking Channel that they wanted to air the RSC, she'd do it.

"Thank God," Claire said fervently.

"Yeah. Major catastrophe averted."

Narrowing her eyes, Claire asked, "So why did you not explain these circumstances to your handsome pastry chef? It was certainly in his best interests as a contestant that you keep all three judges happy and willing to work!"

Eva screwed up her face. "I don't know. I didn't want to tell him! It would've sounded like making an excuse, or something."

"It would've been a good excuse!"

Crossing her arms over her chest, Eva set her jaw. Her father hated excuses, and Eva had learned early on that the best way out of almost any infraction was to own up to it.

Claire shook her head, the overhead lights glinting off the threads of silver just starting to appear in her luxuriously thick chestnut hair. "It worries me, this fondness you have for men who disapprove of you."

"What can I say? I enjoy a challenge."

In fact, the challenge Daniel Lunden presented fired her nerves with more energy than she'd felt in the last two months, months she'd spent traveling from New York to Atlanta, San Francisco, Austin, and Chicago to oversee the qualifying challenges that had decided the teams of chefs who would represent their regions in the Rising Star Chef competition.

It had been more grueling than she'd anticipated, the endless traveling, and Eva wasn't normally one to stay put for longer than it took to unpack a suitcase. Maybe it was the eliminations—it was a lot tougher than she'd ever thought it would be, telling hundreds of chefs they wouldn't be moving on to the next round.

Crushing dreams was hard work, as it turned out.

And then there was the second-guessing, trying to convince herself she'd made the right call when she'd picked the judges, that the judges were choosing the best chefs, that the ever-present tension between Claire and her fellow judges was still at a low simmer rather than a dangerous boil, that the television producers weren't going to back out on their promise to film the competition for the first time . . . really, Eva felt as wrung out and twisted up as a discarded string bikini, and the RSC hadn't even started yet.

But when she'd seen Lunden standing in the doorway of the plane, long-fingered hands on lean hips like an avenging warrior, all the exhaustion and nervousness and self-doubt went up in a firestorm of excitement and lust.

The way the chill of condemnation clashed with the unmistakable glitter of instantaneous hunger and sparked his eyes to a bright, sizzling blue called to the fighter in Eva. She wanted to stoke the fire of that hunger, feed it craftily and carefully until it flamed up and overwhelmed the disapproval.

Until he couldn't help himself, and he had to let go and enjoy her.

Claire's quiet voice burst the happy bubble of Eva's fantasy. "That's what Theo always says. Take care, Eva. You are your father's daughter . . . in more than one respect."

Neither the azure-blue Michael Kors wrap dress nor the delicate lace unmentionables beneath it were armor against Claire's warning. Her oldest friend and mentor never seemed to have trouble finding the tenderest spot on Eva's well-defended underbelly.

Eva loved her father madly, had explicitly modeled herself after him—but Claire had been pretty vocal over the years after Emmaline Jansen's death about Theo's parenting skills.

Or lack thereof.

"So?" Eva demanded, snatching the latest issue of *Restaurant USA* from her white leather satchel purse, her movements jerkier than she liked. "I don't see why that's a bad thing. My father is wildly successful, both personally and professionally. Why shouldn't I try to be like him?"

"Hmm. Perhaps because he's miserable?"

That brought Eva's head up, but when she found Claire's gaze, it wasn't mocking or sardonic, despite her tone.

"What makes you think Dad isn't happy?" Eva asked, her silly heart jumping into her throat.

The softness in Claire's gaze made her look tired, and a little sad. "I have known many men like your father, none of them happy. When I came to America at twenty, I worked for a man very much like Theo—powerful and confident. Older than I. He was my first affair of the heart . . . and very nearly my last."

From the way Claire's mouth turned down at the corners, Eva didn't think it was because the guy was so wonderful that he ruined her for all other men. "It ended badly?"

"It ended predictably. The man was married; I was nothing more than a bit of fun, something to brag about, a demonstration of his prowess to the other men at the magazine." Voice sharpening with her need to make Eva understand, Claire turned in the seat to face her more fully. "That is why I caution you about starting something with this pastry chef, Eva. Romance is distracting, at best . . . catastrophic and humiliating at worst."

Eva sat frozen, starting at her oldest friend. A zillion questions zipped through her brain, too many to ask. "You never told me any of that before."

"About the affair? But no, it was not my finest hour. I tell you now only so that you may learn from my mistakes."

"Mistakes like dating my father." Eva pressed her lips together, instantly wishing she could call back the words.

But Claire didn't get upset. "I can never regret my time with Theo, because it gave me you. Even if, yes, in many ways your father reminds me of my first lover—a man who seeks only the thrill of passion, not the comfort and steadiness of love."

It would've been easy for Claire to make that a criticism of Eva's recent—and future—behavior. But all Eva saw in her friend's face was sympathy, concern, and the warm affection that had sustained Eva for most of her life.

"I'm sorry that first love affair sucked," Eva said, not even trying to hide the hoarse rasp of emotion in her voice. "And I'm really, really sorry it didn't work out between you and my dad."

Overcome with the need to give Claire something in

return for the secret she'd shared earlier, Eva said, "You know, I was mad at him for a long time for screwing things up with you. I'm not sure I've forgiven him yet, actually."

She flipped blindly through the magazine in her lap, page after glossy page of restaurant industry news, food trends, and insider gossip.

"You should forgive your father." Claire laid one hand on Eva's, stilling her manic page turning. "I forgave him long ago for not being what I needed. However, I admit I still get angry, sometimes, when he is not the man *you* need him to be."

When she was sure she could keep her voice even and steady, Eva said, "It was hard for us after Mom died. You know that. Hard for me—but for him, too. Everything at home reminded him of her, including me. I understood."

Claire's voice was as soft as her face had been. "How sweet you are beneath the spoiled-princess-of-the-restaurant-world facade. You know my only wish is for you to be happy."

Eva forced herself to meet Claire's too-perceptive stare. Calling on years of training, Eva arranged her mouth into her brightest smile and said, "Happy and sweet, that's me. Or it will be, once I get a little sugar from that hot pastry chef."

Claire's lips tightened, and for a breathless moment Eva was afraid she wasn't going to let her get away with it. But then, mercifully, all Claire said was, "I give up. There is no reasoning with you. Simply promise me you'll be careful, and do nothing you'll regret."

The heaviness of those last words made Eva pause and eye her friend with concern. "Don't worry," she said slowly, studying Claire's shuttered expression. "I won't do anything to mess up the competition. The RSC is my top priority. No matter how hot Daniel Lunden is, he's just a bit of fun on the side. Like whipped cream! Fluffy and light and sinfully tempting."

"A little whipped cream can be fun and harmless. Too much will make you unhappy—and it's not always so simple to know when you've had enough."

Eva wasn't blind. She'd seen the way their young celebrity judge, rock star and famous foodie Kane Slater, looked at Claire. Fifteen-year age difference or not, Eva had known she needed to monitor the situation, and she thought she had.

Choosing her words, she said, "You're starting to sound fairly dire. Is there something I need to know?"

The shrug Claire gave rang alarm bells in Eva's head—jerky and stiff, it lacked Claire's habitual Gallic grace.

"Nothing you need to be concerned about. Only a slight difficulty between Kane Slater and me."

"Difficulty," Eva repeated, trying not to push too hard.

Claire ran a hand through her hair, disordering the loose auburn waves. "It is my own fault. I blame no one but myself. Oh, don't look at me like that, it's nothing apocalyptic. Only . . . let us say I indulged in too much whipped cream, and it didn't agree with me."

There was definitely a story there, but it would have to wait for another time. Eva could tell by the tightness around Claire's mouth that she'd said all she was going to—for now.

"Speaking of your father," Claire said, in an unusually clumsy subject change. "He's been calling me without cease."

"Oh really?" Interest prickled along Eva's nerves.

"Yes. He is worrying about you and the competition. You know that he wants to fly to Chicago to check on us?"

The tightness in her throat had nothing to do with the fact that her father didn't trust her abilities. Really.

"I hope you told him we didn't need any hand-holding."

Claire crossed her legs. "Yes, I told him. I don't know that he listened, but I told him. He seemed concerned that the television filming might fall through."

"It won't." Eva had to fight for a calm, even tone. "I promised him I could make it happen, get the RSC on the Cooking Channel, and I will."

"Well. That's good, then."

Rolling her eyes at her friend's bland reply, Eva said, "It *will* be good. I know you're not into it, but I think Dad's right. This is the way to take the competition to the next level, and it's my chance to finally make the RSC look more like my mother's vision of it."

Claire snorted. How did she make even that noise of disdain sound elegant? "This version of *the next level* involves ridiculous grandstanding, fistfights, backbiting, and all those other lovely reality show staples."

Eva's stomach clenched in automatic denial. "No way," she protested. "We're going to keep it classy. The show is going to be all about the food, all about the craft and technique of some of the most talented chefs working today. And the more popular the show is, the more of those chefs we can help."

Claire sat silently for a long moment as the engines throbbed to life, filling Eva's head with white noise.

"I hope you're right," Claire finally said, her gaze searching Eva's face.

Eva, who also very much hoped she was right, turned on her most brilliant, confident smile—the one that banished the doubts from every potential restaurant investor and made the local health inspectors blush.

"Come on, you know I'm going to pull it off. It's the

RSC! My family's thing. I'm not going to let it go to pieces, or turn to shit, the very first year Dad lets me get involved with it."

Suddenly Patrick the flight attendant appeared at Eva's elbow like a wonderful magical sprite, holding a tray of long-stemmed champagne flutes.

Eva accepted her mimosa with a conspiratorial wink, and passed one to Claire.

"Drink up, *ma chérie*," Eva said, purposefully using her ugliest American accent to make Claire grimace, then laugh. "We need the fortification before the RSC starts in earnest."

Clinking the cheap glasses together put a little sparkle back in Claire's brown eyes. "Yes. Here's to overcoming challenges."

"And to throwing down some challenges of our own."

Tipping her head back to let a sip of the tart-sweet cocktail slide down her throat, Eva enjoyed the blend of dry sparkling wine and sweet orange juice. This early in the morning, the sugary alcoholic goodness gave her a bigger lift than the air under the plane's wings.

Somewhere back in coach, Daniel Lunden was sipping a plain old ginger ale, surrounded by giddy passengers swilling down their mimosas. She pictured him glaring at them, those brows drawn down tight over his brooding blue-gray eyes as he silently condemned them for letting her buy their forgiveness with brunch drinks.

Eva drained her glass and licked the sharp taste of anticipation from her lips.

"Let the games begin."

Chapter 3

Chicago didn't look at all like he'd expected.

Blinking up through the cab window at the short, squat high-rise office buildings—high-rise? Medium-rise, at best—Danny contemplated the stainless-steel gray of the October clouds and wondered why he felt so unsettled.

Apparently he looked as weirded out as he felt, because his brother clapped him on the back hard enough to send him sprawling against the car door, if Danny hadn't already been bracing himself against the freaky vertigo of seeing so much sky stretching over the tops of the buildings.

"Buck up, Danny," was Max's helpful advice. "Chicago's a great town. You're gonna love it."

Danny shrugged, leather-jacketed shoulders squeaking against the cracked vinyl of the taxi's backseat. Even the cab looked all wrong, drab gray instead of bright orangey yellow. "We're not here to love Chicago. We're here to cook. It doesn't matter what city we're in—once we're in the kitchen, we could be anywhere, and the only sight I want to see is my marble pastry board set up all nice and cold and in one damn piece."

One of Max's brows quirked up in that annoying way he'd had ever since they were kids, whenever Danny was being a moron. Which, according to Max, was often.

"Come on, Dan. I never pegged you for one of those New Yorkers who refuses to leave the city."

Danny tensed. "Not everyone feels the need to spend half their life wandering the globe playing with their auras and trying to find themselves. Or whatever new-agey crap gets you out of bed in the morning."

Eyes wide, Max backed off, hands held up in front of him as if Danny had pointed a gun at his chest.

"Boys, play nice," Jules interjected from Max's other side. She didn't raise her voice or anything, but then she didn't need to. Her genuine distress at seeing her best friend and her boyfriend squabbling like . . . well, like brothers, was enough to simmer Danny down.

Except this thing with Max was more than plain old vanilla sibling bickering, and Danny knew it. They'd hashed out their differences enough to be able to work together, but sometimes the issues simmered over and blew the lid off their careful, stilted relationship.

A pang of guilt shot through him, but before he could apologize, the weird, non-yellow taxi swerved to the curb—at least the cabdrivers seemed to have gone to the same driving school as the ones in New York—in front of the hotel that would be their home base for the first leg of the Rising Star Chef competition.

Paying the cabbie and dealing with the fact that some of their luggage seemed to be missing from the trunk allowed Danny and Max to skim over the awkward silence that had started cropping up between them anytime they got into an argument lately.

The cab carrying Beck, Winslow, and the missing gear pulled up, and in the ensuing confusion of bags and luggage carts, Danny managed to shake off his worries and get juiced about the start of the competition.

The irrepressible Winslow Jones was a big help with that.

"Man, can you believe this joint?" The youngest chef on the team stared up at the vaulted ceiling of the lobby, jaw hanging open in exaggerated awe. "Now this is what I'm talking about. Lunden's needs more shiny. Marble floors and what not."

Danny reached over to rub Winslow's smooth shaved head. "Sure. You can be in charge of polishing," he dead-panned, cracking Win up, and smiled his way over to the reception desk.

The Gold Coast Arms, a four-star hotel in the swanki-est part of downtown Chicago, was the home of one of the city's best restaurants, Limestone—which also happened to be one of the Jansen Hospitality Group's biggest stars. Rumor had it that Eva Jansen had strong-armed—or sweet-talked, depending on whom you heard it from—the ritzy hotel into sponsoring the preliminary round of the RSC, which was usually held in a bare-bones convention center somewhere.

Glancing around at the opulent decor—even the walls were shiny, patterned with some expensive-looking gold-leaf stuff—Danny shook his head. He would've preferred a basic, utilitarian setup to all this luxury. It was unneces-sary and distracting, when distraction was the last thing he and his guys could afford.

A scuffle drew Danny's attention to the far side of the lobby where an enormous glass-and-steel doorway arched almost to the ceiling. In the course of his explorations, Winslow had managed to bump the chrome easel beside the door, knocking the sign it held onto the floor.

Win got it back on the easel, realized it was upside

down, and turned it right-side up, apologizing profusely the whole time and just generally making a spectacle of himself.

Danny's amusement faded into concentration when he read the sign, though, which proclaimed in bold letters that the acclaimed hotel restaurant Limestone was temporarily closed in preparation for the Rising Star Chef competition.

That sign, and the knowledge of what it cost a restaurant like that to simply shut down business for days, brought it home to Danny for the first time.

This was really happening.

It was another half hour before they were installed in their rooms. Jules and Max were holed up in what everyone was already calling the Honeymoon Suite, even though it was just a regular room.

Danny, Beck, and Win were bunking together.

The Gold Coast's sponsorship did extend to comping the contestants' rooms—but hotel management had definite ideas about how many people fit in one of their two queen-bed deluxe superior rooms.

"Thank the sweet Lord we've got a chick on our team," Winslow said fervently, slinging his oversize packing case onto one of the beds. "Until they saw Jules, I think they were fixing to cram all five of us in here, two to a bed and one in the bathtub."

"Hey, at least we've got a great view of the Water Tower." Danny held the gold-striped curtain back to point at the very top of Chicago's most famous historic landmark, just barely visible from their window.

Win sucked his teeth and squinted in Danny's general direction, but Beck, who'd efficiently unpacked his one small bag into the three narrow drawers in one of the bedside tables, stood up and said, "It's fine. Lots more space than some places I've slept."

So evidently Beck's claustrophobia didn't extend to slightly cramped luxury hotel rooms.

"The Water Tower's kind of cool, I guess," Win grudgingly admitted, stepping over to the window.

"It's one of the few structures that survived the big fire in 1871, the only one that's still standing. Supposedly because it's made of limestone."

Win brightened. "Hey, like the restaurant!"

"I think there might be a connection," Beck said. His expression never changed, but somehow Danny knew he was teasing.

Fondness for his teammates suffused Danny with warmth. "Come on, guys. No point hanging around the room all day. Let's go down and check out the competition space, see what this Limestone kitchen looks like."

"Good idea." Winslow sat down to put on the pristinely white sneakers he'd removed the instant they got into the room, and nearly slipped right off the slick damask seat cushion. "Maybe they'll have the ingredients for mimosas lying around. I could really go for one of those."

Groaning, Danny threw his head back to stare at the ceiling. "Seriously? Enough with the mimosas!"

"I just don't see what would've been so heinous about having one," Win sulked. "Everyone else on the plane got one."

"Everyone else let Eva Jansen buy them off for the price of a mixed drink. I don't want to speak for you, but personally, my time is worth a little more to me than five bucks."

"And me drinking my complimentary spicy tomato juice was the perfect *fuck you*. I guess we showed her!"

Win's snarky tone usually got a smile out of Danny, but not this time.

He knew it was ridiculous to stand on principle in a situation like this. So Eva Jansen was a spoiled brat who threw money at her problems to make them go away. So what? That was her business. The smart move would've been to shake her hand, sit down and enjoy his tasty champagne cocktail on her dime, and let it go.

But something about her got under his skin, in the most inconvenient way possible.

He'd been off his game to begin with, Danny comforted himself, because he was worried about Beck. Danny cast a glance at his normally stoic friend. Looking at him now, all stern face and bulging muscles, no one would guess Beck had spent the first hour of the flight putting ten finger-shaped dents in the plastic armrests between their seats.

But Danny couldn't quite forget how messed up the guy had looked while they waited and waited for the plane to take off, and he added *Watch out for Beck* to his mental list of responsibilities as they trooped out of the room and down the plush carpeted hall to the bank of elevators.

"So what was Eva-the-Diva wearing?" Win asked, pressing the button with the down arrow.

Danny blinked. "Huh? I don't know, something blue. A dress."

Winslow sighed. "God. You're such a straight boy. I need details, man! Eva Jansen is the style icon of the restaurant world. People are going to want to know what she had on. They're going to ask me, and what will I tell them?"

"Maybe it was purple," Danny offered, feeling helpless. "Come on. I'm not Joan Rivers, I didn't ask who the designer was. I had other things on my mind."

"But you knew it was designer." Winslow pounced,

looking triumphant. "That's something. And I'll just bet you had other things on your mind. If I swung that way, I'd be all over Miss Eva Diva. She is something way beyond fine."

Danny couldn't help it. He sputtered. "I'm not all over her! I mean, I wasn't. Damn it, Win!"

Even Beck snickered a little when Winslow started snapping his fingers and singing. "It's just . . . ah! A little crush . . . ah!"

"I do not have a crush." Even Danny was surprised by the amount of growl in his voice. Still, it was enough to shut Winslow up for a second, which wasn't easy, so Danny couldn't feel too bad about it.

"Look, she's hot," Danny admitted, moderating his tone. "I'll give her that for free. But spoiled little rich girls using Daddy's money and rep to play with the lives of hardworking chefs? Not really my type."

"Ouch," Win said, wincing. "Snap judgment much? I thought she seemed pretty cool when she emceed the regional finals."

"Come on, Beck, back me up." Danny turned to their large, silent teammate.

The guy blinked in that slow, assessing way he had, ripped arms crossed over his broad chest. Not for the first time, Danny wondered when the hell Beck found a spare four hours a day to lift weights, because surely there was no other way to get cut like that. He didn't look a walking ad for steroids or anything, but still.

"Win's right. It's bad tactics to form an opinion based on rumor and preconceived notions—you run the risk of underestimating someone."

Winslow did a quick hip-shaking boogie. "In your face, Lunden!"

Unable to hold in a laugh, Danny conceded the point

rather than continue arguing. "Fine, fine. Eva Jansen could quite possibly be the smartest, savviest, hardest-working woman in the restaurant industry for all I know. Happy? That doesn't change the fact that none of us needs a split focus right now. The competition is all that matters."

"Someone tell that to Max and Jules." Winslow shook his head. "If either one of them can focus on something besides each other for longer than ten minutes these days, I'll be freaking amazed."

Danny sighed. "You're not wrong. But they're in love. They're happy, which is a great thing, but they're both professionals. I'm sure they'll snap out of it when we hit the first challenge. Until then, we just need to pick up the slack for them, a little. It's going to be fine."

He refused to contemplate what he'd do if they didn't snap out the haze of fluffy bunnies, twittering birds, and prancing unicorns that currently surrounded them in time to help the team kick ass in Chicago.

As Beck stepped forward, frowning, to jam his finger into the DOWN button again—where the hell was the elevator, anyway?—Winslow sidled closer to Danny, his startling green eyes intent on Danny's face.

"You know," Winslow said softly. "It's okay to feel a little shitty and left out when you see Max and Jules together. I mean, they're not my BFF and my older brother suddenly sharing this deep forever twoo-wuv connection, and sometimes I want to yell at them to get a room and leave the rest of us poor singletons in lonely, solitary peace!"

"I'm happy for them," Danny said. He was vaguely proud of that fact that it didn't sound like he'd spoken the words through gritted teeth.

"Well, sure." Win shrugged. "I'm happy for 'em, too. That ain't the issue. But you and Jules used to be super close, and now she's all wrapped up in Max. It's normal to feel left out."

Danny forced a laugh. "No one should be as in touch with his feelings as you are. It can't be healthy."

Win's eyes narrowed on Danny's face. "I'll tell you what I think you're interested in getting in touch with: the lovely Miss Eva-the-Diva."

"You're way off base," Danny told him as the elevator bell dinged. "All I'm interested in is winning."

Danny breathed a sigh of relief. This conversation was treading dangerously close to some of the shit he wanted to suppress and avoid.

Yeah, okay. The woman in charge of running the entire Rising Star Chef competition, one of the most successful restaurateurs in the country, was hotter than a pan full of caramelizing sugar. Which didn't make her a sensible option for relieving the annoyingly persistent ache he felt when he looked at his brother cuddled up to his best friend.

Used to be super close, Win had said, and Danny couldn't lie to himself. There were times when he missed being the man in Jules's life, and having her be so present in his. But she deserved someone who could love her for real, not just as a friend, and Danny was happy for her. For both of them. He was.

And he definitely wasn't lonely or pathetic enough for pointless, impractical fantasies about Eva Jansen.

"Just remember what they say." Winslow threw an arm over Danny's shoulders as the doors swished smoothly open, and hauled him inside. "All work and no play makes Danny a Cranky McCrankypants."

Pulled off balance, Danny laughed and shoved at Winslow, who stumbled back into the immovable wall of Beck, who grasped his shoulders and set him gently on his feet.

"It's like watching a Marx Brothers routine," a lazy feminine voice said from the corner.

With a start, Danny realized they weren't alone in the polished wood box. Standing there all gorgeous and sexy in her bluish purple mummy-wrap dress and that ever-present curl of a smile was Eva Jansen.

That figured. No wonder the elevator took so long to arrive. She'd probably had the doors held open for ten minutes, waiting for her to finish powdering her nose or something.

"Well," Eva purred, tilted gray eyes slitting like a cat's on the prowl. "Fancy seeing you here."

Chapter 4

Completely against his wishes, Danny's body responded to the low seduction of her voice. He shifted uncomfortably. Why did she always have to sound like she'd just gotten out of bed?

"Hi, Ms. Jansen!" Winslow stuck his hand out, all chirpy and bright-eyed, sure of his welcome. "Love the dress." He slanted a look at Danny. "Michael Kors is the master of wearable beauty, I always say."

"Do you?" Eva arched one perfectly arched brow as she shook Win's hand. "Thanks. Where'd you get that T-shirt? If you say at a concert, I'm going to die of jealousy right here in the elevator."

Danny did a double take. Yep, he'd remembered it right—Winslow had on a battered Rolling Stones shirt, the original black faded to gray after repeated washings.

"You're a Stoner?" Winslow was beaming now, all but bouncing up and down on the balls of his feet.

"What can I say? Mick Jagger is hot."

There, he told himself. *See? She isn't the perfect woman—she's every bit as shallow and superficial as you thought.*

Which wasn't as comforting as Danny would've expected, not when he was face-to-face with the slender curves of her unabashedly female body bound by that tight little dress.

Danny had his shallow and superficial moments, too.

Win got thoughtful. "I was always more into Keith, myself. That boy can really rock a head scarf."

Beck cleared his throat, drawing Danny's attention from the Stones lovefest in the corner. The big guy's face was taking on that grayish hue under the olive skin, and in a flash Danny realized the elevator doors had closed, but they weren't going anywhere.

"Hey," he broke in sharply. "Now that we're all best girlfriends, does someone maybe want to pick a floor?"

Suppressing his immediate guilt at the hurt that flashed across Winslow's face, Danny turned to Beck.

Keep him talking.

"What floor is the kitchen on, man? Do you know?"

From his friends in the hotel restaurant biz, Danny knew that you couldn't count on the kitchen occupying the same floor as the dining room. Worst-case scenario, they could go down to the lobby and ask, but Beck was starting to sweat.

"Oh, are you going down to Limestone to check out the kitchen?" Eva stepped smartly up to the elevator's control panel and pressed the button for the second floor. "I'm on my way there, too."

"Small world," Danny muttered.

"Small hotel," she replied, sending him a look from the corner of her almond-shaped eyes.

The rest of the ride down to the second level took about fifteen seconds, but they were some of the longest, most tension-filled seconds of Danny's life.

Beck looked miserably stoic, Winslow was uncharacteristically subdued, and somehow Danny felt responsible for both.

He tried not to hate himself for the way he couldn't drag together enough focus to do anything about it—not with Eva Jansen standing less than three feet away from him, the only person in the elevator who appeared completely at ease.

Every time Danny drew in a breath, the lush, complicated scent of her perfume teased his nose and kept his nerves on edge.

When the elevator slid to a smooth halt, Beck was the first one out the doors, followed closely by Winslow.

Cursing the manners his mother had drilled into him, Danny put an arm out to keep the doors open and stood aside to let the lady behind him pass. One heartbeat, then two, and he finally glanced back to see what the hell he was being kept waiting for this time.

However, Eva wasn't fixing her hair or fiddling with her cell phone or any of the other obnoxious things he'd imagined in that instantaneous flash of annoyance.

No, nothing so mundane. Instead, she was leaning against the brass rail that ran along the back of the elevator, arms spread out to the sides, red-tipped fingers curled gracefully around the horizontal rod and mile-long legs crossed at the ankle in front of her.

The elevator buzzed loudly, jolting Danny out of his paralyzed contemplation of the way Eva's dark, dark hair swung against the milky paleness of her delicate jaw.

At his jump, the corners of her candy-apple lips tilted up even more. Pushing away from the wall, she sauntered forward. Danny braced himself for the moment when she'd brush past him, her body so close and yet so untouchably far.

But again, as if she'd made an advanced study of how

not to do what Danny expected, Eva stopped just inside the elevator doors. She lifted one white hand to Danny's tensed bicep—the thick waffle-print cotton of his sleeve did nothing to blunt the electric spark of the touch—and trailed those slender fingers along his arm until she'd managed to tug his unresisting limb away from the door.

The elevator stopped buzzing, although Danny hardly noticed what with the buzzing in his ears, and the doors slid shut, enclosing the two of them alone in the tiny, opulent box. With a soft whir, the elevator began to ascend, called by someone on a higher floor.

Never breaking eye contact, Eva leaned in. Danny's heart kicked against his rib cage and his breath sped up, but she reached right past him and pressed some button that made the entire elevator jerk to an immediate stop.

The suddenness of the maneuver woke Danny out of whatever pheromone-induced coma she'd put him in with her perfume and her dress and her wickedly curved mouth.

"What are you doing?" he demanded. It came out less sharp, more hoarse, but he couldn't do anything about that.

"I wanted a moment alone with you." She never lost that look of calm, detached amusement, and just like on the plane, it set Danny's temper on fire.

"Next time, you might think about asking."

"I was pretty sure you'd say no," Eva returned calmly, her gray eyes flashing silver with amusement.

As much as Danny might have wanted to refuse to spend a moment alone with this woman who shook his composure and made him forget himself . . . "You're one of the most powerful people in the restaurant industry, plus you hold the fate of this competition in your lily-white hands. You really think I'm dumb enough to blow you off?"

Whoops. That came out a bit more aggressive than he'd intended.

One dark brow winged up. "I didn't peg you for someone who cared a lot about authority," she said, mildly enough considering the tone he'd been using. "And I know you don't have much respect for me, regardless of how much power I supposedly have."

Danny took a deep breath, trying to loosen the pressure in his chest, get back some semblance of his usual control. "Look, I'm sorry if I've offended you or whatever."

That stung a little, but it was worth it if it kept her from forming some kind of grudge against his team.

Instead of looking grateful for the apology, however, the minx had the balls to laugh at him. "Nice. You're not sorry you were rude—you're just sorry I didn't like it, right? Well, you can relax, Mr. Manners. I'm not that sensitive, and I've been looked down on by bigger men than you and come out on top in the end."

It was more of an I-am-woman-hear-me-roar speech than a flirt, but somehow she said the words in that smoky honey voice of hers and all Danny could picture was the two of them laid out on the nearest available surface, with Eva straddling him like a pony.

He swallowed hard. "What, exactly, did you trap me in here to talk about?" With some extra jaw clenching, he managed it without sounding like a sex-starved teenager or something.

"Actually," she said, with that half-smile that made it look like she was enjoying a joke no one else was in on, "I wanted to apologize again to you for holding up that plane. I noticed the way your friend—the fish cook for the team, right? I could tell he didn't like being in the elevator, and it made me wonder if the airplane upset him the same way.

And then I thought maybe, before, you were worried about him and that's why you were so annoyed that I held up the departure. Because you're the one who takes care of everyone on your team, I think. I bet if you were the one with claustrophobia, you wouldn't have even come up to the front to complain to the flight attendant. Anyway, I wanted to say I was sorry for making it harder for you to keep your team calm and happy. But we got off track, somehow, and you ended up apologizing to me. Sort of. Sorry!"

Against his will, Danny stiffened. Her unexpected insight struck way too close to the bone and left him feeling raw and exposed. "So. That's one for me, and one for you. As far as I'm concerned, we're even now."

Eva sent him a knowing look from under insanely long, curling lashes. "Are you sure you won't let me make it up to you?"

Without conscious volition, Danny's feet carried him forward, slowly closing the gap between them.

Eva didn't move, just tilted her head, her steady gaze never wavering for an instant. This was a woman who knew what she wanted and wasn't afraid to go out and get it.

They were so close now, they were sharing the same air, passing one breath back and forth between them in a long, heated moment of suspended time. He could smell the heady sweetness of her perfume, but underneath it was something even more addictive—the warm, earthy tang of clean skin and woman. It went to his head like some sort of toxic, mind-altering smoke, blurring reality and fuzzing out his will to back off.

The desire he'd been repressing roared back to the forefront of his consciousness, voracious as a starved wolf and twice as unwilling to be denied. Eva's stillness, her lifted chin, should've indicated submission, or at least acceptance, but instead there was something about her steady regard and curved lips that felt like a challenge.

Unable or unwilling to ignore it, Danny ditched the last vestiges of his common sense and reached for her with both hands.

Her mouth under his was soft, yielding, but Danny didn't miss the flare of triumph in her eyes before she shut them and moaned, giving herself to the kiss. Her body molded effortlessly to his, her heat pressed firmly along the length of him. Those pretty white fingers of hers returned to his arms, this time trailing up, pausing to squeeze his shoulders before clasping at his neck.

Danny wanted to stop this, he really did, but somehow he couldn't make his fists unclench from the sweet roundness of her hips. All his focus was on the meeting of their lips, the slick slide of their tongues, the ferocity of his need for her taste.

She made a sound deep in her throat, rough and unashamed, and immediately pure unadulterated high-octane lust flooded his system. He'd been hard since he'd seen her splayed out against the back wall of the elevator, but when she growled like that, the rush of blood through his body made his cock throb so thickly he was momentarily afraid he'd pass out.

Heart beating like it did at the top of the tallest roller coaster at Coney Island, Danny finally managed to pry his fingers loose and take a step back, gulping in some much-needed air.

Eva let him go easily, staring up at him with her mouth flushed and swollen from his kisses, but still, freaking *still* looking about half a second from a smirk.

"That was fun," she said throatily, smoothing her perfectly smooth hair.

"That was idiotic," Danny gritted out. His body, high

on adrenaline and sex and the slight edge of danger, already ached to be mashed up against Eva's softness again. "And risky. Eventually, someone in this hotel is going to notice this elevator's not running."

"The risk is part of what makes it fun." Eva bent to snag her purse from the corner where she'd dropped it before making her big move. Shooting him an arch glance as she located a compact mirror, she said, "Oh, please. I hope you're not going to try to convince me you didn't enjoy that."

Watching her reapply her lipstick sent a weird pang shooting through his midsection. It was so . . . intimate.

Turning away, Danny located the EMERGENCY STOP button and punched it forcefully, releasing the temporary hold on the elevator, then hit the button for level two.

Without looking at her, he said, "Yeah, okay. I'm a guy. I enjoyed the hot grope. Sue me."

Shit, part of him thought. *I hope to God she doesn't sue me. She can afford way more flesh-eating lawyers than my family can.*

But Eva only laughed again, this time with an edge he couldn't identify. "I didn't mean the kiss."

I will not ask her what she means, I will not ask her what she means, I will not ask her what she means . . .

The elevator stopped at the ninth floor, but whoever had called it must have long ago given up and taken the stairs or something, so Danny jabbed at the button to close the doors and send the car back down to the kitchen.

Danny kept his gaze on the light flashing through the numbers above the doors, counting down the floors. Just as the 2 button was illuminated and the elevator began to slow, a charged heat along his side warned him that Eva was next to him.

Her breath brushed his ear, tickled through the strands

of hair at his neck, sending a shudder of savage, un-quenched desire down his spine.

But it was her words that gave him the biggest chill.

"It wasn't the kiss that turned you on," she murmured. "It was the naughtiness of it. The fact that you broke your own rules and played by mine, even for a few seconds, got you hotter than you've ever been in your whole life. And there's more where that came from."

Danny's lungs locked up tight. He couldn't move, could only stare as the doors slid open and Eva walked past him and out into the golden light of the hallway.

"You coming?" She tossed it over her shoulder as if she didn't even care, but even in his moment of shocked paralysis, Danny registered the slight stiffness of her slim, elegant form.

Somehow, the knowledge that she wasn't quite so nonchalant as she wanted him to think made it easy to breathe again, and to stride down the hall at her side.

He let them get to the huge double doors that marked the entrance to the hotel kitchen before he stopped and said, "I'm a pastry chef. I'm good at rules—good at figuring them out, and figuring out ways around them, ways to bend them, ways to break them."

She hesitated, one hand on the door, and for the first time a note of uncertainty crept into her confident gaze.

"Just a friendly warning," Danny said, reaching past her to push the door open. "In case you thought you were the one setting up the game. I'm here to win, sweetheart. And I don't mess around."

Chapter 5

It was only October. How was Chicago already a bleak frozen wasteland ripped by icy winds? Kane Slater zipped his black hoodie up all the way to his chin and wished he'd been smart enough to bring a real coat.

But damn, it never got this ball-shriveling cold back home in Austin, not even in the dead of winter. And in fucking LA, where he lived now, people wigged out and started wearing those ugly-ass furry boots if it dropped below seventy-two.

Still. He should've known it would be chilly up here. He hummed a snatch of the new, half-formed melody he couldn't get out of his head and huddled down into the worn fleece of his sweatshirt, making sure his thick black sunglasses were perched firmly on his nose, hiding his distinctive blue eyes. His hood was up and pulled tight, too, and he'd pretty much found that if people couldn't see his blond hair and blue eyes, they didn't know who he was.

At the very least, no one on the streets of Chicago seemed to recognize him, and Kane sent up a hymn of thanks to whatever gods looked out for rock stars who'd slipped the leashes of their handlers for an afternoon.

It was stupid, maybe, but after the rocket-ship launch of his last two years of Grammys and music video awards and world tours and screaming girls throwing their panties onto the stage, Kane needed a break every now and then. He accepted the restrictions, the bodyguards, the eyes watching his every move as part of the whole fame package, and usually it was a decent trade-off. He knew he'd make the same deal with the devil a thousand times over if it meant he got to live and breathe music every day.

But the huge, smothering, never-receding wave of attention made it hard to get a minute alone to think.

And Kane had some shit to work through.

Okay, he told himself as his rubber-soled Converse All Stars pounded the sidewalk, the thin canvas doing nothing to block the slushy leftovers of last week's snow. *Man up. You made a commitment to the RSC, to Eva, and to yourself. Don't let the fact that you're all whipped and mopey over a fellow judge stop you from doing your job.*

Also, he decided as a gust of frigid air whipped down the canyon formed by the tall buildings and neatly sheared off the top layer of Kane's skin, *maybe don't be such an emo loser that you stalk around in the ice cold contracting pneumonia or something.*

Conceding his defeat to Chicago's famous blustery weather, Kane wrapped his arms around his torso and shouldered his way into the first coffee shop he saw.

Warmth hit him like a feather pillow to the face, so soft and welcome his bones actually ached with it. The abrupt transition stole his breath for a long instant, but the jingle of the door behind him and the press of another caffeine-deprived customer jostling into him got Kane moving again.

The place looked nothing like the bright, airy cafés of LA, all big panes of glass and clean, modern lines and self-consciously designed furniture. And it wasn't much like the well-used, well-loved downtown shabby-cool hipster coffee bars back in Austin.

And it couldn't have been more different from that one place on the Upper East Side of Manhattan—the Parisian-style coffee shop where he'd first told Claire Durand he didn't care how much older she was, or what people would think. Where he told her exactly how much he wanted her.

Forcing the memory from his mind, Kane looked around at the cracked plaster walls covered in aging yellow posters for things like Vienna beef hot dogs and chocolate-covered Twinkies. It was a small place, narrow and long, with a bank of red vinyl booths running along the left side. Customers lined up to the right, giving their orders to a smiling young woman with colorful tattoos climbing both bare arms.

Kane was willing to bet she didn't call herself a "barista," and that the cups of coffee came in small, medium, and large. He grinned.

More than anything else, it reminded him of the diner back home in the Texas Hill Country town where he grew up.

Feeling calmer and more at ease than he had in months, Kane risked pushing his sunglasses up onto the top of his head so he could read the menu. Sure enough, his options were limited to drip coffee, espresso, or latte, and none was offered in Italian sizes.

He thought the girl working the counter might have recognized him—behind her cat-eye glasses, she went a little wide and shocky—but she handed over his beautifully boring plain coffee-flavored coffee without any hassle. Grateful, Kane stuffed a twenty in the tip jar and went in search of cream.

What he found was the one woman he'd been doing his best to figure out.

There, sitting at the booth in the corner behind an open laptop and a mug topped with snowy white frothed milk, was Claire Durand.

She'd been on his mind so much, Kane had to pause for a moment and blink furiously to clear his vision and make sure she was really real, really there.

But it seemed she was, elegant and classy in her dark red sweater set, with a gorgeous patterned scarf knotted carelessly at her neck. She was like something out of those magazines Kane's mom used to get, the ones that had articles like "Where to Summer This Year" and "At Home with Princess Grace."

And it had to really be her, he reasoned, edging closer to her table, because if it were all in his head, surely he'd picture her the way she'd looked stretched across the sheets in his hotel room back in New York, her slim, toned thighs and slender arms reaching for him, her mouth deeply pink because he couldn't stop biting at her lips, her gorgeous hair spread over the pillow like a blanket of fallen autumn leaves.

Feeling a little dazed, Kane raised his mug to his lips. The bitter burn of unadulterated coffee jolted him awake. He never did find the cream, did he?

But now that he'd seen Claire, he was locked into her magnetic gravitational pull like a satellite orbiting a small planet. Drifting closer, he stood right over her. She glanced up from her work with a frown of concentration still knotting her auburn brows.

The frown smoothed into a look of pure surprise. Kane savored it for a bare moment before setting his coffee down on her table and sliding onto the bench seat across from her.

"We've got to stop meeting like this," he said, as easy and breezy as you please.

The memory of that day, weeks ago, in a small café on the Upper East Side flickered across her beautiful face briefly, then was gone.

She hesitated before she replied, and Kane experienced a quick, silent panic that she'd call him *Mr. Slater.* Which would mean he'd have to do something drastic to remind her that since they'd seen each other naked, last names were just creepy, but then she said, "Kane. How nice to see you."

Not the most enthusiastic greeting he'd ever received, but the leap of heat in her eyes told a different story.

"I like your office." He gestured to the scuffed tin poster hanging above her head covered in a stamped advertisement for Jolly Good Doughnuts.

"What? Oh. Yes, well, the room I've been given at the Gold Coast is sufficient for sleeping, but it doesn't provide a large enough desk, or a steady supply of hot coffee. We featured Blue Smoke Coffee in the magazine earlier this year in an article about the new trend in scaled-down coffee bars."

"Hey, I read that article—I think I even tore it out of the magazine and pinned it to the wall of the tour bus. I had every intention of visiting all the places y'all listed. What are the odds I'd stumble over this one completely at random?"

"I couldn't say." Claire narrowed her eyes at him, clearly a bit on the disbelieving side of *incredible coincidence.*

"My mama always says I was born under a lucky star." He gave her his best disarming smile and leaned back in the booth, locking his arms behind his head to stop them from reaching for her.

She was just so perfect and whole within herself, with an inner stillness born of knowing exactly who she was and what she wanted. Claire Durand sometimes seemed more like a monument or a statue made of marble and steel than a flesh-and-blood woman.

But Kane knew she was made of silky smooth flesh, and that she was hot-blooded through and through. He'd had that firm, creamy skin of hers under his hands, his mouth. He'd tasted it.

The contrast between the Claire in his head, how she'd been that night, and the Claire sitting straight-shouldered and distant across from him made Kane's head spin harder than a shot of espresso on an empty stomach.

"Anyway," Kane barreled ahead. "I would've thought you'd be a-okay with running into me here . . . off the competition site, away from everyone who knows us." He spread his arms along the back of the booth. "There's no one here to care if I get inappropriate."

He waggled his eyebrows to take the edge off his words, but the unhappy curve of Claire's mouth told him he'd failed. "Kane . . . all I asked was that you be a bit more . . . circumspect. More aware of our surroundings. This is not a vacation from my real job—this is an enormous and highly visible part of my real job. I can't be seen as one of your . . . what is the word? Groupies."

Stung, Kane dropped his elbows to the table and leaned in. "Okay, A? You're not a groupie. Nobody in their right mind would mistake you for one. And two, that's not totally accurate."

She closed her eyes briefly. "I'm sorry. I didn't mean to imply that you don't take your duties as a judge of the RSC seriously. But it is not your career, Kane."

He winced. "Uh, no . . . actually, that part was pretty accurate. And I see your point. I do. But you didn't just ask me to be circumspect. You asked for time. Apart. And that's hard for me."

The raw honesty in his voice must have gotten through to her, because everything about her softened, from the line of her shoulders to the look in her eyes.

Reaching a slim hand across the table, Claire let her fingertips rest gently on his rigid wrist. "It's hard for me, too. I have missed you."

Kane could relate. After that first night together in New York, followed by weeks of banter, flirting, kissing, and making love across the country as the judges traveled to the other regional finals to pick the teams from the Midwest, South, Southwest, and West Coast, Claire's request to cool things down once the actual competition began had come as a shock.

Although, looking back, he could sort of see where there had been clues . . . the way she always wanted to meet after hours, away from the rest of the RSC crew, the way she stiffened when he forgot and touched her in public.

But they could figure that stuff out, he thought. It didn't have to be the end of everything.

Giving her his best cocky grin, he flipped the wrist she'd touched and grabbed her fingers. "So if you miss me, and I sure as hell miss you, then hot damn! I've got just the solution."

Claire blew out a breath that stirred the wave of auburn hair over her high forehead.

"You aren't listening. Or perhaps you simply do not wish to hear. Fine. Let me be plain. Kane, what we have between us, it is . . . how do you say? *De trop.* Too much, of everything except common sense and rationality."

Kane's foolishly hopeful heart perked up. "I make you

feel too much. That doesn't exactly sound like a catastrophe to me."

Her mouth quivered as if it wanted to laugh. "For you? I would imagine no. You are one of those men who lives at a faster pace than the rest of the world, always searching for the new thrill, the new sensation."

He had to admit, she had his number there. "So I skydive and eat blowfish." He shrugged. "I like to feel alive. Don't you?"

Her eyes sharpened like arrows on his face. "Ah, but I don't need to risk my life and sanity in order to feel alive. And in affairs of the heart, it is the same. You chase the big risk, the big emotion. For me . . ." It was her turn to shrug, and he watched with a stirring of desire in his gut as she made a much more elegant job of it.

"For you?" he prompted he when she fell silent.

A shadow moved across her face, like a curtain dropping over a well-lit stage, and she said, "You Americans. You suppress the body and its desires, and treat the heart as if it is a wild animal to be tamed, so that when those things are awakened in you, they have the strength of ravenous lions, too long imprisoned."

Caught by the imagery, Kane felt a line of lyrics unspool in his head, perfectly shaped to fit the melody that had been rattling around in there for a day and a half.

Burning with it, he snatched the pencil he always carried in his back pocket and leaned across the table to steal Claire's unused white paper napkin.

Scribbling furiously, he fought to get the words out of his brain and onto the paper before they vanished into the air. "Go on," he said tensely, hand cramping from how tight he was holding the pencil. "I'm still listening. Lions. Go."

Amusement colored her voice the same red as her cashmere sweater. "You see? Nothing is simple for you. But I learned, when I was younger than you are now, the way to happiness is balance and moderation—the needs of the body are important, yes, but they do not rule the entire self. Take your pleasures where you find them, enjoy them, then leave them there so they do not overtake you. I believe in this, Kane, the way some people believe in heaven and hell."

God, that voice of hers. The way she used words. If he hadn't already known she started out at *Délicieux* as their star feature food writer before being promoted to editor in chief, he would've been able to guess on the strength of this conversation.

Everything she said, every single image, slid between his ribs and pierced his heart. He didn't want this to be the end of everything between them, but if it turned out to be, then he'd have one last reason to remember Claire Durand, because she'd made even this moment beautiful, and if there was anything Kane believed in as strongly as heaven and hell, it was the idea of beauty.

"So you took your pleasure with me." His voice was more of a strangled gasp than his usual strong baritenor, but he forgave himself, this once. "And now you're ready to move on. Just like that."

Claire shifted in her seat, the leather creaking under her hips. After a moment of visible internal struggle she said, "No, not just like that. And not for the reason you're thinking."

Kane's brain had gone to a very visceral place at the sound of her moving against the leather.

Yeah, this was a make-or-break conversation in which he was seriously emotionally invested, but he was still a guy.

"I promise, you have no idea what I'm thinking," he told her.

Something in his voice, some hint of the X-rated memories playing out in his mind's eye like the best-ever porn, made her dark brown gaze snap to molten hot chocolate in an instant.

"I need to pull away from this"—she gestured between them languidly—"because when I'm with you, I lose my balance. I don't feel calm and happy."

She leaned forward, and Kane swallowed down his immediate urge to leap across the table and crush her thin lips under his.

"When I'm with you," Claire said, her accent rolling through the words like distant thunder, "I am a starving lion, raging at my captivity."

And as she sat back, the fires in her eyes banked again while she gathered up her laptop and left, Kane realized two things.

He'd never wanted to be eaten up so badly in his life.

And if Claire could still look at him like that, then nothing—*nothing*—was over.

Chapter 6

Eva was supremely grateful she spent a good portion of her life strapped into ridiculously high heels. If these Louboutins were out of the norm for her, there was no way she'd be able to keep upright after that knee-weakening, eyebrow-singeing, no-holds-barred kiss back there.

The kiss itself had thrown her off balance with its intensity, the immediacy of the connection between them. It felt . . . real, in a way she wasn't used to, and wasn't a hundred percent sure she liked.

But if the kiss had her wobbling, it was his parting shot that nearly knocked her flat. The idea that Daniel Lunden might make new rules for the game they'd just started, a game she hoped, more than ever, would continue—it gave her chills.

Maybe good, maybe bad. Who could say at this point? All Eva knew was that she felt something, something interesting and unusual and worth exploring.

Although not right at the moment, maybe, because holy crap, what did I just walk into?

She'd taken a moment, no more than thirty seconds, truly, to untwist her metaphorical panties and de-wobble her knees. Half a minute after Lunden went on through to the kitchen, Eva stepped in after him.

And plunged directly into the middle of a fistfight.

That tall, heavily muscled chef from the East Coast Team crouched in the middle of a knot of kicking, punching Limestone chefs. The Limestone executive chef, and head of the Rising Star Chef competition's Midwest Team, lay on the rubber mats at Muscle Man's feet, clutching his jaw and spitting curses. The other East Coast chef, the cute black kid with the freckles and green eyes, had a bruise coming up along one cheekbone, but was valiantly engaged in a struggle with the Limestone saucier on the edge of the fight.

Beside her, Daniel Lunden yelled, "Break it up, guys. Come on." Which, of course, accomplished nothing other than to add to the din of crashing bodies, loud insults, and heavy breathing. He must've known they were past the point when talking could solve things, because before the words were out of his mouth, he was pushing up his sleeve and grabbing hold of the nearest combatant.

Assessing the situation in a blink, Eva dropped her Chanel purse safely to the left of the door and prepared to wade into the fray.

"What the fuck are you doing?" Lunden snarled at her as he strong-armed his flailing opponent away from Eva. "Stay out of this."

"Like hell," Eva said, ducking a flying fist. "I run restaurants for a living. You think this is my first kitchen brawl? All right, boys, that's enough!"

She stuck two fingers in her mouth and whistled, loud and shrill. The sound guaranteed to bring a New York taxi screeching to a halt in front of her made the Limestone chefs freeze in their tracks long enough to realize their boss was in their midst.

The only one who didn't seem to notice or care about her presence in the kitchen was the big guy in the middle of the fight. Eva was close enough to the center of the action now to see the mindless rage, layered over with something sharper, like pain or fear, clouding Muscle Man's dark eyes. With his chin-length hair lashing around his face and his warrior's stance, he looked absolutely wild, like a bull skewered with a Spaniard's sword.

Eva didn't allow herself even an instant of hesitation.

Just as he drew back his meaty fist for another right hook, Eva stepped directly in front of him and tilted her head back to look him in the eye.

"Enough," she said as firmly as she could, doing her level best to radiate calm and confidence in spite of the fact that her palms were slick and clammy with nervous sweat.

Vibrating with anger, every visible muscle clenched, the big chef blinked down at Eva, fist still pulled back and ready to strike.

"Come on, Beck," Lunden said into the silent tension. "Whatever it is, let it go for now. We can figure this out, but only if you calm down and let us help you."

Shuddering like a wounded bear, Muscle Man, aka Beck, lowered his fist. His massive shoulders drooped, and Eva let out an unobtrusive sigh of relief, adrenaline still flooding her veins. She felt as if she'd averted disaster, and, glancing around the kitchen, it seemed the feuding chefs had managed not to destroy any of the ovens, blast chillers, or salamander broilers.

Thank God they hadn't knocked over the liquid nitrogen tank in the corner. That would've been a bitch and a half to explain to the insurance people.

"This meathead attacked me," slurred a voice from around Eva's knees. She looked down to where Ryan

Larousse, Chicago's brightest young culinary prodigy—and hottest-tempered chef—sat pressing an open palm to the swelling line of his lower lip. One of the Limestone chefs reached a hand down, and Ryan scrambled to his feet. "I want him thrown out of this kitchen, and I'm definitely pressing charges. That psycho should be in jail!"

Before Eva could do anything to calm the troubled waters, Daniel Lunden jumped right on in and started splashing around.

"Hold on just a minute there, Gloria Allred. No one's going to jail." He pushed through the crowd to stand at his teammate's side. Eva wished he didn't look so damn sexy while stirring up trouble and making her life harder, but it was hard to deny that the sight of him, all alpha male and inflexible, beautifully lean arms crossed over his chest, got her thinking decidedly and deliciously inappropriate things about handcuffs.

"I know my boy, and Beck isn't some hotheaded kid out looking for action." Lunden sneered that bit, giving Ryan Larousse a once-over that made the younger chef flush as red as the blood trickling from his split lip. "If he jumped your skinny ass, you damn well did something to provoke him."

Having dealt with Ryan Larousse before, Eva had no doubt that this was true. Still, in the interests of fairness. "Ryan? Is this true?"

The quick slide of his gaze told her everything she needed to know before he replied with a surly, "No way. We were just talking. I mean, what the hell."

Beck remained as silent and immovable as a monolith, except for the rapid rise and fall of his rib cage as his breath returned to normal. Tilting her head to one side to get a different angle on him, Eva said, "Beck. Anything to add?"

The crackling flames had died away from Beck's expression, so Eva wasn't surprised when his only response was to stand there stolidly, meeting her gaze without blinking.

Lunden didn't like it much, though. "Come on, Beck. Tell her what happened, so we can sort this thing out." Casting a frustrated look at the third member of the East Coast Team, he said, "Win, you were here. What went down?"

Win straightened up guiltily, unhappiness in every curve of his wiry body. "I don't know," he admitted reluctantly. "I mean, we came in, introduced ourselves, tried to figure out where you two had disappeared to, and started shooting the shit about the other teams in the competition. Trading stories, getting background info." He shuffled from one foot to the other. "You know how it goes."

Oh, Eva knew, all right. Whenever a bunch of chefs got together in one room, the first thing that happened— after the requisite dick measuring, of course—was gossip.

The restaurant industry was fairly small and tight-knit, even across state lines. Lots of chefs were nomadic, traveling to new cities chasing opportunities in new restaurants, and they tended to all know one another, or at least know of one another.

And from the way that little sweetie pie Win was blushing, Eva could guess at one other component of the gossip.

Some chefs' conversations sounded a lot like they could've been overheard around the watercooler at the offices of TMZ or *Star* magazine. The only kind of stories those chefs considered worth trading had to do with who'd slept with whom, and how good—or bad—the sex was.

Eva happened to know that the East Coast Team wasn't the only one with a female chef.

"So who is she?" Eva asked, watching Beck closely.

He didn't move. Not by the flicker of an eyelash did he betray a reaction, but Eva knew she was right.

The dawning realization in Win's wide eyes as he darted a glance at his stoic teammate was just the cherry in the Manhattan.

"Okay, it sounds like this was all a big misunderstanding," Daniel Lunden said, spreading his open hands in front of him and giving a big, hey-we're-all-buddies-here smile. "Sorry things got out of hand, but you know, it's a competition. Tempers are high, we're all feeling the pressure." He quirked a brow at the hulking Beck. "And hey, the show hasn't even really started yet. Just wait until there are cameras all over the place and twenty-five chefs sharing one kitchen! This was nothing compared with the clusterfuck that's going to be. No need to borrow drama when tomorrow's going to bring enough of its own. Am I right?"

Eva caught several of the chefs—the ones who'd had to put up with Ryan Larousse the longest, probably—nodding. The tension in the room had broken like a stick of dry pasta, brittle and weak in the face of Lunden's charisma.

She had to admire his style—from kissing the stockings off her in the elevator to defending his teammate to keeping the peace.

Or almost.

"No fucking way," Ryan spat. "This isn't over just because you say it is, Lunden."

"Actually," Eva said mildly, taking one casual step forward to interpose herself between Ryan and Lunden, "it's over because *I* say it is. Come on, Ryan. You wanted to stir some shit and, congratulations, you made shit soup. It's not my fault if you're unhappy with the way the dish turned out."

From the corner of her eye, Eva could tell Ryan wasn't the only chef gaping at her in astonishment.

Yes, fellas. The lady knows how to swear. Get over it.

"That's pretty stand-up of you, Ms. Jansen," Win said. His tentative smile made Eva want to smile back, but she squashed the urge. They weren't getting off so easily as all that.

"Yeah, thanks," Lunden added, although his jaw was so tight it looked as if it must've hurt to get the words out. "I think it's time for us to go. We'll see you all tomorrow."

Interesting. He didn't like it when he wasn't the only one defending his pack. Or maybe he just wasn't used to it. A little shiver of anticipation tightened everything in Eva's body for one luscious instant.

There were so many intriguing layers to Daniel—that name, so formal, didn't seem to suit him—Lunden.

He was like an artichoke, she mused, watching him skillfully extricate his boys from a roomful of men who'd been doing their best to kill them not ten minutes before. Lots of tasty layers.

And Eva couldn't wait to peel all the way down to the heart of him.

So close. They were so close to getting out of this mess with no harm, no foul, but just as his hand touched the door, he heard, "Not so fast."

It was Eva.

Turning slowly, he arranged his features into his best pleasant expression, eyebrows arched over innocent eyes, slight smile stretching his mouth.

What now, damn it?

Eva stood in the center of the kitchen, surrounded by men who were taller than her and outweighed her by at least fifty pounds.

It said something about her that Danny had felt no compunction leaving her alone in the midst of all that raw, seething, thwarted aggression. Ryan Larousse might be a violent little punk who resented the hell out of authority, but he was no match for Eva Jansen.

Holding up one scarlet-tipped fingernail in a silent command for them to wait, Eva turned away from the East Coast Team and focused her high beams on the Limestone chefs.

"You boys have better things to do than pick fights in my kitchen, I'm sure. And since you know the layout, you've already got the advantage on the rest of the teams. So unless you're in here booby-trapping the place—yes, Larkin, I said *booby,* try to keep it together—I suggest you head up to the rooms we've so graciously provided for you, and get some rest. I expect great things from you tomorrow. Go!"

They went.

Danny watched the scarred, tattooed gang of kitchen hooligans march past and tried not to envy them.

Ryan Larousse, clutching one hand to his lividly bruising chin like a drama queen, gave Beck a nasty stare on the way out. Beck, back to doing his normal impression of an oak tree, didn't appear to notice. Not for the first time, Danny wished he could borrow a little of the guy's invincible poise.

"Now," Eva said when the other team had gone. "I don't need to know what this was about—since I know Ryan, I can make an educated guess. And as he's technically my chef, I'll apologize for him."

Approaching the unapproachable mountain that was

Beck could be unnerving at the best of times. When he was like this, sweaty and disheveled and strung wire-tight from a fight? Put it this way: Eva's quick, fearless stride right up to him earned her some respect in Danny's book.

She held out her hand, head tilted way back to be able to make eye contact with Beck. "For whatever he said about her, however he mocked what she means to you, I'm sorry."

Danny still had no clue how or why she'd gotten the idea that this whole scuffle was over a woman. That seemed way out of character for gruff, unsentimental Beck—but instead of setting her straight, Beck actually took her hand and said, "Thanks. I shouldn't have lost my cool like that."

She nodded, dropping his hand but never his gaze. "You don't have to tell me what's going on, but you should probably let your teammates know, so they can watch your back and keep this from happening again. Because Ryan is not the type to let up on something once he knows it bothers you. And I don't need to know what that is." Her voice hardened, and her eyes went flinty. "But I do need to know that a fight like this isn't going to happen again. Not while I'm in charge of this competition."

Danny held his breath for Beck's response. The guy had proven himself unpredictable today, after all. But he shook his head, shoulders back and straight like a prisoner at a parole hearing. "I get it. I take full responsibility. It won't happen again."

"I know it won't." Eva's voice was gentle again, and she smiled as she leaned down to scoop up her shiny leather satchel with the big interlocking C's on the side. She slanted a glance at Danny. "I'll be watching you carefully to make sure of it."

"Well, bye, see you tomorrow, Ms. Jansen," Win chirped abruptly, his delighted gaze darting back and forth between them as he grabbed Beck by the sleeve and started towing him toward the door. "Danny, take your time. No rush!"

Danny winced. The little shit must've watched *Yentl* on the plane or something.

And then he was alone with Eva Jansen for the second time in a single hour, and honest to God he wasn't sure his heart could take the stress.

"I like that," she said, running the tip of her pretty, pink tongue along her plump Cupid's bow of a bottom lip. "It suits you."

Dazed, wondering if he'd missed something crucial to the conversation while zoning out on the many uses to which he'd be happy to put her tongue, Danny said, "What does?"

"Danny."

How did she manage to make the name he'd been called since kindergarten sound like pure, filthy sex?

Shutting down that thought, hard, Danny attempted to get his brain back on track. "Thanks for being so cool about the fight. We're here to compete, period. Everything else is just meaningless distraction."

Arching her brow and giving him a who-are-you-trying-to-convince look, Eva said, "This wasn't the first time Ryan Larousse crossed a line. But he's a brilliant chef, so up till now we've put up with it."

Slinging that purse up onto her shoulder, she sauntered past him, hips twitching and fucking mesmerizing in that tight little skirt.

"A couple pieces of advice?" she offered languidly over her shoulder. "Keep your eye on Ryan. He's a prick, but he *is* talented, and after today he'll be very motivated to kick your ass in the competition."

"Already planning on it," Danny said. "What was the other piece of advice?"

Flashing him a sultry grin that made his heart kick at his rib cage, she said, "Don't discount meaningless distractions—sometimes they're just what the doctor ordered."

And then she was gone, leaving a cloud of perfume and a very conflicted pastry chef behind her.

Chapter 7

"Which one is Ryan Larousse again?" Max asked out of the corner of his mouth as they trooped into the kitchen, fumbling with the wireless microphones the production assistant in the hall had handed out. "Man, I can't believe you guys got into a scrap. You should've waited for me!"

"It wasn't fun," Danny said for what felt like the hundredth time. "It was stupid and pointless and could've gotten us disqualified from the competition."

What he held back, for the hundredth time, was the observation that Max would have been there if he could tear himself away from sucking face with his new girlfriend long enough to actually lead the team he was supposedly in charge of.

Or maybe Jules was supposed to be in charge. Who could keep track, at this point? Danny felt the Rising Star Chef title, the competition, his family's restaurant, and his father's legacy slipping out of their grasp, and while he was clinging desperately with his fingernails, Max and Jules were billing and cooing in their love nest like a pair of mated swans.

Or something.

It was possible Danny had some issues to resolve, once this whole thing was over. *But see?* he wanted to say. *I'm a fucking professional, damn it. I put my personal shit aside until the cooking is done, because that is what it means to be a freaking chef.*

And people thought pastry chefs were wimps. They had no clue.

"Aw, Dan-the-Man. You never would've let that happen to us," Max said, with his usual cheery disregard for the limits of Danny's supposed superpowers.

Jules gave him a sympathetic look, but before she could say anything Danny gritted his teeth around a smile. "Maybe we'd better get everyone situated? I think the judges are going to be in soon to talk to us about the first challenge."

"Good idea," Jules said, standing taller. "Guys, huddle up. Max?"

Winslow bounded over like a young basketballer moving down center court, Beck following more slowly. Beck had been slow, in general, since the fight the day before, and it had Danny worried. Not about lingering injuries or anything—Danny hadn't seen much of the fight for himself, but by the time he'd stepped onto the scene, Beck had been pretty much wiping the floor with that snot-nosed band of jumped-up wannabe badasses.

But Beck seemed to lack his usual laser focus; the impenetrable fortress of calm surrounding him had definitely been penetrated.

As Max started his inspirational speech about what a great team they were and how much it meant to him to get to cook alongside such talented blah blah blah, Danny swept the other teams gathering in the kitchen with a critical gaze.

There were the Limestone guys, competing for the Midwest region, leaning against the stainless-steel countertops along the back wall like a gang of roughneck kids staking out a street corner. Their various black eyes, cut lips, and bruised cheekbones only added to the look. They had the home-field advantage, and they knew it.

And it was not nothing, that advantage. As Danny took in the massive size of the kitchen, which he hadn't really had a chance to do yesterday, what with one thing and another, he realized how helpful it would've been to have familiarized themselves with the layout.

Much less to have cooked in it every day for years—to know it better than their own apartments, the way the Midwest Team did.

Keeping one ear open for the pauses in Max's speech-ifying that might signal a cue to nod or cheer, Danny studied the wide, rectangular room. It was set up with five rows of freestanding prep tables, one row for each team. Five large white cutting boards per table interrupted the spotless gleam of stainless steel.

The back wall, behind the lounging Midwest Team, was all corner-to-corner convection ovens, black and serious looking. A bank of refrigerators occupied the wall to Danny's left, while a line of gas cooking ranges under enormous ventilation hoods marched along the wall to his right.

An opening in the back right corner must lead to the dry-goods pantry, where things like sugar, flour, honey, and rice lived, and the walk-in coolers that housed eggs, milk, proteins, and veg.

Three of the Lunden's Tavern kitchen could fit in the main room alone, easy. Maybe four if you counted the pantry and walk-in areas.

Danny's guys, used to the complicated choreography of moving with one another in the cramped confines of a Manhattan restaurant kitchen, weren't going to know what to do with all the extra elbow room. He worried that it would be a major stumbling block. He worried that they'd get lost, lose their drive and intensity, in the open air of the high-ceilinged room.

But most of all, he worried that the unblinking lens of the video camera glaring from the front of the room would spell disaster.

So much could go wrong. Danny pressed his lips together and rolled his shoulders, cracking the tension from his neck. He'd just have to make sure to keep everyone together, pointed in the right direction, and going strong. The same thing he did every night at dinner service back home, basically, only this time in front of three renowned celebrity judges, a camera crew, and the woman whose flashing gray eyes and delicate floral scent haunted him.

That perfume she wore was the only delicate thing about her, Danny mused, finally letting his gaze fall on the one person he'd been studiously avoiding ever since entering the room.

Eva Jansen stood at the front of the kitchen in deep consultation with a schlubby guy with a mustache, wearing a wrinkled short-sleeved button down, and a headset. She'd already been here when the teams started filing into the competition kitchen, giving marching orders to that slight, willowy assistant of hers, Drew something with the black-rimmed Ray-Ban glasses and even blacker hair.

Danny remembered Drew from the regional finals, because Win had struck up a friendship with the guy. Maybe more than a friendship, Danny remembered thinking, although Win denied it now, said it was all casual, just for fun, shrug, no Big deal.

Eyes sliding from assistant to boss, Danny watched the way Eva moved, purposeful and powerful in a dress red enough—and tight enough—to stop the traffic on Michigan Avenue.

With the memory of that superheated kiss playing through his mind, Danny had a hard time understanding how to turn anything that felt like this into casual fun.

Fun? Hell yes. Casual? Not unless the definition had recently expanded to include the unquenchable desire for more—more touch, more kisses, more skin, more breathy little noises panted in his ear. More of Eva.

And that was exactly the problem, wasn't it? Danny had no idea how to be casual, but he suspected that when it came to matters of the bedroom, Eva "The Diva" Jansen was rarely anything but.

Not that she looked all that casual at the moment. That body-skimming dress was cinched in with a shiny black belt that matched her shiny black shoes with the pointy toes and even pointier heel. With her glossy dark hair and flawless face, she looked ready for that camera to zoom in on her at any second.

Although she should probably take a minute to replace the aggravated scowl with one of those big, toothy smiles people on TV were so fond of. She had nice teeth, Danny had reason to know.

He didn't have time to consider what might be going on with the television guy to put that wrinkle between her perfectly arched brows, because at that moment Max reached the conclusion of his motivational rah-rahing, and Danny had to tune back in long enough to clap him on the back and shake hands with everyone.

"Yeah, what he said," Danny put in, with a wide smile. "We rock. We got this. Let's go out there and show them New York City is home to the best chefs in the world!"

Max blinked. "Or . . . I could've saved my breath with the ten-minute cheerleading session and just gone with that. Thanks, Danny."

"But it's not in the bag yet," Jules warned. Always a

worrier, his Jules, Danny thought fondly, before Max looped an arm over her shoulders and Danny remembered, oh yeah, she wasn't really his Jules anymore. Not that she ever had been.

"Aw, Jules," Winslow whined, nearly levitating out of his sneakers with excitement. "I'm all pumped now, can't we save the reality check for later, after we kick some ass?" Danny shot him a tense, narrow look, prompting Win to hold his hands up in surrender and add, "Culinarily speaking, of course. Metaphorical, hypothetical, allegorical ass. Whatever—not the real deal. Because fighting is all kinds of wrong and violence solves nothing, and all that jazz."

Danny relaxed back onto his heels, glad Win remembered their little chat from the night before. It was one thing to defend his guys against outsiders, but when it came right down to it Danny wasn't putting up with any nonsense that might get them kicked out. He just couldn't have it. And now both Beck and Win understood why.

"No, reality can't wait," Jules said, impatience in every line of her tall, athletic body. "This is the big times, and we're up against the best of the best from around the country. Come on, what do we know about them?"

Under normal circumstances, Jules Cavanaugh would've made sure the Lunden's team did a background check on its competitors that would rival the best FBI profilers. She'd always been a big believer in knowledge as a source of power; she loved information, learning knew things, and putting them to good use.

In the weeks since the Lunden's crew had been named the East Coast Team, however, she'd fallen down on the job a little. If Danny were forced to guess—and if it weren't a gag-inducing image—he'd have to say that his old friend was probably learning a lot of new stuff and putting it to use. It was just that she was mostly learning new ways to make Max even more ridiculously smitten than he already was.

Ever since the other chef contestants had been announced, Danny had intended to look up more about them than the widely publicized names of the restaurants they hailed from, but in the frantic rush to get Lunden's Tavern staffed for the absence of its core group of chefs, there hadn't been time.

Family lore held that Max had inherited their father, Gus's, passion and drive, while Danny took after their mother, Nina, whose infallible judgment about people made her the family's de facto head of hiring.

With Max and Jules distracted, Gus out of commission after recent heart surgery, and Nina spending more time than usual taking care of him—to the extent the grouchy bastard would let her—most of the prep for this adventure had fallen to Danny.

Yeah. Even in his head it sounded like a lame excuse for not knowing more about the chefs they were about to pit their skills against.

Shame licking at his insides, Danny scrutinized the other teams arrayed against the rows of tables.

"The row behind us has got to be the Southwest Team," Win muttered out of the corner of his mouth, eyeing the colorfully striped fabric of their knife rolls and the sun baked tan of their skin.

Danny nodded in agreement. "All I know is that their restaurant's called Maize, they're from Santa Fe, and Paulina Santiago is the head chef."

The only woman on the Southwest Team was short and plump, with a pleasant, round face and kind eyes at odds with the battle-scarred thickness of her broad fingers as they competently arranged her knives along the side of her cutting board.

In a sudden flash, Danny wondered if this was the woman whose name Beck had been unable to bear hearing trash-talked by Ryan Larousse. But a quick study of Beck's dark, impassive face made Danny think Paulina Santiago wasn't the reason behind the fight. Although, the way Beck stood, with his feet apart and his arms crossed, he did sort of appear to be bracing for impact.

"I know the guy heading up Team South," Max said, nodding at a tall, lanky chef with a buzzed head and striking blue eyes standing two rows back. "Ike Bryar. He's fierce, I went up against him once in a head-to-head at the Edinburgh Food and Wine Festival. Good guy. Good knife skills."

In kitchen lingo, that was almost redundant.

Danny considered the other players on the southern squad. Couldn't be anyone on that team who'd lit that fire under Beck—no female chefs filled out their ranks.

The fourth row of tables, in front of the bored, leaning Midwest crew, was empty.

"Guess the West Coasties are late," Jules observed. She had her eyes on the wall clock ticking down the minutes to eight AM, their appointed kitchen call time, so she missed Beck's minute flinch.

But Danny'd been watching for it, hard enough and close enough that he jumped like a popcorn kernel hitting a hot pan when it happened.

Okay, he told himself. *Calm down. This is good. Now at least you know what direction the storm is rolling in from.*

He snuck a peek at Eva Jansen, who was also watching the clock. Making a little pout with her mouth—Jesus, was that the best she could do with a frown on those plumply curved lips of hers?—she checked the time against the slim watch on her wrist.

The click of her heels was muffled against the cork flooring as she strode to the center of the oasis of empty kitchen space between the camera and the chefs' tables.

"Does anyone know where the West Coast Team might be?"

A nasty chorus of laughs from the back of the room had Danny tensing right along with Beck and Winslow.

"Maybe their team captain had a . . . rough night."

Danny didn't need to turn around to know that sly, insinuating voice belonged to Ryan Larousse. For one thing, he slurred the *p* in *captain* a little, as if his mouth were too sore to make the sound properly.

For another, he'd seen that exact same look of exasperated impatience on Eva's face when she was dealing with her star chef yesterday.

Instead of addressing Larousse, however, she put her hands on her hips and scanned the room. "Does anyone have anything *useful* to contribute?"

A clatter at the kitchen door had every eye—including the camera—turning to catch the entrance of a ragtag band of chefs unlike any Danny had ever encountered.

Most kitchen crews were rough around the edges. They tended to be made up of outsiders and outcasts, people who didn't make good office drones and didn't care too much about conforming to "normal." Of the chef contestants standing in the Limestone kitchen at that very moment, at least ninety percent of them sported body art of some kind.

This new group? Put them all to shame.

Clearly they'd never met a tattoo or a piercing they didn't like, but even more than that, they gave off an almost palpable air of *different*.

From the lean, whippy Asian guy with orangey red dreadlocks down to his waist, to the gypsy-skirted, bangle-ankleted strawberry blonde with the killer curves filling out a faded blue T-shirt emblazoned with a stylized crying sun and the word SUBLIME, they didn't look like anyone Danny knew.

And coming from New York City, he thought he'd met all kinds.

"I'm so sorry we're running behind," Strawberry said, hurrying toward Eva with her hands outstretched. "It's totally my fault. I slept right through the alarm on my phone—I must've been exhausted!"

A loud, derisive laugh shot from the back of the room, and Danny put a cautionary hand on Beck's arm, just in case.

"I take it that's her," he said under his breath.

Beck didn't answer, but the granite tension of the muscles under Danny's palm spoke for him.

Confusion crumpled Strawberry's pretty face for a moment as she sought the source of the cruel laughter, but that sunny smile came back out when Eva distracted her with a bright, "Don't worry, you're not too late at all! Nothing officially starts until eight o'clock. And the judges aren't even here yet!"

With a quick, warning glance at Danny, Eva took the woman's arm and started to lead her, and her band of misfits, to the open row.

I've got it under control, Danny tried to tell her with his eyes, something in his chest warming at this moment of silent communication and teamwork.

But, as it turned out, Danny had nothing under control. Because from the minute the pretty hippie-lady chef passed by the Lunden's table and turned her head far enough see Beck, all hell broke loose.

And there wasn't a damn thing Danny could do to stop it.

Chapter 8

Okay, so far so good, Eva told herself, tugging at the arm of the executive chef of the Queenie Pie Café and resolutely keeping her gaze away from the cameraman in the corner.

All chefs were finally present and accounted for, and presumably ready for action. Now if the judges would just show up before Ryan Larousse had the chance to continue his campaign to turn every single one of Eva's hairs gray.

She had no idea what had caused the bad blood between Larousse and the teams from the East and West. Coastal envy? She didn't know, and she didn't care, so long as she could get her competition off the ground without any further drama taking the focus off the—

Eva looked down at her empty hand, then back a few paces to where Skye Gladwell, the final addition to the pool of contestants, stood staring, openmouthed and wide-eyed, at the Lunden's Tavern team.

"Henry?"

Eva didn't miss the way every head at the East Coast table swiveled to take in their teammate. "Hold up, who the hell is 'Henry'?" Winslow demanded, but no one looked at him.

Skye Gladwell lifted one trembling hand toward Beck, but didn't touch him. "Is that really you?" Her voice was disbelieving, as if she couldn't trust the evidence of her own eyes.

Eva took a suspicious inhale and frowned at the West Coast chef nearest her, a stocky man wearing a canvas artist's smock and eau-de-marijuana. If Skye had been hitting the hash pipe as hard as her sous chef here, she was probably right to doubt what her wide, shocked eyes were telling her.

Except that the tall, dark chef Skye stood blinking up at happened to be the same one who'd gotten into a fist-fight the day before—and the stony look on the guy's face couldn't quite hide the flash of recognition in his black eyes. Recognition and something more dangerous, Eva thought.

"Skye." The tall chef acknowledged her with a nod.

"I didn't know you were going to be here," Skye said, sounding dazed.

"Surprise."

Eva's gaze snapped back to Skye, making her realize that she, along with everyone else in the kitchen, was following the tense exchange like a match point at Wimbledon.

Uh-oh. Is the camera already rolling?

"Oh my God," Skye muttered, red spreading up the back of her neck, all the way to the tips of her ears. "This is unreal. I can't believe you came."

A sly voice from the back of the room called out, "I bet that's not what you were saying last night! Boo-yah!"

Eva had seen Beck in full fighting mode the day before, but it was still startling to watch the berserker rage take him over.

"You piece of shit," he snarled, turning and lunging toward the back table as if he'd hurdle all the tables and chefs between him and his prey.

The Midwest guys followed Ryan Larousse into a round of loud, jeering laughter, while the chefs at the front table exploded into action, trying to keep Beck under control, and the tables in the middle erupted with excited chatter. In the blink of an eye the entire kitchen was in an uproar.

"Stand down, Beck, come on," Danny commanded, getting one arm around his teammate's straining chest to hold him back.

Eva took a moment to appreciate the way the muscles and tendons stood out along Danny's hard forearm before shaking herself and sticking two fingers in her mouth. But her usual earsplitting whistle barely made a dent in the fracas.

Just as Eva was wondering whatever happened to that air horn her father had insisted she keep in her purse when she went off to college, the three judges walked into the kitchen, and the torrent of conversation stopped as if some giant hand had brought down a cleaver.

Skye Gladwell and her crew scurried to their places, not making eye contact with anyone, and Eva telegraphed a warning to Danny Lunden, who managed to unobtrusively wrestle Beck to a standstill in the front row.

Intensely aware of the cameraman, who was suddenly standing behind his camera and avidly filming rather than slouching around looking bored, Eva let her biggest TV-ready smile spread across her face, checked to make sure her mike was hot, and stepped forward to greet the judges.

Time to get this situation under control, before the Rising Star Chef competition turned into a three-ring circus.

Danny met Eva's gaze and for one blazing moment of connection, he knew they were thinking the exact same thing.

Let's get this show on the road.

Apparently, the judges were of the same mind-set.

"Welcome to the seventeenth annual Rising Star Chef Competition," said the celebrity chef judge, Devon Sparks, to a round of applause. He flashed his gleaming grin, dimple winking into view, and vamped to the camera a little bit. Even though he'd recently quit his mega-hit TV show, playing to an audience was clearly second nature.

"You've all worked hard to get here," Sparks continued, warming to his theme. "You beat out hundreds of chefs in your regions of these great United States for the honor of competing today. This is the chance of a lifetime—the chance to prove yourself the best of the best. And make no mistake, Chefs, that is the true prize."

"Although, let's be honest," the other male judge, Kane Slater, drawled with a winning smile. "The actual prizes are pretty much made of awesome."

Kane Slater wasn't a chef or food professional, of course, but he was one of the most famous amateur foodies around. Given the teeniest opening, Winslow would rattle on for hours about the rock star's legendary feasts and food-themed costume parties.

Some people had questioned the choice of Kane as a judge, but Danny didn't have a problem with the guy. He'd certainly seemed to know his stuff at the regional competition finals.

Although when Eva threw the blond-haired, blue-eyed

rock god a wink and a wave out of the camera's sight line, Danny thought he might have to revisit that opinion.

Smoothing the frown out of his expression took so much energy, Danny barely heard the actual recitation of the prizes. The sack of cash from the sponsors would be nice, and Danny wouldn't turn down the brand-new car, although he wasn't sure where he'd park it in the West Village.

But the personal chef write-up and restaurant review in internationally renowned food magazine *Délicieux*? Now, that was a prize worth fighting for.

Danny perked up his ears as soon as Claire Durand, the editor in chief of *Délicieux,* spoke.

In her lightly accented voice, Claire began, "*Bonjour.* I hope you have slept well, because last night was perhaps your last chance to do so."

Danny's muscles tightened in anticipation, his shoulders stiff enough to snap, but there wasn't a peep from the hecklers in the back row. Guess even Ryan Larousse was smart enough to keep his ugly gob shut when Claire Durand was talking.

"The next few weeks will be grueling as we begin to winnow out the losing teams. A series of culinary challenges await you, and you must do your utmost to meet them. Those who fall behind will be eliminated. Those who rise above will advance to the next round, and the opportunity to cook . . . how do you say?"

Her elegant brows drew down over her regal French nose.

"Mano a mano?" suggested Kane Slater.

She shot the younger man a look Danny couldn't decipher.

"Head-to-head," Devon supplied, crossing his arms

over his chest meaningfully. "The final round will be one chef from each of the two teams left standing."

A ripple of excitement passed around the room like a high-stakes game of telephone. This was a new development—past years had seen the final challenge continue on in much the same vein as the earlier rounds: teams competing against one another for a whole-team win.

"In this moment, however," Claire said, seizing control of the conversation once more, "the team is key. Yes? You will find teamwork to be vital to all the challenges in this round of the competition—and the way you work as a team will tell us much about you as chefs. Good luck."

She looked back to Eva, who was clearly continuing in her role as mistress of ceremonies.

Tucking a sleek wing of dark hair behind her ear, Eva turned to the chefs. "The United States is a country as diverse in fabulous local foodways as it is in cultures, languages, and ethnicities. But a few cities stand above the rest as leaders in the culinary world. The rivalry between New York and San Francisco is well established, but we chose to begin the competition in Chicago for two reasons."

She paused dramatically, giving Danny time to notice the way she filled out that red dress. Style-wise, it probably shouldn't be that sexy an outfit, he thought. It wasn't particularly low-cut; the sleeves went down to her elbows, and the hem was somewhere around her knees. But somehow, every time he looked at her, he could barely breathe for wanting her.

Eva wasn't showing a lot of skin, but what skin she did have on display was choice.

As if she could hear his thoughts, Eva's eyes fastened on Danny's face. They'd taken on that special sparkle he was already becoming familiar with—the one that said she had him right where she wanted him.

"The first reason we came to Chicago was because, out of all the teams who won the right to compete, the Midwest Team from the restaurant Limestone, right here in the Gold Coast Hotel in Chicago, scored the highest in the final round of judging."

A stir swept through the kitchen as chefs on every team glanced at one another and reevaluated their competition.

Danny kept his gaze straight ahead, locked with Eva's, while his mind raced to assimilate the new information. He couldn't help feeling as if she was throwing this out there as a personal challenge to him, even though he knew, rationally, that wasn't true.

Obviously, this was something they'd planned out way in advance. Long before Eva had set her sights on him, for whatever reason. And it made sense, from a publicity standpoint—if Eva wanted the Cooking Channel to broadcast the competition, she had to give them some drama.

Casting the Midwest Team as the front-runners and everyone else as underdogs was a good start.

"And the second reason," Eva continued, a cat-in-the-cream-pot smile on her face at the stir she'd caused, "is that we wanted to celebrate the exceptional diversity and exciting freshness of the Chicago food scene.

"There are several foods and techniques Chicago is famous for. In your first official challenge, we'd like each team to prepare a three-course meal that best represents your team's talents—Chicago-style. You have two hours to plan and shop this morning, then four hours to prep this afternoon. You'll have two more hours to cook tomorrow, before the judges come back to taste your food. Oh, and Chefs? One more thing."

The air felt electrified, and Danny's heart was beating hard enough to shake his whole chest. What kind of curveball was she about to throw at them?

"This will be our first elimination challenge," Eva said gently. "The team the judges choose as their least favorite will be going home tomorrow night. The other four teams will progress to the next round. So, with that said, are you ready?"

A chorus of voices shouted yes, the adrenaline of the room spiking hard as every contestant tensed, poised for action. Danny could feel his muscles twitching, his hands almost shaking with the need to be cooking, stirring, measuring, plating.

Eva swept one red-clad arm to the side, pointing at a digital timer mounted on the wall beside the clock. "Go," she barked, and the timer flashed on, red numbers counting down the seconds and making Danny feel as if he were already behind.

Everyone scrambled to put their heads together while the judges trooped out of the kitchen, leaving the chefs behind with Eva and her camera crew.

Because he couldn't stop himself and his focus was for shit, part of Danny's brain tracked her as she efficiently unclipped her microphone from the back of the shiny black leather belt cinching her slim waist and snagged the rumpled camera guy for another intense discussion.

"Are we boring you?" Max's laughing voice in his ear brought Danny back to earth.

Cheeks stinging with embarrassment, Danny cleared his throat and resolved to ignore Eva Jansen, no matter how unreasonably hot she was. "Sorry. What've we got so far?"

"So far we've named two things Chicago is known for," Jules said, pencil poised above the notebook she carried around in her back pocket for jotting down menu ideas. "Steak and hot dogs."

"Sausage, in general." Beck crossed his arms over his chest. "Chicago is the hog butcher for the world."

The line caught Danny by surprise, made him give the guy a closer look. Somehow, he hadn't expected big, scary Beck to be quoting from a Carl Sandburg poem.

"Pizza, too," Winslow added. "That weird deep-dish kind."

Chicago-style pies—with their thick, doughy crusts and mountainous piles of toppings—were so different from the typical New York slice of floppy, deliciously greasy pizza, they hardly seemed like the same category of food at all.

"I'm not confident about our ability to get a Chicago-style deep-dish pizza right," Danny said. "What else do they have going on in this town?"

"There are a few places—Limestone is one of them—where Chicago chefs are taking experimental cooking to the next level," Beck said, his gaze fierce and intent on the notepad in Jules's hand. He seemed to be working extra hard to concentrate, and Danny felt a brief, searing moment of admiration for the guy.

Whatever unresolved mess existed between Beck and that San Francisco chef, Skye Gladwell—Beck was handling it like a pro.

Better than Danny was dealing with his unwelcome attraction to Eva Jansen, at any rate.

Focus, asshole.

"So the Midwest Team is likely to stick to what they know and do something avant garde and crazy with garlic foam, basil ice cream, and tomato water, or whatever," Max said. He'd always been good at strategy. It used to drive Danny crazy when they played board games, but now he was glad of it.

What Danny was good at was research. "I've been reading up on Chicago, actually," he said, carefully avoiding Max's eye. Max liked to give him shit for it, but it had saved the team's ass on more than one occasion. "And the current big trends here are brunch and comfort food. Smaller restaurants in the hot neighborhoods like Bucktown and Wicker Park get lines out the door and around the block for fancy waffles and a good omelet, and everybody in town has their own version of chicken potpie and mashed potatoes."

"Great!" Jules's eyes lit up the way they did when her imagination was sparked. Scribbling madly, she asked, "Any other thoughts?"

"Oh!" Winslow jumped as if he'd been goosed. "I know another thing Chicago's known for—jazz. Jazz, clubs, Prohibition, the mob, lounge singers, soul food . . . hey!"

As always, Win looked surprised that his seemingly random brainstorming had produced a real idea, but Danny was no longer shocked by it. "Good one, man," he said, clapping the younger chef on the back.

"Yeah, but I bet the southern team will think of it, too," Win said. "And my mama might be black, but she grew up in New York City, and so did I. Food that feeds the soul at my house is take-out pad Thai and delivery Chinese dumplings."

Danny tilted his head back to stare at the ventilation-hooded ceiling. "It's a little early in the competition to start trying to beat the other teams at their own game. We need to stick to what we know and love to cook—which is steak."

Lunden's Tavern had been the go-to spot for a great steak in the West Village for decades. Their family had served everyone, from Ronald Reagan to Luciano Pavarotti. Up until his death, they'd kept a special supply of a certain type of canned Italian sardines on hand, just in case Frank Sinatra blew through town.

"But we did steak at the regional finals," Jules argued. "It's too obvious to do it again so soon. Even if we didn't replicate Max's soy-lacquered tenderloin, I think it's too similar, makes us too much of a one-trick pony."

"Ms. Jansen did say we're supposed to show who we are as chefs and as a team with this dish," Win reminded them. "So it's all about what do we want to show. We got talent here, folks. No need to cook ourselves into a corner this early on."

Despite the sharp stab of nerves that always assaulted Danny at the idea of breaking away from the familiar, he nodded firmly. If everyone already agreed, he wasn't going to be the one to make waves. "You're right. No steak for this challenge. So what do we do instead? What's left on the list?"

Silence descended while they each ran through the options they'd already brainstormed. Danny's brain whirred through the choices at lightning speed, adding and tossing ingredients in different combinations and configurations. It was hard to work out what he'd be doing for his dessert course until he knew what the main would be, because all three courses needed to flow together seamlessly to create one perfect, coherent taste experience.

When Beck was the one to break the pause, they all looked at him with varying degrees of startlement. It wasn't that Beck never spoke, but he was on the strong-and-silent side, more a supporter than a leader.

But something was different about him today. Danny studied him closely, trying to figure out what it was that made the guy seem more . . . there, and present, than he usually did.

"I've got an idea," Beck said slowly, his deep voice rumbling over the words like tires over gravel. "What if we did a breakfast-for-dinner thing? There's this seafood sausage I've been wanting to try my hand at . . ."

And just like that, a world of possibilities opened up.

Danny licked his lips as the potential swirled through him. Around him, his teammates were all lit from within by the fire of a great idea, talking excitedly and sketching plans on Jules's notepad.

They had a shot. They could win this thing, Danny knew it down to his bones.

And as the wall timer ticked down, Danny looked up to catch Eva Jansen's eyes on him.

One moment of eye contact, the suggestive curl of her shimmery red lips, had Danny hardening in a scorching hot rush.

Okay. They could win this thing—if he could manage to keep his dick in his pants and his mind in the kitchen.

Somehow, as he watched the way Eva's hips rolled while she sauntered around the room making sure each team had what it needed, Danny thought that might be easier said than done.

Chapter 9

As soon as the judges left the kitchen, Claire handed her wireless mike to the PA and took off down the hall without a single glance back.

Kane clenched his fists and forced himself to pay attention to what the other male judge, celebrity chef Devon Sparks, was saying.

"You're my wife's favorite singer. She's beyond pissed that I get to hang out with you all over the country for the next few weeks. Almost as pissed as she is that I'm leaving her alone to deal with morning sickness and cravings for peanut butter and fried pickles." Devon smiled, and unlike the brilliant grin the cameras loved so much, this one went all the way to his electric blue eyes.

It made Kane pause, breathe in, because Devon was clearly talking about something—someone—that mattered to him, and Kane had promised himself a long time ago that he would never, ever be the kind of person who ignored what mattered.

It was a hard promise to keep when he existed between the shallow, glittery world of LA parties and the surreal eternal road trip of touring, but he did his best.

Ignoring the fact that Claire was waiting for an elevator, about to slip out of his reach, Kane returned Devon's
smile and said, "Congratulations on the baby thing! And
thanks, man. It never stops being awesome to hear about
someone listening to my stuff. What's your wife's name?"

The guy's almost-too-perfect face melted into something human, right before Kane's eyes. "Lilah. Lilah Jane
Sparks, and she listens to your music so much—if I didn't
know she loved me, I would've tossed every one of your
CDs out in the street a long time ago."

The deep, comfortable assurance of his wife's affections gave Devon a settled, grounded air that affected Kane
strangely.

He was curious about it—what would it be like to know
yourself to be loved, completely and utterly, by someone
other than your family?—but he was curious about a lot
of things, so that wasn't weird. What was weird was the
way Kane was simultaneously attracted to and repelled
by the idea.

To be loved . . . sure, who didn't want that? But to be
settled and grounded. Ugh. Kane suppressed a shudder.
That wasn't for him. He had too much to do, too much to
see and experience and accomplish, to take a dive, clip
his wings, and start shuffling through the dirt.

Song lyrics tickled at his brain, distracting him. "Well,
I'm glad you didn't," he said vaguely, trying to blink the
fuzziness away. "You . . . want me to sign something for
Lilah?"

"Actually, I had a different favor to ask," Devon said,
looking sheepish as he pulled his phone from the pocket
of his perfectly tailored camel blazer. "Today is her birthday. Would you mind . . . ?"

Kane relaxed. This was easy. "Sure, man, no big. Dial
her up for me, and I'll take care of the rest."

Devon tapped the phone's screen once, then handed it to Kane. A sweet molasses voice drawled in his ear, slow and husky with sleep, "Mmm, time for my morning sugar. How do you always know just the thing to make me feel better?"

Sending Devon a smile, Kane started to sing into the phone, to the accompaniment of shocked silence followed by a bit of squealing and laughing. By the time he'd made it to "And many moooore," Devon was beaming, Lilah was practically in hysterics, and Claire was long gone.

Suppressing a sigh, Kane brushed off Devon's thanks and said good-bye to Lilah.

"You're the best, Slater. I won't forget it. Catch you later!"

As soon as Devon got his phone back, it was clear he and his wife needed a little alone time—and after witnessing their connection up close and personal, Kane kind of wanted to be alone, too. He waved Devon away with a smile and stuck his hands in his pockets, wandering the hallway in front of the hotel kitchen doors.

He was trying to decide if he could stomach the idea of using his famous face to pry Claire's room number out of the chick working the reception desk upstairs when Eva slipped into the corridor, pulling the doors gently closed behind her.

"Hey, babe," Kane greeted her, glad of the distraction from his increasingly circuitous and unhappy thoughts. "How's it going in there?"

She brought a hand up to her mouth as if she wanted to bite the nail of her index finger, but as soon as she realized it was shellacked with red paint, she twisted both hands behind her back. "It's going okay. Maybe. I don't know. God, what made me think I could pull this off?"

"Aw, now." Eva never failed to move him to big-brotherly tenderness when she dropped that shark-like armor and showed her vulnerable white belly. "It can't be as bad as all that. The chefs looked like they were ready and raring to go when we left 'em. C'mere. You're doing good."

He gave her a one-armed hug, squeezing her shoulders tight. With her in those spike heels, they were almost the same height. It made Kane wish nostalgically for his old, scuffed-up cowboy boots to give him an extra inch or so on her, but he'd left those behind when he left Texas.

"The chefs are crazy. They're fighting already and we haven't really even gotten started yet," Eva wailed, turning her face into his shoulder and probably smudging makeup all over it. "And the cameraman is driving me bonkers—the producer from the Cooking Channel keeps saying he's not sure there's enough action and drama even to make a B reel for if they do the live feed from the final challenge in San Francisco. What does he expect?"

"I don't know, I think things have been pretty action-packed so far," Kane said. "What about that fistfight yesterday?"

"But I don't want them to air stuff like that," Eva wailed. "That's not what the RSC is about!"

Kane put his hands on Eva's shoulders and set her back a step so he could look into her face. "Hey, hey. Come on, now, sugar. 'Fess up about what's really eating you."

She fidgeted for a second, which made her look awfully young. It reminded him of the Eva he'd first met, five years ago at a holiday bash at some skeevy record producer's house—a wild child with long, mink-brown hair and an irrepressible need to have the attention of every man at the party.

Not because she wanted to have sex with them, Kane had seen at a glance. But because it fed some deeper need hidden under her sparkly tank top and tight little jeans.

Eva was a wanderer, a seeker, like Kane. He'd known

it instantly, in one of those freaky moments of understanding, and when she'd gotten in a little too deep—vodka tonics and handsy rich guys made a bad combo—Kane had stepped in and rescued her.

She'd been his soul sister ever since. And even now, half a decade, two platinum records, and a successful restaurant empire later, he still didn't always get what made her tick. Which was, of course, part of her considerable charm.

"There's this guy," she told him, then smacked his arm and sulked when he laughed.

"Baby, with you? There's always a guy," he said fondly. "That part, I knew already. Tell me what's messing you up about him."

Her mouth twisted and she got a faraway look in her eyes. "He's not . . . like the others. I don't know how else to describe it. I just . . . I want him."

Kane shrugged. "So go get him, girl." For Eva, it was usually exactly that simple, and if he couldn't help the pang of envy, he could at least keep it from showing on his face.

But Eva didn't seem to agree. She shook her head, sending her short brown hair lashing against her chin. "It's complicated. He's one of the contestants."

Well, now, Kane thought. *Like father, like daughter.* But he knew it would hurt her to hear that, so instead he asked, "And that's a problem for you?"

"Not usually," she admitted. "I mean, it's just sex. It's simple biology, right? You build up tension and stress— you need to open a valve somewhere and let it out, or you'll explode. Nothing deep and emotional about it, just a bodily function. Like sneezing."

"Sure," Kane said, nodding sagely. "Coed naked sneezing. The next wave in porn."

, shut it. You know what I mean, and I know you agree with me. Don't try that soulful artist thing with me; I've seen the way you blow through women, like a flu patient with a box of tissue."

"Gross," he told her. "What is it with you and mucus today?"

Her eyes got big and anguished. "I don't know!" she cried. "I'm totally off my game. I got him to kiss me in the elevator, and it was perfect, all hot and bothering, but then . . . he made me feel something. And he just walked away afterward, like it was nothing!"

Hmm. It sounded as if The Diva had met her match. Kane put on a sympathetic face. "Would it have been better if he tried to ravish you in semi-public?"

"Yes!" Eva set her chin stubbornly. "I mean, at least it would've been normal. Now I don't know where to go from here."

Once again, he and his soul sister were on the same cosmic wavelength. It would've been funny if it weren't so sad. Kane sighed, "Tell me about it, babe. I'm a little stumped, myself."

Her gaze went from dejected to crafty in about half a second. "Oh, I think I've said enough. It's your turn. Why don't you tell *me* all about it, and I'll see what I can do to help?"

"Unless you can convince an extremely intelligent, very stubborn woman that I'll be worth going against her very nature, you're no good to me."

"You are worth it," Eva declared, ever loyal. "And Claire should give you a chance to show her. I can't convince her, myself, but I can make it possible for you to have a shot at it."

Heartbeat quickening, Kane grabbed for Eva's hands.

"Oh, baby girl. If you do that, I promise I'll name the first hit single off the next album after you."

She grinned. "Hey, if I can't get a handle on my own love life, at least I can help you with yours. Claire's in suite thirty-two eighteen; I upgraded her this morning after she complained about the lack of a desk in her room. I bet she's up there right now, settling in with the bottle of complimentary champagne I sent up."

Kane waggled his eyebrows, deliberately blanking out the fact that this was exactly the sort of thing he'd promised not to do. "Maybe she could use some company."

"Go get her, boy," Eva said, giving him a little push in the direction of the elevators. "And remember, she's French, so she thrives on being contrary. And beware the pout! If she pulls out the big guns, you'll know you're getting to her. *Bonne chance!*"

Kane blew her a kiss and stepped onto the elevator, heart lifting as he began to rise up through the hotel, closer and closer to Claire Durand.

Bonne chance, indeed.

He was going to need all luck he could get.

Eva watched her friend rush off to make sweet nookie with her other friend, and struggled not to feel abandoned.

It's not always all about you, she lectured herself.

Well, okay. She was the pampered only child of a wealthy man who'd lost his best friend and his moral compass when he'd lost his wife, and who had therefore spent most of her childhood and teen years leaving Eva alone in their Long Island mansion, then showering her with guilt gifts later.

So really, it kind of was all about her. Or at least she came by the feeling honestly.

She checked her watch. The sapphire-blue minute hand had barely progressed at all.

Ugh, this waiting! It was interminable.

She'd left the kitchen to get some distance from the frenetic energy of the chef contestants in full planning mode, but in less than half an hour it would be time to pile them all into the cars for the trip over to the grocery store.

Not for the first time, Eva felt a glow of accomplishment at the fact she'd managed to woo Lincoln as a sponsor. The car company was not only providing a brand-new SUV as a prize for the final winner, they were also lending several Town Cars as transportation to get the chefs to and from the different challenge venues. Whipping out her phone, Eva called to make sure the cars and drivers were pulled around to the front entrance of the hotel, and that they knew the address and best route to get to the grocery store.

After another glance at her watch, Eva decided she'd better get back in there and hurry the chefs through their final minutes of planning time. With a little, very minor manipulation and wrangling, Eva was sure she'd manage to arrange matters so that she and Danny Lunden had a car all to themselves for the drive over to Fresh Foods.

Time to stop feeling lost and nervous, she told herself. She was Eva Jansen! Successful restaurateur, millionaire playgirl, and all-around catch. Just because some hotshot pastry chef made her special lady bits tingle, that was no excuse for morphing into a silly, starry-eyed girl.

I do better on the offensive anyway, she mused as she called time on the chefs and herded them out to the waiting Town Cars, where she maneuvered Danny into her limo and locked the doors behind her.

"Drive," she told the uniformed man up front before twisting in the comfy leather seat to face Danny, whose look of startled confusion changed to narrow calculation in the space of a single heartbeat.

"You again," he said. "Why do I get the feeling I'm being stalked?"

Adrenaline and excitement pumped through Eva's veins, warming her blood and filling her with that fun recklessness she loved so much. The thrill of the hunt . . .

"Because you are," she told him, settling back into the cool embrace of the deep car seat and crossing her legs very deliberately. An air-conditioned breeze chilled her legs where the hem of her dress had inched up, but she didn't make a move to pull it back down.

Sure enough, Danny's interesting blue-gray eyes flicked down to take in the newly bared expanse of silk-stocking-clad thigh—but only once, and so quickly that if she hadn't been watching for it, she wouldn't have noticed it.

But Eva noticed everything Danny did.

"I'm not sure if I should be freaked or flattered," he said, angling himself to face her. The backseat of the car was spacious and comfortable, but Danny's long legs and rangy frame took up quite a bit of it.

His legs sprawled naturally, and the dark denim of his jeans rubbed teasingly against Eva's knee when she shifted. Danny's gaze went hooded and intent, sending a shiver down Eva's spine.

"Oh, flattered, definitely," Eva said, a little dismayed by her own breathlessness. "I have very discerning tastes."

Okay, that wasn't always true. Eva had more than her share of wince-worthy men in her past. But in this case?

She watched the way Danny Lunden commanded the backseat of this borrowed car as if it were the throne room of a palace, his handsome face made intriguing and appealing by the slight rasp of stubble along his jaw, the firm set of his extremely kissable mouth.

No, this time, Eva was sure, she'd have absolutely no regrets.

"I don't know if you're aware," Danny said, very politely, although his eyes flashed with something sharper and more dangerous. "But I'm in the middle of a culinary competition that could make or break my career, and restore the reputation of my family's restaurant. Now isn't really the best time for me to be concerned with getting my rocks off."

"Please." Eva dismissed that as the weak excuse it clearly was. "Now is the perfect time. You're stressed, tense, uptight—you need some release, hotshot, or you're going to burn out."

"Or I need to concentrate on what really matters."

Eva uncrossed her legs slowly, letting her left calf brush along his right shin. The contact sent a shower of invisible sparks through the car, charging the air with electricity. Eva's breath quickened, and from the way Danny's chest rose and fell, she thought his had picked up, too. Eyes locked on his dark gaze, Eva slipped her feet out of her Louboutins and curled her legs beneath her on the seat so that she knelt facing him. Her dress rode up farther still, almost high enough to show him what color undies she had on.

"Danny," she said, exhaling his name on a sigh. "Don't kid yourself. This matters." And she leaned forward, braced one hand on the strong round muscle of his shoulder, and kissed him.

He was motionless under her touch for a single, agonizing heartbeat before he broke with a growl like a wolf caught in a trap, and hauled her into his lap.

His mouth opened, sharp teeth nipping, tongue caressing, and Eva sank into it with a purr of satisfaction. It was every bit as good as it had been before—better, even, because this time she was prepared for the sudden jolt of lust, the frenzy of hunger to taste all of him, immediately and deeply and more now yes please more more more.

Her dress had rucked up high enough to get her legs around his waist, so she straddled him. Framing his scratchy cheeks between her palms, Eva pressed her hips into his, making them both shake with need.

It took everything she had not to rub herself against the stiff fabric of his pants, the enticing hardness of his thick erection pushing between them and driving her wild.

The physical proof that Danny wanted this as much as she did enabled Eva to take a deep breath and center herself. Circling her hips slowly, she found a rhythm that made him shudder and bite at her mouth. The fragile, damp silk of her underwear was no shield against the onslaught of sensation.

Tremors raced through her, little lightning shocks of pleasure and need zipping up and down her spine. Thank God she'd had the foresight and planning to push Danny in the direction of a car without a cameraman. The last thing she needed was for a sex tape to start making the rounds of the Internet.

Panting into the kiss, Eva clutched at the short, soft spikes of Danny's light brown hair and let herself move hard and purposefully while his hands swept up her back and around her sides to cover the swells of her breasts.

Rearing back to gasp in a breath, Eva stared down at Danny. Desire was obvious on his face now, the lines of his cheekbones and mouth stark with hunger.

Eva savored the intensity of his focused gaze, the wet sheen on his chiseled lips. His desire fed hers like dry kindling stoking a fire, and when Danny palmed her breasts and flicked his thumbs over the hard points of her nipples, she let the moment take her and shatter her into a million pieces.

"God, you're beautiful," he rasped, eyes shining up at her as he watched her come apart, and his words sent another shiver of delight all through her, a rich echo of the explosion.

"Mmm." She smiled and slumped, boneless, against him. It was perilously close to cuddling, but she was too smug and satiated to care. "You're not so bad yourself."

The insistent jut of his erection nudged the notch of her thighs where she was wet and so, so sensitive, making her sigh and wiggle closer. She snuck a hand down between them to pet at the straining length.

Danny sucked in air, his lean belly going taut against her reaching arm.

Oh, she liked that.

Looking for more reaction, Eva leaned her head on his shoulder and curled her fingers, fighting the stubborn fabric of his jeans to get a better grip. His neck smelled like salt and smoke, with an underlying hint of sweetness, as if his skin were dusted with a fine coating of powdered sugar.

"Wait," he said, voice strangled. "Don't—" Eva lifted her head to frown at him, but before she could make it clear she had no intention of leaving him hanging—she didn't play that way—her phone blared a few menacing bars of Darth Vader's theme music, loud and jarring even from the depths of her purse. It was her father's ringtone.

And . . . the mood was officially killed.

Great. Only Eva's dad could cockblock her from three states away.

Chapter 10

"I have to take this call." Eva sat up abruptly. Danny could only be grateful that she seemed aware of how much damage she could do to a man in his condition, even as she scrambled off his lap and dove for her purse.

While the ominous orchestrals faded and began to cycle back up for a repeat, she managed to wrestle the phone free and get it up to her ear.

"Hi, Dad," she said, and wow. That was exactly what Danny needed to hear.

Instant soft-on.

Although if he wanted it to last, he really couldn't look at her, perched on her knees in the seat beside him, red dress up around her hips and showing tantalizing glimpses of her flimsy, expensive-looking panties, all black satin and red lace edging dark against her creamy white skin.

Or the delicate pink flush of arousal still staining her cheeks and neck, and the lush fullness of her just-kissed mouth . . . Danny shifted uncomfortably and pressed the heel of his hand against his painfully renewed erection.

He tuned back in to Eva's conversation in the hopes that it might have the same effect on him as before.

"No, everything's going great," she was saying brightly, confidence in every syllable.

But, Danny noticed, her knuckles were white with tension where she gripped the phone.

"Dad. I've got this handled—the RSC is going to be bigger and better than ever this year! And the TV thing is going to work out. You don't have to worry . . ." She broke off for a moment, eyes going wide with dismay. "No! I mean . . . I know how busy you are . . . I'd love to see you, too, but Dad . . . look, let's plan something for after the competition, okay? . . . oh. No, of course you'll be at the finals. I'm not trying to keep you away, I just don't need my father checking up on me!"

That mouth of hers that always seemed half a beat away from a smirk didn't look quite so sleek and teasing now. In fact, it looked like she was having to work to keep it from trembling and giving her away as she turned a little toward the window and lowered her voice.

"You said you trusted me to run the show this year, to take things up a notch. Are you going back on that?"

A long, taut moment strung out like a coiled wire, until suddenly her shoulders relaxed and she closed her eyes.

Danny let out the breath he hadn't even been aware he was holding. What the hell? This was none of his business. He shouldn't even be listening in.

Which didn't stop him from straining to catch her last, quiet words to her father.

"Thanks, Daddy," she said, sounding truly grateful. "I promise I won't let you down."

It hit Danny like a ten-pound sack of flour to the head. How many times had he said that exact same thing to his parents? Well, he didn't call his father *Daddy*, but other than that . . . it was pretty much the refrain of Danny's entire life.

Eva said good-bye and hit the OFF button on her phone, and this time when her shoulders dropped, Danny was pretty sure it was relief. He watched her take a deep breath and turn back to him, the carefree, come-hither look on her face carefully constructed, perfectly beautiful . . . and completely fake.

"Now," she said, dropping her phone back in her purse, and slinking over to him. "Where were we?"

"You can put the womanly wiles away," he told her. "I was just about to tell you I'm fine. No need for reciprocation."

She looked confused. It was kind of adorable. "But. That's not how it works."

And then it was kind of sad. Danny gentled his voice; it was easier to do now that her conversation with her father, and Danny's own unwilling empathy, had completely trumped his urge to mate. "I don't know who you usually date, or get busy with, or whatever you want to call it—but sex doesn't always have to be about an equal exchange of orgasms. We're not talking about the free-market economy here. It's pleasure. And believe me, I got plenty out of watching you lose control like that. So we're good, sweetheart. You don't owe me anything."

"I know I don't owe you," she said testily, jerking her hem down her legs and unfolding herself into a more normal sitting position. Danny didn't want to be charmed by the annoyance in her voice, but he couldn't help it.

"Do you?" He leaned back and studied her. It was gratifying to be able to so thoroughly discombobulate her. He'd bet it didn't happen often.

"I'm not some innocent little virgin," she said, digging through her huge purse—how the hell did she find anything in there?—and coming up with a tube of lipstick. "I know all about sex, and pleasure, and what two consenting adults can do together."

While she efficiently reapplied the slick red lacquer he'd—oh man—kissed off her, Danny struggled to maintain his cool.

"No virgin kisses the way you do." His voice came out on the hoarse, growly side, and Danny swallowed hard. "Besides," he went on. "Can you honestly still be in the mood for nooky when you just got off the phone with your father?"

She stiffened, but he pretended not to notice. "Because I have to say, even thinking about my parents . . . well, that pretty much puts my sex drive in neutral every time."

Eva smiled, as he hoped she would, and relaxed a bit. "I guess you couldn't help overhearing."

"It's a nice car," Danny said, "I've never been in a backseat that actually has one of those privacy shields like in the movies. But it's not quite big enough that I can pretend I didn't catch the gist of your conversation."

"My father founded this competition almost twenty years ago," Eva said. "I guess you probably know that already. Actually, though, it wasn't his idea. It was my mom's."

Now, that was interesting. Danny racked his brain for what he knew about Eva's parents.

Theo Jansen was a legend in the restaurant world—his empire stretched from upscale French places in New York City to glitzy celebrity chef outposts in Las Vegas. Pretty much everything the man touched turned to caviar and champagne.

But his legend extended beyond the dining room. Theo Jansen was reputed to be the consummate ladies' man. He showed up at restaurant and club openings with a different socialite or supermodel or Broadway starlet every night of the week, and the stories about what he got up to with those ladies . . . well, Danny had never thought about what it would be like to hear salacious gossip starring his own father, but he didn't see how it could fail to fuck a kid up.

When he considered it from that angle, it wasn't any wonder that, according to the culinary gossip hotline, Eva was doing her level best to follow in her father's footsteps— both in business and in pleasure.

But try as he might, Danny couldn't remember a single story about whatever had happened to Eva's mother. He couldn't even think of the woman's name.

If he'd been asked to guess, Danny would probably imagine she'd been a trophy wife, or something, and was living out her generous alimony settlement in some Italian villa.

At least, that would've been his default before this moment, in the close, intimate confines of this car's backseat, across from Eva Jansen—who still looked recently ravished, and smelled like sweet, satisfied woman. Something about the way Eva hunched in on herself, so different from her usual brash confidence, told Danny there was more to it than that.

"Oh yeah?" seemed like the safest response he could give.

"She loved to cook, the skill and technique and artistry of it, and she thought it was horribly unfair that there was no venue for chefs to hone their talents by competing against one another, and be recognized by the entire nation for their accomplishments."

Loved. Past tense.

Oh, Eva.

Swallowing past the lump in his throat, Danny said, "She was right. There are so many chefs in cities across America, doing good work, putting out fantastic food. The

RSC does a great job of showcasing those people and giving them a place to shine."

"And a chance at an even bigger future," Eva said, conviction brightening her eyes and making them sparkle. "That's what I want to do—make my mother's dream a reality."

Danny had no idea why it surprised him to find out that Eva was a true believer under all her glitz, glamour, and ruthless maneuvering; he already knew she was a living, breathing contradiction in terms.

"For what it's worth," he told her, "I think you're doing a pretty good job. So far."

Shit. Good thing that wasn't awkward, or anything.

But Eva gave him a small smile. "Actually, it's worth a lot. Thanks. I know you wouldn't say it if you didn't mean it."

Danny had about two seconds to wonder how she knew that about him before he registered the fact that the car was slowing to a stop in front of a giant Fresh Foods grocery store.

"Looks like we're here," he said, unnecessarily, but damn it. The atmosphere in the car was still pretty thick with embarrassment, overlaid by the taunting aroma of sex and hunger, and Danny wasn't exactly functioning at his best.

This was why he was supposed to keep his distance from Eva Jansen, he reminded himself. She was the world's most dangerous distraction.

Shaking his head in self-disgust, Danny popped the lock on the door and started to get out, only to be stopped by a slim hand gripping his elbow.

"Wait . . . before you go." Eva glanced down, then up at him through her sooty lashes. It was a very pretty picture she made, softer and more vulnerable than he was used to seeing her. "I just wanted to say . . . thanks. For everything. And if you could keep this whole thing to yourself, I'd really appreciate it."

A ball of nausea coiled in his belly. He'd never been treated like a disposable sex toy before.

It wasn't as much fun as he would've imagined.

"Don't worry about it," he said curtly. "I don't kiss and tell."

Her head came up, silvery cat eyes widening in what looked like shock. "Oh! No, not about the kissing. I don't care, tell the whole world. I meant about the call. With my father." She glanced to the side, fingers fidgeting with the clasp of her shiny watch. "I'd rather keep it quiet, that he has his doubts about me taking over the competition. That's just. Well, it's very personal."

This had to be one of the strangest encounters of Danny's life. Nothing ever seemed to go the way he expected when Eva Jansen was involved.

What kind of woman didn't regard her own sexual exploits as "personal"?

Reeling a little, Danny nodded at her and escaped from the car. The sick feeling was gone, but it had been replaced by the much scarier sensation of falling through space—and the expectation of a hard landing.

Somewhere between the Gold Coast Arms and the Fresh Foods parking lot, Danny was afraid he'd lost any ability to keep his distance from Eva Jansen.

The grocery expedition was more like full-on battle than a shopping trip. The butcher counter was mobbed immediately by three separate teams, which made Danny extra glad they had decided not to go that route.

Beck didn't even need to use his considerable bulk and intimidation factor to get up to the fish counter, so that saved them some time. Jules and Winslow hit the produce section, while Max and Danny ran for the baking aisle. They hadn't had a chance to really inventory the hotel kitchen's stores, but Danny was assuming they had basics like bread flour and yeast. He needed buttermilk and dark brown sugar, among other things.

Periodically, when the fierce current of the action, fighting the crowds and racing around the store looking for the best product took him past the checkout lanes, Danny caught a glimpse of Eva.

She had one arm up, her gaze on her watch, as she counted down the minutes of their timed shopping trip. Hair immaculate, lipstick as red and unsmudged as ever; no one looking at her would guess that not forty minutes before this, she'd been in the throes of a gorgeous, moaning, head-thrashing climax in the back of a limo.

But Danny knew. The image was imprinted on his brain as if it had been carved there like an etching in granite, right alongside the vision of Eva, momentarily downcast and unsure, her lashes dark moons against the fairness of her cheeks.

Danny had seen the real Eva Jansen, the one behind the elegant predator. And the bitch of it was, even if he could, Danny wouldn't go back and unsee it.

She fascinated him, in a way that nothing had fascinated him since he first discovered the magic alchemy that turned flour, butter, and sugar into cookies.

He wanted her. And an innocent, oh-so-reasonable voice kept repeating in his head: *Is it really so bad to want something for yourself?*

Chapter 11

The throb of pleasure still thrummed through Kane's body like the backbeat rhythm of a song—something slow and intense, pulsing with meaning and joy. Heavy on the high hat.

He'd collapsed to the side in an effort not to crush Claire's trim, small frame—Kane wasn't tall, but he was compact, with more lean muscle mass than it maybe seemed like. Or so that *Cosmo* interview had said.

Anyway, Claire was safe and uncrushed next to him, the sheen of sweat still drying on her skin. Every shallow, panting breath brushed her high, perfect breasts against Kane's arm where he'd curled it around her rib cage to keep her close.

"*Mon dieu*," she breathed. "What are we doing?"

They were the first words either of them had spoken since Kane knocked on the door of her suite and Claire hauled him inside, pressed him back against the wall, and kissed him.

They weren't exactly the words Kane had been hoping for, either.

"Whatever feels good," he said firmly. "Wait. It felt better than good to me, but did you not, um . . ."

She opened her eyes to stare up at the ceiling. "My God. How young you are. Yes, Kane. I ummed. Thank you for that."

In a single instant Kane went from totally irresistible stud to knock-kneed virgin fumbling after his prom date.

Confusion and hurt curdled together in his stomach, leaching the warmth of his orgasm from his skin. Kane shivered and pulled his arm away from Claire's body.

So much for afterglow.

"You're welcome," he said shortly. "I guess this means you're kicking me out, now that the lion's been fed, huh?"

He moved to get off the bed, maybe find his pants so he didn't have to finish this conversation with his bare ass hanging out in the breeze. Some part of him hoped for Claire to clasp a hand to his forearm and tug him back down beside her, but she didn't.

"And now you're angry. Should I not mention your age? But you are young."

"In years, maybe," Kane allowed, stretching to pluck his jeans from the top of the dresser where they'd been tossed. "But not in experience."

Back when he was seeing that double-jointed fashion model, he'd done the entire Kama Sutra. Twice! Somehow, though, that memory didn't give him the good, wicked tickle of satisfaction it usually did.

This thing with Claire—it was as if it overshadowed everything, made him rewrite every song he'd ever sung to try and make sense of the new things she showed him about himself. It wasn't an altogether comfortable sensation, but then, if Kane wanted comfortable, he would've stayed put in Austin, playing gigs in dive bars for free beer and barbecue.

If Kane wanted comfortable, he wouldn't have gone on that skydiving trip last year, or bar-hopping with that crazy coked-up socialite in San Sebastian, or on his most recent, intensely grueling international tour, and he certainly wouldn't give his mother his new cell number every time he changed it.

Comfort was overrated.

"Put those pants down and come back to bed."

Claire's slow, exquisitely accented voice jolted Kane back into his body—which, he realized, was standing motionless and naked in the middle of her hotel suite, with a sock in one hand and a pair of inside-out jeans in the other.

Dropping both, Kane turned to face her. The quick flare of desire in her deep brown eyes reminded him of the power of the human form, of how strong it felt to stand there in front of her, bare and unashamed, secure and present in his compact, muscular body.

Kane looked damn good with no clothes on, and he knew it.

But if desire were all he saw on Claire's flushed, dewy face, he would've snatched up his pants and gotten the hell out of Dodge, because Kane Slater was nobody's blow-up doll.

Sex symbol of an entire generation? Sure. But to Claire, he was beginning to realize, he wanted to be more.

And that indefinable more was exactly what he saw in the trembling of her kiss-swollen mouth and the flicker of uncertainty in the downward sweep of her long, coppery lashes.

Even still, Kane had to force his seized-up lungs and vocal cords to do his bidding.

"I came up here today, even though I knew you wanted us to cool things off. And I'm not sorry. I want to be with you—and I'm pretty sure you want to be with me, too. So . . . how about it? You positive you want me to stay?"

He tilted his head to one side and held his breath.

Her soft, French-accented tones were as perfect, pure, as the opening notes of his favorite piano solo.

"Yes. Stay. But, Kane, this doesn't mean I'm prepared to be completely open about our . . . thing, as you call it."

All he heard was *yes*.

Warmth bloomed under Kane's breastbone as if he'd swallowed a star. Or a shot of good tequila.

The sheets were cold against his skin as he slid between them, but they heated up fast once he rolled to his back and pulled Claire over him.

"Mmm, better than any blanket," he said, relishing the way the soft, slight weight of her pressed his legs apart, pushing their hips together.

She squirmed against him and smiled. Kane loved that every one of her rare, reluctant smiles felt like an accomplishment, like winning a prize.

"You understand, yes?" she murmured, running one slim thigh between his. Her voice was slightly muffled where her mouth nuzzled into the curve of his neck. "The idea of people talking about my intimate, private business, what should be only between you and me . . ."

"I totally get it." Kane petted at the silky fall of her hair and smothered the jaw-cracking yawn that took him by surprise as all his muscles seemed to melt into the mattress. "No worries."

The last thing he was conscious of before sleep dragged him under was the quiet sigh of Claire's breath against his shoulder.

There was something energizing about the frantic bustle of a competition kitchen, Eva mused, even if you weren't one of the chefs cooking your heart out and cursing the temperamental stovetops and slipping in spilled olive oil.

She mostly tried to stay out of the way, of both the chefs and the range of Bernard Cheney and his camera in the front left corner of the kitchen, while her heart performed an aggressive series of kickboxing moves against her rib cage.

It was hard to breathe, although that could've been the heat. When her father designed the Limestone kitchen for the Gold Coast hotel, he must've skimped on the ventilation.

Really, though, Eva had never been in a fully functioning professional kitchen that didn't feel like the inside of an active volcano an hour into dinner service.

The combination of roasting ovens, salamander broilers blasting heat, fryolators spitting hot oil, grills throwing flames at the ceiling, and a lot of intense, stressed-out chefs made for a toasty working environment.

She'd already done the rounds of the different groups of chefs, trailed by the surly cameraman, to find out what each team planned to serve the judges.

The Southwest Team was stuffing sausages for their spin on hot dogs; the Southern Team was playing with soul food. Danny's guys—the East Coast Team, she corrected herself; it wouldn't be good to start slipping up and referring to them as "Danny's guys" on camera—had a whole riff on the Chicagoans' love of brunch that sounded like fun. If they managed to pull it off, it would probably be a stunner.

Good food made for good TV, and that was all she was hoping to serve up today. But Eva's hopes for a clean, classy challenge appeared to be in some danger when it came to the teams from the Midwest and the West Coast.

Biting her lip, she watched as Skye Gladwell and Ryan

Larousse collided in front of the walk-in pantry for about the fifth time, both having run there in search of ingredients for pizza dough.

Both teams planned to present pizzas—and the sparks were already flying.

"Out of my way," Ryan snarled, scrambling to catch his balance and haul himself into the pantry with one hand on the doorjamb.

"I'm pretty sure there's enough yeast for everyone," Skye retorted, hurrying in after him. "Or don't you keep this place well stocked?"

That was rough stuff, coming from her. At the beginning of the prep period, every time Ryan challenged her for an ingredient or shoved her out of his path, she'd smiled a tense little smile and let it go.

By this point in the afternoon, however, three hours and counting down, even hippie-crunchy-granola Skye had clearly reached some sort of limit with Ryan's behavior.

If Eva had to guess, she'd bet it was the malicious gleam of frustrated anger in Ryan's eyes that had started to get to his competitor. The guy was infamous for being able to hold a grudge—people still told stories about the lengths he'd gone to in order to revenge himself on his first boss, an old-school chef who dished out a lot of abuse in the kitchen.

And after suffering such ignominious defeat at the hands of the East Coast Team yesterday, Ryan was out for blood.

However, he also wasn't an idiot. Which made him more dangerous, because as she'd been warned when she'd hired him to run Limestone, Ryan Larousse could be subtle and sly when he was after something. He wasn't always a hot-tempered brawler.

No, Ryan was a schemer. A planner. And today, his

plans seemed to include driving Beck crazy by torment-ing Skye Gladwell.

As a special bonus, the storm clouds gathering around Beck's head appeared to be driving Danny to distraction, as well. His concerned gaze darted from Beck to Skye, and back to Ryan, even as his hands swiftly and methodi-cally peeled the dusky purple skin from a pile of damson plums.

Beside Eva, Bernard Cheney stuck his pencil behind his ear and leaned over his camera to get a shot of Danny's jaw clenching down tight, his furious glance in Ryan's direction.

"Now, that's good television," the producer muttered, rocking back on his heels.

Eva pressed her lips together for a moment, then said, "Look. I know it's your job to wring as much drama out of this situation as you can, and that's how you get audi-ences and ratings and publicity—I know all of that." She paused, not even sure what she wanted to say, but know-ing that it had to be said or she'd go nuts.

"I just . . . is it necessary to focus so much on the per-sonal lives of the chefs? I'd think the food would be enough."

Cheney snorted. Disgusting man. "You'd be dead wrong. The food's just a prop. It's stage business. The real meat of the show—ha ha—is always going to be the per-sonal shit. The laughter, the tears, the fights, the jealousy, the sex. That's what sells."

"Sex sells? How original."

Cheney turned one squinted eye on her, bushy brows lowered. "It's a cliché because it's true. And without the extra juice from a good scandal or a fierce rivalry, there ain't no way my bosses are going to be interested in air-ing your little cooking contest."

Eva's gut clenched, her breath choking in her lungs.

She'd sworn she could bring the RSC into the public eye and capture the imaginations of the Cooking Channel generation. Filming the competition—and the competitors—was key. Her father had made that very clear.

So maybe she didn't like the idea of delving into the contestants' backgrounds . . . maybe it was cheap and crass.

Okay, there was no maybe about it. But she didn't have any choice.

"Film what you need to," she ordered Cheney, ignoring his satisfied grunt.

Desperate for a distraction from the sinking sensation in her chest—*so this is what selling out feels like? Ugh*—Eva scanned the kitchen for her other major gambit in the battle for the hearts and minds of the masses.

Kane Slater, Eva's glittering supernova of a celebrity judge, waltzed into the kitchen looking disheveled and tired and very pleased about it.

Claire was close behind him. She was slightly better put together—at least her hair had been brushed and her buttons were all done up correctly—but a similar aura of satiation haloed her head. Interesting.

"Are we late?" she asked, her heels clicking quickly across the floor. "No, I see Devon has yet to arrive. *Bon*."

The judges were scheduled to film a quick tour of the kitchen before the contestants finished for the night. Eva couldn't remember whose idea that had been. Whoever came up with it hadn't taken into account that acute ratcheting up of tension that occurred whenever the judges were in the same room as the contestants.

As if this kitchen needed any more tension.

The clanging of pots slamming down on the stovetop and whirring buzz of food processors seemed deafening, suddenly, the chefs shouting back and forth to one another with instructions and status reports, frantically trying to reach the end of their prep lists before Eva called time.

Ryan Larousse was at the grill station stoking up the fire to fantastic heights in preparation for searing off some meat. Even he'd reached the point of desperation, finally, focusing more on the task at hand than on his gamesmanship. Relief at being able to stop watching out for the guy made Danny light-headed.

Pastry chefs didn't usually spend a lot of time in the thick of dinner service. Most professional restaurants called their pastry guy in early, like seven in the morning, and had him or her out of there by five.

But with his family owning the restaurant where he worked, and his father counting on him more every year, Danny's hours had never been quite that cut and dried. He was used to working through the rush, keeping tabs on everyone in the kitchen with one corner of his mind while the rest concentrated on executing meticulously perfect crème brûlées.

No dinner service at Lunden's Tavern could have prepared him for this balls-to-the-wall insanity.

If he trusted every cook here, that would be one thing. He was used to cooking with guys who had his back, who respected the hell out of each other and worked hard not to let each other down. And even in those circumstances, putting out a perfect menu in this compressed amount of time would've been a bitch. Add in the fact that they were competing against a whole slew of talented fuckers who were also sharing their kitchen space, and Danny's orderly, control-loving mind spun off into orbit.

There were too many things to keep track of. The consistency of the plum compote, Win racing around, Max and Jules playing off each other as if they were humming a duet in perfect harmony, while Beck seethed like a storm about to break every time that assmunch Larousse looked sideways at the chick from the West Coast team.

And, of course, Eva.

In short, Danny's focus was shot, and time was almost up. A quick glance at the timer clock showed fifteen minutes left and counting, and they had to have their stuff finished off or at a good stopping place, and packed away for the night, when the clock ticked down to zero.

Just as Danny was getting ready to let the whole problem of Ryan Larousse go fuck itself, he noticed the strawberry-blond hippie chick, Skye Gladwell, rounding the corner of the back tables with a huge, obviously heavy pot of something emitting billows of steam clutched in her hands.

The space behind the grills was one of the prime pathways for getting from one end of the kitchen to the other, but it was ridiculously narrow. And made narrower by the ebbing and flowing tide of bodies in perpetual motion as chefs moved between their stations, the pantry, and the walk-in coolers.

"Behind, hot," she yelled, the standard warning to the guys hunched over the grills that they should refrain from stepping back for a few seconds to give her time to pass.

Ryan Larousse was still at the grills, Danny noticed with a leaden sensation tugging hard at his stomach.

It was like watching one of those crazy Japanese TV shows where they made people run up inflatable rubber staircases and avoid giant swinging hammers and leap onto rotating platforms for a prize, only without the entertainment value of watching nutballs get swiped off the obstacle course and into a pool of water.

Although what happened next in the Gold Coast hotel kitchen somehow felt every bit as inevitable as the cold dunking of those reality show contestants.

Skye dodged an arm holding a knife and heaved her smoking stockpot out of the way of a chef bending down to grab a bottle of olive oil from the shelf below his station. She moved fast, one eye on the ticking clock and a look of intense determination firming her soft mouth.

She was halfway down the line when Ryan Larousse made his move.

Chapter 12

An instant before it happened, Danny caught the twitch of a sneer on Larousse's mouth, the hint of anger putting red flags on his cheeks. Before he'd even consciously registered the intent, Danny was moving to intercept.

His shoes squeaked on the rubber matting as he whirled and threw himself toward Larousse, who smoothly, deliberately, stepped into Skye Gladwell's path, forcing her to swerve and bobble the heavy pot.

"Oh, behind you," she cried, knuckles white on the handles, but it was slipping, and Danny was still a few feet away.

An enraged roar from behind him told Danny that Beck had become aware of the situation, and in the next breath the big chef barreled past him and into Ryan Larousse like a rampaging bull.

Beck knocked Ryan to the floor and out of the way just as Skye's fingers slipped on the pot handles. Danny had only a brief instant to take in her round face, white with panic, before he dove for the pot.

Pain seared into Danny's fingertips as they made contact with the scorching-hot sides of the pot. It slipped between his palms, which felt as if he'd stuck his hands in the blue flames of a gas stovetop, but Danny ground his teeth and clamped down hard.

Boiling chicken stock sloshed over the edges, spattering down onto his wrists. "Fuck me," he gritted out, bending his knees to lower the pot gently to the floor.

"I'm so, so, so sorry," Skye said in a rush, kneeling down beside the pot and reaching for one of his red, burned hands. "Your poor fingers! Oh my gosh, if you hadn't caught that, it would've splashed all over me. Third-degree burns from head to toe! Thank you."

Before Danny could respond to her gratitude, he heard the distinctive sound of a fist smacking into flesh and bone behind him.

Clambering to his feet, he saw Skye's face go from grateful to horrified in the blink of an eye.

"Stop it! Oh stop that, please. Henry, don't!"

Bangle bracelets jingling, she rushed past Danny before he could catch her, arms outstretched entreatingly toward the two men wrestling on the floor.

Beck the Berserker was back, Danny saw. An eerie calm had blanked Beck's face; he didn't appear to hear a word Skye said. His entire focus was on the man he had pinned to the rubber floor mats.

Shit, there was a camera rolling, catching all of this, Danny remembered with a sickening surge of panic. "Beck, man, come on," he said urgently, reaching for the guy's broad, rock-solid shoulder. "Let him up."

"She could've been hurt," Beck said, his tone oddly detached. "He tried to hurt her, Danny."

"But I'm fine, Henry. So it's time to let him up, now," Skye said. Her voice was gentle, but there was an edge of steel running through it that made Danny look at her sharply. This sweet-faced woman wasn't as soft as she looked.

Beck hadn't yielded to Danny's hand on his arm, no matter how strongly Danny tugged at him. He was about to put his back into it, really haul the guy to his feet whether he was willing to stand or not, and no matter how much it hurt his own scorched palms, but then Skye reached past him and laid her hand on Beck's back.

A shudder rocked the big man's frame. Beck's voice came out sounding like boulders rolling down a mountain. "You're okay?"

"I'm fine," she repeated. "But even if I wasn't, you shouldn't have done that, Henry." Then there was that knife-edge of hardness in her voice again as she said, "I will not be your excuse for violence. Don't put that on me."

Beck looked up at her, and the mute misery on his face tied a knot in Danny's throat. But he loosened his hold on Ryan, and Danny felt his own shoulders sag in relief, the sudden draining of adrenaline from his body making him aware of just how fucking much his hands hurt.

"All right, get them up from there." Eva's clipped instructions jolted Danny, and he blinked at her stupidly, almost swaying on his feet.

Max and Win were there, suddenly, pulling Beck off the floor and hustling him out of the kitchen, presumably to dunk his head in an ice bath and shock some sense into him. Skye watched them go, a strange, pained expression on her face, one hand covering her bloodless lips.

She turned back to Danny, looking ready to start spouting thanks again, but before she could open her mouth, Eva was there.

"Hugo? Take Ryan back to your hotel suite, and for God's sake, stay out of trouble for one damn night."

"Me?" Ryan protested, a grimace twisting his boyish features. "It was just an accident. A stupid mistake."

He actually looked as if he regretted it, and for a moment, Danny almost felt sorry for the guy, who was, after all, pretty immature and reckless, and maybe just hadn't thought his actions through.

But then, of course, Ryan had to ruin it. "Talk about breaking the rules! I'm the one who got attacked. Again! That guy is like a rabid dog, he oughta be locked up or put down."

Anger roiled through Danny's belly, but he didn't have a chance to blast the guy because he blinked once, and Skye Gladwell was all up in Larousse's face.

"You shut your mouth," she hissed. "Henry Beck is ten times the man you'll ever be."

Ignoring the little shit's sputtering, Skye turned her back on him and leaned up to kiss Danny's cheek. He raised his eyebrows, and she smiled, saying, "I'd shake your hand, but I don't want to hurt you."

"I appreciate it. These are starting to sting like a bitch."

Concern and remorse clouded over Skye's face. "Here, let me see—"

But abruptly, Eva had angled her body between them, gray eyes flashing dark as iron. "I'll take care of him. You should get your team together and head up to your rooms. I'm calling time early for today; we'll give you all an extra ten minutes tomorrow."

There was some grumbling from the other teams while they moved to pack their prepped food away and clear down their stations, but Eva didn't appear to notice or care as she held out one imperious hand. "Palms up," she said briskly, lips tight. "Let's see the damage."

"It's fine," Danny protested, curling his fists to hide the worst of the redness. Which, of course, pulled at the skin just starting to blister. He couldn't help his wince, and Eva pounced.

"There's no need to keep playing hero," she said, grabbing for his wrists. The tartness of her words contrasted dizzily with the gentleness of her touch. "I had the cameraman stop filming when it looked like Beck might strangle that idiot, Larousse."

"I'm not a hero," Danny said, annoyed. "But thanks for turning the camera off. Video evidence would've made it hard for Beck to plead not guilty on a murder charge."

"That might have made for scintillating B-reel footage on our Cooking Channel Special Event program, but I'm not quite ready to sign over every scrap of integrity to the television producers." Eva traced over his hypersensitive, flinching skin with delicate fingertips.

"Your concern for my teammate is heartwarming," Danny said, trying not to stumble. He was crashing hard, head spinning like the dough hook on his stand mixer, set to KNEAD. He blinked and shook his head, trying to jar himself back into clarity.

"Hey. I'm concerned. I'm planning a celebrity singalong, a telethon, and a charity ball in his honor, right after you guys pull your shit together and get through the rest of this competition. But in the meantime, let's get you checked out by the paramedics."

Whipping out her high-tech phone, she touch-typed something into it at lightning speed, too quickly for Danny to follow. But he didn't really need to know exactly what she was saying. He knew where he needed to be.

"No, thanks," he told her. "I'll be fine. I just need to go check on my guys, make sure they're all right."

"Not so fast, buster!" Eva tucked her phone away, eyes wide and determined. "You're not going anywhere. Your guys will survive without you—Beck didn't have a scratch on him, and he's got your brother and two other chefs to help calm him down. They don't need you."

A spike of panic punctured Danny's pain haze. "Yeah, they fucking well do," he gritted out.

Her eyes softened. "That's not what I meant," she said, her voice going low and regretful. "But they need you whole and with all your bits in good working order. Think you can hold a whisk with those fingers?"

Danny's hands clenched spasmodically, sending shards of fire streaking through his palms and up into his wrists and forearms. The pain was a blur now, hard to tell where it ended and he began.

Burns sucked.

"I guess a little aloe or something couldn't hurt," Danny admitted, trying to keep his hands still.

"That's my boy." Eva tucked her arm through the crook of his elbow and steered him out into the cool chill of the hotel hallway where a short, scruffy man in scrubs stood waiting.

Danny shivered in the aggressive air-conditioning, the contrast of temperatures from the inferno of a busy, crowded kitchen to this empty hall making his head spin.

"Oops, better sit down," Scrubs said, pushing Danny over to the bench between the elevators. Embarrassed at how easily his knees folded and plopped him into a sitting position, Danny resisted the hand trying to get him to bend over and stick his head between his knees.

"You're a little shocky," the paramedic explained, relentlessly urging him over. "A bad burn stresses the whole body."

Blood rushed to Danny's head and sloshed around like his skull had turned into a giant snow globe. It distracted him from the questions the paramedic asked, Eva's answers, and the paramedic's gentle but efficient probing.

When they finally helped him sit back up and the blood drained back down where it was supposed to go, his hands were wrapped in white gauze and the searing pain had settled to a low throb that kept time with his heartbeat.

Danny blinked. "I look like I'm about to go ten rounds in the boxing ring."

"Or a kid about to get into a snowball fight," Eva suggested, accepting a clipboard from the paramedic guy and signing some papers.

"You couldn't have wrapped my fingers individually?" Danny had never been a big fan of mittens.

"For tonight, keep them wrapped like that. Don't get the bandages wet. Tomorrow, we'll check and see how the burns are doing, and maybe we can see about cutting down on the padding."

"Sure thing, Doc," Danny agreed easily, leaning his head back against the wall. No matter how the burns were doing, these mittens were coming off tomorrow. He needed his hands.

Eva gave him a look like she knew what he was thinking, all arched eyebrow and smirking mouth, but she didn't rat him out to the paramedic. Danny smiled at her, and when the guy handed her a miniature bottle of pain pills and took off, Eva smiled back.

Shaking the bottle to make the pills rattle, she said, "Want one of these?"

Danny cracked his neck from side to side, taking stock. His hands ached, but it was surprisingly manageable. "Nah, I'm good for now. Whatever that gel was that he smeared all over my hands seems to be doing its job."

"Well, the pills are here if you need them later." He watched her slip the bottle into her purse.

"Um. Not to be a wimp or anything, but I might take one before I pass out tonight."

"Good," she said calmly, slipping the purse strap onto her shoulder and putting a hand under his elbow to steady him as he stood. "I think you should. Rest is important to recovery, and getting decent sleep will keep you sharp in the competition tomorrow."

"Yeah. I agree. But it's going to be kind of tough for me to take one of those pills tonight if you're holding them hostage."

"Not at all," Eva said, pressing the UP button and standing back to wait for the elevator. "Since I intend to hold you hostage as well."

He blinked and saw himself spread-eagled, tied to a bed, with Eva standing over him. Another blink, and she was the one on the bed, silk scarves holding her wrists and ankles wide, her body white and lovely against the sheets.

Danny shook his head vigorously as a different sort of fire raced through his blood at the lightning-fast images.

"I should get back to the room," he said, "see how my guys are doing." But even Danny could hear the lack of conviction in his voice.

It certainly didn't escape Eva's attention. The curl of a smile at the corners of her red mouth took on a satisfied look.

The elevator doors shushed open and she wasted no time marching them both into it and pressing the button for the top floor.

"You can call them from my suite," she said, determination in every line of her slender body. "You need someone to look after you tonight, Danny. And if you go back to your teammates, it'll be the other way around. You'll be taking care of them."

"It's not like that," Danny started to protest, then stopped. Where the hell did his conviction go, anyway? It was as if it had been boiled out of him by the hot stock.

"It's exactly like that," Eva contradicted, pulling out her phone and texting while the elevator zoomed silently upward.

A hard kernel of resentment popped in Danny's chest. Maybe she was right, but that somehow made it worse. "So fucking what? I take care of my friends. I don't see how that's a bad thing."

"It's not," she said, without looking up from her fingers tapping away at the keypad. He kind of wanted to grab the phone out of her hands and stomp it. "Especially if the caretaking is a two-way street."

Danny forcefully kept himself from clenching his stiff hands into fists. "I'm not a little kid with a skinned knee. I don't need to be taken care of."

"Tonight you do. The paramedic said so."

"For fuck's sake," Danny exploded, "do you think maybe the texting can wait until we're done with this conversation?"

Her cheeks went pink, but she clicked a button hurriedly and put the phone away, her eyes finding his. The pretty silvery gray was dark with compassion and something that looked a lot like earnestness. "Sorry, I was ordering some stuff up to the room."

"What stuff?" Danny asked, wary.

"Food, mostly. And I got the concierge to send someone out to fill your prescription for more of that pain-relieving gel."

Danny closed his eyes, hating himself. "Sorry," he said. His gruff voice sounded weirdly like his dad's, when Gus Lunden apologized to his infinitely patient wife for one of his bursts of temper. It made Danny sigh. "I'm not great at letting people help me. More used to dealing with shit on my own, I guess."

Something like recognition flickered in her gaze. "I know. Come on, Danny, let me do this. I want to."

Her quiet plea broke through Danny's resistance, and he felt his shoulders slump just as the elevator slid to a stop.

"I guess the team can do without me for a little while."

Her smile was brilliant, blinding in the warm, atmospheric light of the hallway she led him into to. A set of double doors faced the elevator bank, and Danny craned his neck to look up and down the short hallway. They were the only doors on this floor.

"The penthouse?" he said, incredulous, as she pulled out a key card and slid it into the door lock. "You're in the penthouse suite?"

"The hotel insisted," she said, pushing the door open and waving him in. "It's empty a lot of the time, so when VIPs come through, they like to comp it for us."

"Must be nice to be a VIP," Danny said, stopping two paces into the room to stare around him. He was standing in a foyer—an actual, honest-to-God foyer, in a freaking hotel room—lit by an angular brass chandelier that cast a soft glow over the green-gold watermarked silk covering the walls. The floor under his dirty, spattered kitchen clogs was white marble, inlaid with something that looked an awful lot like jade in an abstract, swirling pattern. Danny followed it into a large, spacious sitting area, complete with two deep, green leather couches, a glossy wood writing desk with spindly legs, and a round glass coffee table covered with papers, folders, and an open laptop.

There was more brass in here, a couple of table lamps, and yet another chandelier over the . . . holy cow.

"There's a dining table," Danny said, gesturing as if Eva might have missed the mahogany monstrosity camped out in the left-hand side of the suite.

"I know." She didn't sound terribly impressed.

Danny counted the ladder-back chairs tucked under the gleaming, expansive tabletop. "It seats eight. It wouldn't fit in any room of my apartment, even if I threw out my bed."

"It's just a table, Danny." Amusement colored her voice as she disappeared into a side room Danny hadn't noticed. There was the familiar sound of a refrigerator opening, and she reappeared in the doorway with a glass carafe of orange juice in her hand. "Want a drink? I'd offer you something stronger, but I think a little fresh-squeezed is a safer bet."

Danny peered over her head as she got a couple of glasses out of a cabinet, and felt his jaw drop. "Well, suck me sideways. There's a whole fucking kitchen in here!" And not just a minimal kitchenette, either, but a full-on gourmet kitchen with granite countertops, top-of-the-line appliances, and more counter space than some professional kitchens Danny'd seen.

"I'd think you'd be sick of kitchens, at this point," Eva said, slipping past him with two glasses of orange juice.

Taking one last, fascinated look around the perfectly appointed space, Danny joined her on one of the couches. The tufted leather looked like it was going to be hard and uncomfortable, but instead Danny sank into it like a lover's embrace, the cool depths of the sofa's arms and back reaching around to enfold him.

He sighed in contentment, head lolling back. "I could fall asleep right here."

"That's only because you haven't seen the bedroom yet." Eva's voice was serene, even bland, but everything inside Danny went on red alert anyway.

Yet.

Sitting up straight was a challenge when all he wanted

was to melt into a pile of exhausted bones in the corner of the couch, but Danny managed it. Clearing his throat, he said, "That juice looks pretty good."

"It is," Eva said, taking a sip without dropping her gaze from his. "Tart, sweet, refreshing. You want?"

Danny licked his lips. "Yeah. Only I'm not sure how to pick it up."

He could just picture himself bobbling the slick glass between his bandage mitts, spilling sticky juice on this couch, which probably cost more than the mortgage on his parents' West Village apartment building for a year.

"Here," she purred, scooting closer to him and leaning over his lap to pick up the glass from the side table. "Let me help you."

Danny sucked in a breath at the sudden soft press of her lithe body against his, the quick brush of her breasts against his arm as she sat up.

Eva tilted her head, the look in her gray eyes coy, inviting, and Danny couldn't help but shake his head at her. "This was all part of your plan to get me up here, wasn't it?"

"Yes," she told him, tipping the glass up to his lips and letting some of the icy, sharply sweet juice trickle into his mouth. "I asked Ryan Larousse to throw boiling liquid on you so I could have my wicked way with you. And you walked right into my trap! Bwa-ha-ha."

The juice was perfect, cold and shocking, a wake-up call for his senses.

"Mmm," he moaned, chasing a stray droplet with his tongue. "If this is your wicked way, I'm in. More, please."

Her cheeks were flushed, and her eyes sparkled with laughter as she brought the glass back to his lips. The moment felt very delicately balanced, the soft, supple weight of her suspended over him, dripping juice into his mouth as if he were some kind of ancient king and she was his serving girl.

Danny could get into this, he mused, in a big bad way. "How are you feeling?"

The words brushed his cheeks softly, stirred the hair at his temples as she shifted to curl up at his side.

"Better now," Danny admitted, gazing at her.

Happiness lit her up from within. "I told you. Didn't I tell you? I'm good for you." She felt so right, so there with him, as if she fit into his empty places and filled them up with light and softness and lust and fun and all the other things Danny didn't usually let himself have.

"You know what would be good for me?" he said, in a voice gone rough with emotion and desire. "A kiss."

She squirmed against him in a very distracting way, looking tempted. But she said, "I don't think that's what the paramedic had in mind when he said you needed to rest and be looked after."

"Ah, but it's what you had in mind," Danny said. "And it'll relax me. Don't you want me to be relaxed?"

Okay, so *relaxed* wasn't the best word for how he was feeling—especially a certain, completely irrepressible part of him that didn't care about pain or exhaustion or anything other than how throbbingly hard and cramped it was, pressed up against the zipper of his jeans.

Eva didn't buy his oh-so-innocent face for a second, that much was clear from the adorable way she wrinkled her nose at him, but Danny didn't care because in the next instant she was kneeling up again and leaning over him to put the empty glass back on the side table. She was so tempting, hovering over him like a hummingbird taking sips from a flower, and Danny couldn't help it if he was more of a Venus flytrap than a rose.

He reached for her unthinkingly, encircling her with his

arms and tumbling her into his lap, which was awesome, but the move put pressure on his aching palms, which was less awesome.

Danny winced and bit back a gasp, but Eva caught it.

"Oh, be careful," she said, wriggling around in his lap as if she were trying to pull away.

"Just . . . stay where you are," Danny managed as she ground her hip into his aching erection. "Don't move."

"Are you in a lot of pain?" She was so anxious and concerned, Danny couldn't take it.

He made no effort to hide the rough desire in his voice. "Why? Are you going to kiss it and make it better?"

Chapter 13

Eva had to wonder if someone had been in her room, messing with the thermostat. How was it so hot in there?

Maybe it had something to do with the solid wall of living heat pressed up close beneath her, melting her bones and enticing her to wind her arms and legs tight around him like a creeping vine.

Danny Lunden was the hottest thing she'd ever had under her—and Eva had once walked the rim of an active volcano on a dare.

With his taunt about kissing still ringing in her ears, Eva leaned up, relishing the way it jostled their lower bodies together.

This wasn't her first rodeo—she knew exactly what part he was hoping to have kissed. And she wasn't averse to it—but first . . .

Smiling down at him, she took his poor, bandaged hands in hers. Gently, delicately, she feathered light kisses over the gauze, feeling the tension in his stiff wrists as he fought not to pull away. Surprise glinted in his stormy blue eyes as the connection between them spun from pure sex to sudden intimacy.

Eva could relate—she wasn't prepared for it, either. But when he left his hands lying in her grasp, docile as a sleeping wolf, her heart squeezed so tight she had to lean forward and kiss his handsome mouth, just to buy herself a minute to process.

Of course, that turned out to be a big mistake, because once her lips were moving against his, the kiss was all she could think about. Hot, deep, just wet enough, with strong strokes of that agile tongue setting every nerve ending on fire. Eva moaned into his mouth and wrapped her arms around his neck. Danny's arms stayed at his side, tense and rigid enough to distract her from the ravishment of her mouth.

Why wasn't he holding, stroking, caressing, easing the ache of desire that kept bursting between them like solar flares?

Oh, right.

With one last nip at his luscious mouth, Eva pulled back slowly, her mind struggling to grapple with the logistics of making love to a man whose hands were covered in second-degree burns.

"This is ridiculous," Danny rasped, chest heaving, eyes glittering with frustrated desire. "Help me take off these fucking bandages."

"Not an option," Eva said instantly. "The paramedic was very clear. Besides . . ." She drew her hands down his shoulders, across his breastbone, feeling the pounding of his heart and the bellows-blow of his breath as he panted like a racehorse beneath her touch.

"This has definite possibilities," she murmured, letting her fingers wander lower to tease at the worn waistband of his jeans.

"I can't touch you." Danny sounded beyond frustrated at this point. His steely thighs tensed and trembled under her bottom.

"Ah, but I can touch you," Eva said, savoring the moment like a sip of fine champagne.

His eyes widened, his mouth opened, and she flipped the button on his fly.

Danny's mouth snapped shut on a groan, and his back arched hard, making the leather of the sofa creak. Eva was panting now, too, every breath filled with the heady, intoxicating scent of clean male sweat and hot, musky sex.

"You wanted me to kiss it better," she said, breathless. "I'm just taking care of you, like I promised I would."

With that, she slid down his zipper and eased his pants open around the prominent bulge of his trapped erection.

Eva went down to her knees, thankful for the thick, lush pile of the hotel suite's carpeting. The denim covering Danny's legs was rough against her palms as she ran her hands up to his hips, the friction sensitizing her skin.

He lifted his ass off the couch when she urged him up, and twisted awkwardly to help her get his pants and underwear pulled down far enough to expose the gorgeous, flushed thickness of his cock.

This was a moment Eva loved—the hush of expectation, the crystallized joy of anticipation and want and closeness all focused on her.

Propping her elbows on the couch on either side of Danny's hips, Eva smiled up at his taut, strained face and bent to press a single, soft kiss to the plump red head of his penis. His groan was loud enough to make her glad they were the only people occupying this floor of the hotel.

The transparent shock and pleasure in his expression tightened everything low in Eva's body, sending tremors down her spine and into her pelvis. Swaying her hips back and forth, she relished the way her skin was beginning to slicken with the heated, silky liquid pooling between her thighs.

Right about now was when some men, impatient to get to "the good part," might slide their hands around her head and grip her hair, or pet at her shoulders, or do any one of a dozen things calculated to make her get on with it.

Whether it was his smarting palms or the innate patience required of a high-level pastry chef, Danny did nothing but stretch his arms along the top of the sofa and stare down at her intently.

There was something both exquisitely liberating and deliciously submissive about kneeling here for him, without a single touch to ground her in the moment but the brush of her own hands against the bare skin of his lean hips. She felt powerful, wielding the strength of his own desire to make him sigh and move at her whim.

Needing more, she dipped down and took the head of his cock in her mouth. He was hot, so very hot, skin soft and velvety where it stretched so tightly over the throbbing flesh beneath.

He tasted salty, warm. Delicious.

She swallowed more of him, loving the way he moved thick and heavy over her tongue, the way he pressed his hips into the couch to keep from thrusting and choking her.

Such control you have, Danny, she wanted to say.

It made her reckless, made her want to be the one who forced him to lose it.

He hunched over to brush his mouth against her hair, a butterfly kiss that made her shiver. Her greedy fingers sought out the tense, hard washboard of his stomach muscles holding him in the awkward position.

"You're amazing," he said into the top of her head. "But

you have to stop now, or this is all going to be over way too fast."

Eva made a muffled noise of protest and sucked harder.

A bolt of triumph shot through her when he tensed and moaned at the onslaught, but then his voice came again, so soothing, but commanding, too. "Come up here, sweetheart."

The endearment pierced something in Eva's chest, some giddy inner schoolgirl that had never gotten over the secret desire to be called something sweet in that exact tone of voice. With one last, lingering stroke of her tongue up the throbbing vein on the underside of his cock, Eva pulled off with a delightfully obscene *pop* and looked up at him.

He should've looked ridiculous—most men she'd been with would have—sprawled there on the leather couch with his pants halfway down his hips and his erection spearing up out of them, so hard that it curved tight to his muscled stomach.

He didn't look ridiculous. He looked edible.

Licking her lips, Eva prepared to ignore Danny's demand and dive back in for more of the addictive smoke-salt flavor of him, which she could still taste on her tongue. But he shook his head, stopping her, and stroked the backs of his bandaged hands down the sides of her face.

It was a strange sensation, the soft cotton gauze not as warm or as rough as his callused fingers, but it was the expression on his face that melted her insides. Danny looked as if he thought she was the edible one—and he was starving.

"Up," he repeated, that same compelling blend of inflexible command and coaxing softness.

No wonder his team listens to him, Eva thought dazedly as she found herself pushing off her knees and standing before him. It scared her a little, how much she wanted to just listen, let him tell her what to do, and trust that it would be good for both of them.

Struggling to find some measure of control, she arched a brow and sent him her best sultry smile as her fingers went to the black patent-leather belt at her waist. A little striptease usually reminded everyone just who was in charge of the scene.

Danny leaned back, heat flashing in his eyes as he watched her slip the tongue of the belt free of the buckle. Dropping it to the floor with a soft clink of metal, Eva felt her balance returning. Putting a little dance into her hips, she imagined the pulsing beat of music at her favorite club and closed her eyes, inching the hem of the tight red dress up her thighs.

"No," Danny said quietly, jarring her from her fantasy. "Zipper first."

Eva dragged in a breath, aware that her heart was flapping in her chest like a baby bird fallen from its nest. His focused gaze trapped her, wouldn't let her retreat into her safe, comfortable imagination.

Instead, she raised shaking fingers to the zipper at the back of the dress, feeling every moment of the clumsy contortion, every extra second of silence as her fingers slipped and fumbled before finally getting the zipper all the way down. The sleeves, tight down to her elbows, kept the dress up in front, but in back she could feel the draft of the climate-controlled air wafting against her bare shoulder blades.

"When I get these damn bandages off," Danny said conversationally, "I'm going to undress you slowly, revealing one inch of skin at a time, tasting every part as I uncover it."

Eva started to pant, suddenly so hot she could hardly

bear the constriction of the sleeves around her arms, the dress around her waist and hips. She wanted to peel the whole garment off, but she hesitated, desperate to know what Danny was about to say.

"You're so insanely gorgeous like this," he said, his voice no longer casual. The rough, guttural truth of the words scored along her skin like fingernails scratching up her back, and Eva gasped for air and shimmied out of the dress so fast she almost fell over.

She must have looked like an idiot, but she didn't even care, because the chill air felt so good against her overheated body, and Danny's eyes flared with desire when he saw her black lace panties and registered the fact that she wasn't wearing the matching bra. Or any bra at all.

Eva had never been so happy to be flat-chested.

And she congratulated herself on picking out a dress that morning that was structured enough that she didn't need anything underneath. Because it meant that right now, there was nothing between Danny Lunden and her breasts but cold air making her nipples tighten into little knots of aching need.

"Come here," he said, his whole body poised as if all he wanted in the world was to leap off the sofa and grab her.

But he didn't, he couldn't because of his hands, and Eva realized with a start that if she didn't undress him, no one would. Galvanized into action, she threw herself back onto his lap, knees spread on either side of his hips, and seized his mouth in a hungry kiss. Their tongues met and fought for control, sliding and stroking, while Eva's busy fingers moved to the snaps on his white chef's jacket.

Taking hold of the sides, she ripped the coat open with a satisfying sound. He had on a plain white T-shirt underneath, and they had to break the kiss for long, painful seconds to wrestle him free of both jacket and shirt without jostling his injured hands too much. But after a bit of cursing and a couple of frustrated laughs, Eva was able to wind her arms around his strong neck and press her naked breasts to his equally naked chest, and boy, oh boy, was it ever worth it.

Danny had the kind of body lots of men spent hours and tons of money to achieve, but Eva knew his muscles came from the grueling grind of lifting heavy pans, kneading bread dough, and working hard. The planes of his chest felt different under her than some model or actor's sculpted perfection.

Everything with Danny felt more real.

Tearing his mouth away from hers, he gasped out, "Up, kneel up, I want to taste you."

Unsteady but more than willing, Eva braced her hands on his broad shoulders and pushed up. Danny didn't wait for her to get settled; as soon as she was close enough, he angled his head and took the tip of her breast into the wet heat of his mouth.

Someone had tied a cord from Eva's nipple to her clit, and with every suck of Danny's talented mouth, every lash of his rough tongue, the cord pulled taut. Eva gasped and squirmed, her knees wobbling. She couldn't believe Danny was making her feel this way without ever touching her with his hands.

Who needed hands with a mouth like his?

He made a hungry sound against her breast, the vibration sending shivers cascading down her sides, and pulled his head away. Eva squirmed some more, and suddenly the damp, throbbing head of his cock was thrusting against her inner thighs, hot and seeking and so close to where she wanted it.

Mindless with need, she reached for it, loving the heavy throb it gave as her fingers clasped the base and stroked all the way up to the head.

"Gah," said Danny, eyes rolling back in his head.

Eva grinned, feeling wild and fierce, and wished she were wearing breakaway underpants. Since she wasn't, in fact, a professional stripper, she had to work to shimmy out of the black lace panties, but Danny didn't seem to mind the way she wriggled around his lap to get it done.

When she was completely naked, Eva pushed in close for a victory kiss, trapping his erection between them and rubbing shamelessly while she let Danny conquer her mouth.

"God, you are the hottest thing I've ever seen," he said, when she let him pause for a breath.

"You're pretty hot, yourself," Eva replied, running her hands down his beautiful abdomen to circle his cock once more.

Danny's eyes were slits of blue-gray in his tense, flushed face. "Good. That feels good. Fuck, I wish I could touch you."

"Me too," Eva agreed fervently. There was an emptiness down there—she was so wet and open, she ached. Whimpering a little, she rocked her hips helplessly.

His eyes opened wider, inspiration burning into them. "Be my hands, Eva. You do it, and let me see."

Chapter 14

"What?" Eva felt slow, as if all the foreplay had turned her brain to tapioca.

The forceful tone bled into his voice, his jaw as hard as marble, as he said, "Hold up your right hand. Index finger."

Clumsily, she complied, and he praised her with a soft, "That's good. You're perfect."

Warmth filled her at the approval in his voice, and a languid sort of heat stole over her as he propped his feet on the coffee table behind her, raising his knees as a support for her back. She relaxed against his strong thighs, the denim rubbing her skin sensitive and hot, and waited for his next request.

"Beautiful," he said, and she didn't know if it was a compliment or an endearment, but either way, she liked it. "Take that finger and touch yourself. I want to see how wet you are."

The boldness of it, the straightforward way he stared at her and invited her to participate in stoking her own passion appealed to Eva.

She'd never been shy. Or, if she had been, it had been

many years since she acknowledged it or let it stop her from doing whatever the hell she wanted. So the blush that heated her face and neck surprised her as she trailed that finger down the centerline of her body toward the slippery, tingling flesh between her legs.

Her cheeks were hot, as hot as the tiny cluster of nerves at the top of her slit when she searched it out and made herself shudder.

Danny watched every move she made as if he were going to be quizzed later, and Eva let the attention cover her in a mantle of confidence. When Danny's lips parted and his breath sped up, Eva's natural exhibitionist came roaring to the forefront of her consciousness.

Holding his gaze, she let another finger come into play, delving deeper, playing through the slick folds and circling her clit. It felt incredible, better than when she did it alone, as if Danny's presence, his watchful eyes, gave the familiar act an extra kick.

Shuddering, hips pulsing ever so slightly, Eva let herself writhe in his lap like a cat begging to be stroked. Her head tipped back over his knees, the long line of her throat bare and vulnerable, her belly quivering softly with every wet slide of her fingers.

"You're driving me crazy," Danny told her, thrusting up so that the rough teeth of his zipper scraped at the bare flesh of her buttocks. The move tilted her hips forward far enough to tap his erection against the back of her hand. Seizing the opportunity, Eva pulled her fingers free of her body and wrapped them around his hard thickness, pressing the length of it solidly against her weeping sex.

That hardness, heavy and hot and right there, felt incredible. It was exactly the friction she wanted, better than any fingers in the world. It must have felt good to Danny, too, because he squeezed his eyes shut and thrust his hips again, shoulders pushing into the back of the couch as his back arched.

"God," he said. "Too close. Can you reach my wallet?"

Keeping his cock where she wanted it with her right hand, Eva craned forward to kiss him, sloppy and hot, while her left hand burrowed into his back pocket.

"Got it," she breathed against his mouth.

"Condom," he gasped. "Get it on me."

Eva had never been so eager to obey in her whole life. She found the condom and ripped the wrapper open with her teeth. The grip of her hand as she rolled the latex down over his straining erection brought another shuddering groan out of Danny.

Feverish with need, desire wound so tightly inside her that she was afraid she'd explode, Eva lifted herself up and, holding Danny steady with one hand, brought herself down over him.

She moaned at the nudge of his cock head against her entrance, thick and searing hot, even through the condom. He was big, wide and uncompromising, and she wanted every inch of him.

Pushing herself, Eva let gravity do most of the work, concentrating on relaxing enough to let him all the way inside.

"Careful, sweetness," Danny said, concern wrinkling his brow. "Not too fast. We've got the whole night."

It didn't feel that way to Eva, who wanted him inside her now, all at once, filling her up and making her fly.

With a gasp she felt herself stretched to the limit as her hips slammed down, grinding her pubis against the hard bone of his pelvis. Her brain shorted out in a shower of sparks, and the whole world became nothing more than rocking and moaning, clutching and gasping and straining toward something perfect, just out of reach, until suddenly, with a tightening of muscles and a last rough thrust, she was there.

When it was over, she blinked her eyes open to find her forehead pressed to Danny's sweaty shoulder, her thighs quivering tiredly, muscles sore from being held apart for so long.

He groaned and shifted, as if he might be sore, too, and that one tiny movement sent aftershocks fluttering through her entire lower body.

"God. This competition is under protest," he breathed. "I call shenanigans. The founder's daughter just drained all my strength out through my dick."

Eva snickered into his collarbone, licking a little at the salty taste of his skin. "Lucky for you, I've got nothing to do with the judges' decisions about anything, or your competitors would be the ones calling shenanigans."

"Hey." Annoyance crept into his satisfied tone. "I wouldn't have slept with you if it would look like I was trying to fuck my way to the top."

Opening her mouth lazily, Eva sucked at his neck. Not hard enough to leave a mark and cause questions neither of them wanted to deal with, but definitely hard enough to feel, if the way Danny stretched against her was any indication.

"Okay, uncle," he said on a strangled gasp. "Maybe I would've slept with you no matter what. You are hell on my good intentions, woman."

"Good intentions are for the boring," Eva told him, reaching an efficient hand down to deal with the condom. There was something kind of dirty and fun about playing nurse like this.

Danny snorted as she moved off his lap and tossed the used condom in the direction of the trash can beside the desk. "I've been considered boring by lots of people."

"Stupid people," Eva dismissed, collapsing back against the couch with a gusty sigh. "People who've never had sex with you. God, I needed that." Rolling her head far enough to the side that she could see him, she said, "And so did you. Admit it. I took good care of you!"

"I admit it, I'm glad I followed you up here," Danny deadpanned. "None of my teammates would've employed your particular method of pain relief."

"Mmm. I'm better than a bucket of ice and an aspirin? You sweet-talker."

Buffeting his bandaged fingers against the sticky mess at his crotch, a spasm of annoyance crossed his face. Danny growled low in his throat. "I think I mentioned once before, when I first met you—I might be a pastry chef, but I'm not as sweet as I look."

"Here, let me help with that." Eva got kind of a thrill out of the easy way he lay back and let her tuck him back into his pants. She did up the zipper but left the button undone, purely because she liked the look of it.

She liked being the one who got to see him that way.

The thought was frightening in its intensity, and Eva shied away from the revelation as if it were a light shining too brightly into her eyes. Silently cursing her still-shaky legs, she wobbled off the couch and started a fruitless search for her underwear before giving up and heading across the living room to the French doors that led to the bedroom.

When she came back to the living area a few moments later, swathed in one of the hotel's complimentary thick terry-cloth bathrobes, it was to see Danny pushing himself off the couch with his elbows, his soiled shirt hooked over one bare, muscular arm.

Despite her own instinct to flee the scene, some contrary portion of Eva's heart tugged with disappointment at the sight of Danny poised to make his getaway.

Leaning one shoulder against the doorjamb, she had to work to make her voice smooth and light. "Going somewhere?"

Danny stopped, bent halfway over and tripping on the trailing hems of his jeans. "Just trying to take a hint," he said, as casually as he could manage.

Which wasn't very casual. He grimaced, irritated by his own inability to just be cool and not care, for once in his whole, stupid life.

Fingering the tie holding her robe closed, Eva slanted him a look from under her lashes. "Maybe you should check your clues one more time. The hint could just be that you need a shower."

Happiness poured into the hole that had opened in his chest when Eva left him there on the couch without a backward glance. Danny waved his useless baseball-mitt hands and said, "Can't get 'em wet, remember?"

Eva sauntered toward him, her whole body moving in a sinuous, slinky way that reminded him of her unself-conscious abandon as she took her pleasure. "I'm disappointed, Chef," she said. "I would've thought you'd be a little more innovative than that."

Danny felt his mouth go dry as she picked apart the knot at her waist and let the robe fall open to frame her lovely, smooth skin. "Any man whose brain works at peak capacity around you is either gay or dead."

She gave a delighted laugh. "That doesn't make any sense."

"Proving my point!"

"Come on." Eva grabbed his elbow, managing to knock his shirt and chef's whites to the floor. "I've got a big, gorgeous, deep spa tub in the master bathroom."

Danny's eyes followed his clothes down and snagged

on the telephone resting beside the couch. He frowned. "I should really call my guys and check in."

Eva's fingers tightened, but her voice went sultry and low. "The tub's big enough for two . . ."

Danny swiveled his head back to her in time to catch the moment when Eva dropped the robe in a pile over his discarded chef's jacket.

Completely comfortable in her own skin, she turned and swayed those perfect little hips over to the double doors she'd disappeared through before, casting one flirtatious peek over her pure white shoulder as she slipped into the next room.

Danny followed her without another pause.

He was pretty sure the guys would understand.

When he blinked his eyes open the next morning and stared up at the gold-leaf motif on Eva Jansen's swanky penthouse ceiling, Danny was suddenly less sure about how understanding his team would be.

They'd no doubt spent the night dealing with Beck's anger issues—and what the hell was up with him and that chick from California?—and worrying about the coming day of cooking. He should've been with them, not here, lounging around in the lap of luxury, waiting for someone to peel him a grape or something.

Sitting up abruptly, Danny twitched his fingers to check for soreness. The bandages had loosened during the night, what with one thing and another, and he was able to curl his hands into fists without too much pain. It was only by resolutely sitting on his memories of exactly what "one thing and another" had entailed that Danny was able to push back the cover and climb out of the bed, careful not to disturb the slender lump in the sheets beside him.

He moved smoothly, wincing only a little when he had to brace one hand on the corner of the bed to bend over and pick up his jeans. Annoyed by the bandages, Danny set his teeth to a trailing end at his right wrist, and tugged until he could begin to unravel them.

"What are you doing?" Eva's sleepy voice matched her tousled brown hair and heavy-lidded eyes.

Danny couldn't look at her without wanting to dive back into bed and lick her all over, so he went back to his bandage. "I'm taking these off so I can see what the damage is," he said calmly. "The paramedic said to check."

Eva pursed her pretty mouth, looking skeptical, but she couldn't really argue. "Here, let me. You're making this harder than it needs to be."

Bemused by her constant desire to nurse him, Danny obediently held out his hands and enjoyed the gentle, meticulous way Eva unwound the white gauze to reveal his reddened, blistered palms.

She sucked in a horrified breath, but Danny flexed his hands and said, "Hey, no. They're better than they look. A little of that magic hand lotion, and I'll be ready to cook."

"Don't they hurt?"

Danny shrugged and snagged his jeans from the floor. "Well, yeah. But it's workable. I can push through."

"I don't like it," Eva said.

Jesus, civilians.

"This is what chefs do," Danny told her. "Come on, you've been around chefs all your life. You must have seen this kind of thing before. We get injured—put a hand down on a burner, chop off a fingernail, what have you—and we keep cooking. My dad once dropped a hotel pan piled with twenty pounds of lamb shanks on his foot and busted four bones. He swelled up like a balloon, but he limped his way through the rest of that dinner service and never once fell behind or complained."

Eva sat up in bed, pulling the sheets to her chin and

resting her elbows on her raised knees. With her tangled, messy hair and perfect makeup-free skin, she looked like a little kid.

"You love him a lot, don't you?"

Danny had lost the thread. "What? Who?"

She made an impatient noise. "Your father. The way you talk about him—you're proud to be his son."

"I never thought about it that way, but yeah." Pulling on his jeans took some time, the denim harsh against his stressed hands, and Danny used the extra moments to duck and hide from Eva's too-perceptive gaze. "He's a good man and a great chef. He's always had a lot of faith in me."

"Must be nice." The bitterness in Eva's voice made Danny glance at her swiftly, but her mouth was curved in a soft smile. "My dad and I are close, too. It's been just us, for a long time—I mean, if you don't count his legion of girlfriends, hookups, and one-night stands. Which I don't."

Danny was beginning to get a picture of Eva's childhood, and it wasn't a particularly pretty one. His parents might drive him nuts, on occasion, but he'd never doubted that they loved each other and their kids more than anything—with Lunden's Tavern running a close second.

Before Max left home, he'd accused their father of loving the restaurant more than his own children, but Danny knew that wasn't true. He'd seen the way his father grieved for those lost years with his eldest son, and no amount of Danny picking up the slack at home and at the Tavern could quite erase the shadow of pain in the old man's eyes.

Thinking about his brother got Danny worried about the time again. He checked the clock beside the bed.

Shit. Later than he'd thought.

Tick-tock went his internal timer, and he knew he

needed to get back to his team and get ready to face the day, but damn it. He was not the guy who could leave Eva Jansen huddled alone on her bed, looking like she didn't have a friend in the world.

Also, she was naked. Really, there was no way he was going anywhere. What was he, superhuman?

Knee walking back over to her, Danny wrapped his long arms around her and pulled her tight to his chest. She came easily, burying her face in the crook of his neck, and Danny tried not to let his heart squish too much at the trust the gesture implied.

Max was right.

Danny was a sap.

Chapter 15

Eva buried her face in Danny's broad chest and wondered when, exactly, she'd turned into a snuggler. Not that she was usually into the wham-bam-see-you-around type of encounter, but she did prefer to have control of the situation, so she usually invited guys she liked back to her place or her hotel room.

Like last night. Nothing unusual there. What was unusual was the fact that Danny was still here the next morning. Eva didn't kick her dates to the curb or anything, but there was usually a pretty mutual sort of understanding that, post-condom-removal, it was easier to just go their separate ways.

When Danny tried to leave last night, though . . . Eva shivered, remembering the tense roil of panic in her gut when she'd seen him gathering his things. It was weird, she reflected as she breathed in his scent—wood smoke and warm cotton and that ever-present hint of powdered sugar— but then, this whole thing was weird. Different.

Remembering the conversation with Claire on the plane, Eva thought her friend might even approve of the way

things were going with Danny Lunden. It was possible that
up till now, Eva had let herself get into a little bit of a rut.

It was just that sex had always been so easy. Fun, meaningless, no muss, no fuss. She enjoyed men, she enjoyed
the attention they gave her. And she'd never been ashamed
of that, although there were moments when she remembered how things had been between her parents, before
her mother's death.

She knew there could be more between two people than
fun and easy.

But why would anyone want anything other than fun
and easy? She'd never met a man who shed any light on
the answer to that question.

Danny tucked his knuckles under her chin and tilted her
head up for a soft, closed-mouth kiss, just a silken glide of
warm lips, and Eva had to clutch hard at his shoulders to
keep her sudden attack of vertigo from pitching her off
the bed.

Danny Lunden made her wonder what she'd been missing all these years.

Before she could catch her balance, leap from the bed
and brush her teeth, or forget about morning breath and
just wrestle him back down under the covers, she heard a
tiny, tinny beep emanating from the other room.

Eva instantly identified it as her phone's voicemail
alert—and as soon as she registered the sound, she realized it had been going on for quite some time. Ever since
she'd rolled over and opened her eyes to the beautiful
morning sight of a naked Danny Lunden shaking his tail
feather around the foot of her bed.

"Shit," she said, scrambling out from under the covers.
"I didn't charge my phone last night. I always plug it in
next to the bed, always! I can't believe I forgot."

"Then we're even," Danny said, going back to looking

for his clothes. "You distracted me from calling my team last night and finding out how they were doing."

"No, we are not even," Eva yelled over her shoulder as she jogged into the living room to retrieve her phone from her purse. "Because your team is safe and sound in their hotel rooms. But my team, by which I mean the enormous staff running this whole competition, has been up since before dawn working and putting out fires and wondering the where the hell I am. Balls, look at this. Seven missed calls."

"I'm sure everything is fine," Danny said, appearing in the bedroom doorway in his jeans and nothing else. Padding on bare feet to the kitchen, he bent to cast a critical eye over the meager contents of the fridge. "Man. I was thinking about cooking you breakfast, but there's not a whole lot to work with."

"Breakfast?" Eva melted a little. "That's my favorite meal of the day."

"Oh, yeah?" Danny sent her a smile to rival the early-morning sun peeking through the blinds. "What's your favorite breakfast treat?"

"Crêpes," Eva said instantly. "Or, as we used to call them in my family, French pancakes. When I was little, my dad made them every Sunday morning, and he had to double the recipe to keep up with me. Five years old, and I could pack away eight or ten at a sitting, rolled up around strawberry jam and sprinkled with powdered sugar." She closed her eyes, remembering the sweetness of those lazy mornings.

"Damn. Now I'm starving."

Her phone beeped again, and Eva's eyes popped open, her heart racing once more.

Shit, shit, shit.

She didn't realized she was repeating her mantra aloud

until Danny came over to put his hands on her shoulders and say, "Sweetheart, it's okay. You're fine."

"Stop it," Eva said, shrugging him off and picking up the bathrobe still lying next to the sofa, where she'd discarded it last night. "Stop doing that thing you do."

"What thing?" He did the wide eyes at her, as if he didn't know.

"That soothe-the-wild-beast thing," she said, pulling on the robe. "It's very nice, especially when you do it to your teammates. But it makes me feel like your little sister or something, which, I think you'll agree, is gross in light of last night."

He arched a brow and put his hands on his lean hips, abandoning the search for his underwear. Eva's breath sped up. Hot damn, but he was fine.

"Jules Cavanaugh, on my team? She's like a little sister to me. And, you know, maybe a sister-in-law someday pretty soon. Either way, I can categorically state, for the record, that I've never had a night like last night with her." He shook his head, the one tuft of golden brown hair sticking up funny on the side of his head glinting in the light of the rising sun. "To be honest, I don't think I've ever had a night like last night before. With anyone."

Eva couldn't help but grin and waggle her hips at him. "We were pretty phenomenal weren't we?"

"If I'd been wearing socks," he told her, "you would've rocked them."

Feeling herself start to melt, Eva shook her shoulders and set her face in a stern expression. "Enough! I see what you're doing, mister. You are not as sneaky as you think."

"Oh?" He dropped his arms and started stalking toward her like a big cat after his prey.

"No." Eva backed away, holding her still-beeping phone in front of her like a shield. "Regular soothing didn't work, so you're trying to sweet-talk me out of my panic attack. But I refuse to be calmed! I will be frantic and upset and worried and—"

Danny rushed her and Eva ended her half-laughing diatribe in a shriek that turned to a muffled squeak when he swung her up into his arms and kissed her.

A knock on the door broke them apart for long enough for Eva to call, "Come back later, please!"

"You don't want housekeeping to come in?" Danny asked. "Your sheets could probably stand to be changed."

"It can wait," Eva said, threading her fingers into his hair and angling her head for another kiss just as the doorknob rattled and the electronic lock beeped.

Several things happened at once. The door opened, Eva squawked and clamped her naked legs around Danny's denim-clad waist, and Danny turned his back to the door to shield her from the eyes of the maids. Or maybe to shield the poor, unsuspecting maids' eyes from the unexpected sight of Eva Jansen's lily-white ass hanging out in the breeze.

Which was a lovely sight, Eva was sure, only it could be considered a bit much for first thing in the morning.

Laughter bubbled up uncontrollably and Eva had to hide her face in Danny's shoulder to keep the hysterics contained.

Still facing the wall, Danny said, "Can you please come back later?" in his calm, polite way, which only made Eva laugh harder.

Until a familiar voice replied, "No, I most certainly will not come back later. We're in crisis mode, and it has to be dealt with immediately. Who the hell are you? And . . . is that my daughter clinging to you like a barnacle?"

Oh, shit.

Eva lifted her head and stared over Danny's bare

shoulder, directly into the snapping steel-gray eyes of Theo Jansen.

"I'm guessing that's not housekeeping," Danny said.

"Somebody better start talking." The voice was gruff, growly, clearly belonging to an older man very used to giving orders.

"Hi, Dad," Eva said, confirming Danny's worst fears. "You want to give us a second? As you can see, we were right in the middle of something."

Danny stiffened, some part of his brain waiting for the cold press of a shotgun barrel between his shoulder blades, but all he heard was the sound of the hotel door closing.

"He's gone, you can let me down, now," Eva said blithely, as if she weren't embarrassed at having been caught climbing him like a vine by her very own father.

Then she exploded. Not embarrassed, evidently, but righteously pissed. "Damn it, damn it, damn it! What is he doing here?"

She moved fast to grab the bathrobe and swirl it around her, but Danny still had time to notice that she wasn't blushing. Not even a little. The only red on her cheeks looked like pure anger, and it was the light of battle that brightened her eyes from gray to silvery blue as she marched over to the door and threw it open before Danny had a chance to retrieve his shirt from the floor.

"That was quick," Theo Jansen said, eyes still on the phone in his hand.

Apparently, Eva had inherited her attachment to electronic devices from her father.

"You know me," Eva said, hooking an arm through her father's elbow and guiding him over to the couch. "All work and no play, isn't that what you used to say?"

Danny found it best to look up at the ceiling while

carefully blanking his mind of any and everything that might have occurred on that couch the previous night.

"I'm glad to hear you absorbed some of what I tried to teach you," Theo said, bypassing the couch for one of the throne-like chairs flanking the coffee table. "And a bit surprised, since I can only assume you've been letting work slide completely, based on the crisis situation we now find ourselves in."

Eva flinched, and without thinking Danny moved to stand behind her, drawing Jansen Senior's gaze for the first time.

Theo scowled, his trim dark beard making him look like a statue of a Roman warrior Danny had seen at the Met on a school field trip when he was a kid, all rough-hewn jaw and flinty gaze.

If Roman statues wore charcoal pin-striped suits and carried handmade leather briefcases.

The man was intimidating, not only because he was a legend in the restaurant business, with a reputation for making and breaking chefs' careers with a single stroke of his fountain pen, but also in his person.

He wasn't particularly huge, although he looked to be in pretty good shape for a business-type in his late fifties, but his presence loomed large enough to take up most of the hotel suite. Danny was uncomfortably aware of the fact that he wasn't wearing a shirt, and his pants were unbuttoned and threatening to slide down his hips at any moment.

Clearly having zero desire to let on that she had no idea what this crisis situation was all about, Eva dodged. "Want some coffee, Dad? Danny and I were just about to order room service."

Somehow, Theo Jansen conveyed sardonic disbelief with only a slight smile. "Is that what they're calling it these days? Yeah, sure, coffee would be great, and while you're at it, how about a little privacy? We have business to discuss."

Wow. Danny had never been dismissed so thoroughly in his life, and he'd been through school only two years after his brother, Max the Magnificent.

"Give it a rest, Dad," Eva said, rummaging around on the desktop. "God knows, I've had to sit through enough excruciatingly polite breakfasts with your one-night-stand morning-afters."

That hurt more than he thought it would. Danny fought to keep his face impassive. Forcing his movements to be smooth and unhurried, he leaned down and snagged his T-shirt. He thought he'd feel better with more covering, but the chill that had settled under his skin wouldn't dissipate.

Collecting his dirty, flour-streaked chef's jacket, he said, "You know, I've got to be going, anyway."

Eva looked up from the room service menu she'd been perusing, eyes wide, but Danny didn't give her a chance to protest. He needed to be gone, away from this crazy, rich, entitled family with their offhand, no-big-deal attitude about sex.

Danny had never been able to work that way. Last night with Eva . . . that had been a big deal to him. He wasn't surprised that she didn't feel the same way; he hadn't gone into it expecting more than a single night of pleasure. Leaving it at that was turning out to be tougher than he'd planned, that was all.

Maybe one day when Danny learned how to be cool and uncaring, he'd give Eva a call. Until then, the only smart thing to do was to get the hell out, before he got himself in any deeper.

"Eva. I'll see you around."

Since he hadn't been introduced to Theo Jansen—and really, wasn't that better? He didn't need a guy like that associating his family name with bed-hopping booty-call boy toys—Danny didn't bother to say good-bye to the man.

Heading for the door, he was surprised when Eva slipped into the hallway after him, grabbing for him with the hand that wasn't holding her bathrobe closed.

"Wait," she said urgently, remorse tightening her voice. "I didn't mean—"

"It doesn't matter." Danny shook her off gently. This wasn't her fault, not really. They came from totally different worlds. Glancing over her shoulder into the opulent suite, all marble and gilt and antiques, his stupid heart clenched.

Eva lived in a fantasy, where everything was beautiful and she could have whatever she wanted delivered to her doorstep with a simple phone call. And she was a woman who knew what she wanted, and went after it. Danny could respect that. He respected, too, the fact that she'd never hinted at wanting more. She'd made no promises, and if one night wasn't enough for him—well, he had no one to blame for that but himself.

Really, the only surprising part of all this was that she'd been interested in a guy like him for even one minute.

Trying to be grateful for the time they'd had, and not blame Eva for the way he'd misunderstood—or willfully ignored—the rules of an encounter like this one, Danny kept his voice gentle.

"Go back to your dad. Sounds like you've got some kitchen fires to put out, and I've got to go find my team. This was fun, but it's time for me to head back to reality now."

She reared back as if he'd slapped her, a pang of something flashing through her eyes so quickly, Danny couldn't read it before she recovered her balance as gracefully as a dancer.

"It was fun," she echoed, expressionless and bland, as if they were talking about a trip to the zoo or a walk through Central Park. "Of course, that's what I'm known for. The original Good Time Girl, that's me. Well, playtime's over, babe. See you in the kitchen."

Danny frowned at the sour note that curdled her voice, like a cup of buttermilk spilled into cake batter, but he was frowning at her back because she'd already turned away, on to the next challenge.

She shut the door behind her with a careless kick of her heel, leaving Danny staring at the blank white wood paneling and wishing it could be so easy for him to move on.

Chapter 16

Eva took a moment, with Danny's good-bye punctuated by the click of the door latch still echoing in her ears.

Fun. Why did that suddenly sound like an indictment? It was all she'd ever wanted or offered, before. But somehow, when Danny Lunden said it, her soul shriveled up like a sun-dried tomato.

Blowing out a breath, she ran her hands through her hair, fingers snagging on the tangles. She had to pull it together; her life had gone far enough to shit already without letting her father see her lose it over some guy.

As he'd be very happy to tell anyone who'd listen, Theo Jansen had never allowed emotions to get in the way of business.

Half an hour after his wife's funeral, he'd been in a business meeting with the realtor who'd eventually found him the property that became his first three-star restaurant.

Claire liked to sniff and say that Theo Jansen hid in his work, like a small boy afraid to face his bedtime, but Eva had never seen where that was such a terrible thing.

So what if Dad could teach a master class on repression? It gets the job done.

Working to control her own wayward emotions, Eva counted her breaths and fumbled in the pocket of her robe for her phone.

Flicking a quick finger over the screen, she scrolled past the voicemails to the frantic text message from her assistant, Drew.

SOS. Sparks on flight back to NYC.
Fam emergency. No return date!!!

Eva's heart stopped, every extraneous thought and feeling cramming down to make room for the enormous bubble of panic expanding in her brain.

Whipping the phone up to her ear, she dialed Devon Sparks's number, but it rang through to voicemail.

Tapping her toe, she waited for the beep and blurted out, "Devon, oh my God. I'm so sorry, I just heard. Please let me know what's going on with you and Lilah. Take care of each other!"

"Getting up to speed, are we?" Theo asked as Eva thumbed the phone off and staggered over to drop down on the couch.

"Is it something with the pregnancy?" Eva couldn't imagine the terror of that. She didn't even know Lilah, really, had only met her a couple of times, but she'd seemed sweet and funny and down to earth, completely unlike the women Devon usually dated.

"She fainted. Her blood pressure spiked, from what I understand. I'm sure bed rest will take care of it."

Eva's heart sank, even as she sent up a prayer of thanks that it wasn't something more serious. "But the reality is, it doesn't matter if she's all better tomorrow—after a scare like this, Devon's not leaving her again. It took every ounce of persuasion I've got to talk him into it the first time. Which means we're down a judge."

Theo leaned forward, resting his elbows on his knees. "You've still got Claire as the voice of authority, and you've got your token color commentator, that musician who throws the wild parties." He shook his head, clearly baffled by Kane's popularity, and Eva bit her tongue. Now was not the time to defend her friendship with Kane Slater. Theo had agreed that including him as a judge would increase the mass appeal of the competition, so there wasn't really any more to say.

"But Devon was our celebrity chef judge, our best link to the restaurant world." *And our famously good-looking chef that thousands of women swoon over every time his show comes on the Cooking Channel,* she added silently.

Eva slumped over, running a hand through her tangled hair. The night's lack of sleep was catching up with her. She felt sluggish and slow, mired in doubt and fear. "How are we going to find someone to replace him on such short notice?"

She looked at her father, so calm and collected, so in control, and felt a quick spurt of gladness that he was here to get her through this.

Of course, she hated herself for it—this whole thing was supposed to be about proving how capable she was on her own, damn it—but the feeling was there all the same.

Her father, riding to the rescue, taking over, having his opinion about her abilities confirmed . . . She could feel everything she'd been working toward slipping away, her father's respect draining through her cupped hands like water.

No.

164 LOUISA EDWARDS

Stiffening her spine, Eva sat up straight and yanked her brain into focus. God, she needed coffee.

"Our new judge needs to be someone the Cooking Channel will see as a big draw," she muttered, flipping furiously through her mental contact list. "But the problem is, most of those chefs are booked solid, months in advance."

Theo's silvery brows drew down in a frown of concern. "Are you still having trouble convincing the Cooking Channel of the RSC's television appeal? Eva, we've been over this and over this—"

"I know," she cried, the sharp, sickening tug of failure getting a stranglehold on her. "It's under control! Or at least, it was. Before Devon left."

Theo sighed his Eva-is-so-dramatic sigh and reached out to pull her against his side. Kissing the top of her head, he said, "Okay, honey. It's going to be fine. We'll find a great new judge, and in the meantime, I'll fill in, so we can keep the competition going."

A flicker of hope warmed Eva's chest. "That might work. As a stopgap solution, of course—not that you don't have the potential to be a big Cooking Channel star, Daddy."

She grinned up at him, her world coming back into balance, but Theo didn't smile back. Instead, he let her go and stood up from the couch, pacing a few steps back and forth in front of the coffee table.

"Eva. You're not going to like this, but it needs to be said."

Clutching the bathrobe more tightly around her, Eva struggled to present as upright and business-like an image as she could. Considering she was barefoot and naked under the robe, and her hair probably looked like someone had stuck her head in a blender.

"Go ahead, I can take it," she tried to joke. "It can't be worse than everything else that's happened today."

"Well, it's early yet." Theo gave her a quelling look, pressing his lips together tightly. "Look. I know I'm the last person who should be lecturing anyone on the subject of romantic entanglements . . ."

Eva's stomach sank down to her knees. "Dad—" she protested faintly, but he held up a hand to stop her.

"I know," he repeated forcefully, eyes snapping with determination. "I've slept with my share of RSC contestants over the years."

Her father, Eva reflected with a shudder, had a weakness for pastry chefs, too. He enjoyed the female variety, but still. Ugh.

"And it's a damn stupid double standard," he continued, "but the fact is, this year's competition faces an unprecedented level of scrutiny. It's what we wanted, what we worked for—but it means that the eyes of the world are watching everything we do."

Eva shot off the couch. "So let them watch! I haven't done anything wrong. I'm not a judge; nothing I say or do has any bearing on which teams advance to the next round."

"I understand that." Theo shook his head impatiently. "But it's not about actual wrongdoing. It's about the public's perception—and you have to admit, Eva, from the outside, it doesn't look good for the panel moderator to be carrying on with one of the chefs."

I don't care, she wanted to shout. *I don't care how it looks, or what people think! I just want Danny!*

But . . . all Danny wanted was a night of fun, and he'd had that already. He couldn't get out of there fast enough, eager to get back to his team, his friends, the people who mattered to him.

What, exactly, was Eva fighting for here?

As if sensing her wavering, Theo put a comforting hand on her shoulder. "We agreed, Eva. This is our year. The year when the RSC finally gains the recognition it deserves."

The year when Eva finally got the chance to extend the reach of her mother's legacy.

Eva closed her eyes briefly, but nodded. "I know. You're right." She tried out a smile. Shaky, but passable. "This is our year."

My year.

"And look," Theo pointed out, "it doesn't have to mean you can never see him again. Once the competition is over—"

"No." Eva cut him off, unable to listen to any more. Shaking back her hair, she started the process of steeling herself for the long day ahead. "It's fine. Last night was just . . . stress relief. Nothing serious."

Fun.

Ignoring the clutch of pain in her chest, Eva smiled again, and this time she felt the familiar security of her polished, professional mask slip over her face.

"Not to worry, Dad. It's over. I've got everything under control."

Chapter 17

The mood in the competition kitchen was tense that morning, although it was impossible to know if that was due to the timer ticking relentlessly down toward the moment when the judges would sample the final dishes, the knowledge that one team would be going home after today's elimination, or the lingering looks of hatred aimed in Beck's direction by a bruised, infuriated Ryan Larousse.

Or maybe it was just Danny, who felt tense because he'd walked into his team's hotel room to find all four of them pissed off at him.

And when he'd tried to apologize for not checking on them and making sure they were okay, they'd gotten even more upset.

"For fuck's sake, Daniel," Max had finally growled. "We didn't need you here propping us up and calming us down. We just needed to know you were okay."

Taken aback, Danny hadn't known exactly what he was supposed to say. "I was fine."

"None of us saw you or heard from you after you did your white knight thing and caught that pot of boiling stock," Jules pointed out, arms crossed stiffly over her chest. "For all we knew, you had to go to the hospital or something. And you didn't have your phone, so we couldn't even call you!"

Part of Danny had wanted to lash out, hit her back with a sneer and a sarcastic "I'm surprised you even noticed I was missing."

Jules had been pretty out of it ever since she and Max got together, and as for Max, himself—well, Danny had learned not to count on his brother years ago.

But that would start a whole big fight, and what would it accomplish? All it would do would get everyone riled up and at each other's throats right before they went into the biggest culinary challenge they'd yet faced.

So instead, he'd ground his back teeth until his jaw clicked, and smiled as he spread his hands out to the sides, trying not to wince at the stretch of his red, blistered palms. "Obviously, I'm fine."

In the end, the only way Danny could get them to shut up and quit acting like he was some fragile little invalid who'd needed nursemaiding was to promise to break competition rules by carrying his cell phone into the kitchen, in the pocket of his black jeans.

He figured as long as he didn't actually use it to look up a recipe or a technique or something, and it didn't go off in the middle of the challenge, it was probably okay.

Winslow hadn't said anything in front of the rest of the team, but the minute everyone trooped out of the room to head down to the kitchen, Danny had found himself staring into his friend's arch, slyly amused face.

"So . . . Miss Eva took care of you, did she?"

Danny'd stiffened, ready to stonewall, but it didn't matter. Win patted him on the shoulder and said, "No need to confirm or deny, sweet thang. I got your number, and my lips are sealed."

"There's nothing to keep quiet over, and nothing to deny," Danny insisted. "It was just a thing that happened, a one-time-only type of deal, and now it's back to real life. Back to reality."

Reality, in Danny's case, meant the meticulous, careful, safe, comforting world of pastry. Although baking on a challenge deadline, with judges waiting and a television crew taping, admittedly took some of the comfort out of it.

Forcing down a snarl of pain when one of his raw palms accidentally scraped over the rough edge of his marble pastry board, Danny cursed himself for the millionth time this morning for running out of Eva's suite without grabbing that magic lotion the paramedic had used.

Beside him at their team's allotted pair of gas burners, Winslow sent him a worried glance, his hands never slowing in his measured, steady stirring of the vanilla bean custard. "You okay?"

"I'm fine." Danny couldn't help but grin at the pains Win took to speak out of the side of his mouth, as if he was terrified the camera might pick up on his comment. "How's that custard coming?"

Lifting his wooden spoon, Win watched critically as the warm creamy liquid dripped from the back of it. "Not quite set yet. Few more minutes."

Winslow was their swing guy, a jack-of-all-kitchen-trades, from butchering to delicate pastry work. He'd flitted from station to station today, helping out wherever he was needed. They were damn lucky to have a chef as multi-talented as Win on the team, and Danny knew it.

He felt especially lucky right at the moment, as Winslow took the tedious, finicky job of stirring the custard in its double boiler, making sure it didn't scorch over the very low flame, and left Danny free to deal with caramelizing the plums he'd macerated the day before in sugar, lemon juice, and fresh thyme.

Running to the coolers, Danny checked on his yeast batter for the buttermilk waffles that would serve as the base of his breakfast-for-dinner dessert. He'd planned a sort of breakfast sandwich of waffles enclosing caramelized plums suspended in custard, but when he peered into the huge stainless-steel bowl holding his waffle batter, his heart seized with panic.

It was a mess. Watery and separated, with ugly clumps of what looked like congealing flour, and it sure as hell hadn't looked like that when he put it away the night before.

Grabbing the bowl from the cooler, Danny hauled it over to his team's table and peeled back the clear plastic wrap to get a better look.

"Christ, what happened there?" Max asked as he jogged past holding a bunch of grapes.

"I don't fucking know." Danny scrabbled for his wire whisk, dragging the balloon shape through the odd, chunky batter and whipping the whole thing into a furious froth.

"Are you going to be able to salvage it?" Jules huddled close, pausing in her construction of miniature towers of perfectly blanched, thinly sliced potatoes. Her version of home fries was going to be the essence of refinement, Danny had no doubt.

He did, however, have his doubts about this freaking batter. "I don't think so," he replied, giving it another good whisk and watching bubbles of stubborn flour balls break the surface sluggishly. "Something's off, maybe the yeast was bad, or the bowl wasn't perfectly clean and had some vinegar or lemon juice in it that soured the batter. Impossible to say, and it doesn't matter now, anyway, because this whole dish is fucked."

Danny resisted the urge to fling the bowl of nasty stuff across the kitchen, like his father in one of his temper fits.

Turning to face his worried teammates, who'd gathered around like mourners at a funeral, was the hardest thing Danny had ever done. "I'm sorry," he said, almost choking. "I let you all down."

"Hey, no. Don't say that. The custard's still good," Winslow pointed out desperately, still stirring like a machine. "And those plums are the bomb, man, I can't stop swiping tastes of 'em."

"Yeah, seriously. Shut the eff up, Danny," Jules said. "You haven't let anyone down."

"It's just time for a little reconceptualizing." Max's eyes had that same twinkle he used to get when they were kids and he was about to lead his hero-worshiping brother into some terrible mischief or other.

"Oh no," Danny moaned, bringing one hand up to cover his eyes. Peeking through the gaps between his fingers, he glared at Beck. "What, you've got no advice or platitudes for me?"

Beck paused, his expression grave. "Never give in," he finally said. "Never surrender."

Winslow snorted. "What is that, a *Star Trek* reference?"

"No, man," Jules shook her head. "Wasn't it in that *Star Trek* spoof movie, *Galaxy Quest*?"

"Winston Churchill," Beck told them, turning back to his own work of stuffing forcemeat into sausage casings. "I'm paraphrasing, but . . ."

For a moment, the silence was punctuated only by the shouts and cooking noises of the other teams.

"The point is," Max said, "all is not lost. Far from it!

Come on, we've got these awesome components, the custard and the plums, and about—" He glanced at the ticking timer. "Geez. About an hour left. Holy crap. I've got to get back to my red wine sauce. Danny, you've got this, man, right?"

"Yeah, I've got it," Danny said, waving them away.

He so didn't have it, but the last thing they needed was to go down for all three of the main dishes being incomplete because everyone was standing around kibbutzing about Danny's failed dessert.

"Um, what should I do?" Winslow asked hesitantly.

"Just keep stirring." Danny regretted his terseness, but Winslow hopped to the job anyway, moving that spoon through the thickening custard as if the fate of the world hung on it having a perfect, silken texture.

Poor kid, he could probably read Danny's uncertainty in every line of his body, but what could he say? Danny had never been the creative one, the man with the plan. He was a foot soldier. He executed. He didn't come up with ideas.

The kitchen doors opened with a bang that drew Danny's attention. He was jumpy, distractable, that's all—it certainly wasn't that he'd been wondering where Eva was, or that he was hoping to see her now.

Danny knew he was lying to himself the instant his heart lifted into his throat when she stepped through the doors. She was immaculate as always in a pair of soft, tight-fitting pants the color of a perfectly ripe Italian eggplant and a creamy confection of a shirt that wrapped around her slender form, revealing nothing, but somehow leaving nothing to the imagination.

He'd never known any woman as effortlessly sensual and seductive as Eva Jansen. A rush of desire and he was hard in his jeans, aching with the need to touch her.

So he was nothing but a convenient sex toy to her. Maybe he could live with that.

The guy who walked into the kitchen after her, however, put a very effective dampener on Danny's libido.

"Shit, what is *he* doing here," Danny muttered.

"Who?" Win wanted to know.

"The old guy," Danny said, jerking his head toward the new arrivals. "That's Theo Jansen."

"And where's Devon Sparks?" Winslow's sharp eyes had noted the one absence from the normal crew of judges as Claire Durand and Kane Slater marched in, followed by no one.

Danny shrugged, watching from the corner of his eye as Eva finished her consultation with the TV producer and stepped forward, hand raised. "Looks like we're about to find out."

"Chefs! Can you gather around for a second, please? We'll stop the wall clock, so you won't lose any time."

Danny followed the gaggle of sweaty, red-faced, food-stained men and women up to the front of the kitchen.

It was stupid—these were his people. He was just one of the crowd, and he blended in with them perfectly in his chef's jacket smeared with ruby-red plum juice and with a drying patch of batter crusting down one sleeve.

Still, he stood in front of Eva and her distinguished father, and felt like digging his toes in the ground and brushing at his dirty clothes like some urchin off the street.

"As some of you may already know, the man to my left is my father, Theo Jansen. He ran this competition for twenty years, and he's here to lend us his expertise, so please welcome him!"

There was a polite round of applause, but looking around the room at the other competitors' faces, Danny was pretty sure the prevailing reaction was impatience to get back to cooking.

Theo Jansen stepped forward, smiling like a benevolent uncle. "This is the first year I've stepped back and let someone else take control—my daughter, Eva. And from what I can see, she's doing a fantastic job!"

The false heartiness of his voice grated in Danny's ears, and he thought he saw a quickly suppressed wince from Eva. But her face stayed smooth and pleasant, camera-ready, even when Theo continued, "But I have to say, I'm glad to be here, so I can keep an eye on things."

Plastering on a smile that Danny knew was fake the same way he could tell imitation vanilla from pure vanilla extract, Eva moved up to stand next to her father and took a deep breath. "Chefs, I also have some upsetting news, which is that Devon Sparks has had to leave us."

Interest rustled through the room as chefs glanced at one another, eyebrows raised. "He and his wife are expecting their first child together," Eva explained, "and there have been some complications. Nothing life threatening, but Devon feels that he needs to be there for his family at this time, and of course, we understand."

"So who's going to be the new third judge?" Jules muttered, just loudly enough for Danny to hear. "Crap, we did all that research on Sparks, his likes and dislikes, and now it's for shit."

"I know you're wondering who will take Devon's place," Eva said, still wearing that imitation vanilla smile. "In the interests of moving forward, not losing any time or momentum with the competition, we need to get someone in that third judges' chair quickly, so . . . my father will be stepping in as a judge."

A shiver of dread worked its way down Danny's spine. Somehow, this didn't feel like good news.

"I'll still be running the competition, and of course I'm the panel moderator, so I'll be tasting your food right alongside my father and the other judges." She glanced over at Danny as if she couldn't help it. He stared back, unsure how he was even supposed to react.

"Okay. Playtime's over," Eva concluded, swallowing hard, and Danny had to work to contain his flinch. Flexing his fingers, he concentrated on the pain of his burned hands, using that focus to keep his face blank and emotionless.

Theo Jansen stepped forward, his hearty voice booming out over the assembled chefs. "So get back to cooking—you've got less than an hour left on the timer!"

Everyone scattered, grumbling about sauces that had been left on the stove too long, but Danny lingered for a moment, his guts clenched into a knot at the way Eva's throat moved convulsively as she swallowed, her eyes shadowed dark gray with what looked an awful lot like regret.

Her hand grasped the sleeve of his chef's jacket, a quick, glancing brush of the fingers that was enough to stop Danny in his tracks.

"Danny," she said softly, flicking a glance at the television camera against the wall, filming the action by the ovens.

No one gave a shit what they were doing, Danny was sure—all anyone cared about was the relentless ticking of the timer as they rushed to get their dishes finished. Still, he jerked his head in the direction of the walk-in cooler.

Once they were out of the line of camera sight, Eva seemed to relax a little, her shoulders sloping down as she let out a breath.

"I know you don't have any time to spare," she said

quickly, not meeting his eyes. "But I had to make sure we were on the same page—"

"Don't sweat it." Danny was proud of how even his tone was. "I know exactly where I stand, and what last night was about. And if the page you're on says it can't ever happen again, then we're definitely reading from the same book."

She stiffened. "Good."

"Great."

Her gaze flashed to his for a second, and Danny had to flex his fingers again, clenching them down tight and aching to keep himself from asking her if this was really the way she wanted to play it.

But it was. Of course it was. Eva knew exactly what she wanted—it was pretty much her defining characteristic. And she never let anything stand in the way of getting it.

Clearly, she didn't want Danny.

Not the way he wanted her.

Nodding decisively, Eva lifted her chin, took a deep breath that did interesting things to that shirt she was wearing, and marched over to consult with the cameraman, heels clicking a staccato beat against the tiled floor.

Danny watched her go, every muscle locked in the desire to grab her, shake her, make her admit that the fire they'd started was too hot to burn itself out after one night—but Eva had already put him out of her mind.

She had a job to do, and in her own way, Eva was every bit as hardcore as any chef Danny had ever known. Admiration glimmered through him, and a kind of bone-deep recognition.

This was probably a no-brainer for her. Ditch the chef contestant, avoid complications with the competition. Or maybe not—maybe she felt the same serrated edge of unfulfilled hope and wasted potential slashing at her insides that Danny did.

But both of them knew it didn't matter.

Eva would keep going. She wasn't a quitter. She wouldn't walk off the line and leave her staff fumbling around, trying to play catch-up without her. She'd stick it out, nut up, and get it done.

In that moment, Danny knew he was a goner.

Chapter 18

Cheney waggled his bushy eyebrows at her, pen stuck in the gristly hair behind his ear. Waving his clipboard at her, he said, "Hey, if I'd known we were going to get this kind of drama on a daily basis, I'd have pushed for more cameras."

Eva felt a burst of frustration that threatened to bloom into a full-on rage. It was as if the entire universe were conspiring to make this the crappiest day possible.

"Look, Mr. Cheney," she gritted out, her jaw so tight it hurt. "I told those visionless pricks at the Cooking Channel months ago that this competition had the potential to be their hottest new show, or at least a special-event program that could pull in millions of viewers."

"That's right," Cheney nodded. "And they sent me to check it out, get some B reel, and assess whether there's enough here to bother bringing in a full crew. Which is expensive, as I think I don't have to probably remind you."

Eva put her hands on her hips, digging her fingernails in until she could feel tiny crescent moons of pain stinging through the clingy wool of her trousers. "So if you've already assessed us as 'worth the bother,' where the hell is the rest of my camera crew?"

Cheney made a clicking noise with his tongue and the inside of his jowly cheek. "Well, that's where it gets dicey. Things were going great, with that fight and everything, and that lady chef from San Fran making eyes at the big, scary dude from Manhattan. There was some story there. And that other New York chef, the one who tackled the soup and saved the girl? That was pure gold! Until you made me shut off the camera. And now this thing with Devon Sparks leaving . . . I don't know."

"What, exactly, is it that you don't know, Mr. Cheney?" Eva tried not to sound too homicidally annoyed, but it was tough, because the primary alternative was to let him see how desperate she was. "Because the competition is going forward, with or without Chef Sparks as a judge, and I can assure you the drama is only just beginning."

"Oh, I'm sure that's true enough." Cheney cast a jaundiced eye over the rush and bustle of chefs in the last hour of the challenge's countdown. "I've been shooting for the Cooking Channel a long time, and let me tell you, there ain't nobody got more drama than a big group of chefs. The gossip and backbiting and sleeping around and egos clashing all over the place—I tell you what, it's a dream for an honest TV producer, looking to make a few bucks."

"Again, I have to ask, Mr. Cheney. What is the problem?" She gestured out at the frantic kitchen, hotter than the steam room at her fitness club, and twice as sweaty, full of shouts and near-collisions, and at least fifty enticing smells competing for her attention.

He stuck his clipboard under his arm and rummaged around in his pocket, coming up with a pack of gum. After

Eva refused a piece with a quick shake of her head, he shrugged and popped one in his mouth, chewing thoughtfully. "The problem is, you don't seem to be on board with the kind of program this wants to be. You got to get the viewers to turn on their TVs or set their TiVos, or whatever it is. You got to get the butts in the recliners, is what I'm saying. And the quickest way to do that is star power."

"But we have Kane Slater," Eva protested. "He's a multi-platinum recording artist! He's on every magazine's list of hottest guys out there!"

"Yeah, he was a good get," Cheney acknowledged, sucking on his gum. "But he's not a chef. Cooking Channel viewers? They tend to get their panties wet mainly over hot chefs. That's sort of the whole point."

Eva gave him her best unimpressed look. "If you're trying to disgust me, you should know, I'm fairly unshockable. And I don't grant your premise, at all. Kane has universal appeal!"

"To music nerds, maybe." Cheney snorted, but Eva thought she saw a spark of respect in his eyes that hadn't been there before. "Look, I'm not saying there's zero crossover potential. But I can tell you right now, my bosses aren't going to think it's enough. You can't argue with demographics, at least not to TV execs."

"Mr. Cheney. We are, of course, in talks with several major Cooking Channel stars, trying to work it out with their schedules so they'll be able to come on as judges. My father is only stepping in temporarily. Can't you give us a few more days to make that happen?"

The naked plea in her voice must have penetrated his thick, crusty exterior, because Cheney softened minutely. "Look, I'd like to help you out, but every day I'm here, filming stuff I won't be able to use, it's costing the studio money. Here's an idea—If you can't give 'em a hot chef at the forefront of the action, here, you're going to have to go for the other big audience draw—reality show staples like catfights, secret affairs, that kind of thing. You got any of that to offer?"

Eva felt like pulling her hair out. Except then she'd be bald, on top of everything else, and her life was shitty enough already.

"No! That's not the kind of show I want to do. That's not what this competition is about."

Before Cheney could do more than roll his eyes, her father's smooth voice cut into the conversation.

"Mr. Cheney, give me a moment with my daughter. I'm sure we'll be able to put our heads together and come up with several ideas that will interest your superiors at the Cooking Channel."

Chewing hard, Cheney squinted back and forth between Eva and her father. She stood as tall as she could, refusing to show any emotion.

She wanted Cheney to stay—but was she desperate enough to give in to his demands? Eva didn't know.

She'd have to figure it out, though, and fast, because the obnoxious little man turned back to his equipment with a terse, "Fine. I'm kind of curious what they're making, anyway. But after that, if you can't offer me another hot chef judge or something juicy, and I'm talking front page of *US Weekly,* I'm out of here."

"Thank you, Mr. Cheney." Eva gripped her father's elbow and steered him toward the kitchen doors. "You won't regret it."

"Eva, please," Theo said with a glance at the timer on the wall. "The challenge is almost over. We don't have time for this right now. Cheney has agreed to stay, there's nothing more we can do for now."

Battling back tears of frustration she would not allow

to fall, Eva tried to get her breathing under control. "Really, Dad? We don't have time for you to explain why you're trying to sabotage me?"

Theo got that pained look on his face, the one that told Eva she'd reminded him of her mother, somehow. She'd stopped asking for specifics when she was around eleven, but the expression never failed to clutch at her heart.

"So dramatic," Theo murmured, letting her pull him out into the hallway. "I'm not trying to sabotage you, honey. I'd never do anything to hurt you. But you swore you could get the RSC onto the Cooking Channel, and so far, it seems like you're just not willing to do what it takes to make it happen."

Eva's throat felt scratchy and tight, as if she'd swallowed shards of broken glass. "Dad. I'm trying . . ."

"Not hard enough. As the head of Jansen Hospitality, I'm like an army general. I need to know that when I tell my lieutenant to take that hill, that damn hill is as good as taken. No excuses. No waffling. The fact that you can't seem to close this deal with the Cooking Channel, well . . ."

He pressed his lips together so tightly, they disappeared in his trim salt-and-pepper beard. "It makes me wonder how ready you are to take over Jansen Hospitality. Honestly, it makes me wonder if you'll *ever* be ready."

The words hit her like a slap in the face. Her knees almost crumpled, but Eva dug for the strength to stand up straight.

"You were right," she said through numb lips. "This isn't the right time to discuss this. Come on, let's go back inside."

Remorse glimmered through Theo's dark gray eyes. He put a large, warm hand on her shoulder—the same hand that had clumsily braided her hair, and tenderly dabbed antibiotic ointment on a scraped knee, and pulled her close for a hug after she graduated from college.

Throat aching, eyes burning, she stepped away to open the doors. Theo let his hand fall back to his side, and Eva tried to pretend she didn't hear his sigh of disappointment.

So dramatic, she heard in her head, her father's voice equal parts nostalgia, pain, and irritation.

Dramatic like her mother, she guessed, although Eva didn't really know. Her main memories of her mother were of soft arms, and kisses that smelled waxy and left bright red imprints of smiling lips against her cheeks.

Eva didn't feel dramatic. She felt brittle, like sugar spread thin and burnt to a crisp, as if all it would take was one sharp tap and she'd shatter across the kitchen floor.

Okay, maybe she was a *little* dramatic. But damn it! Could this day get any worse?

Danny had to push hard to get his dish finished, but once he'd gotten his brainwave, it was downhill work from there.

He'd watched Theo take Eva out of the kitchen for a confab, and when they came back in, Eva had that look. The too-perfect, put-together face that hid everything vibrant and real about her behind a facade of serene professionalism.

It was Eva's game face.

Danny felt an unwilling tug of sympathy. He knew from personal experience, nobody could tear into you, make you bleed and cry, like family. And he had what he considered a really good relationship with his parents.

From what he could tell, Eva would say the same. She obviously loved her father. As much as he held her position in the family company over her head or hurt her feelings or fucked around with a lot of women, she adored him. And it made sense. Theo was all she'd had, ever since she was little.

It made Danny remember the story she'd told him, about her dad cooking French pancakes for her when she was a kid. The memory had been a happy one, he knew, a moment in time when she and her father had been in perfect harmony, the sweet and bitter of life balanced and blended, rolled up in a crisp-tender, golden crêpe and dusted with confectioner's sugar.

French pancakes, he thought, a grin tugging at his mouth. He loved that she still called them that, even after a lifetime of five-star French meals and trips to Paris.

And then, as if Eva had waltzed over and whispered it in his ear, Danny knew exactly what he was going to make.

It was risky—crêpe batter was supposed to sit in the fridge for at least an hour after you mixed it up, to let all the tiny air bubbles pop and settle so the crêpes were easier to handle, less likely to tear. But there was less than an hour left, no time to lose, and Danny would just have to execute his crêpes perfectly. There was no other option.

Racing to the walk-in, he grabbed eggs and whole milk, snagging a blender on the way back to his team's table. Win, finally done with the custard, ran to gather up the dry ingredients Danny shouted out to him, returning at a jog with his arms full of flour, sugar, salt, and baking powder.

Danny measured them into the blender, whirring the batter liquid and smooth, while Winslow rustled up two identical sauté pans. He clanked the things down, covering two of their team's allotted burners.

"Guys?" Danny wrestled the blender pitcher free of its base and trotted over to the range. "I need these burners. We good?"

"Yeah, I can make it work," Beck said, moving at double speed, his hands going so fast, Danny couldn't even see what he was doing with those sausages of his.

"I gotta have one for the fried eggs," Jules shouted from across the table. "But not until ten minutes before zero hour."

Max was already plating, setting out the white rectangular plates they'd chosen for presenting the first course. "You're good to go, Danny boy. Kill it!"

Danny wasted no more time. "Win, crank it up, we've got to get these pans heated and it's going to take a minute."

"What are you thinking, boss?" Winslow twirled the knobs on the stovetop and checked the color of the flames under both pans, like the smart chef he was.

Cooking in an unfamiliar kitchen meant that the things that were automatic in your own restaurant, like where to set the gas range knob for the level of heat you wanted, became fraught with peril and the possibility of scorched food.

"Crêpes," Danny said, tapping the blender sharply against the counter to help the bubbles float to the surface of the batter. "I'm thinking a mille crêpe cake, actually. Hey, can you check that the blast chiller has room in it? And add a little starch to that custard, let's thicken it up to a pastry cream."

"You got it." Winslow saluted, his sneakers squeaking on the rubber floor mat as he took off.

Adrenaline pumped through Danny's veins, but his hands were steady as rocks while he found a ladle and an open container of vegetable oil.

When a couple of drops of water danced and jumped when he flicked them onto the pans, he knew they were hot enough. Moving carefully but quickly, he ladled out enough batter to thinly coat the bottom of the first pan.

This was the critical moment—without a proper crêpe

paddle, the flat, wooden implement used at crêperies all over France to smooth their batter into perfect, uniform circles, Danny had to judge exactly how much batter to use.

Too much, and the crêpe would be pale and flabby. Too little, and it began to cook too quickly, before he could tilt the pan far enough to fill in the holes.

There was no time; Danny had to get both pans going at once, and he had to watch them for any signs of smoking or scorching. Fiddling with the height of the flame under the back burner, he almost missed the cues to flip the pancake on the first burner.

One strong flick of his wrist, a quick few seconds of browning and crisping up on the other side, and the first crêpe was done. Sliding it onto the plate Winslow held out, Danny rushed to ladle the next cup of batter into the empty pan before the second crêpe began to burn. And it went on like that, Danny establishing a rhythm of dip and flip and turn and slide that was almost like a dance, or the graceful, smooth moves of tai chi that Max had tried to teach them all a few weeks ago as a calming meditation technique.

Danny had sucked at tai chi—maybe if Max had explained that it was just like the moves in the kitchen, the way your muscles learned the pattern of flex and tense and sway, and your mind could float away, above it all, working on the problem of how, exactly, to build this crêpe cake.

A mille crêpe cake was, literally translated, a thousand crêpes stacked into a single dessert. Its layers were stuck together with any of a variety of ingredients, from lemon curd to whipped cream. What Danny had was Winslow's beautiful vanilla bean custard and some gorgeous caramelized plums worked into a deep amber compote shot through with streaks of ruby.

"Win, come here," he said, once the stack of thin, fragile pancakes was starting to get respectable. "Damn it," he swore as he flipped too gingerly and the crêpe folded in half.

"Whoops." Win bounced up next to him.

"Tell me about it." Danny rolled his eyes at himself. He could waste a bunch of time trying to get it back into the pan and on the correct side to brown without ripping it to shreds, or he could simply accept that it was over and move on. He dumped the crêpe.

Re-oiling the pan, he scooped up a new ladleful of batter and said, "My fault. I was too wimpy with it. You've got to show those crêpes who's boss."

"Where did you learn to make these?" Win's face was fascinated, the way it always got when someone showed him a technique he'd never seen before. "At the FPI?"

Danny had taken classes at the French Pastry Institute in New York, but he'd never gotten certified as a pastry chef. Couldn't take the time away from Lunden's Tavern.

He shook his head. "Nope, my mom. And Julia." He grinned, remembering his mother sitting down with him to watch old episodes of Julia Child's public television show when he was a kid. They'd both loved quoting Julia, parroting back to the TV, "You must have the courage of your convictions!" in that high, fluty voice.

"Man, that chick got around," Winslow said. "So, what do you need from me, boss?"

Danny filled Winslow in on the plan and watched the kid's startling green eyes get bigger. He looked surprised, then hungry, which Danny took as a good sign.

"Okay, go, go, go," he urged as he scraped the blender bowl for the last of the crêpe batter.

"We've got fifteen minutes," Jules called out, and Danny automatically responded with their normal kitchen acknowledgment, "Heard!"

Fifteen minutes. It was enough, but only barely. They'd have to work fast and clean, not the easiest when dealing with tender, paper-thin, still-warm crêpes, but it could be done.

A sense of infinite possibilities expanded Danny's rib cage, making him light-headed and invincible.

He stole half a second for a glance up to the front of the kitchen where Eva stood with the judges, talking to them about who-knew-what. The color had come back into her cheeks, but she still looked drained, diminished in some indefinable, wordless way.

She hadn't looked like that last night. She'd looked intense, passionate, alive . . . she'd looked happy.

He'd been happy, too.

Why were they both so willing to give that up without a fight?

Clenching his jaw, he went back to work, finishing the final crêpes with a flourish to distract himself from the way his wrist ached from the constant, repetitive flipping almost as much as his palms stung where they gripped the handles of the pans.

He'd do it. He'd finish this damn cake, and it would be the best thing Eva had ever tasted, and she'd give him that smile, the one that chased all the shadows out of the room and made him feel like he'd borrowed one of Winslow's too-tight T-shirts and his chest was about to burst out of it.

Eva thought she could dismiss him, turn Danny into just another notch on her bedpost, but she was wrong. There was more to him, more to them, and he wanted the chance to figure out exactly what that meant.

He wanted the chance to make her happy again—and to be happy himself.

It was good to have a goal, he told himself, running over

to Winslow with the final batch of crêpes stacked high on a platter.

Never mind the fact that there was sort of a built-in goal when you were cooking in a timed challenge as part of the Rising Star Chef competition.

He wanted to help his team win, no question. But at the moment, the reward of Eva's smile felt more real and urgent than any prize.

Chapter 19

Kane Slater was not having the time of his life.

First off, he was thrown. That nice lady he'd sung happy birthday to was in some sort of trouble that no one wanted to talk about too much, even though Kane wanted to tell them, *Y'all, I grew up with a single mom and five older sisters, I know about feminine issues.*

Not that it was his business, really, but he was worried. She'd seemed nice, and Devon Sparks had always been a stand-up guy to Kane. He liked the way the older chef lightened up whenever anyone mentioned his pretty, new southern belle of a wife.

But that was only the first thing that intruded on Kane's personal happy day parade, and he had to keep reminding himself that it was the worst—the most important, because whatever Lilah Sparks was going through had scared Devon enough to hightail it out of Chicago on the first plane back to New York, and that shit was real.

It was definitely a bigger deal than Kane's little, bitty, silly problem accepting the fact that he was going to be spending quality time with one of Claire's exes. One of the ones who mattered, he was pretty sure, after watching

Claire light up with a fond sparkle the instant Theo Jansen walked into the room.

No, Kane told himself as he watched the older man step over to stand way too close to Claire, his trim, distinguished body angled in such a way that all his intense attention was clearly focused directly on her. *This is no biggie.*

The past, over and done with a long time ago, according to what he remembered from when Eva gave him the scoop on the other judges before he'd agreed to come on board.

"Claire's a peach," she'd said, cheerfully unaware of Kane's embarrassingly massive, stupidly persistent crush on the editor in chief of his favorite food magazine.

"She's been more of a mom to me than any of the steps," Eva went on, referring to the progression of ever-younger women her father continued to marry and divorce every few years. "Or maybe I should say she's like a big sister, at this point. I still think of her a little in the mommy way, though, because she almost got stepped! That's how I met her, my dad dated her for a few months when I was a kid. But Claire was too smart to get on the step train, and when she broke up with him, I cried so hard! I thought I'd never see her again. But she didn't break up with me—she'd take me to high tea at the Pierre every couple of weeks, talk to me about school and boys, God, everything."

Eva had smiled, a softer look than Kane was used to seeing on this wild-child party buddy who'd become a friend. "She took me to get my first French manicure, and complained the whole time about how much better they did it in Paris," Eva reminisced. "She bought me my first tube of red Chanel lipstick."

"And thus, a monster was born," Kane intoned with

maniacal laughter, ducking the punch Eva threw at his arm.

But he'd known right then that if he ever actually met Claire Durand, he'd be in trouble.

If his crush was this bad, based only on her picture and smart-as-hell letters from the editor in every issue of *Délicieux,* how would he withstand a real live woman who'd cared enough to befriend the motherless daughter of a man she'd dumped?

And of course, he'd been right.

Really, he had nothing to complain about. After all, how many foodie nerds with hopeless crushes ever got to actually meet the object of their long-distance affections? Talk and hang out? Seduce and kiss and touch and see them naked in real, living color?

Kane was lucky. Always had been, one of the luckiest bastards on the planet, and he knew it.

So this thing with Theo Jansen showing up, it shouldn't have caused a ripple in the smooth, crystal-blue waters of Kane's lucky, lucky life. And if Claire had treated him with the disdain due an obnoxious ex-boyfriend, or if Theo had been less charming, dapper, witty, urbane, and above all interested, Kane would probably not be sulking right now.

Probably.

He was moody, sometimes, he'd been told. To which he usually replied that he had to keep up the rock star image somehow, and since he wasn't interested in heroin and loved his guitar, Betsy, too much to smash her on the stage, he was left with mood swings.

But this felt worse than one his moods where he was sure he'd never make another record or come up with another good lyric, and the space in his head that was usually filled with music was quiet and dark and scary.

This actually felt *worse,* and that was a total nightmare, because up till now he would've said the musicless brain void was the scariest shit of all. Now he knew better.

Now he knew that watching Theo Jansen put a light, yet somehow proprietary hand on Claire's slender shoulder—and her not shake it off—was worse.

Eva appeared next to him as if drawn by his misery. She looked none too pleased, herself, and Kane breathed a sigh of relief at the idea of focusing on Eva's mood instead of his for a few minutes.

"Everything okay?" he asked, deliberately turning his back on the tableau of Food Editor Wooed by Restaurant Magnate.

"Not so much," Eva said, trying to laugh, but it sounded more like a choked sigh. "My father is . . . it's complicated."

Kane, who'd turned back to Claire and Theo at the first mention of Eva's father, as if he were physically unable to compel his body to obey instructions that might increase his sanity, blinked his eyes closed and zeroed in on his friend. "I'm good at complicated," he told her. "*Rolling Stone* said so in their review of my last album. 'Layered and textural, with hidden levels of complication and emotion woven into every verse.'"

He paused. "Not that I memorized it, or anything."

Eva rolled her eyes. "Of course not." But she laughed when she said it, and Kane felt like, hey, mission accomplished.

Thrusting his hands in the back pockets of his jeans, he lifted his chin toward the wall clock steadily ticking down. "It's almost time. You think they're ready?"

Eva followed his gaze up to the timer. "If they're not, they're disqualified."

Man, that would suck. Kane hadn't been so consumed

by adolescent jealousy that he'd missed how hard everyone was working in that kitchen, running their asses off, shouting back and forth.

Even a good ways back from the stoves, it was hotter than Austin in August in there, a wet, overpowering, killing heat that got into the lungs and made it hard to breathe. Everyone was sweating, including the judges, but some of those poor chefs looked about ready to pass out.

It was a total kick to be there, to see it up close, and Kane pressed his lips together, determined not to waste this opportunity to learn from some of the country's best young culinary talent.

So Claire was flirting with her ex—or at least, not shutting him down when he flirted with her, in that sedate, dignified, grown-up kind of way. So what? Kane was in Chicago, one of his favorite cities, immersed in one of his favorite things in the world—food.

As the buzzer went off, loud and startling, and Eva yelled, "Knives down!" Kane promised himself he'd quit mooning and start experiencing.

With that firmly in mind, he was the first one out of the kitchen and across the hall to the conference room the hotel had set up as an elegant private dining room with a large oval table decked out in white linen, gleaming silverware, spotless crystal glasses. The works.

No food yet, though, and Kane rubbed his flat stomach, congratulating himself on the stellar decision not to eat breakfast that morning.

Okay, it had been more of a choice between having a bagel and rolling Claire over and having *her* one more time, but he was confident he'd made the right decision.

Especially considering, for all he knew, that might have been the last time. Shaking himself free of the morose thought that he should've joined her in the shower afterward, too, Kane threw himself into a chair and stared into his water glass.

The other judges followed after him, and Kane tried not to care where Claire sat. He supposed he could've arranged things the way he wanted them by sitting in the middle chair, but that felt too much like childish game playing to him, and God knew, he didn't want to do anything else to make Claire think of him as a stupid kid.

Not with the perfect example of a handsome older man on hand to provide comparison.

Unbuttoning his sleek, tailored sport coat, Theo Jansen stepped forward and pulled out the center chair, making Kane grit his teeth in annoyance. And then again in embarrassment, because Jansen had pulled the chair out for Claire, like a gentleman, like a guy with manners who wasn't raised in a barn, and Kane could just hear his mama screeching in the back of his head.

Trying to sit up straight instead of falling into his normal, comfy slouch, Kane was glad he'd ditched his hoodie today. Not that the crumpled gray cotton shirt with the sleeves rolled to the elbows was the epitome of class and taste, like ol' Jansen's pin-striped suit, but at least, you know, it had buttons instead of a drawstring and zipper.

Eva was the last one in, and she hurried over to the chair beside Kane's just as the first team of chefs trooped in with their dishes.

"You okay?" she whispered in his ear.

"I'm fine," Kane promised, splaying both hands flat on the tabletop to make them quit twitching and moving.

Imagine this is a stage, and you're having an off night, but these people paid for the Kane Slater Experience, and they are by God going to get it.

He smiled at her, the bright, star power one. "I'm just hungry. And no offense, but I kind of hate your dad."

Eva snorted. "None taken. At the moment, I'm kind of right there with you."

She looked gutted, and no wonder. The guy swoops in, all charming and shit, and undermines her in front of everyone involved in the competition, while simultaneously putting the moves on Claire. What a douchewad.

Man. Kane hated feeling so negative. He'd never understood people who wrote those achy-breaky-heart songs, or why the radio-listening public lapped them up like ice cream on a hot day, but now he thought maybe he got it. The only thing he could imagine doing with all this crazy emotion was to pour it into a song.

Look on the bright side, he told himself. *This is fodder for the next album. People will call it my Blue Period, and I'll get to look like a true artiste.*

The thought was less cheering than it should've been.

Kane didn't really perk up until the Southwest Team set their plates down in front of him. Time to get down to the serious business of eating.

The southwesterners had done a play on the famous Chicago-style hot dog, replacing the standard steamed all-beef dog with a spicier, almost chorizo-esque sausage heaped with fun stuff like avocado and Mexican crema. There were pickled jalapeños to balance the richness with a little sour, and the soft, pillowy fresh-made bun elevated the whole thing.

It was kind of a huge mouthful, though, and Kane only managed about a quarter of his, hoping to pace himself for the future teams' offerings. The dessert was a little disappointing, a sort of soupy ice cream that the team revealed they hadn't had time to chill properly.

"Which one of you is the pastry chef?" Kane asked.

Blank looks were his only reply, until a short, hairy guy

on the end piped up to say he'd been in charge of the ice cream.

Huh.

As the next teams cycled through, it became clear that they hadn't brought a true pastry chef along for the ride, either. The southern contingent presented a kick-ass homage to Chicago's soul food, although their fried chicken wasn't as good as Kane's mama's. Their take on buttermilk pie was more successful than the ice cream, but the crust was pitiful, too thick on the bottom, soggy and tasting of raw flour.

The West Coast Team had a pastry chef, but she was young and kind of rabbity nervous looking—for good reason, as it turned out.

The first two dishes, a salad and a vegetarian, distinctly California version of Chicago's famous pizza made Kane feel like he'd never look at vegetables as boring and uninteresting again. Their food was a revelation to Kane, who had a tendency to go big and bold rather than simple—but simplicity, when executed as perfectly and as masterfully as Skye Gladwell's crew did it, took the fresh, delicious, completely un-exotic ingredients to whole new heights. They were Kane's biggest surprise of the day.

But that poor little pastry chef. The molten chocolate cake she served for dessert was a total flop. The oozy, liquid center was too sweet, the sugar almost grainy on his tongue, dissolving to an unpleasantly bitter aftertaste.

The Midwestern Team was the one Kane was the most excited about. They'd scored the highest in the final round with a very impressive meal full of the latest techniques using the hottest new gadgets—smokers and semiconductors and liquid nitrogen and a metric ton of other stuff that Kane had written down to acquire for the kitchen in his house back in LA. Assuming he ever spent longer than three days there again.

And the Limestone chefs didn't disappoint. Every dish was a knockout, putting together bold, gutsy flavor combinations Kane had never thought of, would never think of, but that forced him to redefine the whole idea of *delicious*. Their presentations were fanciful, full of playful details like serving their pan-seared lamb chops on a parchment paper pillow filled with burnt hay, so that as the pillow slowly deflated, the scent wafted up and infused the lamb with the flavor of a backyard bonfire.

The dessert was a sweet beet sorbet mounded beside a chocolate mousse with a port sauce. The whole thing was sprinkled with smoked sea salt, and it wasn't made by a pastry chef, but it was competent, an avant-garde little creation that Kane didn't love. But he could tell it was well done, and Claire and Theo sure seemed to like it, so it was probably one of those no-accounting-for-tastes things.

Or maybe he was just getting full, although that would suck, since there was still one team left to go.

In the break before the last team presented, while the hotel staff quickly and efficiently cleared away the dishes, Kane leaned over to Claire and said, "So, aren't each of the teams supposed to represent a whole restaurant? I'd think that would mean having at least one guy who can whip up an in-your-face dessert in a pinch."

Pushing a hand through her loose hair—she'd given up on the bun half an hour ago, and the curling waves of auburn were driving Kane bonkers—Claire said, "It's always this way. They think, to win, they must put forward only their strongest chefs. And many chefs are contemptuous of pastry. They do not understand the delicacy of it, the way it is more science than art, but also still creative.

They think it's so simple, but they're wrong. As we have seen."

"A few of the teams do have pastry chefs," Eva put in quietly, with a darted glance in her father's direction. "For instance, this next group."

Chapter 20

The next team knocked and entered, and under the table Eva's leg started bouncing up and down as if her stiletto heel had suddenly been rubberized.

Kane tilted his head and studied the last team of the day. His schedule said they were from the East Coast, which was the first team they'd chosen, however many weeks and a zillion hopeful chef competitors ago. Now that he thought about it, he remembered them from the finals in New York.

This was the team that Claire had jumped all over him for what she perceived as him helping out the pretty lady chef, who'd choked a little during the trivia contest.

What was her name? Jules Something, he thought, giving the athletic, leggy blonde a smile. She grinned back at him, then sobered up to address the judges' panel.

"What we have for you today is a tribute to one of Chicago diners' favorite things: brunch. All over the trendy neighborhoods like Bucktown and Wicker Park, brunch places are popping up and drawing crowds—and let's face it. Breakfast is the most important meal of the day." She winked, and Kane heard Theo Jansen chuckle.

"What do you have for us?" Claire said briskly.

"We're starting you out with a little appetizer that packs a lot of punch," said the chef with the buzz cut, light brown hair and a possessive gleam in his eye whenever he glanced at Jules. "Jules and I wanted to play with Chicago's famous steak, but we didn't want to do something too familiar, like from the Lunden's menu. So we got one of the cheap, stringy cuts and braised it in wine and some herbs until it's falling apart. Then we fried a farm egg in brown butter and laid it over the top."

He stepped forward, carefully placing a tiny oval dish in front of each of them. A single perfect egg quivered gently in Kane's dish, dotted with droplets of golden butter and flecks of green herbs.

A film covered the yolk like a white veil over the brilliant orangey yellow, and when Kane dipped his spoon into the center, the yolk broke and ran out over the white like a river down a mountain. He peeked under the egg to see the shredded beef. It didn't look like much on its own, but when Kane lifted the spoon to his mouth, he had to work hard not to moan like a kid discovering what his dick was for.

The first taste was creamy perfection, the warm yolk and brown butter a wonderfully rich contrast with the tender, wine-soaked shards of meat. And as he went on eating, the egg mixed in with the beef even more, creating a sort of sauce that was nutty with brown butter and satisfying with the egg yolk and just generally one of the best things he'd ever had.

Thank God he didn't need to worry about pacing himself anymore, Kane mused as he stared sadly at his empty plate. He only wished he had some bread to sop up the streaks of egg and red wine left in the dish.

And there was something surprising in there, too—what was it? Capers?

"I've never thought of red wine as a breakfast thing before," he said. "Champagne, sure. But a nice, full-bodied red?"

"If you ask me, red wine is always the right answer," the chef said, grinning at him.

Kane smirked. Apparently, he was forgiven for ever looking or smiling at Jules. "You know what's always the right answer? A play on steak and eggs. Nom."

"Interesting," said Theo from the other side of the table. His voice matched the rest of him, modulated, refined, and a little amused. "With the Cabernet notes, the dish reminded me more of *oeufs en meurette.*"

"What the hell is that?" Kane whispered to Eva, even as Claire turned to Theo with a rare light of approval glinting in her eyes.

"Eggs poached in red wine, with a demi-glace sauce," Eva whispered back.

Okay, that made sense. Made Kane feel like an idiot, too, but that was incidental.

"What's next?" Claire said, setting her spoon down beside her half-full dish. Kane eyed it, wondering if anyone would notice him doing a quick switch, swapping out his empty plate for Claire's.

But then he forgot about it, because the tall chef with the chin-length brown hair tied back from his hard-jawed face came forward with a new dish. This one was more clearly entrée-size, small round slices of a whitish sausage, browned and crackling at the edges, stacked in a tower over a bed of something green. Smears of red slashed the plate like a painter's brushstrokes.

"Seafood sausage," the guy said. "On sautéed escarole with walnuts and red wine vinaigrette. Red wine gastrique on the plate."

"Ah, sausage. One of my favorite Chicago specialties. Did you make it yourself?" demanded Jansen.

Tall Guy nodded, hands behind his back, face as serious as if he were being interrogated by a police detective, but Kane had already moved on to the food.

Wow, okay. That was kind of amazing.

Kane stared at his empty fork as if it might provide some answers about what was going on in his mouth. The sausage was meaty and substantial, yet delicate and briny with the taste of the ocean. He'd never had anything quite like it. The kale had a bite to it, a toothsomeness he enjoyed, and there was something sweet-tart that jumped out at him every couple of bites—currants? raisins?—to contrast with the buttery richness of the toasted walnuts.

Spearing another round of sausage and smearing it through the red wine gastrique, Kane marveled at the way the red wine had reduced to a thick, almost vinegary syrup that shocked the tongue and brought out the flavors of the sea.

Across the table, Eva pushed her plate away nearly untouched, which made Kane frown. He guessed since she didn't get an actual vote in who won the challenge, and who went home, it didn't technically matter if she tasted everything.

But no one should waste food like this. It was almost a sin.

The other judges were nearly finished with their sausage plates, so Kane tucked back in. He didn't want to be left behind just because this dish was threatening to put him into a happy food coma.

Forcing himself to stop with a few bites left on his plate, Kane looked up at the East Coast Team with undiluted anticipation for what they might serve next.

These guys were good—but the West Coast and Midwest Teams had both been pretty stellar, right up to the dessert course.

The last pair of chefs stepped up, a slim young black man with shocking green eyes and a smattering of freckles, and a guy who looked like he might be related to the first chef. Same blue-gray eyes, same light brown hair, same dimple.

Unlike the first chef, however, this one didn't smile. He was as serious as Tall Guy, but there was a flash of an expression, just a flicker like a snapshot, when he looked at the judges across the table from him.

Beside Kane, Eva's bouncing knee suddenly stilled as if someone had hit her OFF button.

This must be the pastry chef she'd mentioned, Kane thought, sizing the guy up. He had a couple of tough acts to follow. Kane really hoped he lived up to the promise of the rest of his team.

The way the guy swallowed and squared his shoulders as if he were facing a firing squad, Kane thought the guy probably knew. This was the pastry chef's challenge to lose.

It all came down to this last dish.

Eva had never had such a difficult time choking down gourmet food in her life—and she'd been eating at five-star restaurants since she was old enough to digest solids.

Her throat was so tight, her stomach so knotted, she'd barely been able to taste a thing, but she had to keep going.

At least her Limestone boys hadn't disgraced themselves, which was both good and bad—it was nice that the only Jansen Hospitality restaurant in the RSC would probably move on to the next round, but a little dangerous, given Ryan Larousse's penchant for provoking the other teams into kitchen battles that had nothing to do with food.

Eva's mind was a whirl of confusion, arguments against selling out and turning the RSC into the lowest form of television, worries about convincing Cheney to stick around and film it . . . how much she wanted to tell Danny she was sorry.

Not that she owed him anything. Not that he probably cared, now that their night of fun—their good time—was over. They probably would've just gone their separate ways anyway. So why should she feel guilty about cutting off any chance of seeing him again?

When the New York team made their entrance, Eva went on high alert, darting a wary glance at her father, who, after all, had seen one member of the team already, half naked and sporting the most adorable case of bed-head known to man. But other than a slight widening of the eyes when he saw Danny, Theo showed no more reaction to the Lunden's crew than he had to any of the other teams.

No, Theo kept his gaze as level and solemn as a priest's, his roving eye—which Eva had half expected to see land on the sweet-faced, natural beauty of Skye Gladwell, and wouldn't that create some fun "drama" for Cheney's viewers—unusually tethered.

Never one to let the chance at a kitchen dalliance slip past, Theo appeared to be focused more on catching up with Claire—and, incidentally, driving poor Kane bananas—than on his usual pursuits.

But Eva made a mental note to worry about this bizarre little love triangle later. Right now, she had no room in her stress box—aka brain—for anything other than the final course of this round of the competition.

"Hi, I'm Danny Lunden," he said, striding forward with his head held high. You'd never know he'd started off the day skulking from Eva's hotel suite the way her first boyfriend, Steve Janovic, used to sneak out of her dad's house when Theo came home early from a night out on the town.

With graceful turns of his strong, tanned wrists, Danny set a plate down in front of each of them.

Eva wanted to catch his eye, somehow telegraph something—she didn't even know what—but he didn't linger over her place setting, just turned away to step back to the front of the table.

Desperate to hide the sudden burning behind her eyes, Eva blinked down at the dessert he'd prepared. The round china plate held a small, perfect oval of a cake, unadorned save for two dainty branches of thyme crossed and laid on top.

The cake itself had a staggering number of layers, each one so thin it almost disappeared between bands of vibrant red and creamy pale yellow filling.

"Ah," breathed Claire, sounding pleased. "*Gâteau de mille crêpes?*"

Eva looked up quickly, just in time for her heart to lift at the fleeting hint of a smile quirking Danny's handsome lips.

"I call it my French Pancake Stack." He looked right at her, and Eva's breath caught in her chest. "I was inspired by the power of memory," he said, never taking his eyes from hers. "And the beauty of taking something good from the past, and making a new memory out of it. I hope you enjoy it."

Fingertips tingling, Eva fumbled her fork, its clatter against her plate shockingly loud in the vivid, hushed silence of a room full of people taking a first bite of something wonderful.

He made this for me, was all she could think, and it meant . . . what did it mean, exactly?

She didn't know, couldn't parse it out, and then, when her fork sank through the soft layers of cake and brought the sweet to her mouth, she couldn't think of anything beyond the shock to her senses.

The flavors of fall exploded over her tongue. She tasted plums, their deep sweetness developed and layered with the dark, caramel bite of brown sugar. The smooth custard played against the fruit like a duet in perfect harmony, and running through it all was a third note she couldn't place, something fresh and herbal, but also a little playful and complex.

Going back to her plate for another bite, she moved the thyme garnish to the side, and realized—oh. That was the third melody weaving through the dessert. And the French pancakes themselves . . . Eva sighed, entranced by the light, eggy crêpes giving body and substance to the heavenly filling.

Her father was a good cook, when he bothered to get in front of a stove, and she cherished the memory of those mornings together. But he'd never made anything as addictive and soul satisfying as this cake.

Apparently unnerved by the hush that had fallen over the room, Winslow spoke up, bouncing on the toes of his sneakers. "Silence is usually a good thing around a table. Mouths too busy to talk? Point for us!"

The judges looked at him, and the excitement on his face vanished faster than Danny's dessert. "I mean," he backpedaled, "I'm not trying to tell you how to score us! Maybe we got a point, maybe we didn't. Maybe . . ."

"Maybe shut up," Danny suggested, clamping a hand over Win's mouth and dragging his teammate back into line.

"That's all we've got for you," he said to the bemused group at the table, but his gaze landed on Eva, and his eyes softened to something vulnerable that made her curl her ankles around the legs of the chair to stop herself from jumping up and, well, jumping *him*.

"I hope you liked it," Danny said, and she knew that one was just for her. Eva couldn't seem to stop smiling as the East Coast Team filed out of the judges' room.

Danny Lunden was . . . like no one she'd ever met. He was almost too good to be true. Hotter than sin, with a body made for pleasure, and he could cook? And listened when a woman talked, and did something to make her feel better?

"That last dish was dynamite," her father said, more enthusiastic than he'd been all day. "I happen to love crêpes, of course—one of my favorite things to make. Remember, Eva? Even the smell of the batter makes me nostalgic."

He sighed happily, and Eva's heart plummeted into her stomach like a brick dropped from the top of the Empire State Building.

Yes, Danny had listened when Eva talked. And then he'd turned right around and used an intimate personal memory to manipulate the emotions of one of the three people who would decide the fate of his team.

She set her fork down, careful to keep her shaking fingers from knocking the silver tines against the dessert plate.

No. He wouldn't. Would he?

Well, why the hell not? her inner realist snapped. *It's a competition. He's not here to make friends—isn't that what people always say on those awful reality shows?*

He's here to win. And he just happens to know that you and your father—the new judge—share a deep and abiding love of French pancakes.

Eva forced herself to look at the situation the way her father would—with an emotionless, clinical eye that sorted through the facts and came to a logical conclusion, unclouded by silly tangents like the way Danny's body moved against hers, or the way his intense focus during the act had made her feel things, real things, besides the sex things . . .

Stop it, she told herself, fiercely regulating her breathing, as Claire handed her empty plate to a server and reached for her notes to begin the deliberations.

It was time to put everything but the food out of her mind. She'd wait out the judging, and when it was over, she and Danny Lunden would have a little chat.

Chapter 21

"This blows," Jules moaned, pacing the five steps in front of their team's kitchen station before doing an about-face and stomping back in the other direction, hands wringing. "The waiting. I hate it! Why can't they just say what they liked, what they didn't, and put us out of our misery?"

"Come on, deep breaths," Max urged from his lotus position on the floor. Every time Jules reached the end of the track she was wearing down in the rubber matting, she had to pivot to keep from stepping on her boyfriend.

"Don't tell me how to breathe," she growled. "Besides, you're not as calm as you're pretending to be."

Jules had never liked being comforted. Danny remembered when they were kids, she'd show up at his parents' apartment white as salt, shaking with anger over something her flighty, semi-neglectful mom had done—or failed to do—but he'd learned early on that Jules wasn't like other girls. She didn't cry, she didn't want a hug, and she sure as hell didn't want to talk about it.

So when Max unfolded from his meditative pose and intercepted her on the next pass, wrapping his long arms around her shoulders and holding her still against his chest,

Danny fully expected her to open wide and take a giant bite out of Max's cranium.

Instead she leaned her body into his, as if she trusted him to take her weight and hold her up. As if the circle of his arms was the safest place she'd ever been.

Feeling as if he were intruding just by standing there, Danny looked away to give them some privacy. And there was plenty of privacy to be had, since the other teams had all cleared down and gone back to their hotel rooms to wait it out before his crew was even done presenting their dishes. The kitchen was empty except for the East Coast Team.

Well, three-fifths of the East Coast team, anyway. Beck had headed back to the room for a shower; after working with shellfish all morning, it was really the only option. And with a wink and a fist bump, Winslow had taken off to find his buddy, Drew, who also happened to be Eva's assistant.

He'd gotten them the scoop before by hanging out with Drew, because Drew tended to be one of the first to know everything that happened in the RSC. Danny hoped to hell that Winslow's in with the skinny, black-haired kid was as solid as he said. From what Danny could tell, Winslow hooked up with a lot of people and managed to stay friends with them, so maybe.

Win needed to stay friends with Drew, Danny decided. Any way they could possibly get confirmation of whether they'd be moving on in the competition, they had to take it.

The illegal cell phone was heavy in his pocket, a rule-breaking line straight to the information he wanted. He could text Eva. Maybe if he begged her for a hint, some indication about how it was going . . .

Danny cut off the thought, forcing his fingers to leave his pocket without touching the phone.

What was the matter with him? He didn't beg, he didn't plead, he didn't freak out. He was the patient one. The levelheaded one. The one who held everyone else together.

So why did he feel so messed up?

One word.

Eva.

He didn't know where he stood with her, didn't even know exactly where he wanted to stand with her, except that he wasn't ready to let her go—not that he had a choice.

He wasn't ready for this to be over, any of it. Danny wasn't ready to go home yet, damn it.

The thought took him by surprise, nearly knocking him over. Danny loved his home. He loved his family and his parents, and the life they'd planned out for him. So why did it suddenly feel as if going home this soon would be like stepping back into a prison cell after a single afternoon of standing in the sunlight?

"Whatever happens is what's meant to be," Max said, and it seemed to soothe Jules, but it made red flash in front of Danny's vision.

"Oh, bullshit," Danny said, so suddenly that he blinked in surprise to feel the word leap out of his mouth.

"Danny!" Jules looked shocked, which made Danny lift his chin.

"What, I'm the only chef in the kitchen who's not allowed to say *shit*?"

"No, of course not," she stammered, looking to Max as if for an explanation of why his brother had lost his mind. "You just . . . you're not usually so forceful in the way you express yourself. That's all."

Danny couldn't deny it, but it didn't make him feel awesome about himself. "Yeah, well. Just because I don't always share my opinions with the whole world doesn't mean I don't have them."

"Of course you have opinions," Max said. "We're just not used to you sticking up for them quite like that."

Danny clenched his jaw. Jesus, what was he, some kind of doormat? Was that how they saw him?

Was that how Eva saw him? Maybe that was why she hadn't introduced him to her father, or wanted him to stick around for longer than one night.

Looking at the way Max and Jules stood there next to each other, bodies brushing and leaning and supporting, comfortable and secure in each other's personal space, he felt a wave of envy so strong, it nearly choked him.

Danny was sick to death of being the levelheaded one. Maybe it was time to take a risk, go all-out, put everything on the line . . .

"Look," he said, one hand going back to his pocket almost unconsciously to toy with the hard plastic case of his cell phone. "If our number is up and we're the ones who are sent home, you two still have each other. You've got Lunden's, and a life together, and you know what you want from it."

"You have Lunden's, too," Jules reminded him, alarm widening her brown eyes. "And you used to know exactly what you wanted from life. You were always one of the surest people I knew."

"Yeah, well, things change." *I changed.* "And I'm not as ready to give up on this adventure as you seem to be."

They exchanged another one of those annoying, mind-reading glances. "Danny, no one's giving up," Max said, familiar older-brother irritation tightening his voice, before a frown from Jules had him smoothing it out into a soothing cadence. "But there's nothing we can do now, anyway. It's out of our hands. We played our plates and now it's up to the judges to decide where we go from here. All we can do is wait, and accept."

"God, is this what people hear when I talk?" Danny shook his head, disgusted. "You sound like a self-help tape."

"No, you usually sound more like a kindergarten teacher," Max shot back. "Sorry if you don't like it when one of your little helpless chicks rises up and pecks you in the nose, but we are not, in fact, kids here, Daniel."

Jules placed a restraining hand in the center of Max's chest. "What he means is, you don't always have to be the one taking care of us. We can return the favor, sometimes."

Danny snorted to cover the bolt of fear that shot through him. "Right. Because this family's been so successful at that."

"We've done okay," Max said, looking confused, and it just hit Danny like a frying pan between the eyes. Neither one of them had any idea what it was like to hold a family together with their bare hands, to feel as if one wrong word, one stupid mistake, would make the whole thing crumble into dust.

"How would you know how we've done?" Danny said, his voice almost unrecognizable to him, wrecked and hoarse. "You haven't been here. For five years, you're gone, off playing with your inner child or whatever all over Asia, and you have no freaking clue what it was like for us."

What it was like for me, in that house, with our parents missing you every single day, wondering where you were, wishing you'd come home.

I was never enough.

Guilt screwed up Max's face immediately. It was almost too easy. Danny almost felt bad about it.

"I'm sorry, Dan." Max shrugged helplessly. "I don't know what else you want me to say."

He'd heard that before, and he knew it was real. Max felt bad, never meant to hurt anyone, blah blah blah. But he had. And Danny was the one who'd picked up the pieces, like always. Anger warring with his peacemaking instincts, Danny couldn't decide whether to tell Max what he could do with his apologies or make nice.

The decision was taken out of his hands when his cell phone vibrated in his pocket, startling him.

It was Eva.

Heart hammering at his rib cage, Danny answered the phone, angling his body slightly away from his brother and Jules.

"I need to see you," she said. No preliminaries, no hint of anything, and Danny's gut clenched.

Did she know something about their chances of moving on? Something bad, maybe. Without thinking, Danny lowered his voice and made it as neutral as possible so as not to freak out Max and Jules.

"Okay. When and where?"

"Can you come up to my suite? I'll meet you there in five."

Danny agreed and hung up, mind racing with possible scenarios, none of them comforting. Well, okay, there was the one where Eva was just insanely hot for him and phoned him for a midday booty call and would greet him at the suite door wearing nothing but a glowing smile.

But Danny was a realist, so he put that one out of his head. Or at least to the very back, so he could look at it again later. Much later, when his brother and his oldest friend weren't staring at him with identical quizzical expressions.

"What's up?"

Danny didn't question his instinct to protect them from whatever Eva had to say. "Nothing much, Beck just needs my help with something. I'm going to meet him in the lobby. Call me if we find out who won?"

"Sure, Danny," Jules said, her worried brown eyes darting between the two brothers. "We'll call if Win comes up with anything."

"Hey," Max called as Danny's hand hit the kitchen doors. "We're okay, right?"

Danny struggled for an instant with all the things he hadn't said, the emotions he didn't want to acknowledge. "Sure, Max. We're fine."

Fighting with his family always gave Danny a headache. Probably from grinding his teeth and clenching down on the words that wanted to spill out of his mouth.

Checking his phone to see if he had a signal, Danny's fingers hesitated only an instant before pecking out his parents' number.

"Hey, Dad," he greeted the gruff voice that answered.

"Danny! I've been waiting to hear from one of you boys. How's it going over there?"

Suppressing a huff of scorn at the idea that it would ever be Max who thought to call and give their parents the update, Danny said, "We're done with the first challenge, still waiting to hear which team is going home. How's your heart?"

"Fine, fine," Gus said impatiently. "I feel great."

"No pain, shortness of breath? When Mom tells you to take your medication, you're not arguing with her, are you?"

"Oh, your mother's taking great care of me," Gus said, sounding grumpy. "Nothing but oatmeal, grapefruits, and hearts of romaine. She won't even let me put lardons and poached egg in the salad! It's a conspiracy. But tell me more about what I'm missing. First elimination, huh?"

"Yep. Someone's going home today." Danny felt again the pang of fear that it might be him, but he shoved it down.

"You're not worried, are you? Good." Danny could almost hear Gus Lunden rubbing his hands together, looking gleeful. "Let's start narrowing the field. How do you think it went?"

"Well," Danny said cautiously. "I know we put up some solid dishes. But it all depends on how we stack up against the other chefs."

"You'll be the best," Gus said fiercely. "There's not a doubt in my mind."

Danny smiled. "Thanks, Dad."

"How were your waffles?"

"Change of plans; did a mille crêpe cake instead. It was almost a disaster, but I think Win and I pulled it out. Didn't have enough time to chill it properly, but it held together okay when I used the round dough cutter to dish it up, and the flavors were spot-on." Danny frowned, thinking of all the things he could have done differently, done better, but Gus interrupted him.

"I'm sure it was great. You'd never let your team down, kiddo, it's not in you." Gus cleared his throat, going even more gruff as emotion overtook him. "We can always count on you. Always have, always will."

"Thanks," Danny said again, rubbing at his chest, where it felt as if someone had packed a ten-pound bag of flour into his rib cage. The pressure made it hard to breathe for a second, but then his mom got on the phone, and he had to go through the whole thing again for her.

He'd just slipped his phone back in his pocket when he got all the way up to Eva's penthouse and knocked on the door. She opened it, and Danny had a brief moment of disappointment that she was wearing clothes, but he got over it.

It was shockingly good to see her up close, to look into her smoky gray eyes and have her look right back at him. Despite everything, the distance they had to keep, the harshness of that morning's dismissal with her father look-ing on—Danny couldn't help himself. The mere sight of her made him want to smile.

Until she opened her mouth and froze him to the spot with the chill in her voice. "Come in, Chef. But please, leave any recording devices out here. There's no point, anyway, I don't plan to give you any further inside infor-mation you can use to manipulate my father."

What the actual fuck?

Chapter 22

Eva left the door open for Danny to come in, pacing back toward the wet bar in the corner of the living room. She wanted bourbon, but her hands were already shaking. Probably not a good idea. But wasn't alcohol a depressant? Wouldn't that slow her down, dull the spiky edges of her mind, and let her be calm for a second?

Only for a second, so she could breathe.

"What's going on, Eva?"

Danny's sharp voice startled her hand away from the miniature bottles of liquor lined up in the wet bar cabinet.

She whirled to face him, clutching her arms around her middle in an attempt to keep from trembling with rage. "I asked you up here so we could talk about what you did today," she said. The effort it took to keep her voice cold and dead was enormous, exhausting. "But now that you're here, I can hardly stand to look at you. How could you, Danny?"

Brows lowering over eyes snapping with heat, Danny held up his hands. "Whoa. Hold the phones. What, exactly, am I supposed to have done?"

"The crêpe cake," Eva hissed. She didn't want to even

say the words *French pancakes*—it would feel too much like a betrayal. "I told you that memory of my father, and you used it to get ahead in the competition."

"That's not what I was doing!" Danny protested, taking a step forward. He stopped when she backed up, bumping into the bar and rattling the glass bottles on their shelf. Gentling his voice, he said, "Look, Eva. I'm sorry that's what you thought, but it wasn't what I meant."

"No? Because it nearly worked. There I was, sitting there feeling all warm and fuzzy about you listening to me and getting to know me. Something so intimate and personal, a piece of my history that I've never shared with any—" She broke off, her voice cracking and pain leaking through.

Danny stepped forward again, but she couldn't retreat because she was already practically sitting on the bar. "Eva. Listen to me. I didn't use you. Okay, that's not totally true—I did use your memory as an inspiration for the dish. But that's it. I wasn't thinking about exposing something personal about you, or manipulating your father's emotions, or taking advantage of inside knowledge of his tastes. I just wanted to make the best dessert possible in the time I had left after my first idea tanked, and that French pancake story stuck in my head."

He inched closer with every word, hands outstretched as if to gentle a wild animal, and Eva felt the calm that had been eluding her settle into her bones. The tremors in her hands had stopped by the time he stood in front of her.

"Now," he said softly, close enough that the puff of his breath warmed her forehead. "Would you quit pretending to be pissed at me and tell me what's really going on?"

Dropping her shoulders, Eva aimed a halfhearted smack at his broad, solid chest. "I am mad at you," she maintained stubbornly, then sighed. "Or at least, I thought I was. God, you are *good* at this soothing thing."

"Bet I can do even better," he said, hooking one strong arm behind her neck and drawing her in for a hug.

Knowing she shouldn't, that she absolutely had to move away, get some distance, put things back on a professional footing, Eva still sank into the embrace.

One last time, she promised herself, breathing in his scent of smoke and caramel, letting the heat of his body soak into her muscles and pull her head down to his shoulder.

"You know I'm not playing games here," he said, his voice hypnotic and low above her head. "So what's up? What's got you all upset?"

Curling her fingers into the rough poly/cotton of his chef's jacket, Eva said, "I don't know. My dad. The competition and the Cooking Channel, and that stupid producer. And . . ."

She swallowed and pressed her mouth to the front of his shoulder to stop the words.

And I'm going to miss you.

She didn't say it, but she didn't have to. Danny heard her anyway. "Yeah," he said roughly. "Me too."

This was insane. Eve wrapped her fingers around his elbows and tugged his arms down, sidling out from between Danny and the bar. She felt naked and cold without his arms around her, but she'd get used to it. She had to.

"I'm sorry," she said, shaking her head. "I'm a nutjob. I shouldn't have yelled at you, or accused you of trying to cheat. I guess I've spent too much time around people who wouldn't hesitate to do exactly that."

"Including your father?" Danny propped his hip on the bar and crossed his arms, with a sardonic lift to his brow.

Palming the back of her neck, Eva huffed out a laugh. "Yeah, maybe. He certainly likes to have his own way, and he's not too fussed about how he gets it. Whatever works, right?"

Danny hummed noncommittally. He had his head cocked, all his attention on her, and that shiver of awareness, of need, fluttered through Eva again. Could she really give this up? Wasn't there a way she could have it all?

Kicking herself into gear, she said, "Okay. So I called you up here for the wrong reason, but it's good that you're here. I just want to say . . ."

Maybe they could work something out. Maybe once this was all over . . .

Danny nodded. "I know. We can't be together anymore, not if the RSC is going to be televised. I get it, Eva."

The words were still caught in Eva's mouth, and she had to swallow them down before she could croak out, "Right. Stuff like this is never really secret forever, people always find out, and then the validity of the whole competition is called into question, and I can't have that."

She laughed, and this time is sounded like more than a sigh. "God. I'm having a hard enough time convincing my dad I can do a good job."

"Getting caught in a sex scandal with a contestant would probably not help," Danny agreed, pushing away from the bar.

"And my father would be pissed." She slanted a glance at Danny from under her eyelashes. "He warned me to stop seeing you."

Danny's eyes flashed blue and silver sparks. "Did he?"

He all but snarled it, and Eva felt a quickening low down in her stomach. She nodded. "It's like he's completely forgotten my teenage years. I was never very good at staying away from the things that would get me in trouble."

Some of the hardness faded from Danny's granite jaw as his mouth curled into a rueful smile. "Are you saying I'm forbidden fruit?"

She swallowed hard. "The forbiddenest."

"And here I thought you liked breaking the rules."

"Not this time." Eva hugged her arms around her middle. "There's too much riding on it."

Danny *was* forbidden. For as long as the East Coast Team remained part of the competition, at least. Eva licked her lips, the words stuck in her dry throat.

It was so new to her, this yearning to plan ahead, to want more time with someone. Her heart beat loudly in her own ears, and the moment stretched between them, taut and thick with potential . . . and then it was over.

A shadow darkened Danny's eyes, and his smile faded. "I should go, then, before your dad catches me up here again."

She'd missed her chance. He was leaving. Which was what had to happen, she knew that. But somehow, the sight of Danny walking toward the door was more than she could stand.

"Wait!" He turned back, his face so purposefully blank, she knew he was feeling something strong, something volatile.

"What?"

Casting around for something legit to keep him there with her for a few more seconds, she said, "Don't you want to know what the judges decided?"

Interest flared in his blue eyes before he banked it. "I'm pretty sure that would constitute preferential treatment," he said gently. "And I don't think you'd want to count on my ability to act surprised when you make the official announcement to everyone. I'm not a great actor."

"I don't believe that for a second," Eva said. Pulling

out her sultriest smile, she went on. "I mean, here you are, acting like you can't wait to get out of this suite and never touch me again."

There was that smile again, as if he couldn't help himself. "Maybe that's the truth."

"No way." Eva let her hips roll a little as she swayed toward him, one step at a time. Maybe she couldn't figure out how to tell him she wanted him to wait for her until after the RSC—but she knew how to make him want her right here, right now. "There's no way I feel like I could come out of my skin with the need to be touched by you, and you feel nothing at all."

Fascinated, she watched his throat move convulsively as he swallowed. "Eva. Don't."

"Don't what?" she breathed, reaching out to finger the snap closure of his chef's whites. "Don't break my own rules? But I know that's what you like about me."

"How long do we have before the official announcement of who's going home?"

Startled by the abrupt question, she drew back. "My assistant and a couple of runners are gathering everyone in the kitchen." She checked her watch. "The judges are scheduled to meet down there in twenty-four minutes."

"Not long enough," Danny said hoarsely, reaching for her waist and pulling her close, his palms scorching hot through the thin material of her shirt. "But it'll have to do."

Eva squeaked, although she'd deny it with her dying breath. The sound was muffled by Danny's mouth, anyway, as he bent his head and took her breath with a kiss.

"One last time," she gasped against his lips as her knees gave out and he cradled her on the way down to the thick, soft carpet.

Danny lifted his head to stare down at her, his body lean and hard and heavenly against hers. Dropping down to nuzzle at her neck, he said, "One last broken rule, then we'll be good."

"We'll be good," she promised, tilting her head back to give him better access. And as his lips found that spot behind her ear that always gave her chills, making Eva's hips buck and her heart stutter in her chest, she had to wonder if she'd be able to keep that promise.

After all, didn't she live to break the rules?

Chapter 23

As it turned out, there was no need to worry about her will-power, or lack thereof. What Eva hadn't counted on was how much everything was about to change.

She was still producing the show, which meant that all decisions and crises having to do with the actual day-to-day of getting the contestants where they needed to go, getting the challenges set up, making sure the kitchen remained stocked and cleaned and ready for action, fell to Eva.

Not to mention the surprisingly heartbreaking task of sending the losing teams home.

She'd had a taste of how awful it felt to let a group of chefs who'd cooked their heart out know that they hadn't made the cut, back during the finals. As producer and emcee, she was always the one who had to deliver the bad news. And it had always sucked. Every time.

But suddenly, now that there were cameras everywhere, black lenses like unblinking eyes focused on catching every snippet of human drama and suffering possible, it became a thousand times worse.

It started that very first day. After the hottest, most urgent, and intensely satisfying twenty-minute good-bye sex of her life, Eva had rushed to put herself back together and run downstairs to the kitchen where all the chefs and judges were waiting.

Holding her head high and pretending she hadn't just been rolling around on the floor with the East Coast Team's pastry chef was a lot easier when she didn't look said pastry chef in the all-too-handsome face.

So Eva had scanned the rest of the room, taking in the hopeful, fearful anticipation and dread, the heart-pounding, cold-sweating agony of not knowing, and she'd felt her own skin begin to prickle with a chill of unease.

God. I have to tell them their dream is over.

And their reaction would be filmed by Cheney and his damn camera, captured for the entertainment of anyone who happened to flip past the Cooking Channel.

Gulping, Eva grasped for the right words and wondered when her life got so freaking emotionally complex and hard to deal with.

No. Fun.

This first elimination hadn't been all that tricky to decide on, back in the judges' chamber. With relatively little back and forth or arguing among Kane, Claire, and her father, they'd picked a loser. She knew it would get tougher as the competition went forward and they narrowed the teams down to the best of the best.

But it was hard to believe that any elimination announcement could be more difficult than this one.

"It was a very tough decision," Eva lied, clasping her hands behind her back to stop their fidgeting. "And I know no one wants to be the first team to be sent home, but unfortunately, the competition is over for some of you."

An electric current of tension zipped through the room, and Eva dug her nails into her palms.

"After a lot of deliberation, and some dishes and flavors

that truly astonished us from each team, the judges have decided that the four teams moving on in the competition are the chefs from the Midwest, the South, the West Coast, and the East Coast."

A stunned silence met her pronouncement, followed by absolute chaos as the kitchen erupted into whoops of joy and celebration.

Amid the relieved high-fives and the backslapping, Chef Paulina Santiago and her crew quietly trudged back to their table and started packing up their knives and other gear, and Eva couldn't watch them, didn't want to see the way their shoulders slumped and their faces crumpled with disbelief, or the way they comforted each other with arms around each other's backs.

But she forced herself to keep her eyes up and on them. She owed it to them to bear witness to this final moment on their journey toward a dream that she'd had a hand in snatching away.

Kane and Claire congratulated the continuing chefs, said good-bye to the Southwest Team, and left.

Probably to go have fun, happy, sexy times together, since nobody cared if two judges were boinking. Damn it.

Eva, however, had the first of many long nights ahead of her. Summoning her assistant, Drew, to her side, she'd immediately started laying out the battle plan for taking care of getting the Southwest Team back to New Mexico, having the kitchen reorganized with four team tables instead of five, to give the remaining chefs more space, and settling up the hotel bills.

A quick glance at the front corner of the room showed Cheney packing up his camera, and a bolt of panic shot through Eva.

From across the room, her father caught her eye, and it didn't take a lifetime of struggling to live up to his expectations to read the clear message in his tight expression.

She had to keep Cheney interested. They hadn't had any luck coordinating schedules with their potential celebrity chef judges, so far. What could she say to make him stay and give the RSC another shot?

The partying gaggle of chefs was beginning to disperse, calling suggestions about taking it out on the town, finding a chef-friendly bar or pub, and throwing back a few drinks to unwind from the insanity of the last few days.

Her attention was caught when she overheard her own name. "I'm going to ask Eva Jansen to come out with us," Ryan Larousse muttered to the chef next to him.

Eva stilled, but kept her eyes on Drew's inky black hair bent over the iPad where he was entering items in his ever-expanding to-do list.

"Dude." Ike Bryar, the head of the Southern Team, frowned, cutting his eyes at her. "What are you doing? That's like inviting the dean of students to a kegger."

"There wasn't an official winner of this challenge, but I bet if we get her liquored up, we can squeeze some good info out of her on who the judges really liked best." The smug edge to Ryan's voice made it clear which team he thought would've won, if points had been awarded.

"And why the hell would she tell you any of that?" The voice came from behind Eva, who couldn't turn around to see the speaker without letting on that she was eavesdropping, but she didn't need to.

It was Danny.

Mostly, she wanted to smack him—he really wasn't a good actor, if this was the best he could do at pretending nothing had ever gone on between them—but there was a soft, silly, hard-to-deny part of her that wanted to melt when he leaped to her defense.

Especially when Ryan snorted and said, under his breath, "Because Eva Jansen knows how to party, man. Just look at her."

It was nothing she hadn't heard before. Chefs were a raunchy, irreverent, testosterone-fueled group. But something about Ryan's comment caught Eva on the raw edge of her emotions, and she flinched.

Visibly flinched.

Drew looked up, eyebrows raised quizzically. And probably no one else would've noticed anything, except Danny was obviously as attuned to her as she was to him, because she could hear the pure rage in his voice when he snarled, "You take that back, Larousse."

The entire kitchen paused, and Eva couldn't keep pretending she wasn't aware of what was going on.

Casting a quick look at Danny, who was a vision of protective anger, legs braced apart and scorched, blistered hands clenched into tight fists that must have hurt unbearably, Eva's gaze swept past Cheney's corner of the room and snagged on the camera still set up there.

Cheney had gone back to filming.

And in that briefest of moments before the other East Coasters leaped on Danny and held him back, before Ryan laughed that harsh, grating laugh of his and swept from the kitchen, Eva knew what she had to do.

Cheney wanted drama. He wanted hot chefs and kitchen fights and maybe a little romance, to bring the female viewers in.

If Eva wanted to make the RSC the biggest, best competition it could possibly be—if she wanted to open it up to every talented chef in America—she had no choice.

"Drew," Eva said, her eyes never leaving Danny, who was whispering furiously with Beck, flailing hand gestures threatening to take out the rest of his team. "I've got a new job for you, one that should take priority over the rest of that list."

"Go," Drew said, fingers confidently poised over the touchscreen pad.

Eva hesitated, stomach roiling with indecision.

The RSC was her mother's legacy. Emmaline Jansen's dream was to found a competition that would elevate and draw attention to the work of amazing chefs around the United States. And when Eva had agreed to take it on this year, she'd done so partly because she wanted to get back to the roots of her mother's original idea.

Eva wanted to discover and encourage the efforts of all chefs . . . not just the high-profile ones, or the ones who'd already achieved success. And the best way she knew to do that was to raise the profile of the RSC itself, to get bigger, better sponsors with deeper pockets, so that they could expand the competition to be more inclusive.

But was she really prepared to go this far to get what she wanted?

Yes. It was the only way. Everyone would benefit from the RSC gaining greater exposure on the Cooking Channel. She was doing this for everyone, not only herself.

There was more at stake than her career, or her conscience.

"You're friends with that chef on the East Coast Team, Winslow. Aren't you?"

Drew's eyes got big behind his glasses, but he nodded, and Eva felt a slow curl of determination in her belly.

If Cheney wanted drama, then by God she'd give it to him.

Chapter 24

The week following the first elimination was one of the hardest of Danny's life. They all felt the loss of the Southwest Team; Paulina Santiago and her crew were nice people, solid competitors. And the fact that they went home brought it into sharp relief—this was a competition. They were playing for real stakes, and screwups had real consequences.

The chefs were given a few days off to rest up from the previous challenge, but most of them spent the time in the kitchen, anyway, shooting the shit, doodling ideas, and just generally staying amped on anticipation.

Danny didn't do downtime. In fact, he sort of sucked at it.

So he practiced his soufflé technique, experimented with caramels, and watched.

He watched Max and Jules emerge from their lovebird haze and get their heads in the game. He watched Beck studiously not watching Skye Gladwell, who swirled across the kitchen in a dance of flowy skirts and jingly bracelets and curly clouds of strawberry-blond hair. He watched

Winslow getting cozier with Drew Gallagher, Eva's assistant.

But most of all, he watched Eva.

Eva, who flew from one task to another as if her stiletto heels had wings attached. Eva, who hadn't stopped moving since the full camera crew arrived the day before. She was in motion from the moment he first caught sight of her across the crowded Gold Coast lobby as he came in with a sack full of light, flaky croissants from the bakery across the street for the team's breakfast, till she bid everyone a distracted good night and went back to work.

Eva, who was starting to look worn and fragile, like pastry dough rolled out so thin it was see-through in places, and far too easy to tear.

She had a lot to do—the production team was gearing up for the next challenge starting tomorrow, and coordinating everything with the camera crew seemed to be quite the hassle. From what Danny could tell, the preparations involved a lot of phone calls, permits, and wrangling around.

While he and the other chefs had been taking in a little of Chicago—okay, mainly scouting out the local bar scene, but still—Eva had been running herself into the ground.

He didn't like it, but what could he do? He kept his distance, not wanting to give that asswipe Ryan Larousse any more ammunition than he already had, after that stupid blowup over him calling Eva a party girl.

Which maybe she was, or had been, but you couldn't prove it by her behavior during the past week. In fact, tonight was the first time anyone had been able to entice her out to the current favorite drinking spot, a refurbished speakeasy in Wicker Park, Chicago's young, artsy neighborhood.

Danny liked The Blind Tiger because it was unpretentious, serving solid drinks made with high-quality liquor to an eclectic mix of patrons, from off-duty firemen still smoky and soot-stained to older couples sipping from their own beer steins to scarf-and-skinny-jean-clad hipsters out on the town.

It reminded him of Chapel, their favorite after-hours bar in New York, and Danny wondered if this was what it was like to travel the world—no matter where you went, you found something to make you feel at home.

Of course, back home, no one would've hooted and cat-called when Eva ordered a Manhattan. But here in Chicago, even though Danny could see a perfectly good bottle of American rye whiskey behind the scarred oak bar, the bartender shrugged and told her to pick something else.

The Chicago versus New York rivalry ran deeper than Danny had ever realized.

Eva looked the bartender in the eye and said, "I'll have a double shot of rye, a shot of sweet vermouth, and a glass with ice. Oh, and toss in a maraschino cherry. Thanks." Then she turned back to Cheney, the camera guy she'd invited along—without his camera, thank Christ—and said, "What'll you have? I'm buying."

God. Was it any wonder Danny was head over heels for this woman?

Eva accepted her shots and mixed up her own Manhattan right under the bartender's nose, then led Cheney to a couple of stools at the corner of the bar where she casually reached across the dull gleam of wood polished by generations of elbows to snag a couple more cherries from the canister behind the counter.

And . . . it was time for Danny to stop watching her now. He took a pull from his bottle, a local craft beer the bartender had recommended, and checked around the bar to see how his guys were doing. Winslow and Drew were off in a corner, heads bent together, giggling over their drinks like a couple of kids too young to be tossing back tequila.

Max was shooting pool in the back with Beck, while Jules kept Danny company, her knowing stare reminding him of just how long they'd been best friends. And how hard it was to keep a secret from her, when she wasn't distracted by songbirds and pink-winged cupids flying around her head.

"You like her," Jules said, tipping her beer bottle in Eva's direction. "Don't you?"

Danny planted his arms on the bar to steady himself. "Doesn't matter," he grunted.

"You always do that," Jules accused, shaking her head so hard, her messy blond ponytail lashed at Danny's shoulder. "What you want matters, Danny. Your happiness matters, just as much as anyone else's."

Rolling his eyes, Danny slouched down on his barstool. "Spare me the psychoanalysis, Jules. Just because you've been clocked upside the head by Cupid doesn't mean the rest of us are panting for the chance to get all googly-eyed."

"That's not the point," she argued. "I'm not saying you're stoked about it, or that you wanted it to go down like this, but that's not how it works. Maybe you didn't mean for it to happen, but you like her, a lot, or you wouldn't be picking a fight with me about it."

"Fine," Danny conceded. It loosened something in his chest just to admit it out loud to one of his oldest friends, but it didn't change anything. "So what? Maybe I like her, but there's nothing I can do about it. So why torture myself thinking about it?"

"Because you can't stop yourself."

"Can too."

Now it was Jules's turn to roll her eyes. "Danny. You haven't been able to keep your eyes off her since she came in."

Realizing his attention had drifted to the corner of the bar where Eva sat making an impassioned speech to the cameraman, looking more animated and energized than he'd seen her in days, emphatic hand gestures and decisive nods and all, Danny whipped his head around. He took too big a gulp of his beer to cover it, and ended up in a coughing fit with Jules whacking him on the back.

And she was a chef, a damn good one, which meant she had some serious upper-body strength for a girl.

"Ow, damn it, quit that," he gasped as one particularly hard smack nearly toppled him off his bar stool.

Okay, make that serious upper-body strength, period, the end. Girl, nothing. Geez.

"So, you gonna be okay?" she asked.

"Aside from my cracked rib?" he groused, clearing his burning throat.

Giving him her patented Boys Are Dumb look, Jules said, "Not about that. About her."

Danny told himself the ache in his throat was left over from inhaling that mouthful of micro brew. "I'll have to be, won't I? I can't do anything about the fact that she's decided it's too risky for us to be together while the competition is going on."

"And after?"

Danny tensed so hard, when he shrugged his shoulders it felt like he was breaking his own spine. "Who knows? We don't exactly travel in the same circles."

"You come from such different worlds. How could it ever work?" Jules said, sighing in an exaggeratedly romantic way that didn't suit her at all. "Yeah, it's pretty Romeo and Juliet. Star-crossed lovers, and all that. Not that you've slept with her or anything . . . Danny!"

"What?" Danny ducked his head, intensely aware of the heat scorching his cheeks and neck. "Don't make a thing out of it, we stopped a while ago."

"I can't believe I missed it," Jules moaned. "I mean, not that I wanted to watch, or anything."

"Okay, now you're creeping me out." Danny shuddered.

"Oh, shut up. I just mean, God, Danny. All this big life stuff was going on with you, and you never said a word. Never let on for a second."

"You didn't notice because you and Max were off in the Honeymoon Suite, doing whatever it is you do that I absolutely do not ever, ever want to know or hear anything about, or, oh sweet Jesus, you're paying for my lobotomy."

Jules made an unhappy noise. "I'm sorry, Danny. I know we've both been preoccupied, not really pulling our weight . . ."

"It's okay," he said automatically, then blinked. "It really is. I mean, yeah, it was problematic, but I get it. You and Max fought hard to get where you are, and you deserved some time to enjoy it. But no, we had to get on a plane and fly out here and cook our butts off. Whatever bonding and togetherness you managed to sneak in, I'm glad about it."

And he was, he realized as Jules thanked him with a quick hug, her familiar cinnamon and salt smell tickling his nose. He'd never understood it before, but now, with this insane addiction to watching Eva Jansen tugging at the back of his brain, trying to make him turn his head to catch a glimpse of her waving her hands in the air and making his point, Danny really did get it.

"I'm just so happy," Jules sniffed, sounding alarmingly waterlogged. "I want you to be happy, too."

"Hey, no." He patted her shoulder. Tears killed him, just slayed him dead. "Jules, come on. I'm happy. I've got you and Max settled, Winslow's got a maybe-boyfriend, and Beck hasn't punched anyone in a few days. Mom and Dad are healthy, and I don't know if you noticed, but we're doing pretty good so far in this Rising Star Chef deal. What else do I need?"

Don't look at Eva, don't look at Eva, don't look at Eva . . .

"Love," Jules snapped, sitting up and scrubbing at her eyes with a huff of annoyance. She hated crying.

"Look, someone on this team has to keep his head," Danny said, pulling his mouth into a teasing smile. "Between you and Max coming down with chronic lurve, Winslow flirting nonstop with that assistant kid, and Beck performing the strangest mating dance known to man with that West Coast chef, we're full up on interpersonal drama over here."

"Fine, fine." Jules laughed. "I'll back off. For now. But Danny, think about this—we're not going to be in the RSC forever. And when the competition is over, you'll be free to pursue . . . whoever catches your fancy. This isn't Regency England or something—where you come from doesn't have to define who you are. Or her, either, for that matter. So just . . . don't give up hope."

Danny gave her the smile she wanted, but as she squeezed his shoulder one last time and hopped down from her barstool to go check out Max and Beck's pool game, he wondered if that was true.

If they lost, would he ever see Eva again? Jules could joke all she wanted, but he and Eva *didn't* move in the same circles. The restaurant world was small, but it wasn't that small, and Danny didn't go to a lot of star-studded openings and gala parties. He probably wouldn't go even if he was invited.

But if they won, would it be any better?

He'd have more time with her, sure, doing post-competition interviews and whatnot. But would either of them want to risk a relationship that could look, to the outside world, like a reason for favoritism?

While he nursed his beer and thought dark thoughts, his eyes were drawn back to Eva. There was a complicated expression on her face as she said good-bye to Cheney, who got up and left after handing her a thick sheaf of official-looking documents. Obviously, whatever she'd been trying to convince the Cooking Channel rep to do, he'd agreed. So why didn't she look happier about it?

Before he could talk himself out of it, Danny was off his stool and making his way down the bar to Eva's side.

"Buy you another round of Manhattan ingredients?" he said.

She straightened her shoulders immediately, as if alarmed that she'd let herself slump over the bar like a broken-down drunk. Or a broken-down, exhausted heap of culinary competition coordinator, Danny thought, watching the way she could only keep herself perfectly upright for a few seconds before wilting like butter lettuce left out overnight.

Come to think of it, that dress she was wearing was sort of greenish, and wrapped around her body with a lettuce-like ruffle down the V-shaped neckline in front, where it tied at her waist.

Danny stared at the bow. Was this seriously one of those dresses where all he'd have to do would be to pull that string, right there, and the whole thing would fall apart, leaving her naked?

"I don't think so," she said, dragging his attention back to her strained expression. "But thanks. If I have another drink, I'm going to keel over right here and fall off this stool. And I don't have time to go to the emergency room for a broken ankle."

"What if I promise to catch you?" Danny squeezed his eyes shut. "Sorry. Forget I said that. I just . . . wanted to see how you're doing. You look tired."

Eva pouted at him, which was at least as unfair as Danny flirting about catching her. *Touché, Ms. Jansen.*

"Never tell a woman she looks tired," she advised. "We cracked your super secret code a long time ago; we know you mean we look old."

"No, that's not what I mean." Danny slid onto the stool next to her, careful to keep his legs and arms from brushing against hers. He wasn't sure what would happen if they touched, but he was pretty sure it could get them thrown out of this bar and arrested for public indecency. "I'm worried about you. You've been going nonstop since that camera crew got here."

"There's a lot to do." Her eyes went unfocused as if she'd zoomed in on some long, scary to-do list in her head. She sighed. "In fact, I should probably get back to it, now that Cheney's all squared away."

"What about Cheney?" Danny asked quickly, mostly to keep her sitting still for another few minutes. She needed the break, he told himself. It had nothing to do with the electric charge he got out of being this close to her.

Satisfaction crept into her tone. "He's finally convinced he did the right thing, sending for more cameras. We're going to turn this competition into the next big Cooking Channel sensation!" She waved the documents in her hand like a celebratory flag.

"Yeah," Danny said. "I've noticed that the camera

crew seems to have expanded. I thought Cheney was balking on that, though. How did you get him to agree that the RSC should be filmed?"

He was just making conversation, trying to spin out the moments when he got to stand close to her and breathe in the light, floral scent of her perfume, but Eva went weirdly shifty and evasive, her eyes darting away from his while she tapped out a rapid-fire rhythm on the bar with the edge of the stacked legal-size papers.

"I just finally figured out what he was looking for, and how to give it to him. Everybody wins."

Danny couldn't help his grimace. "Yeah. Sure."

Her eyes shifted back to him. "You don't like the idea of being on TV? Most chefs would flip at the chance."

Danny shrugged and knocked back the rest of his bottle, the beer hoppy and bitter as it went down. "It's never been a priority for me. Honestly, I think most of those TV chefs are total sell-outs, corporate shills who've lost everything that's great about being a chef."

"But . . ." Eva really seemed to be struggling with that idea. "But you're in this competition for the exposure for your restaurant! What could be better exposure than appearing on TV? I thought you'd be thrilled about this."

"Who, me? I mean, yeah, the publicity will be awesome. Remind people of what Lunden's Tavern used to be, back in the day, and make it clear we're still there, still in it. Still putting out great food. Just . . . if it were me, you know. Just me. I'd never agree to be filmed."

"Well, luckily for me, you signed a contract when you entered the competition that gives me the right to film whatever I damn well please, for the length of your stay as an RSC competitor." Eva pushed away from the bar and grabbed her briefcase, movements stiff and jerky.

Danny wasn't sure what was going on here, but he didn't want her stalking out, completely pissed at him.

"Eva, wait. Whatever I said, I'm sorry."

Breath coming in harsh little puffs that lifted her rib cage and strained the precarious strings tying her dress together, Eva made a visible attempt to control herself. "It's fine. You're entitled to your opinion." Forcing out a laugh, she slung her purse onto her shoulder. "And it's not like you're the first person to have that opinion. I've heard it all before. TV is evil, it pollutes the culinary arts, la la la."

Now Danny was the one getting pissed. "Oh come on. You're mad that I don't agree with you about the Cooking Channel being the saving grace of this competition?"

"No," she said, slowing her breathing. "I'm not mad."

Except she so clearly was.

Eva's eyes were shadowed in the dim flickering of The Blind Tiger's Prohibition-era lighting. She turned to leave, and Danny's instinctive move to follow her and finish this was stopped in its tracks by the parting shot Eva tossed over her shoulder.

"I'm not mad—but maybe I'm disappointed. I don't expect everyone to agree with me. But I guess I would've hoped that you, of all people, would give me the benefit of the doubt. That you'd believe I'm trying my hardest to do the best I know how, for the good of the competition."

"Eva—"

She paused by the door, her face turned away so all he could see was the pure, pale curve of her jaw. "It's not your fault. It's mine. I should never have expected anything from you. I broke my own rules, and now I'm paying the price."

Chapter 25

Who the fuck does he think he is? Eva fumed, the anger simmering under her skin keeping her warm on the two-block hike over to the Five Points intersection, where she'd said she'd meet Claire.

She stuffed the revised Cooking Channel contracts into her briefcase haphazardly, hands shaking, lost in her furious contemplation of Danny's ungrateful, shortsighted, old-fashioned, hidebound idiocy.

In fact, she was concentrating so hard on suppressing the voice whispering that Danny had only echoed exactly what she herself had always believed, that when a hand landed on her shoulder, she shrieked and nearly pepper-sprayed her poor assistant, Drew.

"It's only me," he cried, hopping back a step, hands raised as if she'd pulled a gun on him. "Can I catch a ride back to the hotel?"

As the sharp shock of fear at being touched on the street, at night, without warning drained from her system, so did the jolt of energy she'd gotten from sparring with Danny. Suddenly remembering that she hadn't had more than four hours of sleep a night for the last week made Eva's bones hurt.

"Sure, hop in," she said, waving a hand at the black chauffeured car waiting patiently at the curb. "As long as you don't mind sharing with Claire and me."

Drew had a long-standing, somewhat debilitating fear of Claire Durand, so Eva felt she ought to warn him. "You might have to make conversation with Claire, since there's a good chance I'll fall asleep as soon as my head hits the leather headrest."

Drew blanched, his white cheeks going even paler until he looked like a ghost by the light of the streetlamp. "Oh, uh, in that case. Can I just talk to you for a quick sec?"

Trying not to sigh audibly, Eva pulled the flaps of her cashmere coat closer to her chin and buttoned the top button.

"Shoot," she said.

"It's just . . . my assignment. With the chefs? I'm not feeling too great about it."

A headache threatened with a lance of pain behind Eva's right eye. "No?"

He shook his head, the porcupine quills of his coal-black hair quivering into spikes. "Winslow Jones and I . . . he's my friend. Maybe more than a friend, and I don't like using him for inside information."

"It's only gossip," Eva pointed out. "Stuff he'd be telling you anyway, probably. And you pass it on to me, same as always. I don't see how this is different from the way we've done things in the past. You keep your ear to the ground; it's part of what I pay you for."

He screwed up his face. "Yeah, for who's leaving what restaurant, and who's looking for a new sous chef, and who's had a fight with their backer. This stuff you want to

know now . . . it's more personal. It feels like I'm breaking a confidence, and I don't like it."

"It's just for a little longer," Eva said, trying not to plead,
but God, the timing could not be worse, here. "I talked to
Cheney tonight, and I promised we'd have something for
him soon. We're so close to getting the television side of
things going—I just need a few more stories to pitch to
him, angles to work with the chefs as they're filming. And
once they get going, it's out of our hands. Whatever the
cameras catch, they catch."

"I know, but . . ." Drew fidgeted with the fringe on his
purple wool scarf, looking unsure.

"I'm not asking you to fabricate anything, Andrew,"
she said. Time for a little tough love. "Just give me a few
more details, things for Cheney to watch out for, and we'll
let the chefs and their inherent ability to create drama take
care of the rest."

"Okay, fine," Drew said, his cheeks red with wind-
burn, or cold. Or maybe frustration. "Tell Cheney that the
East Coast Team pushed Beck to open up about what the
deal is between him and Skye Gladwell, and it turns out
they knew each other. A long time ago, like, ten years
ago, in San Francisco. Win thinks they had a relationship,
but it ended because . . ." He paused uncertainly.

"Oh my God, what?" Eva cried.

"I don't know. Win isn't sure . . ."

"Drew . . ."

"Okay! He doesn't know, but he thinks Beck spent
some time in prison. And maybe that's why Skye dumped
him. There. Happy now? I feel like such a turd."

A shiver ran down Eva's spine, chills prickling her legs
and arms. She'd known it had to be something like this.
"You're not a turd," she said. "That's not, like, some deep,

dark shocker like a secret baby or an evil twin or something. Prison time is a matter of public record."

His face lightened. "So . . . there's other ways you could've found out about it," Drew said. "Not necessarily because I squealed like a rat."

"Exactly. Do some more digging, would you? The more details, the better."

A knocking sound from inside the car made Eva glance at the darkened windows, where a barely visible hand rapped against the glass.

"Good work," Eva said, putting her hand on the car door handle. "This is exactly what Cheney was looking for. You really came through for me, and I won't forget it. Now go back to the hotel and get some sleep. You sure you don't want a ride?"

With a nervous look at the car, Drew backed away, blowing into his cupped, mittened hands. "No, no, that's okay. I'm feeling better about stuff now. Thanks for listening. I'm going to head back to the Tiger, see if Win . . . if the others are still hanging out."

Eva said good night and ducked into the warmth of the car, pushing Claire along the wide backseat.

"What was that about?" Claire asked, irritable.

"Sorry to keep you waiting, but I had an employee with an inconvenient attack of conscience. Don't worry, I squashed it." And she refused to feel bad about that.

Claire raised her eyebrows in that expressive way that had always gotten Eva to confess to whatever youthful mischief she'd gotten up to in the hopes of attracting her father's attention. "I see. Sounds serious."

"Not as serious as my need to get back to the hotel sometime this century. Hey, driver?" Eva leaned forward and tapped on the privacy divider. "Know any shortcuts back to the Gold Coast Arms? There's a crisp fifty in it for you if you get us there in less than half an hour."

She still had about fifty emails to answer that were too involved to get into on her iPhone, and she had to make sure everything was set up for the challenge the next morning—those cars had to be on standby in front of the hotel by six o'clock, or they'd be behind all day, and the schedule was so tight . . .

The car peeled away from the curb so fast, Eva careened into Claire, who righted her with a firm, "Put on your seat belt."

"Yes, Mom," Eva mocked, fumbling for the shoulder harness, but beside her, Claire's graceful limbs went into a stiff, ungainly freeze.

"What?" Eva said, mystified. "What did I say?"

"Mom," Claire replied faintly. "You never . . . I haven't heard that from you before."

"It was only a joke. Ignore me, I'm babbling with exhaustion."

Claire shot her a quick, unreadable glance. "I know. I offered to pick you up so that we would have time to talk, but perhaps it must wait until later."

Intrigued, Eva unbuttoned her coat and got herself situated.

"Talk about what?"

"Have you spent much time with your father since he arrived?" Claire asked.

Not sure if this was a change of subject or the subject, Eva replied warily, "Noooo . . . I've been a little busy running his competition for him. What, has he been complaining that I'm ignoring him? Because the phone works at both ends, you know."

"That is not . . . no. *Merde,* this is difficult. I do not even know how to begin to explain." Angling herself to face Eva, Claire pushed both hands through her wavy, auburn hair, pulling it back from her face and exposing the lovely, strong lines of her bone structure.

"Eva. We have known each other a long time. I watched you grow up."

It had to be exhaustion that was keeping her emotions so ridiculously close to the surface. Swallowing around the hard knot in her throat, Eva said, "You helped me grow up."

Claire's face softened, the lines of tension melting from the corners of her eyes. "That is lovely to hear. You have always been very important to me, in my life. Much more important than I would have supposed, the first time I met you!"

"God, I was such a brat," Eva exclaimed.

"You were a motherless child," Claire corrected. "And in many ways, fatherless, too. You needed guidance and attention—copious amounts of both."

"So, nothing's changed in the last fifteen years!" Eva said brightly. "And even though I've figured out other ways to get the attention I want . . ."

Claire snorted, but Eva ignored it, a growing fear weighing down her words so that they dropped into the silence of the car like rocks into deep water. God, was Claire about to tell her she had cancer or something? "I still need you. You're not . . . going anywhere, are you?"

The confused scrunch of Claire's brows eased the compression in Eva's chest immediately. "Where would I go? No. Listen to me, Eva. It's about your father."

Her accent got thicker, the way it always did when she was upset, and Eva's rib cage squeezed in again. "He has asked to see me again. To give him another chance."

Eva blinked. "Wait. What?"

A spasm of impatience crossed Claire's face. "Your

father is interested in me. Romantically. And I would like to know what you think of that."

Bewilderment spun Eva around so she felt dizzy. "I guess . . . fine? I mean, no. Hold on. This is my dad we're talking about. I love him, but that doesn't mean I couldn't see how bad he was for you, before. Even as a kid . . . when you broke it off with him, I knew why. I didn't blame you, even though I wanted you to stay with us so badly."

Claire reached out and clutched Eva's hand, twining their fingers together. Eva pressed hard enough that it hurt where their knuckles rubbed together, but she didn't want to let go.

"So you think it's a terrible idea?" Claire inquired delicately.

"No, it's just . . . a surprise. And I'm not sure why you're talking to me about it—what did you tell my dad? And Claire, what about Kane? I thought you two were working things out."

Withdrawing her hand, Claire retreated into herself. "I told your father I needed time to think, and to talk to you—that as of now, your friendship means more to me than any fond memories or potential future with Theo. He accepted that. And as for Kane . . ."

She shook her head, staring out the dark window of the speeding car, the lights of Chicago a blur beyond the smoky glass. "He's so young. Whatever he thinks he feels for me now . . . it won't last. It can't."

"Kane's my age," Eva pointed out. "If I found love tomorrow, would you tell me not to bother with the relationship, because I'm too young to know what I want?"

She waited, breath caught in her throat, for Claire's answer. It was silly, how much she cared—there wasn't a relationship for her to defend, because there couldn't be right now, and because once Danny found out what she'd done, the way she'd sold her soul to keep the Cooking Channel interested . . .

Stop it! This is pointless. You're doing what you have to do, end of story.

But she still held her breath until Claire said, slowly and with obvious reluctance, "It would depend. Is this love you have found with someone utterly unsuitable, extremely different from you, and potentially bad for your career?"

Eva's breath left her on a frustrated laugh. "Actually, yeah."

"Then my advice to you would be the same as to myself. Think with your head, not your heart." Claire arched a sardonic brow. "Or other organs. Love is all very well, but I've worked too hard to get where I am now to compromise myself for a fleeting hormonal fantasy. And I've watched you work equally as hard, to win your father's approval and his confidence in you. You're a heartbeat away from achieving your goal."

"I know," Eva said, feeling numb weariness creep over her once more. Scooting around on the bench seat, she leaned her weight into Claire's slim, bony, yet somehow comforting form and let her head drop to Claire's shoulder.

"Maybe I really haven't grown up much since you first met me," Eva said drowsily, her eyes drooping. She yawned so hard, something in her jaw popped.

"Hmm?" Claire's arm came up to steady Eva against her side.

"It's just . . . I know you're right. I get it, about sacrificing and making choices and having priorities. But part of me still clings to the idea that I can have it all."

She felt Claire go motionless against her, but before Eva could rouse herself to see what was the matter, Claire had relaxed again. "I want that for you, *chérie*," she said, a note of wonder in her voice. "And I want it for myself."

The last thing Eva was aware of before she dropped into a deep, dreamless catnap was the hard line of Danny Lunden's jaw, the unexpected lushness of his mouth, and the snap of fire in his blue-gray eyes whenever he looked at her.

She was Eva Jansen, damn it. If anyone could figure out how to have it all, she could.

The ring of his phone jarred Kane out of a two-hour self-imposed isolation session with his guitar. He'd been stuck for the last few days, but tonight he'd felt the stirring of music in his brain, a few snatches of melody and one kicky little phrase his fingers itched to play with, so he'd refused all offers to go out and hunkered down in his hotel suite, with the DO NOT DISTURB sign on the door and his cell phone set to block calls.

Except for his mama, and Claire Durand.

Laying Betsy carefully on the bed, Kane fumbled across his nightstand for the vibrating phone and snuck a look at the screen before answering.

With a grin wide enough to hurt his cheeks, he said, "Did you miss me?"

He had to strain to hear her reply. "Kane. We need to talk."

His heart sank. "Uh-oh. Talking's not our best event. And why are you being so quiet?"

"I don't want to wake Eva," Claire said. "She is finally snatching a few well-deserved, much-needed moments of rest. But we are almost back to the hotel, where I'm sure she'll immediately dive back into work."

"She's a powerhouse," Kane agreed. He knew Claire had been worried about Eva; he'd had a few uneasy moment, himself, wondering if maybe he should say something to get her to slow down before she burned out. "Want me to come up to your suite?"

"No," Claire said, a little too quickly. Kane frowned as she continued, "If Eva works tonight, so do I. But I am not as young and spry as she, so I will need a serious injection of caffeine. Meet me at Blue Smoke?"

Ah yes. Time for their traditional coffee shop heart-to-heart. It simultaneously warmed Kane's heart and freaked him right the fuck out that this non-relationship already had traditions.

He'd never been comfortable with predictability before.

Chapter 26

Of course, Claire wasn't exactly predictable.

Kane arrived at the twenty-four-hour coffee shop expecting to have to argue, yet again, for the merits of their non-relationship thing—this time, in front of the off-duty cops and college kids pulling all-nighters who were the only other customers at Blue Smoke around midnight on a Tuesday.

Claire was already there, seated at the same table where he'd first found her—God, was it only two weeks ago? It seemed longer. Sleepless nights full of hot monkey sex would do that to a guy—with her hands wrapped around a mug of the same order of café au lait, heavy on the foamed milk.

But the look on her face when he slid into the booth across from her. Kane paused and widened his eyes, needing to absorb every detail, make a mental snapshot to take out later for inspiration. Her hair tumbled over her shoulders, soft and sensual. He wanted to run his fingers through it, feel again how slippery and silky it was, smell its clean rosemary and mint fragrance. She was wearing that sweater he liked, the one that looked fuzzy and warm, with the deep chocolate color that made her eyes glow and her skin take on a golden hue.

Claire was beautiful—but then, she was always beautiful. Something was different tonight.

"You wanted to see me?" Kane didn't bother to hide the thickness of his voice, the desire pulsing through his body. She deserved to know how much he wanted her.

"To talk to you," she said, the slight flush that rose to her cheeks telling him she knew what he was thinking.

Kane grinned, feeling the fighting spirit spark in his blood. "Okay, so talk. What is it this time? I'm too young? You're too world-weary and wise? That old guy, Theo Jansen, put the moves on you? What?"

Her hands jerked, sloshing hot coffee over the sides of her mug. "*Merde!* Oh, what a mess." Pinned to the booth by the weight of his own assumptions, Kane couldn't even muster the brain cells to grab a paper napkin and help her mop up.

"Wait. Jansen put the moves on you?"

"Theo Jansen expressed his desire to renew our romantic relationship, yes." She had her head down, eyes on the pile of napkins slowly staining brown in blotches, so he couldn't read her expression. He didn't need to.

Kane hunched forward in an instinctive defensive move, but it was too late. His soft underbelly was already exposed, just waiting for the knife. "Wow. I guess I should congratulate you on finally finding the perfect excuse to ditch me."

Her head came up, something flashing through her eyes too quickly for him to understand it. Not that he could see much through the haze of disappointment clutching at his chest and making it hard to breathe.

Suck it up, Slater, he told himself. *This is no worse than the time you got clocked in the head by an empty beer bottle at that crazy outdoor music festival, and passed out, and had to finish your set with a concussion.*

It felt similar, though, as he pushed blindly out of the booth and went to stand up. Kind of wobbly and sick-making.

Until he felt the warm clasp of Claire's slender fingers around his wrist.

He stared down at their hands for a long moment before looking back at her.

There was that expression again, that face he couldn't read, and all he could do was try not to whimper. "What now? Want to get in a few parting shots about how I'm too young to know my own mind, and I'll get over it, and it's for the best?"

"No," she said. "Because I don't want you to get over it. I want to believe that you know your own mind, and that what's best for both of us is to stop fighting this . . . whatever it is we have between us. And see where it leads."

All of a sudden, that look on her face made more sense. It was the same look he saw in the mirror every morning since he'd met her three months ago in New York.

It was hope.

And fear, too, with a little bit of impatience thrown in, because it was Claire, but still. Mostly hope.

Kane's chest burned and he felt as wired as if he'd inhaled two double espressos in a row. He sat back down, but Claire didn't let go of his wrist.

"You mean it?" Kane was wincing before the words were out of his mouth. How much more of a dipshit could he be?

But Claire's voice was soft when she said, "I do. A very dear friend reminded me of a promise I once made myself not to settle for anything less than everything I want and deserve in life."

Choking on emotion, Kane forced a laugh. "What kind of naughty shit did you do in your last life to deserve me in this one?"

Throwing her head back, Claire laughed, that wide-mouthed, open laugh that Kane loved being the cause of. In this case, he could tell it was least partly relief, the tension and fear of the last few moments leaping out of her.

Helplessly, he grinned back. He wanted to point out that her fear was totally wasted. He'd been hers for a long time, maybe even since before they met. But he didn't want to rock the precarious balance they'd managed to finally, finally reach, so he kept his mouth shut and started writing lyrics in his head while the whole world turned to music around him.

Danny couldn't sleep.

It wasn't that he wasn't tired—the constant state of excitement and nervous anticipation at being out of his normal routine took its toll. He'd been sleeping more deeply, more soundly, for longer hours since he got to Chicago than he had since he was a teenager.

Even now, sleep tugged at his limbs, weighting them down to the sheets as he tossed and turned, but his mind would not get with the program.

Pulling his pillow over his face, Danny groaned in frustration. It wasn't any louder than the protesting squeak and creak of the pull-out cot's springs every time he moved, but it still seemed to disturb Winslow.

Lowering the pillow, Danny squinted through the darkness of the hotel room over to Win's bed. There was some snuffling followed by a sigh as Winslow flopped over onto his stomach and went back to sleep.

Lucky son of a bitch.

All Danny could seem to do was lie awake on his thin

mattress, all lumpy where the coils of the hideaway poked up, and stew about Eva Jansen.

He still wasn't a hundred percent on what part of their conversation had pushed her buttons, but one thing Danny knew for sure—being compared to all the men in Eva's past who'd disappointed her? Not one of his favorite things.

It wasn't fair, though, that she got to ding him for disagreeing with her, then never offer any sort of counterargument, herself. He still thought he was right, damn it! The same thing happened with televised cooking as when they started broadcasting football games, timing them for commercials and yukking it up with the sponsors—all the heart and soul and immediacy was lost.

When TV got involved, chefs started caring more about their ratings than their food, and that sucked.

The words trembled on his tongue, practically burning his mouth with the need to get out there and be in Eva's face, proving her wrong. He wished he'd had the chance to say all that to her, and hear her sputter and try to come up with some reasonably non-horseshit response.

Danny glanced at the green numbers glowing from the alarm clock on the nightstand between Win and Beck's beds.

Three in the morning.

Everyone involved in the competition was probably fast asleep. Which was exactly what Danny should be, except for this loop of an argument running through his stupid chatterbox of a brain.

Fifteen minutes later, he was stalking through the empty lobby of the Gold Coast Hotel in sweats and a threadbare T-shirt with the cracked, faded appliqué face of the Swedish Chef from the Muppets grinning from his chest.

"Excuse me?" Danny hesitated only for a second before tapping the silver bell at the reception desk.

A young girl with horn-rimmed glasses, dressed in Gold Coast livery, popped her head out of the room behind the desk. "Sorry, sir! Just taking care of some filing. What can I do for you?"

She yawned halfway through and Danny held back a smile. He had a feeling that *filing* was synonymous with *sleeping* here on the graveyard shift.

"It's no problem," he assured her. "I'm just hoping you can help me find someone."

Her face went wary. "If you have the guest's room number, I can put a call through for you, sir."

"That's okay, I've already checked her room. No answer."

"Perhaps the guest is asleep."

Leaning on the desk, Danny pretended he didn't hear the broad hint in the little receptionist's tone. "I don't think so. See, this particular guest is in charge of the Rising Star Chef competition, and I'll just bet she's around here somewhere, still working."

Eyes dropping down to the cartoon emblazoned on Danny's shirt, the receptionist said, "Oh! You're one of the chefs. Are you looking for Ms. Jansen? She told me to always come get her if any of the RSC contestants needed something."

Danny smiled at her. "Perfect! Do you know where she is?"

The receptionist, whose name tag read CINDY, looked torn. "I'm not supposed to leave the desk. I guess . . . you probably know where the kitchen is, don't you?"

The kitchen. Of course.

Giving Cindy another reassuring smile, he said, "Don't worry about it. I'm just going to go check on her, see if she needs any help with anything. I can find my own way downstairs."

He got a grateful smile and a little wave to send him on his way to the elevators. Cindy seemed like a good kid—he wondered if it was common practice for hotels to schedule young women to work the night desk alone. It didn't seem safe. Maybe he should talk to someone about it.

Contemplating whether Eva, with her VIP connections, might know the right person took Danny out of the elevator and into the competition kitchen, which was lit up as brightly as if it were a television soundstage.

He glanced toward the front of the room, and indeed, there were already four or five cameras bristling from that corner, lenses down and black, like sleeping snakes waiting to strike.

Shaking his head, feeling the annoyance and righteous indignation that had kept him awake for hours come rushing back, Danny put his hands on his hips and surveyed the kitchen.

It was completely empty.

An extra table had been set up at the front of the room, and was covered in a white cloth. It had to have something to do with the next challenge, and Danny resisted the urge to peek.

Deliberately averting his gaze, he wandered farther into the kitchen, poking his head into the walk-in cooler— they had fail-safe latches so no one could be locked inside by accident, but you know, just in case—and called out, "Hello? Eva?"

Maybe she'd gone to bed after all; maybe she was asleep in her room like a normal person. Or maybe she'd been awake in her suite, but had spied him through the peephole and decided not to open the door. Maybe—

A rustling noise drew Danny's footsteps around the corner toward the dry-goods pantry. He pushed the door ajar with the side of his palm and peered inside, his heart going soft and sticky like brioche dough at what he saw.

He'd found Eva. She was asleep—her delectable little bottom propped on an overturned plastic tub, the top half of her body reclining awkwardly against the tall tiered wire racks holding containers of sugar, salt, and different types of flour. A clipboard was wedged into her lap, but her pen had fallen to the floor.

She was paler than the box of sugar behind her head, and there were purple bruise-like shadows under her eyes, stark and dramatic against her white skin.

Danny hesitated. Should he let her sleep? If he woke her now, she'd probably just try to go back to work, and she clearly needed her rest.

But that couldn't be comfortable, that position she'd gotten herself into. She wouldn't be able to sleep long, curled up like that, anyway. And when she woke, she'd have a monster crick in her neck.

Decision made, Danny stepped into the pantry and crouched down beside her.

Chapter 27

"Eva?" He kept his voice soft, hoping not to startle her too badly, but she jarred awake as if he'd pinched her.

"What?" She blinked slowly, squinting against the light and smacking her lips in an innocently bewildered way that made Danny wonder what she'd been like as a little girl.

"You fell asleep in the kitchen," he told her, glancing down at the clipboard still clutched in one of her hands. "Doing inventory? Geez, Eva. Don't you have people to do that for you?"

What was the point of being rich and powerful if you still did the shit work yourself?

Shaking her head as if to clear the sleep from her brain, she said, "I do. But I made a last-minute change to the challenge, and I'd already sent everyone else to bed. Just had to check a few things." Frowning down at herself and smoothing a palm over her wrinkled skirt, crumpled from the way she'd been sitting, she said, "I only sat for down for a second. I can't believe I fell asleep."

Danny manfully held back a really rude noise, the kind that would've earned him a smack to the back of the head from his mom. "Eva. Come on, you've been running on fumes for the last three days. You need to sleep."

Scrunching up her face in denial, she said, "I need to finish this! The next challenge is, what?" She checked her watch and moaned. "God. Four hours away."

"And everything's ready," Danny said. "I saw the table out front. Your plans are made, your pieces are in place. Whatever this checklist is, just let it go."

"So if there's not enough Maldon Sea Salt for everyone tomorrow, I'll just shrug and say, Oh well, sucks to be you, but I needed a nap? No."

"Any chef who can't figure out a substitute for sea salt deserves whatever he gets," Danny said firmly. "Part of the competition is about thinking on your feet, right?"

"Right," Eva said, drawing the word out unhappily. "I am pretty tired, and it's kind of ridiculously late. Which . . . hey, what are you doing down here? You should be getting a good night's rest before the next challenge! It's a big one, you know. The one that'll decide which three teams make it to the final round in San Francisco."

"I came down here to pick a fight with you, actually," Danny said, laughing. Whatever lingering resentment and anger had been boiling under his skin evaporated the minute he saw her. "Or, more accurately, to pick up where we left off."

"The television thing again? I guess you saw the cameras out there." She looked momentarily guilty, her eyes shifting away from his face.

"Yep. All set up and ready to capture every nuance of our facial expressions while we cook."

Relatively mild mockery, Danny thought—hardly the scathing commentary he'd mapped out in his head while tossing around on that torture device also known as a pull-out bed, but Eva's expression tightened into one of defiance.

"That's not what it's about. And if you weren't so ludicrously old-fashioned and conservative and ignorant, like you think the camera's going to steal your soul or something, you'd be able to see that."

Danny stood up and held out a hand to help her to her feet. "You mock, but that's pretty much exactly what I think. Having those cameras in the room, it changes things. It changes the focus from the food to the chefs."

"But that's what I want!" Eva batted his hand away and wobbled to her feet on her own. "This whole competition is about highlighting young, up and coming chefs and their talent. Bringing them recognition and increasing the public's respect for the culinary arts. How can I do that if no one even knows about the competition except for people who are already entrenched in the restaurant world?"

That . . . actually made sense.

"Okay, but it's going to be on the Cooking Channel. The people who watch that, aren't they already riding the chefs-are-awesome train?"

"Some of them," Eva conceded, bending to grab her fancy fountain pen off the floor. "But a lot are just people who happen to enjoy food as entertainment."

"Foodies," Danny said, unable to keep the disgust out of his voice. "Food should not be a spectator sport."

"Why not?" Eva argued, color flooding into her cheeks and replacing the worrisome pallor of a few minutes before. "Not everyone can be a great cook, Danny. But everyone likes to eat."

"First of all, that's bull. If you can read a recipe, you can cook. Second of all, stop fighting with me!"

"You came down here to fight with me! I'm just giving you what you want."

He looked at her, flushed and panting, gray eyes bright as stars with the fervor of what she was saying.

"A fight is not what I want from you," he said. He barely recognized his own voice, pitched so low, but he couldn't do a damn thing about it.

She swayed on her feet, maybe partly from exhaustion, but at least half of it was the same desire to get closer that Danny felt. This wasn't fair. Their resistance was down, it was the middle of the night, they were both working with no sleep and days of frustrated, unsatisfied desire. If something happened between them right now . . . would it even count?

Yeah. It would.

Cursing everyone from his parents for instilling such an inflexible moral code to himself for being unable to just stay the hell away from Eva Jansen, Danny turned and marched out of the pantry.

Leaving her there was the hardest thing he'd ever done.

But when she followed him out of the pantry a few seconds later, the magnetic connection had been broken, at least for the moment, and Danny could breathe again without searching every inhalation for a trace of her scent.

"So, you want the foodies of the world to know about the RSC. I get it. I mean, I don't get it, get it, but . . ."

"No, you don't." The slow, halting weariness of her words made Danny pause. "Foodies aren't the only people who watch the Cooking Channel. Big sponsors watch it, too, and they pay attention to what viewers like. Major appliance companies, brand-name makers of pots and pans, even travel-related companies like airlines and hotel chains—they all have money to spend on sponsorships, hoping to link their brand to whatever's the coolest, most popular thing."

"It's all about money?" Danny sneered. "That hardly makes me more excited about it."

"That's because you work for your family in a business

passed down through generations, with a huge support system already in place," Eva replied, passion still heating her cheeks. "There are restaurants out there where chefs are doing amazing work, experimenting and playing and creating new techniques—but their places are small, just starting out, and the chefs don't have the money to close down for the duration of the RSC. Do you know how much talent we lose out on, simply because the chefs can't afford to even throw their hat in the ring?"

"I never thought of it that way."

"Why should you? It's not your job to see the big picture. It's mine. The bigger and better-funded the competition is, the more chefs we can help to try out. The RSC shouldn't be a contest between the top fifteen percent of restaurants, the solvent ones that have large enough staffs to cover the absence of their competing chefs. It should be for everyone."

Danny breathed quietly and felt the entire world rearrange itself around him. Everything looked different, from the cameras to the cloth-covered table, to Eva standing straight and tall in front of him. Even wobbly and tired, she took his breath away.

And it wasn't just her exotically tilted gray eyes or the pert Cupid's bow of her pink lips or the diabolically distracting curves of her lithe, slender body.

It was her unexpectedly generous heart that took him by surprise and left him speechless with an emotion he couldn't put a name to if he tried.

Eva shifted her weight from one aching foot to the other. "What?" she demanded.

He just stood there, staring at her.

"You're a really nice person," he said, as if it were some major revelation.

Annoyed, Eva tucked her hair behind her ear and went to gather her things up from the table she'd dumped them on when she got back from The Blind Tiger. "Don't get carried away. It's good business to include as many talented chefs as possible."

His face got all knowing and smug. "Sure it is. And I guess it's also good business to run yourself into the ground trying to do six different jobs, instead of letting anyone help you."

Eva ground her molars together to keep from spitting out something about not needing any help, like a hysterical toddler.

My do it, my do it! two-year-old Eva used to scream, according to her father, whenever anyone tried to tie her shoes for her.

Hopefully she'd grown up a little since then. "I have plenty of help," she said carefully. "But this competition is a large, unwieldy event with a lot of moving pieces and parts."

"So delegate some to that assistant of yours."

"Drew has his own tasks," she managed to say without blurting out that one of them was keeping tabs on the gossip about the chef contestants.

"Eva." Danny sighed, running a hand over his stubbled jaw and back around to the nape of his neck. Eva tried not to imagine the way the short, silky hairs there prickled against his fingertips, tried not to wish her hand were there in its place, running through his hair and kneading the tension from his neck.

"I can't believe you came down here," she said, "all righteously indignant and ready to read me the riot act about food TV, and then when I manage to finally explain my position on that, you start picking another fight about my work habits! What is it with you? We can't be together, so you're going to nag me to death in revenge?"

"I am not nagging," Danny protested, looking honestly insulted. "And you might have a point about the TV thing, but I've got a point about you working too hard. At least admit that."

Eva hid a smile. It was way too fun to ruffle his feathers. She held up her thumb and forefinger, pinched together about an inch apart. "Maybe a small point. But Danny, seriously. There's nothing else I can do."

"There has to be someone . . ."

Eva slung her purse strap over her shoulder and worked to keep the green envy out of her voice. "I know you've got people you can lean on, and your team has you. It's not like that for me, Danny. There's no one."

"That sucks," he said baldly.

"I guess. But that's the life I chose. I'm not afraid of hard work, and I have goals." She shrugged, the motion setting off a riot of pain in her tired, overworked muscles. Danny's sharp inhalation said he'd caught her involuntary flinch. She closed her eyes against the anger darkening his face.

"There's a difference between hard work and work that's slowly killing you," he said intensely, his voice suddenly coming from right beside her. He put his hands on her shoulders and hissed as his strong fingers probed the tight knots there.

Eva whimpered, nearly staggering under the pressure of his hands as he kneaded her muscles like bread dough. "It's only for a few more weeks," she gasped. "I can make it."

"Not without help," Danny said, his breath so warm and soft against her hair. His hands burned through the thin, clingy material of her dress, the heat sinking into her muscles and relaxing her better than a bubble bath and a glass of wine.

Almost moaning, Eva tipped her head forward to rest against his broad chest, just for a moment. Her eyes drifted shut. "No help," she slurred, her mind spinning back to that conversation with Claire. Choices. What she deserved. "I want to do it all, so I can have it all."

"Okay. You're not making a lot of sense. I think it's time for bed."

Eva snuggled in closer, wrapping one arm around his hard, lean waist. "Mmmm, yeah. Take me to bed."

Danny's laugh sounded painful, his chest vibrating against her. "God. You're not making it easy to be good, you know that?"

"But you will be, anyway," she muttered, half disappointed and half pleased. There was something solid and steadying about the fact that she knew him so well. Trusted him not to take advantage of this moment of weakness.

"Yeah," he grunted unhappily. "I guess I will. Come on, sweetcakes, let's get you upstairs."

As Danny hooked an arm around her shoulder and half led, half carried her up to the penthouse, Eva tucked her face against his warm neck and breathed deeply, happier than she'd been in days.

Everything was working out. She was so close, mere inches away from everything she'd ever wanted—and with Danny's arms around her, she had to wonder.

Would any of it matter, if she didn't have him?

Before she could reconsider, before her nerves could flutter to life and choke her into silence, Eva blurted, "After the competition. Once the RSC is all over, can we . . . ?"

He paused, glancing down at her with obvious shock.

Plucking up her courage, Eva firmed her mouth and lifted her chin. "I want to find out where this can go."

A slow smile spread across his face, lighting those eyes up like fireworks. "Yeah? So do I."

And that was it. He held her close, kept her safe at his side all the way up to her suite, and Eva felt as if she were floating through the hotel.

It wasn't much of a commitment, she knew—it was vague, unspecified, leaving plenty of wiggle room. But it was more of a commitment than she'd ever managed to offer anyone before, and the fact that Danny seemed to feel the same way?

Well. That was more than the icing on the cake. That was the icing, and the creamy filling, and the cake, and the plate it was sitting on.

It was everything.

Chapter 28

Danny woke up the next morning with the energy of a man who'd slept the sleep of the righteous for a good . . . two, maybe even two and a half hours.

It would've been more, but when he finally fell back into bed, he was hard as a rock from the sleepy sensuality of Eva pressed all along his side, leaning trustingly into him and letting him manhandle her up to her room and under her covers.

Seriously, when they got back to New York, Danny was heading straight for Our Lady and putting in for sainthood.

He still couldn't believe he'd scraped together the inner fortitude to strip Eva out of her executive-sexy garb and tuck her in, then just . . . leave.

Saint fucking Danny, patron of horny, self-denying chefs.

But somehow, as the alarm blared them awake and Winslow grumbled his way to the shower, Danny felt more energized than he had in days. Rested, refreshed, and ready to cook his heart out.

Throwing back the covers, he padded over to the bathroom door, steam already escaping through the crack, and yelled, "Chop chop, Winslow. I've got something I want to do before we meet everyone downstairs for the big reveal."

He just wanted to check in on Eva, make sure she was okay after her late night. Nothing that would get either of them in trouble. But he couldn't stop thinking about how she felt like she had no one to turn to when she needed help. Danny wanted her to know that wasn't true.

She had him.

And part of him wondered if she'd even remember that last bit of the conversation—the part where she'd come right out and told him she wanted to see him when they got back to New York.

She'd been pretty out of it, so he wasn't trying to get his hopes up. But the fact that she'd said it at all, that she'd felt that yearning, even for a brief moment . . . it made Danny twice as eager to see her this morning.

The shower faucet squeaked off. "I'm hurrying as fast as I can. You think this gorgeousness just happens? It takes time to look this good."

Danny sighed. "Fine, but I call second shower."

Appearing in the doorway with a towel wrapped around his skinny hips and another swirled in a turban around his head, Win said, "So what's this errand you want to run? Is it anything like the errand that took you out of our room in the middle of the night last night?"

Crap.

"Sorry I woke you," Danny mumbled, pushing past Winslow and sucking in the misty, moisty air of the bathroom.

"No big." Winslow shrugged, following him in. When Danny paused before dropping his sweats and getting into the shower, Win rolled his eyes and ostentatiously turned his back. "You got nothing I haven't seen before. Up close and very personal. But I promise not to look."

Feeling sheepish, Danny shucked his pants and deliberately didn't rush to get behind the frosted glass of the shower stall. "Sorry."

"You straight boys. So body-shy. Not that you've got anything to be ashamed of. Rowr," Winslow said. He sounded amused, so Danny relaxed and twisted the faucet to hot, luxuriating for a long moment in the scalding fall of water over his bare shoulders. He tried to keep his hands out of the stream; they were mostly healed, but direct heat still stung.

"What can I say? We can't all be as gorgeous as you," he teased.

"Mmm. True. And flattery will so not distract me from my question. What up with you, Daniel? You find yourself a hot mama ladyfriend who somehow needs to be secret from the rest of us?"

Danny barked his elbow on the jutting tile soap dish and swore as tingly pain radiated up his forearm.

"I'll take that as a yes," Win said, his voice sounding weird and distorted until Danny realized he was talking and shaving at the same time. "Okay, keep your secrets. You don't have to spill. Even though I give you all my good gossip. Like, for instance . . . hold up."

There was a pause while Danny squirted shampoo into his hair and worked up a lather. It sounded like the bathroom door opened and closed, then the vent switched on above Danny's head, sucking up steam and laying down a blanket of whirring white noise over the shower.

"I heard," Winslow confided in a stage whisper, "something very interesting about our mysterious Henry Beck."

Danny groaned and rinsed, pushing his face into the

water. "Not another wild theory about Beck being an assassin for the Mossad or something."

"No, this one's legit." Winslow sounded way too excited.

Danny frowned. "Where'd you hear it? And Win, seriously. It's not right to go poking around in Beck's past. If he wants you to know who he is and where he comes from, he'll tell you."

"It wasn't me, I swear. But listen to this, Danny. That Mossad thing wasn't totally wrong—Beck was in the army! Or the navy, actually, but not like a SEAL or an assassin."

Danny blinked water out of his eyes. It made a certain kind of sense. Some of the things Beck had said over the last few months, the things he knew, the way he cooked . . .

"But that's not *even* the juiciest part," Win crowed.

"God. Do I want to hear this?" Danny shut off the water and opened the shower door to grope for a towel.

Thick terry cloth plopped into his hand, and Danny grunted a thank-you, wiping off his face and opening his eyes to see Winslow, now dressed, nearly levitating with suppressed glee.

"You def want to hear this, my man, because it explains soooo much. Like, everything that's gone down since we got here, practically. I mean, we all figured Beck must have known that West Coast chickie, Skye Gladwell, before, right? Clearly. Nobody snaps on a man as hard as he snapped on that Ryan Larousse unless there's something deeply personal going on."

"Okay, true," Danny conceded, briskly rubbing himself dry and making himself a towel kilt before stepping out of the shower stall.

"I thought, hey, he boned her once, maybe. She's cute, if you like that crunchy granola earth mother look, and, you know, boobies."

"Over the line, Chef," Danny warned him, trying not

to grin. "What do you think Beck would do if he heard you talking like that?"

"Beck can't hear me," Winslow said, "or I wouldn't. Because I'd be too scared for my mothereffing *life,* man, because Beck is off the hook when it comes to Skye Gladwell. And you wanna know why?"

"They dated," Danny guessed, heading for the sink and his toothbrush.

Winslow appeared in the mirror behind him, green eyes sparkling with delight. "Way better than that. They were married."

Danny nearly choked on his toothbrush, minty foam clogging his windpipe as he inhaled sharply. His gaze flew to Winslow's reflected grin. "Get out of here. And no comments about my gag reflex, please."

"You're no fun. And oh yeah, baby. Married." Winslow nodded vigorously. "But wanna hear the kicker?"

"Are you really offering me a choice?" Danny asked, spitting toothpaste into the sink, but it was rhetorical at this point. He had to know it all, so he could prepare for whatever fallout might hit the team.

Winslow leaned in, his energetic body almost still, for once. "They split up, but they never got divorced."

Danny turned to face Win, his heart pounding dangerously. This was huge.

"You mean . . ."

"That's right," Winslow said seriously. "Beck and Skye Gladwell are still married."

Holy shit.

Danny's brain didn't want to compute the many ways in which this new information spelled disaster for his crew.

"Are you sure? How do you know?"

"Public record! We found it online. And quit trying to dodge. Now that I've showed you mine," Winslow said, waggling his eyebrows suggestively, "you have to show me yours."

Thoroughly distracted, Danny picked up his razor and stared at it for a moment. Nope. Too dangerous. He'd cut his own throat, the way things were going today. Tossing it back to the counter, he said, "Show you what?"

Win made an impatient noise. "Come on! Spill. Or don't even, just confirm, because I have a theory."

"Of course you do," Danny groaned. "Listen, Win, I don't want to . . ."

"It's Eva Jansen, isn't it!" Winslow pointed triumphantly at the ceiling, like a cartoon detective having an *aha!* moment.

Danny knew he hadn't managed to completely hide his wince when Winslow's blinding white grin spread across his face.

"Okay, yes. I had something going with Eva, before the competition really got started. Nothing serious, and it's over now."

Why did both parts of that final sentence make him feel like a liar?

"I knew it!" Winslow clapped his hands together like a little kid at his first birthday party. The sly, suspicious tilt of his mouth didn't quite fit the image, though. "So if you're not still doing the nasty, why do you have an errand about her this morning?"

"I never said it was about her," Danny pointed out. Crap, what time was it? He needed to get moving.

Pushing out into the chill, dry air of the main hotel room, Danny hurried to his suitcase and rummaged through it for a clean-ish pair of jeans.

Beck was awake, Danny saw, and in the midst of his usual morning routine of push-ups and sit-ups, grunting out a number under his breath after each one.

Danny hesitated after getting his clothes on, eyes on the gleaming expanse of Beck's broad, sweaty back. Should he say something? Like . . . what? There was nothing to say. He still thought it was wrong to nose through someone else's past. Better to wait until Beck decided he needed to unload, someday, or until it turned into a problem.

"It is about her, though, right?" Winslow called from the bathroom. "You owe me, Danny, pay up."

Rushing to stall any further discussion of what Danny owed and why, he said, "Yeah, it's about Eva, okay? I've been worried about her. She's taken on too much with this competition, it's wearing her out."

"So?" Winslow leaned against the bathroom doorjamb, rubbing one palm over his shiny shaved head. "Isn't that her business?"

He gave Win a look that hopefully conveyed his impression of the irony of Winslow Jones not wanting to get all up in someone else's business. Win had the grace to blush, but he stuck his chin out. "I'm serious, man. What are you planning?"

Danny sat on the edge of the bed and stuck his feet into his socks. "I'm just going to make sure she slept, and that she's up in time for the challenge."

"Why?" Beck asked, kneeling up from his floor exercises, chest heaving slightly. With two sets of eyes scrutinizing him, Danny's plan suddenly felt flimsy and potentially stupid. Bending to tie the laces on his black Chuck Taylors, Danny said, "Because. She's . . . I don't know, she's struggling, and I have to help her."

Danny looked up from his shoes in time to catch the worried look Beck and Winslow exchanged.

"You know," Win said, an unfamiliar tentative note in his voice. "Not everybody wants to be helped."

In his deep, slow voice, Beck said, "I have to agree.

Eva Jansen doesn't seem like the kind of person who's looking for a lot of hand-holding and coddling."

"She needs help." Danny stood up and rummaged through his pants from the day before for his wallet and room key. "She doesn't want to admit it, but she's close to burnout."

And Danny needed to see her.

"Maybe, but . . ." Winslow still looked doubtful.

"Guys, lay off," Danny said, with more firm confidence than he actually felt. "It's not like I'm going to go try to get her fired or something, just to give her a break from working. All I want is to check in. Make sure she eats breakfast. That kind of thing. Now, don't be late for the team meet-up downstairs," he reminded them, heading for the door. "You've got forty-five minutes."

Without pausing to listen to any more stupid advice on how he should suddenly stop being himself and taking care of the people he cared about, Danny made his way down to the competition kitchen. He had a hunch Eva would already be up and at 'em.

When he got there, though, there was no sign of her. Instead, Danny found Theo Jansen, and the man was in deep, serious conversation with another guy. Danny cracked the door open and peered through.

It was Kane Slater. What were these two having such a heart-to-heart over? From what he'd seen over the past week since Theo showed up, they not-so-cordially hated each other.

None of your business, Danny, he told himself, shaking his head at the way Winslow's nose for gossip had rubbed off on him.

But just as he moved his hand to let the door swing silently shut, something Theo said rang through his brain like a gong, stopping him cold.

"It's for the best." Theo's voice rumbled, smooth and subtly persuasive. "For everyone, including Eva. I know she's your friend. If you won't think of us, at least think of Eva."

What the hell?

Propping the door open with his foot, Danny checked the hallway. The coast was clear of potential witnesses to this dumb-ass, self-destructive act of eavesdropping.

Which was a damn good thing, because there was no way he could force himself to walk away now.

Kane had been having a good day. Shoot, he'd never been happier. Surrounded by fellow food enthusiasts and awesomely talented chefs, days spent with one of his best friends, and nights with the hottest, smartest, funniest, coolest woman he'd ever met. And Kane had hung out with Madonna! So that was saying something.

He should've known it couldn't last.

If life had taught him anything, it was to grab on to the good stuff and wring every last drop of joy from it, because nothing lasted forever. Had anyone asked, he could've honestly said that he'd tried to do that with Claire, but he didn't know how successful he'd been.

There always seemed to be more to her, more to them and what they could be together, hanging just out of reach like that last, perfect, summer peach way high up at the top of the tree.

When Theo Jansen asked him to meet early that morning, before the challenge began, Kane had assumed it had something to with the competition. He'd bounced in, all chipper and happy, body bruised and sore in the best possible way from the night before. Claire wasn't kidding about that starving-lion thing. She'd pretty much mauled him.

He'd never enjoyed anything more.

But when he got to the kitchen, no one was around, which surprised him. Surely the camera crew had stuff to set up. But no, it was only Theo. Alone and immaculate in the center of the kitchen, staring at the cameras with a smug, self-satisfied expression.

"You wanted to talk to me?" Kane said, feeling immediately awkward and out of place in his scuffed-up motorcycle boots, faded jeans, and plain white T-shirt.

"Yes." Theo turned to face the doors, a solemn, man-to-man kind of look on his face. Kane had to take a moment to suppress his instant gut reaction to that expression.

You're not a kid, and this guy's not your dad. Chill.

Of course, then the first thing out of Theo's mouth had to be, "Thanks for coming down early, son."

Ugh.

"No problem." Kane sauntered into the kitchen, hands jammed into his jeans pockets, and tried not to choke on the fact that he hadn't called the man *sir*. Childhood habits died hard, but they could be throttled back, if he really concentrated.

"I have some concerns about . . . well, about you, actually."

That was unexpected. Not that Kane knew what the fuck to expect from this conversation, but still. Was he messing up during judging or something? "Why?"

"Your relationship with Claire Durand," Theo said gently. "I hope you're not too terribly invested in it. She's an impressive woman, difficult to forget. I should know."

He gave a sheepish, self-deprecating laugh that made Kane want to like him, even as his heart turned to solid ice in his chest. "I am invested," he said. What was this, some kind of protective-ex speech? "You don't have to worry about me. Claire and I have been through all of this.

I may be young, or at least young*er*, but I know what I want."

Theo tipped his head to one side, his dark brown eyes thoughtful. "But have you thought about how what you want will affect the woman you claim to care for so much?"

Muscles tensing as if he were about to run—or fight—Kane had to consciously work to relax each finger out of the fists he'd instinctively clenched. "I don't want to be rude, or anything, but you're way out of line. And maybe you and Claire go way back, but she's with me now. You blew it with her a long time ago."

"Very true," Theo said, holding up his hands in a palm-to-palm, supplicating manner. "Claire made it clear to me, in no uncertain terms, that she'd chosen you."

Kane's heart thawed and flopped around in his chest like a happy fish. "Then I guess this conversation is over."

"Not so fast, son."

Gritting his teeth, Kane said, "I'm not your son."

Theo's stern face softened slightly. "Of course not. My apologies. It's just that you and my daughter are the same age. I've made a lot of mistakes with her—mistakes I'm hoping to begin to rectify."

"I don't understand what any of this has to do with me." Kane's restless fingers found a stray thread at the hem of his T-shirt and worried it.

"It doesn't," Theo agreed. "But it does have to do with Claire. I want her back in my life. Back in Eva's life. I can give Claire the future she deserves. Don't you want her to have that?"

Chapter 29

Kane's happy, flopping-fish heart had just been gutted and scaled. He had to reach for his scattered thoughts, and it took all his vocal training to push them out through his tight, scratchy throat.

"What makes you think . . ." Kane swallowed, worked for it. "That you can give her a better future than the one she chose for herself?"

Reluctant respect flashed across Theo's face for a bare instant. "Claire's a smart cookie. Always has been. And driven! When I first met her fifteen years ago, she was a freelance food writer, doing restaurant reviews for local newspapers and copy editing on the side to pay the bills. She pulled herself up from that to editor in chief of the most important food and lifestyle magazine in the world—and do you know how?"

By being awesome? Somehow Kane didn't think that answer would impress. He shook his head, wanting to see where Theo was going with all of this.

"Claire never let anything get in her way. A lot of women get distracted by things like getting married, having kids." He shrugged. "I'm not making a value judgment about it. It's just the way things are. But Claire was never like that. She knew what she wanted, and she went after it with a laser focus that cut everything else out of her path. She earned a lot of respect that way—not something that's easy for a woman in what's essentially still a male-dominated field."

"You know, I already admired her. You're not telling me anything startling and new," Kane said, crossing his arms over his chest. "What's your point?"

Theo clasped his hands behind his back. "The point is, young man, she got where she is through hard work, determination, and self-denial. The top of the heap—and it's lonely up there. I think we both know a little something about that."

"I don't think you and I have much in common, Mr. Jansen."

"Ah, that's where you're wrong. We both care for Claire, and for Eva, too. And we both know that not only is it lonely at the top, it's also precarious up there. A balancing act. There's always someone scaling the hill just below you, looking to topple you from your perch. And in Claire's case, losing the respect of the serious food community, the restaurateurs, chefs, and advertisers who are the lifeblood of *Délicieux*—that wouldn't just lose her that spot on top of the mountain. I really think it would kill her."

"Mr. Jansen." Kane went to some effort to shake his head in thin, brittle amusement. "The fact that I'm a musician doesn't make me more susceptible to dramatic pronouncements than other people."

It sort of did, though. Was Jansen right? Would being with Kane mess things up for Claire, in ways she didn't want to think about right now?

"By contrast," Theo said, barreling past Kane's retort, "I can give Claire invaluable support, professionally speaking—no one will think less of her for being with me."

Left unsaid was the fact that the same wasn't necessarily true of Kane. He thought of how Claire had objected to their relationship, the things she'd said to talk herself out of it. Was this what she'd been thinking of?

Fear pushed so hard down the back of Kane's throat, he thought for a second he might gag.

"If she's with me, people will talk," he said, feeling suffocated. Kane knew how the paparazzi worked. He was a veteran of the gossip rag wars. They'd say she was robbing the cradle, they'd speculate about her age, their sex life, her weight, and anything else they could think of to drive sales and create a scandal.

"Hardly the image she wants to project as a highly placed, valued member of the professional culinary community."

"No," Kane said. "I can see that."

"And then there's the personal side," Theo went on, gentle and soft and relentless as a pillow pressing down on Kane's face, cutting off his oxygen. "Claire and Eva have always had a wonderful relationship. I want, more than anything, to give Eva what she's lacked for so long—the kind of family her mother's death, and my own dysfunctional grief, robbed her of."

Welcome anger sparked through Kane's blood. "You think playing house with Claire and Eva is going to erase years of being a shitty father to her? Your baby's all grown up, now, Jansen."

Theo actually winced, as if Kane had scored a direct hit. He wished it felt more satisfying. "I know my daughter is no longer a child. But she's still my child, and your friend. And one of the most important people in Claire's life. I'd like to give them an even closer connection—but you need to do the right thing here."

"And what's that?"

"Step aside. Let Claire go. It's for the best." Theo paused, what looked like genuine regret etching lines in his weathered, dignified face. "For everyone, including Eva. I know she's your friend. If you won't think of us, at least think of Eva."

The warm, regretful, hideously sincere tones of Theo's voice rang oddly flat in Kane's ears, a clashing, dissonant chord that jarred him out of his momentary weakness. He felt a frown lowering his brow until he could barely see Theo through the fog of righteous anger.

This asshole was manipulating him. Working on Kane's guilt, his sympathy, whatever vulnerabilities Theo could find, and shredding them like a killer guitar riff.

But he'd gone too far. Theo had woken up Kane's competitive streak—the streak that had pushed him to practice like a fiend even though he could pick out a tune on any instrument within seconds of trying it out, the streak that had gotten him to leave home at eighteen for the bright lights of the Austin music scene, the streak that kept him working, recording, writing, and touring until he was one of the biggest names in the music industry.

Nobody played Kane Slater.

"You want me to step aside? Make me."

Theo blinked. "What?"

"I didn't stutter." Kane dropped his defensively crossed arms to his sides, hooking his thumbs in his empty belt loops. He was a performer, after all. He knew the power of body language.

"Mr. Slater." Theo gave a long-suffering sigh. "Please don't be difficult. You're only drawing out the inevitable."

Kane laughed, fighting spirit surging up into his chest.

"I don't believe in inevitability. The game's not over until it's over. And I'm in it to win it, Jansen. Claire is mine, and she's going to stay that way."

Theo finally dropped the sympathetic-mentor act. A spasm of true annoyance crossed his handsome, weathered face. "You idiot. She's only toying with you. Have a little self-respect. I'm trying to help you, keep you from embarrassing yourself."

"Fuck you, and your help." Kane could feel his face going red with anger, or maybe with the shock of hearing his darkest secret fears voiced aloud.

"Fine." Theo didn't throw his hands into the air in a dramatic gesture, but Kane could tell by the twitch of his shoulders that he wanted to. "On your head be it. But when Claire comes to her senses and realizes there's no possible place in her life for someone like you, I'll be right there, on the spot, waiting to scoop her up."

Kane, who wasn't afraid of dramatic gestures, arched a brow and leaned in close enough to whisper his parting shot into Theo's closed, angry face.

"May the best man win."

Danny blinked, stepping back from the kitchen doors.

He felt like he'd just been buried under an avalanche of new information, and his brain was scrambling to process it all.

Trying to move silently, because he didn't want to find out how epically disastrous it'd be if Theo and Kane realized he'd overheard that whole convo, Danny took another step away from the doors—and had to bite back a yell when his foot landed on something warm and malleable.

He jumped maybe a mile in the air, and came down face-to-face with Claire Durand.

Stupidly, he dropped his gaze to see what he'd stepped on. Oh. Claire Durand's foot.

Claire Durand. The head judge of the RSC. And the subject of the conversation he'd just eavesdropped on.

Raising panicked eyes to her face, Danny relaxed almost instantly. He could've run over her foot with a crosstown bus, he realized, and she wouldn't have registered his presence.

All her attention was focused on the cracked kitchen door and the men beyond it, her face frozen in an eerily blank expression.

A moment later, Kane Slater pushed out of the kitchen, his cheeks red beneath his golden-boy tan.

Wincing, Danny wanted nothing more than to leap out of the way of the oncoming train wreck—unless it was to avoid drawing any attention to himself. Either way, it was moot; he couldn't get his feet to work in the time it took for Kane to barrel to a stop in front of Claire, surprise warring with the militant determination that had fired his whole body into a taut, tense live wire.

"Claire! How long have you been out here?"

When she replied, her colorless lips hardly moved. "Long enough to hear you and Theo fighting over me like two small boys with a toy."

Kane grimaced, but he was still clearly riled, not ready to do what Danny was trying to telepathically convince him to do.

Apologize. Say you're sorry, and mean it. Grovel. Come on!

But instead, Kane shook his head. "Yeah, that got ugly. I wish you hadn't heard it."

Ooh, misstep. Danny squeezed his eyes shut, fading into the background of this debacle as much as possible, but he had to crack one eye to see how Claire was taking it.

About like he'd expected—she was pissed. But in that icy, intense way where she spoke so quietly, he had to strain to hear her.

"Oh, I'm certain you never wished for me to hear you laying claim to me, exposing our private affairs and gloating . . ."

She broke off, something wild and anguished breaking through her frozen mask, and Kane seemed to finally understand that something was really wrong here.

"No! Claire, that's not what I—"

But it was too late. Holding up a hand, she wrestled herself back under such rigid control, Danny wouldn't have been shocked if her bones had shattered.

"Stop." Finally, as Danny had dreaded all along, Claire's eyes shifted to take in their embarrassed audience of one.

"Come on, just let me explain," Kane tried.

"Oh, I think you have brought quite enough outside people into our private relationship." Claire's voice never rose above a whisper, but it was sharp enough to slash right through Kane's justifications.

Unable to pretend he hadn't just witnessed everything that went down, Danny tried on a smile and waded into the fray. "Hey, don't mind me. I was just looking for Eva, but she's obviously not here, so I'm going to go. Away. And let you two talk this out."

Kane shot him a grateful glance, but Claire said, "There is no need. The chefs will be arriving momentarily, and we have judging matters to discuss. Mr. Slater?"

Stalking forward, she pushed open the kitchen door and held it for Kane, head high and face white with suppressed emotion.

There was a long, tense pause in which Kane did nothing, merely looked at her, while Danny held his breath.

Finally, Kane moved. He walked back toward the kitchen, but as he drew level with Claire, he leaned in and said, "Fine. Have it your way—but this isn't over, Claire. You heard me tell Theo I wouldn't give you up without a fight, yeah? I meant every word. Even if the one I'm fighting is you."

Something flickered in Claire's dark eyes, something that made Danny suddenly let out the breath he'd been holding, but before she could respond, a discreet, melodic tone behind them signaled the arrival of the elevator.

Without a backward glance, Kane marched into the kitchen, and Claire followed him. She gave Danny a quick look, lips pursed as if she wanted to say something.

Danny nodded immediately, hoping to show that he understood, that she could trust him to keep his mouth shut about what he'd heard. She nodded back and let the door swing shut behind her just as Ike Bryar and the rest of the Southern Team bounded off the elevator.

Danny rocked on his heels and cracked his knuckles, mind reeling with everything he'd heard.

Bryar, a big guy with a shaved head, wrapped this morning in a Karate-Kid-style bandanna, jerked a thumb over his shoulder.

"What's up with our head judge?"

Danny shrugged, looked away. "They're having a judges' meeting before the challenge; Jansen and Rock Star Boy are in the kitchen, too. It's not quite seven yet, I thought I'd give them a few more minutes."

Ike blew a loud, irreverent raspberry and propped his considerable weight against the door, cracking it open even farther. "Hey, it's seven on the dot, by my watch. Oh! What's this? The kitchen's open! Guess we might as well go on in and get this shitshow on the road."

"Knock yourself out," Danny said, laughing. "I'm going to wait for my guys. We'll see you in there."

He shook his head as the rowdy southern crew packed into the kitchen, all catcalls and cheerful good mornings.

The elevator doors pinged again, and another gaggle of chefs spilled out, raising the noise level in the quiet hotel hallway from peaceful to raucous in seconds, and Danny was swept up in the current of people rushing into the kitchen.

Everyone hurried to their team tables, unfolding nylon knife rolls and setting utensils out across their stations in the places where their hands would know to reach for them, automatically, no thought required.

Eva walked in a few minutes later, gorgeous in a short dress that looked like it used to be tight enough to skim her curves distractingly.

Today the shimmery soft purple fabric hung on her sharp shoulders, bunching a little when she put her arm around her assistant's shoulders and leaned over to whisper in his ear.

The assistant, Drew, grinned and moved smoothly to intercept Theo Jansen, leading him off to the side while Eva went to confer with the camera guys.

"Hmm. She's not giving you the death glare. That's a good sign."

Giving Winslow an irritated look, Danny admitted, "I didn't get a chance to talk to her."

"Good," Win said. "Look at her! She looks great."

Cheney, the guy she'd met with at The Blind Tiger, seemed to be asking her for something, and he looked annoyed when she shook her head apologetically.

Danny scowled. "She's lost weight over the last week. She was perfect already!"

"I'd say you worry too much, but you've heard that before and never paid any damn attention," Winslow said. "So why bother? Hey, at least you know she'll be sitting down and eating something today at the judges' table."

Eva finished up her quiet discussion with Cheney, who turned back to the three new cameramen and had them huddle around while Eva put on her biggest smile.

"Good morning, Chefs!"

Everyone chorused the greeting back to her, with varying degrees of positivity. The West Coast Team looked sleepy, as if they hadn't managed to acclimate themselves to the time difference yet.

Ryan Larousse and his gang looked, as usual, like they'd rather be wielding guns than knives, primed and ready for action.

Danny struggled to get his head back in the game after the morning's drama. This was the moment they'd been waiting for—the last challenge before the finals. Nothing was more important than coming through today and being chosen as one of the three teams to continue in the competition.

His pep talk high lasted him until Eva started to describe what they were about to face.

"Maybe you've noticed, we've got a few extra cameras for the challenge today!" She dimpled at them, pleased as punch. "And with the heightened involvement of the Cooking Channel, we're taking on a couple of other changes. The structure of the judging will be a little different—I'll explain that in a minute. For now, all you need to do is ignore the cameras. Just forget they're there, and cook your best! This is the big one, guys. Good luck to each of you." Over her shoulder, she said, "Are we set, Mr. Cheney?"

"Rolling," he replied, aiming his camera at her.

Flashing the chefs another brilliant, almost manic smile, Eva walked over to the table Danny had seen last night, the long one covered in a white tablecloth.

"Remember what I said at the start of the competition about the importance of teamwork? Well, today, I'm going to divide you up into two teams."

Tension shot through the contestants like a bullet. Danny stared at her, stunned. Team challenges were the worst— being forced to work with your competition added a layer of stress and strategy to an already fraught situation.

Ignoring the murmurs from the chefs, Eva said, "Midwest, you'll be teaming up with the South." Danny had only a second to breathe a sigh of relief that they wouldn't have to deal with that ticking time bomb, Ryan Larousse, on their team before Eva continued, "That means, West Coast? You'll be cooking with the East Coast."

Beside him, Winslow went still, and Danny realized exactly what this meant.

Beck and Skye Gladwell—an estranged married couple—on the same team. Danny felt his pulse leap and his breath start to come short. Was it time to start panicking yet?

"Today's challenge is something a lot of chefs have to face at some point in their careers." With a theatrical flourish, Eva whipped the cloth off the table, revealing a water tank filled with live lobsters, a platter of salmon, steaks, and whole, plucked chickens piled in the back.

But the part that made Danny's blood run cold was the centerpiece—a giant, three-tiered replica of a cake made out of white roses and topped with a tiny plastic couple in black tie and flowing ivory dress.

"You'll be designing and preparing a menu for a wedding tasting!"

Beside him, Winslow stiffened. His gasp was audible.

"Are you okay?" Danny put a hand on the kid's arm, alarmed.

"It can't be a coincidence," Win whispered, eyes round and so wide, the whites were showing. "It just can't. Oh my God. What have I done?"

Eva was still talking, outlining the challenge, something about the traditional things people expected to find at weddings, rubber chicken and over-cooked steak, yadda yadda. Danny already knew what he'd be working on— a fucking wedding cake, the bane of every pastry chef's existence—so he turned all his focus on Winslow.

Who was totally freaking. Win wasn't a silent sufferer; he tended to flip out in tense moments, but Danny had never seen him like this. He looked like he was about to keel over on his cutting board.

"What are you talking about? What did you do?"

Winslow gripped the edge of the stainless-steel counter so hard, the knuckles of his hands stood out white. "I got down with the wrong person, that's what."

Danny followed his gaze to Drew, Eva's assistant, who was standing off to the side of the room, chatting with Theo Jansen.

"I talked to him about Beck and Skye Gladwell," Winslow moaned. "I'm the reason he started looking into it. It was like a game, like playing detectives! Only he found out all that stuff I told you this morning about them being still married, and he swore he wouldn't tell anyone, but God. He must've told his boss, because this challenge is too messed up to be a damn coincidence."

As if feeling two pairs of eyes on him, Drew glanced over at them. When he saw Win's betrayed, accusing glare, he blanched, his whole face crumpling up like parchment paper. Muttering something to Jansen, Drew hurried out of the room, which was all the confirmation Danny needed that Winslow was right. Everything inside Danny sank straight into the ground.

It was a setup.

Eva had used Winslow's relationship with her assistant for information, then she'd coldly, callously designed the challenge that was most likely to lead to fireworks and excitement for her precious Cooking Channel viewers.

One glance at Beck's stony, stoic face, his eyes pools of mute pain burning through the granite of his expression, was enough to send Danny's temper into the stratosphere.

She wasn't going to get away with this.

Chapter 30

"That isn't fair."

The furious voice raised the hairs on the back of Eva's neck. She whirled to face Danny, muscular arms crossed over his white-jacketed chest, eyes snapping with anger.

Eva's heart stopped. He knew.

The instincts she'd inherited from her father sent her smoothly into crisis control mode, even as her heart lurched back to life with a painful thump against her breastbone.

"I'm sorry if you're unhappy with your team's assignment, Chef Lunden," Eva said, her voice coming out cool and blank. "But surely part of the point of this competition is to prove your team can overcome distractions and challenges to produce winning dishes."

"Culinary challenges, sure," Danny ground out. "The distractions of a professional kitchen? No problem. But this is something else."

"What is he talking about, Eva?" Concern drew her father's silvery brows together in to a frown.

"Nothing," Eva assured him distractedly, unable to look away from Danny's cold rage.

"I'm talking about you, using unethically gained information about our personal lives against us." Danny's mouth tightened in a spasm that looked like pain, before flattening out to a hard line once more. "You've gone too far, Eva."

Panic skittered down Eva's spine and up into her throat, a hundred thoughts circling and diving like a swarm of hornets in her chest. Finally managing to drag her eyes off Danny, Eva hissed at Cheney to shut the cameras down.

Cheney scowled at her, clearly unwilling to miss out on the best action they'd seen so far. Beside Eva, her father raised an imperious hand and circled it in the air at Cheney, signaling him to keep going.

"That's right," Danny said, mockery giving his deep, smooth voice a rough edge. "Keep 'em rolling. You'll want to catch all of this good drama to entice the housewives of America to watch your show." His lip curled in disgust. "I mean, what the actual fuck are we doing here? Because it's not about the food, not anymore."

"Danny, stop." Winslow, the one who'd given Drew the good gossip, tugged on his teammate's sleeve, green eyes huge and bruised looking.

"No." Danny's fists clenched, his knuckles standing out white. "It isn't right, what she's trying to do."

"I must agree."

Every head in the kitchen swiveled at Claire's grave pronouncement. Eva stared, unable to believe how quickly everything was spinning out of control.

"Claire," Theo barked, but the narrow look her friend shot over quelled him.

"If this young man is telling the truth, that you somehow set this challenge up to exploit the chefs' personal lives for the sake of creating drama, I must agree with him. You've gone too far."

Eva was intensely aware of that bank of cameras to her right, their unblinking gaze drinking in and recording every beat of this horrible moment.

Hearing the two people whose opinion mattered most denounce her publicly, Eva had no choice but to confront the reality of what she'd done.

Sick with the beginnings of a regret she knew would only grow over time, Eva tried to brazen it out.

The only thing she could do was contain the damage. Keep the competition moving forward, and sort it all out later.

She breathed in deeply and slowly, consciously wiping all expression from her face and voice. Calm. She had to be calm. Defuse the situation. Knowing that it would be exponentially harder if she looked Danny in the eye, Eva faced her oldest friend. She could practically hear her father's voice inside her head, warning her not to back down, not to show weakness . . .

"Thank you for your input, Claire. But as the rulebook states, challenges are entirely up to the discretion of the competition coordinator. Namely, me. And at this point, as unfair as Chef Lunden seems to think it is, it would be equally unfair to the other teams if I were to trade things around based solely on his complaints."

But even as she said it, she could hear how thin it sounded. Swallowing hard against the knot of tension in her throat, Eva glanced back at Danny without really meaning to.

Immediately ensnared in the intensity of his stare, she lost track of what she was saying. Silence beat through the kitchen for the space of one heartbeat. Two. Three.

"Fine," she said, breaking the moment with a gasp of relief, like breaking the surface of a cold pool. "We'll form the teams by random selection. Can we agree on that?"

Without waiting for an answer, she strode over to the supply table and grabbed a wooden knife block and four knives with identical black handles. She stuck the two eight-inch chef's knives and two ten-inch knives into the block's empty slots and studied it. Impossible to tell which knives were which.

Lugging the heavy block back to the center of the kitchen, Eva plunked the thing down on the table directly in front of Danny.

This is the best I can do, she tried to telegraph silently.

Out loud, she said, "Each team send up one chef to draw a knife."

Danny reached out and pulled one of the long knives free of the block with a hiss of metal on wood.

Skye Gladwell came over, the bangles and charms around her ankles tinkling softly. She drew one of the shorter blades and stared at it for a moment. Her expression gave nothing away, but Eva could see the relief on Beck's face. Guilt burrowed its fingers into her chest, but she didn't have time for that now. She beckoned the last two chefs over.

Ike Bryar pulled the other ten-incher, putting his Southern Team with the East Coast. Which left Ryan Larousse's boys working with Skye Gladwell.

Out of the corner of her eye, Eva saw Beck tense up again. She didn't blame him—that combo seemed dangerous to her, too, but hey. Maybe it meant Cheney would get some good footage after all.

Somehow, that didn't seem as important right this minute as it had before.

"The teams are set," Eva declared, stepping back. "Get cooking. I'll be back to check on you in a few hours."

The chefs took off like racehorses hearing the starting gun, and Eva hustled herself out of their way. Only Danny paused for a moment, his gaze heavy on Eva's face. Still angry, despite the team swap. Still condemning her with every flicker of his blue-gray eyes. Still . . . was that hurt? Eva's chest constricted, strangling the breath from her lungs, and when he turned away, she fumbled blindly for the door.

She'd lost him.

The knowledge lodged in her throat like a stone, rough and unyielding. Whatever they'd said last night, whatever he'd felt or wanted then—he clearly didn't want anything to do with her now.

Out in the hall, the air was cooler but next to impossible to draw into her lungs. She needed a minute, just a minute by herself, to process what had happened, the way she'd screwed up everything, the ruin she'd made of her own barely realized hopes. She needed to breathe.

Instead, she found her assistant camped out in a chair by the elevators, his pale face tense and miserable.

"Drew." Concern sharpened her voice. "Are you okay? Have you been crying? Tell me what's wrong."

Ducking his head to hide his swollen, puffy eyes, Drew sniffled. "He's never going to forgive me."

"Who?"

"Win! Winslow Jones." Drew's anguished cry bounced around the tiny space. "He knows I was passing on details and information about them to you, and I'm sure he thinks I was only hanging out with him to get dirt on his friends, but it's not true. I really liked him."

Eva's throat clogged up, her eyes burning as if she were staring directly into a hot oven. The devastation on his young face cut into Eva's heart. She'd justified her actions by weighing the needs of the many—those unnamed, unsung talented chefs who couldn't afford to compete—against the right to privacy of the few, and she'd thought she was comfortable with her choice. Secure in her decision to play the Cooking Channel's game, just enough to get what she wanted.

But she'd never wanted this.

"God, Drew. I'm so sorry. I never meant for you to get hurt."

"I know," he said, still not looking at her. "I'll get over it. I mean, I don't think Winslow was serious about me, anyway. Not the way I was about him."

His voice cracked, and Eva had to hug him again, because hanging heavy and real in the air between them was the unspoken fact that now, Drew would never get a chance to know how Winslow Jones felt about him.

Drew was stiff under her arm for half a second before he sighed and laid his spiky head on her shoulder. Hugging his skinny frame to her, Eva stared straight ahead at the blank hallway wall, and thought about the fact that Drew wasn't the only one who'd lost any chance at finding out where things could go with the man he . . . loved.

Oh, God. What have I done?

Winslow was, as he would put it, a hot mess. After the morning uproar, his concentration was shot, as full of holes as microplane grater, and his nerves appeared to be about as raw as if someone had taken that grater to his bare skin.

Danny propped him up as best he could, but for a team challenge, this was turning out to be very much down to individual dishes. The team with the most dishes chosen by the judges would win . . . and continue on to the finals.

The team with the fewest would lose. And half of that team would be up for elimination.

A quicker challenge than the last, the chefs had been given access to all the ingredients they needed right there in the Limestone kitchen, so they'd avoided the time-consuming trip to Fresh Foods. And as a test of their ability to think and work quickly, they'd had the four hours until lunchtime to prep, and now faced the rest of the afternoon, the final sprint to cook and be ready to present their dishes to the judges by five o'clock.

The biggest switch would kick in when it came time for the actual judging. In ten rounds, the chefs from the two teams would go head-to-head.

There were certain ingredients both teams had to use—lobster, salmon, and so on. Familiar wedding fare, usually boring and uninspired. The contestants' job was to take it from familiar to fabulous.

There were five courses, and each team had to present two options for each course. Two soups, two salads, two entrée choices, and two desserts. By which they meant, of course, wedding cake—something Danny had only attempted in class, never in a real-life setting.

And he was majorly distracted by the implosion that appeared to be shattering his team from the inside.

Calmest of all of them, surprisingly enough, was Beck. When Winslow's knife slipped for the twentieth time, nicking his thumbnail, Beck was the one who left his lobster shells on the table and hustled him over to the sink to patch him up, his huge, silent presence forming a solid protective wall.

Max had taken the bird, and he was off at the end of the table doing weird and interesting experiments with fried chicken skin. Beside him, Jules bent over the endive she was chiffonading to make into a salad to go with her tournedos of beef, one eye worriedly on Winslow and Beck.

Catching his glance, she and Danny exchanged mutual wide eyes and raised eyebrows of concern, but what could they do? They had to push forward.

Jules, at least, had the luxury of not understanding exactly what it meant when Skye Gladwell's whisk leaped from her hand and clattered to the floor in front of Beck as he jogged by on his way back to their table. Jules was oblivious to the deep undercurrents running between the two chefs as Beck picked up the whisk and handed it back to Skye, clean handle pointing toward her, so that his hand got sticky with cake batter and he had to go back to the sink and wash up all over again.

But Danny saw that stuff, and he saw the way Beck's gaze lingered over Skye's hands, bare of any rings or other adornment. He even noticed the wooden, blank emotional withdrawal on Skye's pretty face, so different from the easy sunshine they'd become accustomed to from her.

Danny saw everything, and it filled his chest with blistering rage.

How could Eva have ever thought it would be okay to put Beck and Skye on the same team? Planning a wedding, no less. The fact that they were working with the southern guys now, instead, hadn't cooled Danny's temper very much.

He ignored Eva when she came back to the kitchen to check on them after lunch, and gave them the full rundown on how the judging would go. He also resolutely did not notice her worried glances at her rat bastard of an assistant, or the way she kept a solicitous hand on the kid's shoulder and spoke quietly into his ear.

Probably asking for some more personal, private, intimate, none-of-your-damn-business secrets, Danny thought, turning the stand mixer on high with a vicious flick of his finger. The blades churned to life, spattering melted marshmallow and powdered sugar in a cloudburst.

Danny couldn't resist another quick glare. His narrowed gaze took in Eva's pale skin, the shakiness of her movements, and instinctive worry stirred in his chest before he could crush it.

She patted her assistant, Rat Boy, on the back and pushed him gently toward the door, then paused to scan the kitchen.

Her shadowed eyes found his, and for a long, numb moment, Danny's mind went completely blank. She was just so heartbreakingly lovely, even with unhappiness trembling at the corners of her mouth.

The thought jarred Danny out of his ridiculous mooning. Sneering, at himself more than her, he shook his head and went back to his stupid, temperamental fondant.

If he couldn't get the temperature right, it wouldn't have the right consistency. He'd opted to do poured fondant because it tasted better, but it was trickier to roll out than the kind made with gelatin and food-grade glycerine.

With a ferocious frown, Danny immersed himself in the chemical details and attempted to block everything else out of his consciousness. It worked until Beck loomed beside him, out of the blue, a deep furrow creasing his forehead.

"I know you know about me and Skye," he said without preamble. "Win told me. Everything."

Danny's heart was getting tired of the constant clench and release. Coronary problems ran in his family! He just hoped the RSC competition was going to be willing to pay for his eventual breakdown.

"I'm so sorry, man," he said sincerely.

"Never apologize for things that aren't your fault." Beck was always so freaking calm. "You didn't create this situation. Neither did Winslow, or Eva Jansen."

"How can you say that?" Danny hissed, mindful of the cameras everywhere, microphones at the ready. "She deliberately dug for dirt and then used it to set up this challenge!"

Beck shook his head heavily. "Doesn't matter. I was the one who kept this a secret, and I shouldn't have. I should have let go of all of this years back, but the situation is . . . complicated. If I'd had my head on straight about it, though, and kept myself to myself when that little shit Larousse started talking smack, Eva Jansen would've never known a thing about it. So this is my fault, more than hers. For damn sure, more than yours or Win's. And I need you two to quit taking it on. You're messing yourselves up for nothing."

Danny couldn't have been more surprised if Beck had wrapped those big hands around Danny's ankles and flipped him upside down. "I think that's the most I ever heard you say at one time."

The ghost of a smirk touched Beck's hard mouth. He pointed his stainless-steel double-jaw shellfish cracker at Danny, saying, "And quit making faces at Eva Jansen. She's on the panel tasting our dishes, in case you don't recall. We don't want to alienate her."

With that, Beck was back at his own station, breaking down bright red, boiled lobster and scooping the sweet, tender white meat from the claws.

And Danny was left with a swelling respect and admiration for his teammate—and a need to tell Eva exactly what he thought of her.

Chapter 31

Claire found her in the empty judges' room, sitting at the bare table and staring at the wall.

"*Chérie*? Your cameraman, that unpleasant Cheney person, says to tell you he can't shoot the judging in here—there won't be enough room. Come back to the kitchen, it's almost time."

Eva barely heard her. "Do you hate me? When did I become an awful person?"

Claire sighed and sat down in the chair beside Eva's. "I don't hate you, and you are not awful."

Blinking furiously to clear her eyes of the tears that obscured her vision, Eva turned to her closest friend, desperate to make her understand. "I am, though! I wanted to get the RSC filmed for TV so badly."

Pursing her lips, Claire said, "And why was that, exactly?"

"Um. To increase the exposure of the competition to get more money so that it could be more democratic, let more chefs in."

"Eva." Claire shook her head, the light catching red

and gold glints in the auburn knot of hair at her nape. "I love you dearly, but you must be honest with yourself. If your motives were truly so pure, would you be feeling this guilt now?"

Eva paused. God. She'd been so self-righteous about this for so long, it was hard to dig deeper, down into the dark depths of herself. But Claire's straightforward pragmatism, simultaneously stern and sympathetic, pinned Eva to her chair.

"I do want to be able to open the RSC to more chefs, the way my mother envisioned," she said, uncertainty pinching at her, poking and prodding her to turn just a little to the left and take a good, close look at her own motives.

"I believe that. But you also want to impress your father," Claire said gently.

A hard, complicated truth was welling up in Eva's head, pushing aside everything that she'd thought she understood about herself and her choices.

She'd wanted to make a huge success out of the RSC, because on some level she thought it would prove to her father that she was capable of taking over Jansen Hospitality when he retired.

"Oh my God, I suck," she moaned, dropped her head to the table with a thunk.

"That is just my point, *chérie*." Claire laid a slender hand on the back of Eva's neck. Its cool comfort against her shame-hot skin made it easier to breathe. "You don't suck. You are human, with a human's complex feelings and reasons for doing what you do. You are better than you think. I have faith in you."

Those words, so simple and simply said, fell on Eva's heart like rain on scorched earth.

She hadn't lost everything. She still had at least one

friend in the world—and that friend trusted Eva to do the right thing. Maybe it was time to try.

Maybe she'd surprise herself.

As the timer ticked down toward zero, everyone in the kitchen worked frantically to spoon up one final taste and adjust the seasoning before getting the plating details exactly right.

Danny snuck a quick glance at the other team. Under Ryan Larousse's loud leadership, they'd chosen to collaborate on their dishes, and they were assigning the finished products to different chefs now. Skye Gladwell didn't look happy about it, standing there with her arms crossed over her chest and a mutinous, pinched look around her mouth.

Danny sympathized. It seemed like a weird strategy to him, heavily weighted in favor of whoever was aggressive about picking the best dishes at the end of the day. Which, no doubt, would be Ryan Larousse.

Early on, when Winslow was still freaking out about every little thing, he'd leaned over and said, "Should we have done that? Are we nuts to each make our own dish?"

"No way," Danny had assured him. "We talked enough to the southern contingent to know all our stuff goes together. Beyond that—we're individuals. We each have our own style, and we should showcase that."

Looking at the final results, though, plated up on the teams' tables, he worried. Their team definitely hadn't been quite as cohesive as the other, under Larousse's iron fist. Ike Bryar and his people had done their thing, while Danny and his guys did theirs.

Not exactly a model of teamwork.

The three judges trooped in just as the clock wound down, and Danny kept his gaze trained on the table in front of him, where his take on a traditional wedding cake sat looking gorgeous and hopefully tasting halfway decent.

That was the problem with baking—it was hard to taste-test as he went. Danny sometimes envied the rest of his team and the way they went through a hundred clean spoons sampling every dish in every single phase of its cooking. But in the end, his heart was in the sweet stuff, so he stuck it out.

Their team's dishes looked strong to Danny, with an emphasis on simple, homey classics. Maybe it wasn't fancy or groundbreaking, but with the upheaval and tension of the morning, every chef on the team had naturally gravitated toward comfort food.

The incandescent anger that had lit him up from the moment he'd realized the depths of Eva's betrayal had dimmed somewhat, cooled and calmed by the methodical, familiar process of turning flour and sugar and butter into something refined and delicious.

But there was an issue of self-respect here, right? He couldn't just let this go without giving her a piece of his mind.

So why wasn't he speaking up and denouncing her right now, before the judging even got started?

Danny snuck a glance at the judges, all three of them standing to the right of the bank of cameras, waiting for the signal from the producer. His eye skipped over Eva where she stood beside them, as if his subconscious wasn't ready to deal with her yet, and landed on Kane Slater, who looked less stirred up than he had earlier. But mostly as if he'd lacquered a layer of rock star glitz over the turmoil, and was hoping no one would notice.

Claire Durand, on the other hand, possessed the froidest sang Danny had ever seen, because she appeared perfectly at ease, serene and even smiling at Kane's side. Danny would be willing to bet he was the only person in the kitchen who could see banked fires of anger in her gaze whenever she looked at Kane and Theo.

Who had never seemed more smug, Danny noted, his dignified face registering nothing but approval of the proceedings, and confidence of his place in charge of it all.

Which only left Eva. She had her head bent, her ear close to Cheney's mouth so he could give her instructions or whatever without the cameras picking it up, and Danny couldn't see her face. It sent a shocking lance of pain straight through his chest, and Danny looked away again at once.

He wouldn't say anything yet, he decided on the spot. That much drama and excitement on camera? Please. He didn't want to give her the satisfaction. But after the judging, when they knew which side had lost and the judges went into deliberations on which regional team to send home—that's when he'd say something.

Ignoring the inner voice that mocked him for backing down, Danny braced his legs apart and crossed his arms over his chest, settling in to watch the judging.

It was nerve racking to be last. He didn't think he'd ever get used to it.

"Okay, chefs, time's up," Eva called, striding out into the center of the kitchen. "Knives down."

The judges followed her, arranging themselves on one side of the empty table at the front of the room, which had been cleared of the detritus of ingredients from earlier.

The dreadlocked guy from Skye's team—Danny still couldn't remember all their names—had done a vegetarian cream of parsnip soup with beet chips and saffron-scented crème fraîche. He was up against a more standard butternut squash soup with brown butter and fried sage from one of Ike Bryar's boys.

The judges dipped their spoons and tasted both dishes.

"Good depth of flavor on the parsnip soup," Theo commented. "You said this is vegetarian?"

"Totally," Dreadlocks replied.

"You must have roasted the vegetables for your stock a long while to get that much flavor out of them," Claire said, and the guy nodded. She looked pleased.

"I like the squash soup," Kane said, "but it's a little bland."

"Brown butter usually makes everything better," Theo agreed, "but in this case, it feels too heavy, like it's weighing the soup down."

"I like the fried sage, however. It elevates the dish," Claire said.

Danny couldn't believe how hard his heart was pounding. He hadn't expected it to be like this, hearing the judges' thoughts and reactions as they tasted.

He held his breath, waiting for the verdict as the judges conferred in low voices.

"The point goes to Midwest/West," Eva announced, a subtle flush staining her cheeks.

She still hadn't glanced in Danny's direction, not once since she came in. Not that he cared.

Across the kitchen, the other team exploded in a cheer as Dreadlocks grooved back to their table with a wide grin splitting his cheeks. The unhappy kid from the Southern Team slouched back into line.

"Next up?"

It went on like that, every single matchup filling Danny with tension and anticipation. He had to work hard to keep the score in his head—the other guys won the next point for their second soup, an awesome-looking roasted tomato that beat out Winslow's not-super-inspired English pea and lettuce puree.

And the Southern Team's shaved fennel salad couldn't beat out the West Coast's stunning little number, baby gem lettuces with avocado and grapefruit tossed in a sweet sharp sherry vinaigrette.

But when Beck went up with his salad course, Danny crossed his fingers, almost positive the East Coast/South Team was about to score its first point. It didn't even matter what Ryan Larousse's boy brought—nothing could beat Beck's famous lobster salad.

It was a simple plate of greens dressed up with exotic mushrooms, tossed with champagne vinaigrette, and studded with perfect morsels of butter-poached lobster claw. And then the whole thing was drizzled with tarragon hollandaise. It was killer; whenever they had the stuff to make it back at Lunden's Tavern and offered it as a special, it was sold out within minutes.

The judges reacted pretty much the way the Tavern regulars did—with orgasmic moans and unconcealed pleasure. As Beck returned with his point for their team, fist pumped in the air, Danny felt pride swell his chest.

Yeah, Winslow was off his game, and he'd lost his point, but he hadn't given up. And Beck, who'd been jerked around even more, had powered through and won one for his team.

They were still behind, down two points, but for the first time, Danny let himself believe that this might turn out okay.

They might get to go on to the next and final round, and he should be freaking thrilled about that—so why did he feel so empty?

Points flew fast and furious through the next few rounds, the match wins passing back and forth. The other guys dominated with their first entrée, but Jules and Max both did well, the judges heaping praise on their creations.

Ryan Larousse's picks put up a couple of good dishes, too, and it was clearly anyone's game.

In the end, Max won his point with a fancy Frenched chicken leg, roasted and presented with a perfect little slaw of crisp tender brussels sprout leaves, and a square of fried chicken skin to provide the perfect contrast of crunchy salty texture. And Jules took hers with a duo of beef tenderloin medallions, one in a reduced port sauce, the other touched with a mustardy béarnaise, rich with butter.

Ike Bryar was the one to pull the East Coast/South side out from behind, with his light, crispy salmon croquettes, studded with English peas and big, juicy chunks of tender, pink fish, served on a bed of creamy grits with a side of sautéed kale.

When the judges awarded him that point, the one that brought their teams even for the first time, everyone around Danny roared with delight.

It was down to the desserts. If they could just keep their momentum up, the other guys wouldn't stand a chance.

As the kitchen calmed for the presentation of the last course, Danny realized that Ryan Larousse, himself, hadn't presented a dish yet, which made him nervous. He seemed like the kind of leader who would put himself in the best possible position for praise by choosing the strongest dish as his own. Did that mean they had a decent dessert to show?

The casual slouch of Ryan's body said he wasn't worried. Clapping a hand to the shoulder of the last West Coast team member to present, he sent a smug smirk in Danny's direction.

Alarm shot through Danny. He clenched his fists to stay rooted to the spot, even though everything in his tired, aching body wanted to launch across the kitchen and either punch that sneer right off Larousse's face, or run up to the front and have his cake judged instead.

But they'd decided the order ahead of time, and there was no good way to switch it up now without insulting their southern teammates. And what did Danny know? Maybe the pudgy southern kid's honey custard cupcakes were out of this world. Maybe they'd rock the socks off the . . . shit.

That was one adorable little plate of profiteroles the West Coastie was holding in her hands.

Holding his breath until he nearly passed out, Danny waited for the judges' responses.

"The cupcakes, for me, are not so good. A little too sweet," Claire said, wiping delicately at a smear of frosting.

"I like them," Kane muttered, defiantly finishing his off. Danny wanted to plant a big fat kiss on his stubbled rock star cheek.

"The profiteroles, though," Claire said, a frown of concentration drawing her brows together. "So interesting. And I like that both teams played with the idea of individual desserts, but the profiteroles seem less commonplace to me."

Come on, come on.

Danny's silent plea went unheard and unanswered, because the minute the judges stopped conferring and turned back to face the contestants, Danny knew what they were about to say.

"Point to the West/Midwest." Eva finally, for the first time, looked up and met Danny's gaze. In her eyes, he could see the same knowledge that had just poured over his head like a bucket of icy water.

It was all up to Danny.

Chapter 32

Summing up without taking her eyes from Danny, Eva said, "Team West/Midwest now has five points, while Team East Coast/South has four. The final point will either give a decisive victory to West/Midwest, or we'll be forced into a tiebreaker round. Chefs? Are you ready to present your last dish?"

Danny looked down, unable to bear the weight of emotion in Eva's gaze. He didn't know what she was feeling, what she wanted from him.

He couldn't think about that now. He had to concentrate on keeping his hands from shaking so he didn't drop this fucking cake on the way up to the judges' table. Feeling as if he were marching up the gallows to his execution, Danny made his way forward, the cake stand balanced between his hands, every step keeping pace with Ryan Larousse.

Who was also presenting . . . cake. Cake that looked like a strange piece of avant-garde sculpture, snowy white with flaked coconut and glittering with what looked like diamonds.

Shit.

"I see you opted not to cut the cake before judging," Theo said, nodding at Danny's platter.

He sounded neutral about it, but Danny's defenses shot up. "I wanted you to get the full effect of the decorations on it," he said. "Wedding cakes are at least half about what they look like."

And his cake looked damn good, if you asked Danny. Even considering his hypercritical eye, he was pleased with how it had turned out. The fondant gleamed like raw silk, smooth and gorgeous as it wrapped around the two tiers. Flashy for a wedding tasting, maybe, but this was the RSC. Danny had pulled out all the stops.

He'd spent precious hours fussing with spun sugar and food dyes, crafting tiny sprays of blossoms that looked almost too real to eat. Using more of the fondant, he'd pulled a satiny ribbon of white to cascade down the sides of the cake. The whole thing glistened in the bright lights of the kitchen, a pure, perfect piece of art.

"And it is lovely. But this is a culinary competition," Claire reminded him. "So taste will be important, too."

Swallowing down the heated response that jumped into his mouth, Danny said, "I'm aware of that."

Danny didn't think he'd ever been as aware in his life. Every heartbeat shook his chest and pounded through his body. His breath was shallow, as if the room were low on oxygen and his body was trying to conserve it. A single drop of sweat trickled behind his left ear, sending a shiver down his spine and lifting the individual hairs on his arms.

"And what do we think of Ryan's cake? It's certainly striking." Eva looked at the Larousse inquiringly.

"It's coconut mango," Larousse said smoothly. "We all came up with ideas together on our team, very collaborative, and we wanted to do something out of the ordinary. Not the standard, boring white cake with vanilla frosting."

He shot a deliberate glance at the white frosted cake sitting in front of Danny, waiting to be judged.

"That's why I went with a coconut-inflected cake, very thin layers, with a beautiful mango filling. Enjoy."

Don't enjoy it, don't enjoy it, Danny chanted silently as Larousse carefully sliced and arranged his cake onto separate plates.

But the judges didn't seem to hear him. As each of their faces lit up, Danny's guts twisted into knots.

"Very nice, this cake," Claire said, forking up another bite with a considering purse of her lips.

"The mango," Kane moaned happily. "That's, like, my kryptonite, man. Is there lime juice in it?"

"Yes," Larousse hurried to confirm. "A little bit of acidity brings out the sweetness and complexity of the fruit, don't you think?"

Oh, seriously? Danny bit down on a sneer. *He put the lime in the coconut, did he?*

"Yes, thank you for that input," Eva said shortly, pushing her plate to the side. "Let's try the next one."

Danny couldn't even enjoy Ryan Larousse's brief expression of sullen anger at Eva's dismissal—he was too busy watching every minute shift of muscle on the judges' faces as they took their first bites of his wedding cake.

He couldn't read them. Like, at all.

Sweat prickled at Danny's hairline, and he wanted to scratch at a patch of dried icing on the front of his chef's jacket, but he forced himself still.

"Is that . . . almond infused into the cake?" Kane asked, sounding surprised.

Danny had to clear his throat before answering. "Yes. The filling between the layers is a ginger cinnamon butter cream, flecked with bits of candied almond."

"It's very light. And moist," Claire commented.

"Which is uncommon for a cake with enough structural integrity to stand having more than one tier." Theo looked impressed.

Eva finished her piece first and used the back of her fork to pick up a few stray crumbs. "I love how delicate it is," she said, looking over at the judges. "It's subtle, but beautiful."

Refusing to be placated by Eva's praise—*too little, too late,* he wanted to tell her—Danny kept his chin high and his attention focused on the actual judges. Their opinion would make or break this round of the competition.

His guys were tired. Emotionally and physically, they needed a break. Danny, too, if he was honest. The idea of heading into a sudden-death tiebreaking elimination challenge made him want to throw up, but it was their only shot. He had to clinch this.

The silence stretched unbearably as the judges turned aside and conducted their whispered debate. He didn't want to notice that Eva looked increasingly upset at the direction the conversation was taking.

Resolutely keeping the worry off his face, Danny waited. Finally, the judges turned back to the table. Eva looked pale, something fragile and sharp hiding behind her eyes, as if one more blow might break her.

"This was a tough decision," she said, loudly enough for all the chefs to hear. "But it comes down to a matter of style. And in the end, the judges' panel felt that one chef truly embodied the spirit of teamwork, innovation and excitement we asked for with this challenge."

Danny's stomach wrenched tight. He already knew what she was going to say, the instant before her eyes flicked to him and snagged on his hard stare.

Eva had to swallow once, twice, before she managed,

"The point goes to Ryan Larousse. The West/Midwest team wins."

The world stopped.

Or maybe it was just Danny who stopped—stopped breathing, stopped listening . . . if he could've stopped existing entirely, in that moment, he would've.

Total debilitation, the kind where his head seemed to float two feet above his body and there was no sound beyond the vague thud of his own heartbeat, lasted only a few seconds. Then he crashed back into his body, the familiar aches and pains of hours of being on his feet, racing around a kitchen, standing and bending over a hot oven flooding back, all the more painful for the brief moment of disconnection.

Behind him, Danny heard the rest of the chefs going completely nuts. While the judges congratulated everyone who'd won, shaking hands and offering further praise on their favorite dishes, Danny stood there and tried to take it in.

He'd lost. It had come down to the wire, his father's hopes and dreams for the restaurant that was his sons' legacy riding on Danny's ability to perform—and he'd choked. They might be eliminated today, and have to head home to New York with their tails tucked between their legs, because Danny couldn't get his head together and keep it in the game.

It was all his fault.

Even as the knowledge flooded him, his eyes tracked Eva's stiff body as she made her way around the winning chefs, her usual fluid, energetic grace nowhere in sight.

Yeah, this was Danny's fault. But he'd had help jumping this train right off the tracks, and an iron-cold lump of vengeful bitterness lodged in his chest.

He was startled from his contemplation of revenge by a hand reaching across the wreckage of two wedding cakes sitting abandoned on the table.

Danny blinked down at Ryan Larousse's outstretched palm.

"You put up a hell of a menu," Larousse said, no trace of mockery in his tone.

"But you won." Reluctant respect simmered up in Danny's chest. It made it slightly easier to go on. "You deserved it. You pushed hard, and we folded under pressure. Congratulations, man."

A spasm of dissatisfaction twisted Larousse's features. "Yeah, that wasn't how I wanted it to go. I know I was kind of a dick before, about Skye Gladwell and your boy Beck, but . . ." He struggled for a moment, as if unsure if he wanted to go as far as actually apologizing. Danny wasn't entirely surprised when he went a different direction instead.

Mouth firming, Larousse stuck his chin out and said, "I hope to see you and your team in the final round. I hope you don't get cut. Good luck."

Danny reached out and grasped Larousse's still-hovering hand, shaking it once. "Thanks, man," he said sincerely.

"Actually, it's time for the judges to go into seclusion and discuss exactly that."

Danny stiffened at the sound of Eva's voice from behind him. He felt his shoulders go steely, his spine straight and rigid as he faced her. She was silent for a long moment, lips slightly parted as if she had more to say.

The moment spun out, longer and longer, like heated sugar pulled taut into taffy, but her shoulders slumped and she turned away, breaking the spell. Danny deliberately didn't watch her go, the pain of every glimpse of her like a knife to the back of his neck.

Searching the crowd, Danny found the rest of his team huddled around their worktable. Max had his arm around Jules's slim shoulders. Beck stood a little apart from everyone else, his face so shuttered and closed off, it made Danny realize with a sudden jolt just how far Beck had opened up since he first came to Lunden's.

Not anymore. Beck looked like a stone giant, his expressionless impassivity made all the more noticeable by the fact that he stood beside Winslow, who couldn't keep his emotions off his face if his life depended on it.

Out on the floor, Eva's assistant started rounding the other judges up, herding them toward the kitchen door. He passed Win, who ducked his head too fast to catch the hopeful expression on Drew's face. But Danny saw it, and he saw, too, the way that the brilliant, beaming light behind Winslow's eyes, the life force that made Win such a magnetic presence, seemed to have been snuffed out.

And just like that, anger burned through the guilt and shame, incinerating everything in its path until all Danny could think about was bursting into the judges' panel, throwing accusations around, humiliating Eva the way she'd tried to humiliate Beck, hurting her the way she'd hurt Winslow.

As if feeling his gaze on them, Max looked around, frowning. Something like compassion suffused his older brother's serene expression, and Danny backed away from it, shaking his head to hold Max off from coming after him.

Danny slipped into the hallway just as the judges disappeared into the room down the hall. He breathed in his first breath in hours that wasn't full of the hot, salty air of a furiously working kitchen.

He wasn't ready to deal with Max's Zen platitudes

about everything being Fate or Destiny or Meant To Be, and he wasn't ready to pull himself together and put on a good face for the rest of the team, either.

All Danny wanted was revenge.

Chapter 33

The moment of truth.

Eva had never really understood that phrase until this moment.

Claire's words of wisdom from earlier kept running through Eva's head on an endless loop, forcing her to look at herself and challenging her to be honest about what she saw.

The picture was a little grim.

Not on the outside—she looked pretty good today, she thought. Her lavender silk dress fluttered around her, the perfect shape to soften the accidental new angles of her body.

Stress . . . the ultimate diet!

A casual khaki cotton blazer completed the outfit and professionalled it up a bit, but her shoes were pure indulgence.

Eva'd needed the pick-me-up of white-and-tan spectator pumps with a four-inch heel that morning.

She was vain enough to be glad to look hot, since it might be her last appearance on camera for the RSC.

What she was about to do would change everything. It

would mean giving up on her goal of getting her father to respect her—but it wasn't as if that had been going so great.

And besides, she was a businesswoman at the core. A negotiation where she traded her own self-respect for her father's? That was a shitty deal.

Her heart was a wad of uncooked dough in her throat as she sat at the judges' table and Claire opened the debate about whether they should send home the Southern Team, or the East Coast.

It was now or never.

Pulse pounding in her temples, Eva stood up and turned to face them before she could change her mind or chicken out. "Wait, before you begin, I have something I need to say."

Claire's eyes went wide, then soft with sympathy at the no-doubt strained look on Eva's face. "Now?"

The sick, twisty feeling in her stomach intensified, but Eva pushed it down. "Yes, now. If I don't get this over with, I'm going to wind up with an ulcer or something."

"Shall we leave you alone with your father?" Claire asked, already standing up and reaching for the door behind her as Theo frowned in consternation.

Eva shot her friend a grateful smile, but it collapsed on itself before she could manage to get the first sentence out.

"No, please. Stay. This concerns all of you."

With a quick tilt of her head, Claire paused with her hand on the door, already open enough for Eva to worry that her friend might actually leave her twisting in the breeze, no moral support at all.

But then Claire sat back down and folded her hands on the table. "Go ahead," she said in her quiet, accented voice, and Eva felt warm gratitude suffuse her, driving down the nausea and nerves.

"Well?" Theo quirked a bushy brow in her direction. "What's this new drama about?"

Swallowing hard, Eva tried another smile. This one didn't stick, either. "Sorry, Dad," she said. "You're not going to like this."

A movement by the door drew Eva's attention, just a quick flash of white, but her tired, agitated brain immediately leaped to identify it as the sleeve of a chef's jacket. Breath snagging in her chest, Eva stared at the narrow space where the door hung ajar.

There. Again, a flash of white and movement, and somehow, Eva knew exactly who it was.

"Danny," she called hoarsely. "Please come in. What I have to say concerns you, too."

After a long moment, the door swung open farther. She'd been right. Danny stood there, defiance hardening his handsome face into an almost unrecognizable mask.

"Chef Lunden," her father murmured, a light of understanding coming into his eyes.

Knowing it was even worse than Theo was imagining, Eva swallowed hard and braced herself. Forcing her head high and her gaze direct, she looked at every person in the room, one by one, ending by locking her gaze on Danny's steely blue eyes.

Now or never.

Without dropping Danny's gaze, she reached below the table and opened her briefcase. Hands oddly steady, she pulled out the thick stack of legal documents Cheney had given her.

"These are the contracts I negotiated with the Cooking Channel. They give the producers rights over everything Cheney filmed so far, and everything the cameras pick up between now and the end of the competition."

Danny's eyes flashed angrily, then widened as Eva

took the top few pages and ripped them cleanly down the middle.

"What the hell are you doing?" Theo demanded, his voice booming out into the silence of the room.

"I'm terminating our agreement with the Cooking Channel." Eva said it quickly, but strongly. This was the right thing, she reminded herself as a visible shock wave ran through her listeners.

She managed to tear another couple of pages in half, for emphasis, before her father all but lunged over the judges' table to make a grab for the remaining contract pages.

Eva danced out of his reach, shredding paper as she went, and Theo stopped short. As if realizing that chasing his daughter around the table wasn't the most dignified response to the situation, he took a deep breath and ran both hands over his head, smoothing down his salt-and-pepper hair.

"Can I ask why you would choose to throw away everything we've worked toward since your mother first had the idea for this competition?"

Eva closed her eyes for a moment, the question hitting her like a fist. "Dad." She hated the pleading tone of her voice, but she couldn't help it. She needed to make him understand. "This isn't what Mom would've wanted for the RSC."

"I don't know what you mean," Theo blustered. "But it's what I wanted—and what you promised you could deliver. I'm afraid I'm going to need an explanation for your behavior."

By the door, Danny shifted his weight, drawing her gaze. He could've been carved out of iron, for all the hard blankness of his expression, but despite how it tore at her, Eva found herself glad he was there.

Danny, more than anyone, deserved to hear her admit the truth.

"I made some . . . errors in judgment," Eva said, lifting her chin. "I did things I'm not proud of, all in the name of getting bigger ratings for the competition on television. I compromised myself, my ethics, and this competition."

"Chérie." Claire's soft, unhappy voice nearly did Eva in, but she straightened her spine and soldiered on.

"Everything Danny accused me of . . . it was true. I never meant for it to go so far, and I certainly never intended to influence the outcome of the competition—but I believe that's exactly what happened. My behavior, Dad, has been the exact opposite of everything Mom wanted the RSC to stand for. It was supposed to be about celebrating what chefs can do in the kitchen—not exposing what they do in their private lives. I let her down and I corrupted her legacy, and I'm so, so sorry."

Grief and shame burned behind Eva's eyes, but she held her head high and faced down the shocked gazes of the people she loved most. This was the hardest part.

"So now I'm going to let you all be my judges. If you decide that I should resign from the RSC completely, that's exactly what I'll do—as soon as I tell Cheney and his crew to pack their camera bags and head back to LA. But before I go, I have one last request."

Making herself meet Danny's gaze head on was one of the toughest things she'd ever done, but Eva managed it. "Please don't penalize the East Coast Team for my mistakes. And I'm not just saying that because I . . . I fell in love with one of them."

Danny blinked, jaw loosening as if his mouth wanted to drop open in surprise, but he didn't say a word. In the hearbeats of silence that followed her declaration, Eva felt her heart rip in two, as fragile as the paper she held.

It was over. She'd lost him.

But she wasn't finished yet. Finally allowing herself to look away from Danny should've been a relief, but considering she had to face her father . . . not so much.

"You had your doubts about me taking over running the competition, Dad, but you let me try, anyway. And I really appreciate that, more than you can know. I've loved the challenge of it. And I'm sorry I disappointed you. I'm sorry I failed you. But I failed myself even more." Her voice broke, finally, and Eva felt a red tide of humiliation scorch up her neck and into her cheeks.

This was it. He'd never turn over the reins of Jansen Hospitality to her now. She'd lost everything.

"Oh, Eva." Her father frowned, the lines in his weathered face looking more deeply etched than ever. "Sometimes you have to fail in order to succeed."

That headache was back, throbbing in her temples and driving spikes of pain into her skull. "What does that even mean?"

"It means . . ." Theo sighed. "You're right. Your mother would've hated the idea of televising the RSC, and she would've been beyond angry at the way I've been riding you to get it done. I've been so focused on getting to the next level, I lost sight of what was really important."

Eva nodded, relief trickling down her spine like cool water. "The competition."

Theo grimaced, as if he were in pain. "No, Eva. Not the competition."

Bewildered, Eva clenched her fists, crinkling the papers she still clutched in her sweaty palms. "I don't understand."

"I should've said this to you a long time ago." Theo walked slowly around the table until he was directly in front of Eva. "But until recently, I've been a little too involved in my own issues to notice what was going on. And now, with this whole mess . . . Eva, I want you to know. I . . . admire you for what you did today. It took guts, something you're going to need if you want to succeed in the restaurant business."

Eva tried to smile, her shattered heart spilling over with so much emotion, she couldn't even tell what she was feeling. "Thanks, Daddy."

Putting his hands on her shoulders, Theo stared into her eyes as if he wanted to imprint what he was saying directly on her brain. "Eva. We still need to sit down and talk about what happens when I retire, but no matter what, you'll still be my daughter. I'll still love you."

It had to be the headache making her eyes water like this. Or maybe it was shock. Eva didn't know what to say. "So . . . I guess you're not too mad about me sending home the camera guys, and quitting the competition?"

"I already said you were right about the Cooking Channel. Quit fishing." He still looked the teeniest bit grumpy about it, and the familiar sight made Eva's smile feel less tremulous.

"And you're not quitting the competition," Claire declared staunchly. "No discussion required. I'm the head judge, and I won't have it."

"You mean I can stay?" She could hardly believe it. Eva glanced to her father automatically, part of her certain she'd be punished for going against him this way.

But Theo smoothed down her hair, cupping her cheek in his palm the way he'd done ever since she was little. He smiled back at her, but there were tears trembling in his lashes, too, and Eva nearly lost it. "So . . . does this mean you're not mad at me for being the world's lousiest father?"

"Oh, Dad," Eva sobbed, launching herself into the

kind of hug she hadn't felt like she deserved in a long time.

"The fact that you admitted you were wrong," Theo said, mouth pressed against the crown of her head. "That's one of the first things any good executive has to learn. And one of the hardest for people like you and me."

"How did you learn that lesson?" Eva asked his shoulder.

"Well." She could hear the smile in his voice. "I had your mother to remind me of my extreme fallibility. She never let me get away with thinking I was perfect."

Pain tightened a fist around Eva's throat. "I miss her," she confessed, shaking with the strange novelty of talking to her father about the woman whose loss had shaped both their lives.

"I do, too. Every day. But Eva, she'd be so proud of the woman you've become," Theo murmured into her hair. "And so am I."

Eva clutched tightly to his strong, solid back and let the warm strength of the embrace bolster her courage for the task ahead.

When she reached the tipping point of feeling as if she'd totally lose her shit and start bawling if she stayed put any longer, she pulled away.

"Wow, talk about drama," she said, suddenly intensely aware of their audience. Claire looked misty-eyed, while Kane did his best to look anywhere other than directly at Eva and Theo.

Danny . . . Danny was gone.

Maybe she hadn't lost everything. But she'd certainly lost Danny Lunden.

Forever.

Heart clenching tight, Eva straightened her dad's shirt collar and wiped at the makeup smudge she'd left on his suit jacket shoulder. "I'm going to go talk to the camera guys now, and let you three decide which team to send home."

"Right," Theo said, sitting back down and clearing his throat. "We shouldn't leave the losing team twisting in the wind, waiting to find out who's been eliminated."

"And then, I've got a plane to catch for San Francisco, so I can start setting up for the next round," Eva said, injecting as much brightness into her voice as she could. It sounded pretty fakey-fake to her, but maybe no one else would notice. "There's a ton to do!"

Dark eyes velvety with sympathy, Claire stood and intercepted Eva for a hug as she reached for the doorknob.

"You did well, Eva. I'm proud to know you."

Eva was aware that her smile probably looked more like a grimace. "Better late than never, I guess. And thank you—for being my moral compass when I got turned around. I'll see you in San Francisco."

Waving good-bye to Kane, whose silent presence she'd almost forgotten in the rush of confessions and absolutions, Eva escaped into the hallway and paused a moment to catch her breath.

It was done. She could look herself in the mirror again, and not hate what she saw. And the situation with her father had turned out better than she'd ever dared to hope for, but somehow, even with a clean, unburdened soul and the assurance of her father's love and respect, Eva felt drained. Devastated.

She couldn't kid herself. The way Danny had looked at her earlier, as if she were someone he'd never seen before—and didn't want to meet—told her everything she needed to know about her chances of getting him to understand.

Besides, what was there to understand? Eva knew that in Danny's mind, she'd committed the one truly unpardonable sin.

She'd hurt his teammates. His guys.

If it came down to a choice between Eva and Danny's guys, she had no illusions about who he'd pick.

Every single time.

Chapter 34

Danny's head was a tornado of confused thoughts and conflicting emotions. What Eva had said, what she'd done, what she'd risked in order to put things right . . . He could hardly process it.

When Cheney got a call on his cell and frowned as he jogged out of the kitchen and into the hallway, Danny's breath caught.

She did it. She really did it.

By the time the judges came back, all the cameras were off, and the crew was coiling up wires and putting caps on lenses. But even the general confusion over that couldn't distract the waiting chefs from their worry over which team was about to be cut from the competition.

Poor Winslow, waiting in suspense for the verdict, looked like he was working on hyperventilating himself into a coma.

Throwing an arm around his teammate's shoulders, Danny steadied both of them and took comfort in the solid presence of his guys ranged around them.

A hush fell over the kitchen, even the celebrating chefs

on the winning side pausing as they waited to hear who was going home.

Claire Durand stepped forward, and her beautiful, stern face showed none of the torment of empathy he'd glimpsed in her while Eva made her confession.

Instead she looked cool, completely professional, as she opened her mouth to dispense the judgment.

"First, as you might have noticed, the camera crew is leaving us. We have decided not to pursue televising the RSC, so that we can bring the competition back to basics: the food."

That information sent a minor shock wave through the assembled chefs, but everyone shut up immediately when Claire held up her hand, too desperate for the rest of her announcement to drag out the suspense any further.

"To that end, after careful consideration, the judges' panel has decided that it comes down to the individual dishes presented in the last challenge. Both teams put up interesting food, and gave us much to enjoy, much to think about. But in the end, of the winning points scored by the East Coast/Southern Team, the majority were won by the East Coast chefs."

Danny's heartbeat picked up speed, and he felt Winslow reach up and clutch tightly at Danny's hand on his shoulder.

"Therefore," Claire continued, "with regret, it is the team from Atlanta who will be leaving the competition."

Win sagged under Danny's arm, even as Max shouted with joy and swung Jules off the floor and into a twirling embrace. Beck ducked his head until his hair fell forward and covered his face.

Ike Bryar led his crew up to the judges to shake hands and thank them for the opportunity. He was obviously disappointed, but philosophical about it as he came down and clasped hands with each of the East Coast Team members in turn.

"Hey, someone had to be cut, and this time it was us," he said. Winslow had recovered enough to hold out his fist for a bump, and Bryar grinned. "It was a privilege working with y'all. You go get 'em in San Francisco. We'll be rooting for you!"

Danny thanked him and watched him gather up his team and leave, while the rest of the kitchen exploded back into raucous celebration.

Somehow, Danny didn't feel much like celebrating.

Surprisingly enough, Max was the one who noticed he was missing. "Danny boy! Come down here and get your party on! Ryan Larousse found some bubbly, and we're about to have a toast."

Danny tried to brush his brother off. "I'm not in the mood. You go ahead."

"Not in the mood?" Max looked at him as if he'd sprouted spun sugar flowers from both ears. "Dude. Let me break it down for you. We just moved on to the finals. We came *this* close to having to go home, but instead we live to cook another day! Sorry if you're not in the mood, but you have to have champagne. It's pretty much a moral imperative."

Scrubbing a hand over his face, Danny tried to pull himself out of his funk. "Yeah, you're right. Okay. Lead me to it."

Max paused. "Wait. You're seriously not happy?"

"I'm fine," Danny said. "You mentioned something about champagne?"

"You're not fine."

"I don't want to get into a semantic discussion with

you." Danny started getting annoyed. "You want me to be happy and celebrate, even though we fucking lost? Fine, I'm happy. Let's go celebrate."

Max held the wine bottle behind his back. "Wow, do you suck at being happy."

"What do you want from me?" Danny snarled, reaching the end of his patience.

"I want to know what the hell is going on. Why has Winslow looked half a biscuit away from tears all day? Why is Beck going around even more stoic than usual? And why do you look like someone just tossed you a basketball covered in dog poop and asked you to dribble it up the center?"

"It doesn't matter now," Danny deflected. "We made it through. And you're right, the team deserves to celebrate."

Frustration drew Max's face tight. "*You* deserve to celebrate, is what I'm getting at. You always do this. You take on all the bad stuff for yourself, then pass the good stuff over to everyone else. You set a high standard, man. It's pretty hard to live up to."

Red hazed over Danny's vision, the chaos and fury in his brain condensing down to a single laser point of anger, aimed straight at his brother's head. "Me? What about you? I lived for years in your shadow, Max, and you weren't even there to cast it. There's nothing harder to live up to than a ghost. The fantasy son, who could always be perfect because he wasn't real."

Pain clouded Max's eyes, but his mouth firmed up in that way he always got when he was serious about something. "I hate that you went through that. I hate everything I put you all through when left. But, Danny, I've said I'm sorry a million times. Eventually, you've got to start believing I mean it."

"I believe you're sorry. But that doesn't change how much it sucked. Apologies aren't meaningless, but are they enough? And it doesn't make it any easier for me, now, to trust that people are going to stick around and not leave me hanging."

Shit, where did that come from?

Max, of course, picked right up on it. Eyes narrowing, he pointed the neck of the wine bottle at the cluster of judges talking to the West Coast Team. "Does this have to do with where you disappeared to after the challenge? I noticed you came back alone—and that Eva Jansen wasn't the one to make the final announcement. What's up? Jules says you've got a thing for our lovely competition coordinator."

"Yeah." Danny laughed, the sound dry and rusty. "That's what I've got. A thing."

Max cocked his head. "She's hot. What? I'm in love with Jules, not dead."

"Yep, she's hot." Making a quick lunge, Danny snagged the bottle out of Max's hand and started twisting at the wire cap over the cork. "Also a liar, and a user, and a manipulator."

And she came clean about all of that, a voice in his head reminded him. *She apologized—and she clearly meant it.*

But was it enough?

"Geez. Tell me how you really feel." Max frowned down at the champagne bottle.

But Danny was beyond accepting help. The flood of protective anger rushed over him again, turning his movements quick and forceful. "You want to know why Win and Beck were upset? It was because of her. She hurt them."

With one last, vicious twist, the cork popped out of the

bottle and a spray of sparkling wine geysered up, bubbles cascading to the floor.

Danny stared down at his soaked hand clutching the neck of the champagne bottle, and panted. Max took the bottle from him gently, and said, "Sounds to me like the one she hurt is you, Danny."

"No," he said, shaking his head. "That's not what's important. What matters is—"

"What matters," Max interrupted, a note of steel running through his voice, "is you. Your feelings. You matter, Danny. Quit hiding behind your need to take care of other people."

It was as if Max's words unlocked a door Danny'd kept carefully shut and locked for years. He shuddered, his bones vibrating with the force of it, teeth chattering in his mouth as he tried to make sense of the avalanche of emotion crashing through his system.

Yeah, there was anger at how Eva's actions had affected Winslow and Beck. That was real. But it was mixed in with this monster blend of pain, betrayal, rage, and disappointment that clobbered Danny hard enough to knock him back a step.

Max grabbed him into a hug, his brother's arms strong and fierce and tight, blocking out the rest of the room as Danny's mental defenses crumbled into dust.

Me. She hurt me.

And now that he realized it, he had no idea what to do about it other than stand there and attempt to breathe through the storm.

"Come on," Max whispered tenderly into his ear. "Just let it out."

"Dickweed." Danny shoved at Max's chest, his lungs opening up all at once. "I'm not going to cry, if that's what you're hoping for."

"Aw. Baby brother's all growed up."

"Shut your pie hole," Danny said, laughing and pulling away to run a self-conscious hand through his hair.

Max bumped his shoulder companionably and lifted the bottle of champagne to take a swig straight from it. He wiped his mouth and grinned, but it was the concern in his eyes that broke down the last, cracked bits of the wall Danny had erected to keep his brother out. "Seriously. You okay, man?"

Danny took a deep breath and thought about the question seriously.

Eva had hurt him. But on some level, he understood why. He understood what she'd been trying to accomplish, even though she'd gone way too far. And what she'd said at the end there, the thing that had made him turn around and run before he could give in to the temptation to sweep her into his arms and kiss a smile onto her sad, beautiful mouth . . .

I fell in love.

The memory lanced straight through Danny's chest, filling him with something sharp, jagged, and bright. Something an awful lot like hope.

"I'm not sure exactly what I'm going to do next," Danny said slowly, "but I think I'll be okay. Thanks, Max."

"Hey." Max grinned. "What are big brothers for, if not to tell you when you're being a total knob?"

"You're a good brother," Danny told him. "You always were, even when we were kids."

A shadow crossed Max's face. "Not always. Not when I left."

"No, but . . ." Danny sighed. "You're human. You made a bad choice. Or it felt that way at the time, but who knows? Maybe it was the right thing for you. It made you who you are, the guy Jules loves, the brother I needed right now, today. I can't regret that." He took a deep breath. "And I'll stop asking you to regret it, too."

Max blinked. "Wow. Toss a little emotional intelligence your way, and you take off running with it."

Danny laughed again, feeling lighter than he had in years, as if he'd let something heavy and aching slide right off his shoulders. "Yeah, well. Talking shit out is supposed to be good for you."

"It is," Max said. "When I was at the temple in Japan, they talked a lot about facing your feelings. Sometimes, the stuff they said, it was like watching Obi-Wan talk to Luke about the Force. But I'm pretty sure the monks came up with it before George Lucas." He shrugged and took another hit off the bottle of champagne. "Anyway, when I came back, I wasted a lot of time being bitter and stupid and holding on to my anger—but when I finally talked about it, it was kind of like magic. It fell away. I was like a snake shedding skin it doesn't need anymore."

Danny put his tongue in his cheek. "Okay, now you're getting a little woo-woo for me."

"Fuck off," Max said, grinning. "All I mean is, when someone hurts you, tell them." He waggled the split of champagne at Danny "Don't bottle it up inside, or someday you'll pop your cork and explode all over somebody."

"Whoa," Danny deadpanned. "You're such a poet. Trying to give Kane Slater a run for his money in the lyrics department?"

"You only wish you could be as smart as me."

"It's true, with age comes wisdom. How long until you're thirty again?"

"Oooh." Max clutched at his heart. "Direct hit! Come on, enough of this girlie touchy-feely sharing time. Let's party!"

Danny laughed and shook him off, glancing at the door the judges had disappeared through. "You go ahead. I've got something I need to do."

Max dropped the teasing long enough to give Danny a manly clap on the shoulder and an encouraging eyebrow lift. "Going to try out your newfound emotional coping mechanism on Eva Jansen? Good luck, kid. The first time might sting a little, but it gets better."

Danny doubted it. He wasn't even sure what he planned to say. As he waved good-bye to his shouting, laughing, jumping teammates and slipped out of the kitchen, all he knew for sure was that he couldn't let Eva go without telling her how she made him feel.

Chapter 35

Eva leaned her head against the cool plastic window and wished the plane would take off, already, so she could recline her seat. Every bone in her body ached with a dull, grinding pain that got worse the longer she sat, as if motion alone had kept her joints from freezing up.

Pushing a fist against her chest, Eva frowned. Nothing hurt quite as badly as this yawning emptiness in her rib cage. It felt as if her heart had been scooped out with a melon baller.

It was really over. She'd messed up everything, and even though she'd tried to fix it, she couldn't fool herself. Danny Lunden was never going to look at her again. She closed her eyes and thought longingly about escaping into sleep. Maybe she'd dream something nice.

"Mimosa?"

Opening her eyes, she turned to the flight attendant in the aisle, saying, "No, thank you, I didn't order any . . . oh!"

It wasn't a flight attendant leaning over the empty aisle seat, holding out a glass flute filled with champagne and orange juice.

It was Danny.

"What are you doing here?" she blurted. Dread turned her stomach to lead. "Oh no . . . I can't believe they're sending your team home. Maybe I can talk them out of it!"

She started fumbling with her seat belt, nerveless fingers slipping on the metal clasp, but Danny slid into the seat beside her and covered her hand with his much larger one.

Under the warm, dry clasp of his fingers, Eva stilled—except for the shiver that raced through her at his touch.

Unable to understand exactly what was happening, she stared down at their joined hands, trying to make sense of the sight.

"I'm here for you," Danny said.

She frowned. The words all made sense, but somehow, she couldn't make any sense out of them.

"To yell at me?" she said, feeling suddenly tired again. "Go ahead, do your worst. God knows, I deserve it."

His fingers tightened. "No," he said, intense and determined. "Eva, look at me. Do I look mad?"

Steeling herself, she raised her gaze to trace the sharp lines of his cheekbones, the subtle cleft in his chin, the sweep of his unfairly long lashes, before finally settling on his changeable stormy-sky eyes.

He gave her a smile, and that simple curve of his wide, generous mouth brought Eva's heart back to fluttering, thumping life in her chest.

"If you're not here to yell . . . and you're not eliminated from the competition—you're not, are you?"

Danny shook his head, that smile still playing over his face.

Relief shook her down to her toes. Thank God. She hadn't cost him the competition. It was going to be hard enough to live with herself and the knowledge of what she'd lost—she didn't know how she would've handled it if she'd caused Danny to lose everything that mattered to him, too.

"I got your assistant to give me his seat," Danny explained. "He had some unfinished business to take care of with Winslow, anyway, and I couldn't let another hour go by without telling you I'm sorry."

Eva jerked back hard enough to bang her head on the double-paned window. Danny winced and reached for her, but she evaded his hand.

"What do you have to be sorry for? I'm the one who screwed up everything."

The self-loathing in her voice flayed Danny's nerves like a knife under the scales of a fish.

"Yeah, you messed up," he agreed. "But I know why you did it. And I shouldn't have blamed you for us losing—that was weak sauce. We're chefs. It's our job to work through pain and distractions. One of the first things I remember my dad ever teaching us was to leave my problems at the kitchen door."

"That's . . . extremely generous of you," she said, in a stifled kind of way that made Danny think she didn't really get it.

"I forgive you," he spelled out, watching her closely. Then he grimaced. "So long as you can forgive me for almost going off on you and embarrassing you in front of your dad."

"No, that's not . . . ," she started, then subsided. "Yes, of course I forgive you. But it doesn't seem like the same situation—I mean, you didn't actually do it."

"Because I didn't get the chance," he pointed out. "You threw yourself under the bus before I could."

"Sorry to spoil your fun."

Shit, this wasn't going the way he'd planned at all. "You sure you don't want your mimosa?" he said, a hint of desperation creeping into his tone.

"No, thank you." She settled back into her seat, stony-faced and calm. "If that's all you came to say, Danny—I appreciate the understanding and forgiveness. It's more than I expected from you. Certainly more than I deserve. What I deserve is probably to sit here and take the punishment of having you so close, knowing that I . . ." She faltered, stumbling over the words, and Danny's heart soared as her mask cracked a bit. "Knowing that I have feelings for you. But please. If you truly have forgiven me, could you just . . . do me the kindness of leaving me alone."

Now she was the one who sounded desperate, and the switch raised Danny's spirits considerably. "No, I don't think I will," he said conversationally, settling himself comfortably in his seat. "I haven't been to San Francisco before. Do you think we'll have time to go to the Golden Gate Bridge?"

Shock widened her eyes and brought a mantle of pink to her cheeks. Damn, she was cute when she was annoyed. "Danny! You're seriously not going to get off this plane and leave me be?"

"After making your assistant jump through hoops with the airline to get his ticket changed over to my name? No way. And like I said, I'm excited to see San Fran."

"Don't call it that. Really. People will make fun of you."

"Okay," Danny said agreeably. "How about Frisco? Ooh, let's go to Ghirardelli Square. I like their baking chocolate."

Eva was staring at him as if she'd never seen him before. They sat in silence for a long moment before she finally came up with, "Are you okay? You're acting . . . I can't figure it out."

"Really? I thought it was pretty obvious," Danny said.

"Well, it's not." He liked the tartness in her voice, loved it when she got all brisk and bright, like lemon meringue pie. "So you'll have to clue me in."

"The chef contestants have a week off to rest up before the finals start. I'm spending mine in San Francisco with you, helping set up for the finals. Or wandering around all day and seeing the sights while you set up, whichever. I'm easy."

"Since when?"

Ignoring her muttering, he continued blithely, "But the non-negotiable part . . ." He leaned in, made sure she was listening. "Is that when you get done working every night, you come back to the hotel or meet me at a restaurant, and let me be there for you."

Her breath quickened—he saw the fast rise and fall of her rib cage. But all she said was, "I don't understand. Danny, what are you saying?"

"I'm saying, you're not alone. You don't ever have to be alone again. Not in San Francisco . . . and not in having feelings. You know, for me."

Whoops, a little more awkward than he'd hoped. Maybe he should've planned out what he'd say.

Eva didn't seem to agree. Her eyes were shining, her whole face was shining as hope and fear and relief and love and the beginnings of belief collided in her expression with a starburst shower of joy.

"Danny," she breathed. "You mean it?"

He leaned in farther, brushing her cheek with his nose and nuzzling into the soft, lemony sweet scent of her skin. "Every word."

"But what about your team?" She pulled back, a frown

pulling at her mouth. "You're really leaving them to make their way to San Francisco on their own?"

Danny felt a quick twinge, but he let it go. "They're competent adults. Sort of. Anyway, it's time to cut the cord. I'll always be there for them, but they don't need me to take care of everything. And I don't need them to let me. Not anymore."

Her breath caught, a tiny puff of air against his cheek. "What changed?"

"I found you, Eva. You're the one I want to take care of, from now on."

Even narrowing her eyes couldn't quite dispel the joy radiating from Eva. But her voice was stern as she said, "And you'll let me take care of you, too. Right?"

Danny pretended to think it over. "I'll work on it."

Leaning her forehead against his, Eva closed her eyes. "I can't believe this is happening. When I went into that judging room today, I thought I was about to lose everything. Instead, my father told me he loved me no matter what, and now, here you are."

"Here I am," Danny agreed. "Telling you pretty much exactly the same thing."

She choked a little, and when he kissed her, her lips were salty with tears. Something about the way her mouth trembled under his told Danny that she needed him to spell it out.

"I love you, Eva. No matter what."

Danny spoke the words into her mouth like a secret, but his heart had never felt more open.

"When my father let me take over the Rising Star Chef competition this year, I thought it was my chance. My golden opportunity, the one that would bring me everything I always wanted—and it did. But by far the best thing it brought me was the one thing I never knew I wanted."

The sincerity in her voice, the truth beating behind her words, made Danny's heart pound.

"I love you, and I'm going to keep loving you," she vowed, her eyes shining and wet. "You're it for me, Daniel Lunden."

"Hmm. No more playgirl of the Western world, huh? You're breaking a lot of hearts, here, Eva."

"Pssh. What do I need with all those boys when I have the best one ever, right here in my arms?"

Danny grinned. "I don't know. The parties, the gala events, the men falling at your feet. Maybe you'll miss your wild and crazy adventures."

She arched one perfect brow, that look he loved coming over her face. Wicked, dangerous, seductive, exciting . . . talk about everything he never knew he always wanted.

Eva was it for him, too.

"Who says I plan to give up my wild and crazy ways?" she purred into his ear, with a sinuous slide that brought her body into close contact with his.

Danny shifted in his seat, wishing he'd had the foresight to grab one of those blue airplane blankets to cover their laps.

"Eva . . ."

He actually felt her smile against his cheek. "Don't worry, Danny. All my wild and crazy is reserved for you, from now on. Speaking of which, ever heard of the Mile High Club?"

Groaning and laughing, Danny grabbed her and brought her sly mouth to his. She moved against him eagerly, her lips parting.

"God, you taste amazing," he muttered.

"What do I taste like?" He loved how one kiss made her breathless.

Let's see what two kisses does.

Two kisses had her cheeks flushing pink and her eyes glazing over. Surveying her with satisfaction, Danny whispered, "You taste like hope and happiness, fun and anticipation. The whole wide world I haven't seen, and the chance of exploring it together. You taste like love, Eva."

She swallowed, her tongue darting out to moisten her full, swollen lower lip. "Oh? And what does love taste like?"

Dipping his head again, Danny kissed her once more. "A little tart, a little sweet. Complex. The kind of flavor I can never get enough of, no matter how many times I try it."

She tilted her chin up, silently asking for more kisses. Danny was happy to oblige.

He kissed her as the plane taxied down the runway, gaining speed and momentum. He kissed her as they made the leap that broke the bonds of gravity. He kissed her as they soared up into the clouds, weightless and free.

It would take a lifetime—maybe longer—to discover every nuance of the taste of Eva Jansen's mouth.

And Danny was prepared to give it everything he had.

Some Like It Hot Recipes

MEYER LEMON AND PLUM COMPOTE

2 lbs firm red plums, cut into eighths and pitted
(about five large plums)
¾ cup light brown sugar
½ teaspoon Meyer lemon zest
2 teaspoons Meyer lemon juice
2 branches fresh thyme

Combine the plums, sugar, lemon zest and juice in a large saucepan. Cook over low heat, stirring often, adding more sugar if desired. After 30 minutes, add the branches of thyme and cook for another 15–20 minutes.

When the plums are super tender and the mixture has thickened somewhat, remove from heat. Don't worry, it'll get even thicker and more compotey as it cools. Discard thyme branches and let the compote cool completely. Serve over ice cream or pound cake—or use it as filling between the layers of a French Pancake Stack, along with Danny's Pastry Cream!

DANNY'S PASTRY CREAM

1 whole vanilla bean
1 ½ cups low-fat milk
½ cup heavy cream
3 tablespoons cornstarch
5 egg yolks
½ cup granulated sugar (divided into 6 tablespoons and 2 tablespoons)
4 tablespoons cold unsalted butter, cut into pieces

Combine the milk and cream in a medium saucepan with a heavy bottom. Slit the vanilla bean in half lengthwise and scrape the black seeds into the milk, then add the pod. Stir in 6 tablespoons of the sugar and bring to a simmer over medium heat. As it heats up, give it a good stir every so often to get the sugar all dissolved.

While the milk heats, whisk the egg yolks in a medium-sized bowl until smooth. Then whisk in the other 2 table-spoons of sugar and keep whisking until the whole thing is creamy and the sugar grains are beginning to dissolve—shouldn't take long, about half a minute or so. Then add the cornstarch a tablespoon at a time, whisking after each ad-dition, and—you got it—whisk some more, until the eggs are pale yellow and the whole thing resembles a paste.

Meanwhile, the milk should be about ready to simmer. When it gets hot enough that small bubbles break the sur-face, fish out the vanilla pod and toss it. Then grab a small cup measure and dip out a little bit of the hot milk. Whisk that into the egg mixture—gradually introducing the hot liquid will keep the eggs from scrambling. Keep adding the simmering milk to the eggs in a slow stream, whisking the whole time, until it feels like your arm is about to fall off, or until you get to the end of the milk—whichever happens first.

Transfer the whole frothy mixture back to the original saucepan and set the heat to medium. Keep whisking! I know, your elbow is sore, but it will be worth it. And it's almost over—it should only take about 45 seconds or a minute of vigorous whisking over heat to turn the mixture into a thick, glossy custard.

Take the saucepan off the heat and stir in the butter, a piece at a time. Then strain the pastry cream through a fine-mesh sieve over a clean bowl, pressing the cream through with the back of a spoon or with your spatula. This step seems fussy, but it ensures that your pastry cream is perfectly smooth, no lumps at all!

Cover the bowl with plastic wrap, letting the wrap rest right on the surface of the pastry cream, to keep a skin from forming. Then stick the bowl in the refrigerator! You should let the cream get good and set; 3 hours will do it, or you can make it ahead and leave it in the fridge overnight.

Pastry cream has a lot of uses—it's what goes inside cream puffs and eclairs, or you can slather it over a pre-baked tart crust and top it with fresh berries . . . or you can use it as the filling in the French Pancake Stack!

EVA'S FRENCH PANCAKES

   1 cup low-fat milk
   2 large eggs

2 tablespoons powdered sugar
½ teaspoon lemon zest
¾ cup all-purpose flour
½ teaspoon salt
1 teaspoon double-acting baking powder
Butter for cooking
Powdered sugar for serving

Put all ingredients in a blender, in the order listed, then blend for about a minute. If some flour sticks to the sides, just scrape it down into the batter with a spatula.

The batter will be easier to work with if you let it rest for an hour or so to let the air bubbles settle—but honestly, if you're pressed for time, you don't have to.

When you're ready to cook the pancakes, heat a medium sauté pan over med-low heat. You're going to have to play with the heat a little to see which setting works for you—as Danny explains, make it too hot, and you'll have a hard time getting the thin batter to cover the bottom of the pan when you tilt it. It's better to err on the side of too cool, and ratchet up from there.

Melt about a teaspoon of butter (a third of a tablespoon) in the pan. When the foam dies down, scoop about a quarter cup of batter out of the blender. (That amount will depend on the size of your pan—too much will give you a too-thick pancake, and too little will yield a misshapen crêpe that doesn't go all the way to the edges of your pan.) Pour the batter into the center of the hot pan, quickly tilting the pan to let the batter run out to the sides of the pan and form a circle.

Put the pan back over the heat and let it cook until the edges are curling and crisping. You can take a spatula and slip it under to check for browning, if you like. Then flip the crêpe—either with the spatula, or using the tips of your fingers, or, if you're very adventurous, by jerking the pan à la Julia Child! Personally, I recommend using your fingers—it's the simplest, gentlest way, least likely to puncture or tear the delicate crêpes.

Give the crêpe a good twenty to thirty seconds on the other side, then slide it out of the pan and onto a waiting plate. Repeat until you use up your batter—this recipe makes 8–10 crêpes, depending on the size of your pan.

Guys, I know this sounds tricky, but it really isn't! It just takes a little practice. And the good news is, just about anything you do with the crêpes will hide any imperfections . . . things like rolling them up around jam and sprinkling with powdered sugar, folding them around a squirt of lemon juice and some granulated sugar, or . . . layering them into a French Pancake Stack!

To assemble the French Pancake Stack:

Take the compote and pastry cream out of the fridge an hour or so before you start, to let them come up to room temperature. Slide a crêpe onto a cake stand or plate, and spread with the pastry cream, topping it with another crêpe. Spread that crêpe with the compote, and top with another crêpe, and so on, alternating compote and cream layers until the crêpe cake is the desired height. Double the crêpe recipe to use up more of your compote and cream, and to make a taller stack. Save the prettiest crêpe for the top layer, which won't be spread with anything.

Chill the cake for at least two hours. Just before serving, dust the top crêpe with powdered sugar, then slice the cake into pieces. Use a sharp knife and go easy! The layers should hold together pretty well, but it's going to be more fragile than a regular cake. More special, too! It's a bit of work, but all of it can be done ahead of time, and no individual component is that difficult. This is a great recipe to impress a boss or in-law! Or just to let your family know how special they are . . .

The Rising Star Chef competition comes to a
spectacular conclusion in Louisa Edwards'

Hot Under Pressure

Coming soon from St. Martin's Paperbacks

Beck dusted the chopped tarragon from his fingertips onto the last of the judges' plates just as Eva Jansen said, in her official announcer voice, "Time! Step away from your plates."

The physical act of backing up a pace seemed to cut the cord that had bound him to his work, and Beck felt the rest of the world come back online, background noise and awareness of the other two chefs who'd finished their teams' dishes flooding his head in a rush.

Skye Gladwell was right next to him, her heady, earthy scent of nutmeg and cream hitting him like an open-handed slap to the face. Beck had to close his eyes for a long moment to thank his combat training for giving him single-minded focus and drive.

Because this particular challenge was perfectly calibrated to tap into Beck's primal fight-or-fuck instincts.

Skye? He'd had ten years to get over her, but apparently that wasn't long enough to blunt the edges of his desire for her.

He didn't love her anymore, obviously, but damned if

he didn't still want her as badly as he had at the age of twenty. It had been a surprise to him in Chicago, that unexpected surge of physical need, but he was over the shock of it now, and working to kill the desire as dead as his softer feelings.

Until he managed it, though, he had to acknowledge he was pretty fucked in the head when it came to Skye Gladwell.

The third contestant in this final challenge, however . . . Beck's feelings on that guy were a whole lot less complicated.

On Beck's left stood Ryan Larousse, the cocky, smarmy head of the Midwest Team. They'd already gotten into it once or twice during the competition, to the point where Beck had humiliatingly and completely lost his cool and actually knocked the skinny little weasel on his ass.

Drawing calm blankness around himself was like strapping on body armor, and it helped as Beck worked to slow his breathing and return his heart rate to normal. Eyes straight ahead, waiting for the judges to come over and pronounce a winner.

Feel nothing. Feelings are for people who have the luxury of acting on them. You do your best and accept the rest.

It was a decent mantra, as far as survival went, but Beck couldn't help but feel a mirroring tingle of the excitement in Skye's eyes as she shot him a sideways look.

"This is amazing. I can't believe we're both here," she breathed, her wide, cornflower eyes tracking the progress of the judges, who'd started at the other end of the table with the Midwest Team's plate.

All the work Beck had done of slowing his pulse and regulating his body temperature went up in smoke. "I can't believe you still look at the world that way," he said.

"What's that supposed to mean?" The sudden ramrod tension of her body said more than her stiff words.

Beck shook his head. He'd always loved the innocent pleasure she took from life—but it drove him crazy, too, the way she refused to see the world as it really was, in all its harsh, ugly reality. Especially considering what she'd gone through while their relationship was imploding.

Let it go, he told himself, gritting his teeth. *You're over this, remember?*

"Nothing. Forget it. Congratulations on making it to the finals." Beck thought that was safe. Polite, distant.

"You too," she muttered as the judges exclaimed over Larousse's handmade gnocchi with pea shoots and shiitake foam. "And hey, congrats on finally finding your balls again."

Beck felt his head snap back on his neck as if she'd spit on him.

"What?"

Skye turned to get a better look at his face, brushing the flyaway softness of her red-gold curls against his arm. Beck fought not to flinch, not to grab her and shake her, not to betray his agitation by moving a single muscle.

"Your balls," she said clearly, eyes flashing darker than he'd ever seen them, even that last, awful night. "You must've found them, if you finally got up the guts to show your face in this city again."

The bitterness in her voice stung like lemon juice in an open cut, and Beck had to fight with everything in him not to react.

"Nice talk," he said, unable to help the hoarse thickness of his voice. "You kiss your mother with that mouth?"

She looked away, back to the judges, who were finishing up with Larousse. "I'm not the sweet kid you left ten years ago, Henry. Don't think for even a second that I'm going to go down easy. I'm here to win, not to make new friends or relive ancient history."

"Don't worry," Beck snarled under his breath. "Once this is all over and my team has won, I'll be ditching San Francisco and heading back to the East Coast."

"Perfect," she said. "Except my team's going to be taking home the prize money and the Rising Star Chef title. And before you run back to New York, there is one little thing I'm going to want from you."

The judges were thanking Larousse and sauntering down the table toward Skye as Beck said, "What's that?"

He didn't know what he expected—money, maybe, or a demand that he go to hell. In the furthest, undisciplined depths of his mind, there might've even been a hint of a thought that maybe she'd ask him for one last night together, for old time's sake.

Instead, what she whispered out of the corner of her mouth just before smiling brilliantly and greeting the judges knocked Beck off-balance and stopped his heart.

"I want a divorce."